PRAISE FOR *CHILLY WINDS*

"Mix yourself a gin and tonic, settle into your beach chair, and transport yourself to Virginia's Eastern Shore via *Chilly Winds*, a novel by Brooks Birdwell Yeager. Taz Blackwell is a kind-of-retired negotiator of environmental treaties for the State Department who keeps getting called back into harness and sent overseas to gather intel on nefarious doings involving the Russians and rare earth minerals. Meanwhile, back home on Chincoteague, he stumbles into domestic intrigue and a nasty mining company. Throughout, his romantic life is, well, complicated. Yeager is a deft and entertaining narrator. He knows the corridors of power in DC, he knows his birds and the shore's bars and restaurants, and he obviously knows more than a little about how international environmental affairs are conducted. And he's a dandy writer. *Chilly Winds* is way more than a beach book, but like all good beach books, it's awfully hard to put down."

—Tom Kenworthy, advocate for public lands conservation and former newspaper reporter

"Yeager has produced something remarkable, a tale that is both charmingly picaresque and utterly grounded that captures the high-stakes dynamics of international Arctic politics as well as the local color of life in a small coastal town."

—David Balton, former US ambassador for Oceans and Fisheries

"In this highly engaging first novel, Yeager draws on his vast international and local environmental experience to weave a tale of international intrigue with a surprising finale on Virginia's Eastern Shore."

—William Eichbaum, former senior environmental official in Pennsylvania, Maryland, Massachusetts, and the US Department of Interior

"Yeager's narrative captures the familiar yet alluring machinations of international diplomacy and the unexpected intrigues of a rural, coastal idyll."

—Helen Lewis, Chincoteague Island "come here"

Chilly Winds

by Brooks Birdwell Yeager

ISBN 978-1-64663-228-2

Published by

 köehlerbooks™

3705 Shore Drive
Virginia Beach, VA 23455
800-435-4811
www.koehlerbooks.com

chilly winds

a chincoteague intrigue

brooks birdwell yeager

VIRGINIA BEACH
CAPE CHARLES

AUTHOR'S NOTE

This is a work of fiction. Chincoteague Island, Virginia, exists, but with a few minor exceptions, the events and characters are entirely imaginary.

CAST OF CHARACTERS

In approximate order of appearance

Taz Blackwell	Retired negotiator, US State Department
David Daulton	US State Department
John White	US State Department
Richard Langer	Proprietor, Rainy Day Bookshop
Laney Langer	Proprietor, Rainy Day Bookshop
Moyer Jarvis	Young birder, Dana Jarvis's son
Dana Jarvis	Divorcee, single mom
Silla Berget	Taz's companion in Norway
Ingrid Torson	Arctic shipping analyst
Bren Stokke	Senior official, Norwegian Foreign Ministry
Darly Exmore	Clerk, Accomack County Records office
Soffia Gunnarsdottir	Senior staff, Arctic Council
Roxy Lopez	Bartender, Pony Pines
Tom Axton	Harmonica player, Swamp Possums
Ronny Reed	Guitar player, Swamp Possums
Rodney	Bartender, Ida's
Virgil Waite	Farmer, Tobytown
Bennet Waite	Virgil's son
Russ Antrim	Lawyer
Rick Reed	Security consultant

Irvin Friar	Senior assistant, State Department
Ragnar Skalldurson	Arctic ambassador, Iceland
Nils	Arctic Ocean ship captain
Irina Tsolkin	Mistress to Russia's ambassador to Iceland
Diane McCloud	Bartender, Chincoteague Inn
Ben Shefler	Tugboat captain
Marnie Lowenfeld	Analyst, Russia desk, US State Department
Sergei Goncharov	Russian ambassador to Iceland
Eliza Burke	Reporter
Terry Carter	Taz's neighbor
Suzanne Jarvis	Dana's daughter
Jessica Lansman	Deputy assistant to the president
Brian Radford	Attorney
Gina	Co-owner, diner
Auntie Kate	Elder, Tobytown
Ferdinand Triguet	US embassy to Denmark
Gavin Hart	Economics advisor, UK embassy to Denmark
Robert Lynge	Prime minister of Greenland
Akkanik Olsen	Legislator, Greenland Parliament
Emil Nykvist	Executive assistant, prime minister of Denmark
Paulsen	Prime minister of Denmark
Sergei Lavrov	Foreign minister, Russia
Cliff Curtis	Clammer, Taz's neighbor

CHAPTER ONE

Serve You Right to Suffer

GOOD BEGINNINGS ALWAYS START in the middle. Taz was sure about that much. It was just that he wasn't sure about this particular beginning. He was rubbing his cheek, picking off bits of the decayed rope he had coiled and used for a pillow. It was just before dawn, by the looks of it. Gray in every direction. A light drizzle fell through the mist. Out over the salt marsh the plaints of seagulls pierced the fog. Taz cast a bleary look around the floating dock. Low tide. Smell of damp salt and marsh grass. He heaved himself up to the deck. A deep rumble as a scallop boat thrummed down the channel toward the breakwater at the old bridge. He kneaded his neck. His collar was wet with dew.

Only his mouth qualified as dry. An army in dirty flannel boots had apparently marched over his tongue in the middle of the night.

Fuck me and fuck the whisky too.

Seemed like a good idea at the time. He tried to remember the sequence of events that had led to the brilliant inspiration to spend the night on the dock. Whisky, cigars, and poker with the crew of the *Mary Dee,* one of the scallop boats that made regular refueling stops on the Chincoteague docks. As usual, he had lost more than he had won. Afterwards, a long and unsuccessful flirtation with Roxy.

How'd I even get here?

The Pony Pines, the island's only real bar, the one where Roxy presided, was a good mile-and-a-half away, down the Eastside Road facing the Assateague Channel. Taz looked around, unzipped, pissed into the dark water. At least the town cops hadn't found him curled up next to the Ski-Doos. The only thing for it was to head home and clean up.

He stepped gingerly along the wooden deck on the side of the old restaurant, closed now for two years. Sidled around a few spots where the planking was rotten and he could see through to the oily water. At the back, the deck opened onto a big gravel lot where folks used to park to drink at the old Chincoteague Inn. Not a vehicle in sight. Sharp gravel reminded him that he was barefoot. No clue where he'd left his shoes. Stepping tenderly across the gravel to Main Street, he headed east on Ocean Boulevard. Found his truck next to a yellow front-end loader in the vacant sand lot behind the Dollar Store. A twelve-year-old Toyota. She had once been red. "Rusty but trusty," he liked to say. Old Faithful. She started with the usual cough and growl and stink of gasoline. When, exactly, had he lost his way? And when had we—all seven billion of us—fucked everything up? Irrevocably.

Back at the cottage, he lit a gas burner, pulled a coffee cup out of the pile of dishes in the sink, drizzled what was left of yesterday's coffee into it, and tuned the radio to the local NPR station. Nothing there but bad news. He shut it off and searched for his current favorite record, John Lee Hooker's only album on Impulse, a jazz label. Skipped the boogie-woogie and got right to the title track. He bounced the needle and cursed. A grim smile as he heard the deep, guttural voice, the voice of a man who had seen it all.

"*Serve you right to suffer. Serve you right to be alone.*" The bass throbbed and the reverb on the guitar sounded as ghostly as ever. "*That's why, that's why, that's why—you can't keep from crying.*"

He splashed cold water on his face. Again. The image in the mirror was not bad looking, though it would be unlikely to end up on the cover of a fashion magazine. Wavy brown hair parted on the right, with touches of gray above the ears, just now more than a little mussed.

A red welt on his cheek from snuggling with the ragged hemp rope. Rust-colored stubble beard, shaved close, also flecked with gray. Nose just slightly crooked, broken in high school by a zealous center back. Eyes medium set under brows just prominent enough to give a convincing glower, or arch with a question. Brown with hints of green under unruly eyebrows. He brushed his hair, pulled out some tangles, winced. Hint of a smile as he finished the mental catalogue.

"Your doctor told you to take milk, cream, and alcohol . . ."

Taz rustled up some eggs for breakfast, ran through a quick inventory of the day. The heating ducts in the crawl space needed to be bracketed and taped. Figure two hours on that, then bike to the beach. Look for migrants along the way. September's good for godwits, or maybe a few early teal. Walk up the strand a mile or two. He had found a loggerhead turtle nesting there a week before. Wondered whether Ricky had a good-looking flounder fillet for dinner. Maybe just settle for a slice of pizza from Famous next to the Greek place down at the circle. Then a good stiff drink. Or two.

It wasn't the life he had imagined as he faced the roaring forties, as the Antarctic sailors would put it. Envisioning his future had never been his strong point. Much less designing it. Maybe he had just peaked too early. Policy deputy to the Secretary of the Interior in his early thirties; lead environmental negotiator for the State Department at thirty-seven. Two global treaties under his belt and an invitation to join State's team at the United Nations in New York. Romanced and married the girl of his dreams. High times.

Then the country went crazy, the Supreme Court threw the election to the losing candidate, and Taz's political status changed overnight from up-and-coming to boarding the Siberian Express. Can't blame politics, though. That's like blaming the weather. Politics is something you navigate—or don't. If you wind up facedown in a ditch, maybe you'd better learn to pack a parachute.

CHAPTER TWO

Your Friends at INR

TIME ALWAYS SEEMS TO speed up in the fall. Taz had promised himself to build a trellis for the garden, but right now he was moving rubble at the water line to see if he could restore a patch of marsh grass.

His narrow lot afforded only sixty feet of frontage. Ten or twenty years back, the village, or some well-meaning citizen, had armored it by dumping a few truckloads of broken cinderblocks and chunks of old foundation on the shore. He didn't mind the rubble; it certainly served the purpose. But it was no place for a rail or a baby crab. He worked slowly, using a crowbar to leverage the big pieces, picking up the mid-size and small ones, and trying to create the rudiments of a crescent, so that he could hold enough muck in place for some spartina to get a head start. The water was already cold, and by late morning he was tired. His cell phone started buzzing. He was glad for the break. David Daulton's familiar voice.

"How's beachcombing?"

"It has its moments. Caught four jimmies yesterday and found a colony of baby oysters on a cinderblock this morning. Been traveling, I suppose?"

"Iceland and Brussels. Fishing negotiations."

"What could be more fun?"

"Bastards won't take a quota until we get the last bluefin." He didn't have to say which bastards he was referring to.

"Some things never change. What's up?"

"Your friends at INR want to see you."

"I don't have any friends at INR." The State Department's Bureau of Intelligence and Research.

"Truer words were never said. Still, they'd like to say hello. In person."

"When?"

"Tomorrow."

"Thanks for all the advance notice. You around for coffee before I go in for the barbeque?"

❈❈❈

Taz woke at four-thirty the next morning, brewed some tea, and hit the road fifteen minutes later. Traffic was nonexistent; he was cruising over the Bay Bridge by six-thirty. Annapolis was just waking up. He began to see the first crush of commuters as he crossed the Patuxent River, but his early start had served him well. He parked in downtown Washington on E Street near Twenty-Third and met David at the nearest Starbucks. They ordered double espressos, cut off short and dark, just like the old days.

"So, who's causing trouble this time? Greenpeace terrorize another trawler?"

"No, it's not your enviro friends for once—something more serious."

Taz raised an eyebrow.

"I think maybe they want you to talk to your friends in Norway."

"Must be about the Russians, then."

"Maybe. Look, I was just supposed to let you know to come in. I really don't know any more."

"Okay. How's the wife?" David's wife played cello with the National Symphony.

"Well, at least she's in town. The season starts in two weeks, though, so I don't see her much. Look, I'm not even supposed to be in hearing range of spook stuff. You're on your own from now on."

They finished their coffees and started across the street. David had a morning meeting with the Deputy Secretary; he punched Taz's shoulder and set off at a light run.

At eight sharp Taz walked through the familiar doors on Twenty-first Street and said hello to the receptionist, giving his proper name. "Eustace Blackwell to see John White, INR."

She took his license and eyed him warily while calling upstairs. Taz had put on a sport jacket, no tie.

"They'll be down to get you."

"I'm sure they will."

Five minutes later John White emerged from the elevator lobby like the banker he used to be, making his way through the exit machine. Casually waving his badge in the direction of the guard, he signed for Taz. Managed a smile as he held out his hand.

"Nice to have you in the building again."

You'd have me in a dark room in the basement if you had your druthers. "Yes, good to be back."

"Let's go up—you can see our new offices." State was renovating, floor by floor, corridor by corridor.

On the elevator, White punched the button for the sixth floor. INR was no longer on the seventh floor with the Secretary. That must have rankled. "What happened to lucky seven?"

"We've expanded. There wasn't enough room for all of us."

Taz tried to think of a word to describe White's smile. All he could come up with was *rigor mortis.*

They stopped at a door midway down the corridor, in front of a plaque and a keypad. The plaque said *Assistant Secretary, Intelligence and Research.* White, the assistant secretary, punched some numbers on the keypad. In they went.

Taz recognized the receptionist, a middle-aged woman with one of the warmest smiles that had ever added sunlight to his life.

"Hello, Ellie, how've you been?"

She gave him that signature smile. "Good to see you, Mr. Blackwell. I've been very well, thank you."

He wasn't sure the assistant secretary enjoyed the fact that Taz was pals with his receptionist. White pointed to a door on the left. "I hope you won't mind being separated from your cell phone. You can leave it with Ellie."

So they were meeting in the SCIF, the Sensitive Compartmented Information Facility. Special people, special rules.

"You know I gave up my clearance."

"It's okay. We're getting you reinstated."

"So there'll be FBI agents nosing around?" They were the background check guys.

"No need. It hasn't been that long."

They'd been watching him. Still, he was relieved not to have everybody on the island being interviewed about their new neighbor.

There were a couple of spooks in the room already. He waited for introductions.

"Taz, this is Turner Price, CIA, and Roland Jensen, Defense. Gentlemen, Eustace—goes by Taz—Blackwell." He didn't offer further information. Taz surmised they had already been briefed.

He waited. White spoke again. "Taz, it appears that your northern connections might be useful in a certain, ah, situation we've encountered. Turner, do you want to give the outline?"

Why did the CIA guys always have two last names? Prep-school boys.

Turner got right down to business. "We're hoping you might be willing to take a trip to Norway."

"I like Norway."

"More importantly, the folks we're interested in happen to like you. We'd appreciate it if you'd be willing talk to a few of your old friends. Not just the foreign ministry types. Others as well. Your colleagues who work the offshore circuit, the shipping boys, and your connections in Greenland."

"It'll be good to relive old times. What would you like me to talk about?"

"We'd like to hear the scuttlebutt about Russian activities offshore."

"There's nothing to know. They put all those plans on the shelf when we started fracking the Marcellus Shale. No American market for their gas, and the price isn't going back up anytime soon. Anyway, what does Greenland have to do with it? All the gas is in the North Barents and off the Pechora Peninsula." The trio facing him nodded.

"We're hearing about efforts to cut some kind of secret deal between Rosneft and StatOil," Price said. "The deal is cooking down deep in Rosneft, an obscure office, but they've apparently got lots of money to spend. We've got conversations among officials in Greenland that mention both companies, but they're not conclusive. Still, something is clearly going on. StatOil isn't saying anything about it publicly, but a couple of their top people seem to be on some kind of detail, shuttling between Nuuk and Archangelsk."

Taz thought about the possibilities. Rosneft was the biggest of the Russian state-owned oil companies. *Oil concessions, diamonds, a smelter deal?* The list was endless. Greenland had nothing but ice and world-class mineral deposits, and 50,000 Inuit scattered around the rocky coast in small fishing villages. Nuuk, the capital, had 10,000 residents on a good day. About a thousand of them lived in a couple of old Soviet-era apartment blocks that should have been torn down years ago. The rest of the town was more inviting, like a big fishing village, with scattered wooden houses in bright colors—red, blue, yellow. Small churches, Norwegian-style. Fishing harbor.

The ice had been Greenland's great protector, covering most of it to a depth of 6,000 feet. No roads. You had to fly or float from village to village. Now the ice was melting. Outlet glaciers calving small islands into the Davis Strait, the Greenland Sea, even the Fram Strait way up north. Only a few people understood what that meant. By the time the next generation started to lift its hopeful head, the seas would have drowned North Carolina's Outer Banks, most of the Everglades, and some very valuable real estate in Brooklyn and Manhattan. But that wasn't Greenland's problem. No, Greenland's problem was how to achieve independence from Denmark, and even trickier, how to exercise sovereignty over an island three times the size of Texas. Every oil and mineral company they had to deal with had more employees than Greenland's total population.

A proud people, nevertheless, moving carefully toward independence. The Danes, no longer Viking conquerors but civilized, progressive, cooperating, discussing, negotiating people. The Danish kroner remained the two countries' main link, but if Greenland's home-rule government could lease enough oil, that income might replace the Danish dole. Prime time for the private sector, and the knives and forks were already out.

On his way out, Taz turned to White. "John, make it business class, okay? I'm getting too old for economy."

"We've already bought your ticket. Just keep track of the damn expenses."

CHAPTER THREE

It All Comes Apart

THE DISSOLUTION OF TAZ and Jaclyn's liaison hadn't taken that long, after all was done and paid for. At least that's the way he saw it behind a bottle of Maker's.

Jaclyn's mother had detested him from the beginning. Too uncouth for her daughter. He was from Mineral Wells, Texas, for heaven's sake? Taz might just as well have been born in prison. When her father wasn't on the golf course, he sat or slept in his easy chair behind a bottle of Canadian Club, wearing today's golf cardigan and cream slacks. A commodities broker. He hated his job, but he had made serious money at it. His view was that Taz was not a serious man, not a man who would ever carve a career in the hard world of business.

Not long after the election, things went bitter quickly. One day sun, one day frost. He didn't understand the stress she was under, or the sacrifices she'd made to be on her very conservative law firm's partner track. She couldn't bring him to the firm's spring party because he would undoubtedly say something political and hurt her prospects, or otherwise make a fool of himself. She felt a distance growing between them.

He had been watching a baseball game.

"Why don't you ever want to talk to me?"

"I don't know. Maybe because all of our conversations end so badly?"

She had thought maybe she should take some time for herself, get away, be with her mother for a while. She hated her mother. By that point, it didn't matter.

Less than a year later, Taz was living in his share of their joint assets— an old waterman's cottage on Chincoteague Bay. He had bought it as a summer house for the two of them. Named it *Dachateague*. Now he sat on Dachateague's somewhat ramshackle porch, hoping against hope to find a path forward.

"*Judge decreed it, clerk he wrote it, clerk he wrote it, did indeed Lord— judge decreed it, clerk he wrote it down.*" Gus Cannon and the Jug Stompers. He loved Gus Cannon. Who wouldn't love the man who wrote, "*Everybody's talkin' about a new way of walkin'*"? Still, Taz was left feeling hollow inside.

> *Well, I married me a wife*
> *She's been trouble all my life.*
> *Run me out in the cold rain and snow;*
>
> *Well, she went up to her room,*
> *And she sang a faithful tune,*
> *And I'm going where those chilly winds don't blow,*
> *And I'm going where those chilly winds don't blow.*

CHAPTER FOUR

Tangled Up in Blue

THREE DAYS BEFORE HE had to leave for Oslo, Taz got on his bike, a dented old beater. Pedaled up Main Street towards the new bridge. Rainy Day was open. It was a good bookstore—the first ever on the island. Taz leaned the beater against the wall and slipped into the shop through its back door.

Richard Langer, the somewhat grouchy proprietor, rose from his permanent seat behind the counter. "Where you been? People are looking for you."

"Been around. Who's interested?"

"Tommy came by with his guitar a couple of days back, hoping you might want to play. How're you doing?"

"Day late and a dollar short as usual. I saw a message from Laney. What's up?"

"The roof needs a patch or two. Interested?"

"For money, or books?"

"I'll pay—if your reading list is too long."

"I like money, but my bank likes it even more."

Richard gave a wan smile. "By the way, I'm still looking for that Musil book you ordered."

"*The Man without Qualities.*"

"The very one. The paperback is out of print, but if you want, I can get it in cloth. It's two volumes, so it'll cost you." His eyebrows arched questioningly.

"Sure, go ahead."

"Okay. You playing tonight, or will you be curled up in a fetal position?"

Richard often started grouchy, but he had the acerbic wit to go with it.

"I'll come by—what time?"

"Seven, like always."

Taz liked Richard. Didn't press too hard, except when he wanted to unload some CDs he'd been overly enthusiastic in ordering. Great taste in music; that was where Taz had to hold himself in check, or the bank would be repossessing.

Got back on the beater and headed down Church Street. The produce place might have fresh eggs. Turned out they did, and peppers, too: jalapeños, serranos, dried anchos. The middle-aged woman behind the counter smiled. "Cooking Mexican? How're you liking the new place?" She had a flat Yankee accent. Maybe Pennsylvania or New Jersey.

"Not so bad." Taz answered. Interesting how much people knew about him, even before he had introduced himself.

"The island takes some getting used to." Rolling her eyes.

"Sure. But all the folks I've run into have gone out of their way to be hospitable."

"Aren't you down by Beebe Road? Pretty much a local neighborhood, isn't it?" She was trying to avoid direct articulation of her point.

Taz smiled in her direction. "I guess that's why I like it."

It was almost two by the time he finished work on the ducts. He was sweated up and dirty. Cobwebs in his hair, fiberglass in his fingers. Took a shower and tried to soak out the evil little threads. He was due for a reward.

Taz grabbed his binoculars and baseball cap, got back on his bike, pedaled down Beebe to Ridge Road, up Ridge past the newer houses.

Crossed over to Chicken City, cool breeze in his face, right on Maddox, past the miniature golf courses and the old McReady's Crab Shack, around the circle, up the causeway. The tide was rising, burbling in the little channels of the marsh. He stopped. Scanned the muddy outlet channels for Virginia rails. Saw some telltale chicken-like tracks, but no birds. Over the bridge. Black-capped Forster's terns on their fishing perches didn't bat an eye. Then into the cool pine forest of the refuge. Quieter there. Mid-afternoon still. The overcast sky reluctantly yielding to the spring sun, now warm on his skin.

Headed on to the loop around the main freshwater pond to see what might have come in overnight. A few egrets and ibises captured his attention at the first bend. There were some shorebirds, too, but he didn't stop long enough to identify them with certainty.

Down by the trail to the beach road, a boy was making his way out of the cattails. He had a serious look. An oversize baseball cap and a full rucksack. His heavy binoculars showed just how skinny he really was. Taz pulled up on his bike.

"Mind if I ask what all you've been seeing?"

A little hesitant. "Well, sir, I've seen egrets and glossy ibis just here. But back a ways, I believe I saw something different—like a phalarope." He put the accent on the *lar,* and from his soft drawl and formality of speech, Taz guessed he had grown up in the Carolinas, or maybe farther south.

"I missed that entirely. Was it feeding in a circle?"

"Yes sir, just like the book says, troubling the water with its beak."

"A nice find. I'll have a look on my way back. My name is Taz. What's yours?"

"Moyer, sir, Moyer Jarvis."

"How old are you, Moyer?"

"Eleven, sir."

"From here?"

"Yes, sir."

"Well, I can tell you know your birds."

The boy smiled.

"Do you hunt as well?"

"Oh yes, sometimes my uncle and I hunt the same ones in the afternoon that I watched in the morning."

"I suppose you saw those stilts by the beach road?"

"For sure. They've been here over a week. Avocets, too, some days."

"Well, good luck, Moyer. Which way are you headed next?"

"To the beach sir, to find my mom and sis."

"Okay, ride safe."

"Yes sir. Good to talk to you, sir."

He waved as he rode off.

✵✵✵

Taz waited a while to let him go. Young Moyer looked in your eyes when he spoke. *Not a video game addict*, Taz guessed. He detoured by the more brackish pond to see if he could spot a snapper or maybe an otter. Wrinkled his nose at the whiff of sweet sulfur from the marsh mud. When he finally got to the beach, about twenty minutes later, he saw Moyer in the surf, playing with an older girl. His sister? Taller, but with the same skinny build and sunny face.

Watching them both was a woman standing just above the surf line. She wore a light blue shirt, tied at the waist. From a distance, her hair, cut just above her shoulders, showed an occasional flash of red. She made Taz think of a ruby-throated hummingbird.

Only a few other people were on the beach far in the distance. Taz walked southward. Aroma of sea foam drifting on the occasional light breeze. He dropped the rucksack he'd slung over his shoulder. Rolled up his shirt and pants, tightened the string on the baggy olive-green swimsuit he'd worn underneath. Jogged down to the surf, dove over the first wave and under the second. He made sure to keep plenty of distance from Moyer and his sister. They were lost in their own world in any case. He didn't want to intrude.

There was a longshore current running south. Taz swam out beyond the break, allowed the current to carry him down the strand. Floated on his back for a while, enjoying the lift of the larger swells as they rolled in.

The first few serious rollers broke before they reached him. He swam out another fifteen yards. Bobbed over the next set before he found the wave that was meant for him. He caught it just in time for the long, foaming push across the sandbar. It lifted him high enough that he could use his right arm as a rudder and glide down the swell before the curl closed in around him and carried him towards the beach. He stiffened and stretched his left arm ahead of him to cushion the inevitable tumble into the sand. Arrived in the short surf smiling for the first time that day. Young Moyer saw the ride and waved at him. Taz saluted, headed up to find his towel.

The woman in blue turned toward him as he was buttoning his faded yellow shirt. He straightened and looked up. She was headed his way. Light on her feet, but with a certain determination in her stride. Taz was slightly taller, but she wouldn't have any trouble looking him in the eye. Now he could see that her hair was actually dark brown with a light red sheen. Her gray-green eyes fixed on him intently. She reminded him of Emer, Cuchulain's young queen in the great Yeats play, *The Only Jealousy of Emer*. Taz had played a small part in a college production and, like every other male on stage, had been consumed by Emer. But that queen had nothing on this one.

"You must be the man my son told me about, the one who was talking to him about birds."

"Yes."

No smile from her.

"He's a good birder," Taz added.

"No mind. I don't want you talking to him." Her voice not angry, but firm, with an edge.

He hadn't seen it coming, and it took him aback. "Of course. May I ask why?"

"He doesn't need your kind of trouble. We've had plenty of that already."

He absorbed her words for a moment, feeling himself flush. He took a couple of breaths, recovered his balance. "Well, the last thing I would want to do is to cause you trouble."

It was her turn to flush. Her eyes widened, perhaps in surprise, as she turned and walked away.

Young Moyer and his sister were wading in the surf, trying to catch a wave.

✻✻✻

That night, Taz ate a cold dinner. It was all he wanted. Stuffed his guitar case upside down behind the front seat of the truck and drove to the bookstore. Richard was already on the back porch, with a bottle of Jim Beam. There were a couple of others with him: Ronny Daisey, Tom Axton, and the young fiddler whose name Taz always forgot. He worked at the science center. Ronny played guitar for First Baptist and was a great natural fingerpicker, as well as a good singer and songwriter. Tom played harmonica, loved the old-time, Memphis jug-band songs. The kid fiddled Irish, but he could follow anything but jazz. Taz played a more than competent second guitar and sang on tune, if a bit reedily. Together, they made a decent band.

> *Some got six months, some got one solid,*
> *Some got one solid year indeed, Lord,*
> *Some got six months, some got one solid year,*
> *But me and my buddy, well we got lifetime here.*

Another Gus Cannon song. He led the Jug Stompers, playing banjo and harmonica. Taz had been a fan ever since he heard Gus's voice on a scratchy LP from the long-defunct Herwin Records.

Taz's best friend, Blake Early, had been a harmonica player, too, in the Musselwhite style. He and Taz had worked together on conservation issues in the bad old days when conservation campaigns were long and dollars were short. Over the years, they had become as close as brothers. After Taz's divorce, Blake was the one who had lured Taz to Chincoteague with promises of moonlit kayak trips, endless jams, and Foster's on the beach. The idea of lifetime on the island had depended on Blake.

Now Blake was gone. A drunk driver at T's Corner left a permanent wound in many hearts.

September was growing wetter every day. A mix of tropical gusts out of the Carolinas and westerlies. Sure kept the tourist numbers down. Taz spent the wet days sanding and varnishing his windowsills. The morning after the jam, he biked into town to play chess with Richard and talk with Laney, Richard's wife. This time, Taz had actually studied his copy of *Capablanca's Hundred Best Games of Chess*.

Richard brightened as Taz came through the door, visibly anticipating yet another triumph.

"How's the vagrant today?"

"Cranky as Ezra Pound."

"You know he was constipated, don't you? Didn't take a good shit for three years."

"Well, I figured it was something like that; all that crap about usury."

"Not to speak of the anti-Semitism, or the treason."

"Right. On the other hand, the best versions of Homer since the original."

"There's that," Richard admitted grudgingly.

Richard's heritage was from the Pale of Settlement. Harrowing stories of his grandfather's generation in the Ukraine. His great aunt— his grandfather's sister—had escaped the Nazis through Portugal, but her seventeen-year-old sister hadn't made it.

"There's no balancing. There's only one facet, ugly and unforgivable, then the other, the talent that most poets would kill for."

"No reconciliation."

"Maybe we shouldn't look for one."

Laney came out of the back room. Silver hair tied back. A generous smile. She sidled up to Taz.

"You okay?"

"Not really."

"Well, I wasn't looking for the cosmic answer. A simple *fine* would have been perfect."

"I'll practice at home."

"That's the spirit."

Without Laney, Rainy Day books wouldn't exist. Richard would still be in Alexandria doing PR for the candidate of the month. He's got the vision, she translates it into the real world: commercial space gets leased, customers see flyers, poets are invited to read, coffee on jam night goes for a buck-fifty a cup.

She put her arm through Taz's and they wandered over to the café by the new bridge, not saying much. Laney ordered a cappuccino and Taz an espresso, cut short and dark so there was no foam and little acid. No sugar or milk needed. They sat outside. He savored the coffee's bitter aroma.

Laney took a long look at him. "Seriously, is everything all right? You've been acting kind of weird lately."

"That's new?"

"You know what I mean."

"Well, I ran into this woman the other day."

"And what exactly would be unusual about that?"

"She told me to stay away from her and her kids."

"Oh. Well. That *is* different."

"I mean, she was fierce about it. Didn't want me talking to her son."

"Just being protective; strange men."

"No, it was more. She said her son didn't need my kind of trouble, like she knew something about me."

Laney shrugged. "Everybody knows something about everybody on the island. What did she look like?"

"Gorgeous—gray with flashes of green, ardent. Hair flecked with red."

"Her kid, the one you were talking to. His name Moyer?"

"Yes."

Pause. A sip of coffee.

"Well?"

"You know, I believe there's a storm headed this way."

The mother's name was Dana Bonner. She had come to the island a couple of years back, when her husband, Timothy Jarvis, transferred to the Chincoteague Coast Guard station from a post in the Carolinas. Something had gone wrong. A drunken driving citation, some rumors of abuse. Coast

Guard dismissal under murky conditions. A messy divorce reported in the *Beacon,* the island's paper. Timothy left the island for parts unknown. Not too many people were sorry to see him go. Dana reverted to her maiden name and stayed on with the kids. She worked with troubled families. Her office was in the county's family service center in Accomac.

CHAPTER FIVE

Between Silla and the Deep Blue Sea

OSLO, NORWAY, WHERE THE fast train from the airport stops only blocks from Koenigstrasse and the short walk to the old wood-frame fish restaurants by the harbor. Bergen, with its low colorful waterfront on the fjord. Tromsoe, way up north, whose snow-shouldered mountains loom above the bright modern cathedral across the harbor. But most of all, Silla Berget.

Silla was a researcher at the Institute of the North in Tromsoe. She was everything Norwegians are not supposed to be: sunny, funny, full of life. She was also a great-looking blonde with a dancer's body. It had been four years since Taz had first met her at an Arctic Council meeting in Tromsoe.

Midwinter in the Norwegian north. The sun came up at eleven and set at three in the afternoon. The meeting was a ministerial. The diplomatic heavy rollers. The mayor and the city council had gone out of their way to put their town's best face forward. Among other things, this involved Silla and several of her colleagues performing an avant-garde outdoor ballet in the early evening. They would wend their way silently through the dark streets, waving long red and yellow banners lit occasionally by arc lights, to the tune of strangely hypnotic, synthesized music.

Taz had never seen anything quite like it. He stayed behind as the rest of the delegates drifted back to the hotel for the reception. One of the dancers was changing in an alley behind the sound equipment when he came up to thank her for the performance. She was putting blue jeans over her leggings. Taz turned away, embarrassed to have interrupted a private moment. By then the cold was setting in. He had shivered in his two-button suitcoat. She had already snuggled into her parka and her eyes twinkled as if she were wondering how long he would last outside. Meanwhile, she didn't seem in the least fazed by his garbled Norwegian greeting. She spoke good English, and he had done his best to engage her, shivering the entire time. He lasted just long enough for her to offer a tour of the Finnmark after the conference was over.

Taz was still shivering when he rejoined the other delegates, but he was also feeling a glow from his encounter with Silla. He had changed his travel plans and stayed on four more days.

He'd been back to Oslo twice since then. Each time he and Silla had found something new to explore. They became lovers and then friends. He wasn't much of a correspondent, but she didn't seem to expect that. "Just get in touch when you're headed my way," was how she put it. Either she would be there and available, or she wouldn't.

Now, two years later, she met him at the Oslo airport, gave him a warm smile and, as they embraced, murmured, "It's been too long." They took the fast train into town and headed to Silla's flat so he could drop his bag and take a shower. Then down to the harbor for a walk in the waning sun.

"You said you would be here only a short while."

"Just a few days. I have to go up north."

"Of course—to talk to the oil boys."

"How could you know?"

"Oh please, Taz. Why else would you be here?"

"To see you."

"I'm flattered, but I'm not so naïve as you think. I'd better come with you. I know Tromsoe, and I can help you find the right people to talk to."

It wasn't just that Silla had grown up in Tromsoe and attended its university. After graduation, she had supervised the IT staff for one of the town's midsize oil services. She knew the network of people and power that counted in the Norwegian north.

Tromsoe was more complicated than it looked at first glance—a university town set among the hills above a snug, open-water fishing harbor. Over the ridge was a tidy industrial park that could just as well have been in Bay City, Texas. Oil suppliers, parts manufacturers, pipes, offices, and trucks.

Tromsoe was reaping the benefits of the Barents Sea oil boom. The money end lay just beyond the town's picturesque harbor with the inevitable tourists. The money end consisted of engineering consulting firms, leading-edge geological research institutes and, in Hammerfest—just two hundred klicks up the road—natural gas gathering plants, pipelines from the Sno Vit complex offshore, and tankers waiting to load.

The odd thing was that this place, at the same latitude as Barrow, Alaska—America's little frozen outpost on the Chukchi Sea—possessed a year-round harbor and the flavor of a European university town. All credit to the Gulf Stream. In October, it was still warm enough to allow them to have dinner on the waterfront. They ate cod and drank a bottle of Portuguese red—flavorful, if a little harsh. Taz told Silla about his marriage and subsequent divorce, and then shared some island stories that made her laugh. The way her eyes smiled made him feel there was a reason to be alive. They drank Irish coffees and then walked slowly back to her flat, her arm through his.

✲✲✲

The next morning, they caught the early flight north. Tromsoe was sunny but cold. Taz had booked rooms at the Rica Ishavshotel down by the harbor. The hotel was known for its nice breakfast—pickled herring, eggs any style, crusty bread, and a wild berry jam. There was an attractive bar at the apex of the fourth floor, cantilevered over the water. Taz and

Silla tossed their bags on the bed and went out to walk the harbor and catch the afternoon light.

Silla smiled and reached for his hand. "Taz, I have something to tell you."

He felt a quiet alarm sound.

"I hope it's something good."

"Of course it is, you ninny."

"Well, then?"

"I'm seeing somebody, and I think it might be the real thing."

He felt a sharp pain. At the same time, he couldn't help being happy for her.

"So, who's the lucky guy?"

"His name is Martin. He's an engineer."

"Oil industry?"

"No, he designs tunnels and bridges, that sort of thing."

"How did you meet him?"

"He was here for a conference. My friends and I were doing the registration. It was his first time in Tromsoe. Can you believe that? He's from Oslo. He asked me to tell him which sights to see, and of course I showed him around. He made me laugh—like you do. We have a lot in common. We both love to ski and sail. We even like some of the same books. That's how it started. We wrote emails, then I visited him in Oslo. I met his friends, and we all got along so well. I realized this thing called love might really exist for me after all. And I liked that feeling so much."

She smiled as she said it, but with a hint of sadness in her eyes. For him?

Taz looked at her but could find no words. His right hand reached to replace a strand of her hair that had fallen over her forehead. He felt tears, looked away, and then folded her in his arms.

"Silla, Silla . . . it's great . . . I mean, I'm happy for you."

They continued walking along the harbor front until it became a series of old wooden warehouses. The lane they were in wound behind some clapboard sailmaker shops and then returned to the harbor front. They enjoyed a close-up view of a Norwegian Coast Guard cutter and two sea tugs moored down toward the oil depot. The sun began receding behind the western mountains.

"I thought I might look in on Carl Koster and Bren Stokke. What do you think?"

"Carl's out of the country. Bren might be hard to reach—you know StatOil made him a director."

"I guess I'm not surprised. He was the best mind of the bunch. But I think it's worth a try. We always got along."

"Because you're twins separated at birth?"

"You think we're so much alike?"

She laughed. "He told me one time that you two were like a photograph and its negative—you were the color photograph, and he was the dark anti-matter version."

"He's too hard on himself. I'm not such a bundle of sun myself. Since we can't touch base with Karl, can you find me any of the players in the shipping industry?"

"Only a few people. Maybe it would help if you give me a little more detail about what you're really interested in."

"I want to find out who's focusing on Greenland, particularly if there are plans for any big operations there."

"Still trying to help the Inuit go independent?"

"Something like that."

She thought for a moment. "I have a friend, Ingrid Torson, who works for one of the classification societies. You know about them?"

Taz nodded. They were Norway's private sector guilds that set the insurance rules for the shipping industry.

"She should know if anything big is in preparation. They basically have to get her permission to operate in the Arctic," Silla said.

"Good, let's see her first."

※※※

The next morning after breakfast, they headed across the harbor to see Ingrid Torson. The offices of Det Norske Veritas were in the midst of a tidy row of two-story wooden buildings painted yellow. The letters *DNV* were etched discreetly above a weathered oak door. Silla rang the bell and a young man wearing a tie and sweater vest let them in.

"And you are?"

"Ms. Berget and Mr. Blackwell to see Ms. Torson."

The young man arched an eyebrow and hurried down the corridor. It struck Taz that DNV wasn't in the habit of receiving casual visitors. A moment later, the young man returned and said, "She'll be out shortly." Then he disappeared.

Taz looked questioningly at Silla.

"Don't worry. Ingrid was my teacher at university."

Just then, a tall woman appeared in the hall, elegantly dressed in a gray skirt and cream-colored blouse. She wore her silver hair in a neat bun and looked quizzically at Taz through tortoiseshell glasses. Then she noticed Silla and broke into a broad smile.

"Why Silla, how wonderful to see you. And you've brought me an American!"

Taz offered his hand and introduced himself. "Ms. Torson, I'm Taz Blackwell."

"Call me Ingrid. And I know who you are."

Taz was puzzled.

"I used to assist the Norwegian delegation at the IMO. You were quite a legend there."

Taz smiled. He had briefly headed the US team at the International Maritime Organization—the IMO. After the Amoco Cadiz spill, the United States had joined Norway and Spain in advocating mandatory double hulls and a mechanism for establishing restricted shipping zones in environmentally vulnerable areas of the ocean. But the flag carriers were having none of it. Each country had its own style. The Swedes were fine with double hulls, having already used them in the Baltic; they were more concerned about the impact on shipping of unilaterally designated protected areas. They had offered Taz draft language assuring that shipping companies could comment on any proposed restriction. Basically, they wanted to make sure that their two biggest shippers, Wallenius and Brostrom, got a fair shake. The Russians said little; their companies worked primarily in national waters and were governed almost entirely by Russian regulations.

Then there were the Japanese. They questioned the committee's procedure and defended commercial use of the oceans, which they considered to be under attack by various nefarious forces, including Greenpeace. But most of the time, they had their proxies do their talking for them. Over six months, the foot-dragging by various flag states reached remarkable levels, even for the IMO. Like it or not, the Japanese strategy of building port facilities for small islands and poor countries had bought more than a few votes at the IMO.

After one particularly obnoxious harangue by the delegate from Panama, Taz suggested that he save the self-serving claptrap for his foreign paymasters. Although verifiably true, this was not the kind of fact ordinarily shared at the IMO Experts Committee. The Panamanian delegate stormed out, the Japanese chairman scowled, and the committee suspended work for the month. In Taz's report, he noted that the discussion hadn't been going anywhere in any case. This did not placate his assistant secretary.

"Yes, that was early on. I learned to control my temper better after that."

"I surely hope not. We loved it. Illueaca was never the same again, and he was such a loathsome little hypocrite."

Taz liked Ingrid.

"We were hoping you might be ready for a coffee break."

"That would be delightful. Just let me get my bag."

A few minutes later, they stepped across the street to a little café with stylish, brushed-aluminum furniture. Over espresso and buns, Taz explained that he had come to Norway to get a better feel for the shipping companies working in the Arctic, and particularly in Greenland waters. He was consulting for several clients who were considering investing in the region. They wanted to gauge the regulatory context in which prospective companies would be operating.

This was the background story concocted by the INR team. Taz hated to lie, and worse, he was bad at it, a fact all too well-known to White and his team of spooks. But his cover story was close enough to the truth that he could say it without grimacing. The US government was inclined to support Greenland's desire for independence, which could open up a vast new area for American resource companies. But even the Commerce Department didn't want to duplicate the Soviet environmental mess next door to Labrador. The general feeling was that US companies could meet high standards and would be better off if every company and country had to meet them, too.

Over the course of an hour, Ingrid offered a seminar on current trends in Arctic shipping. Most of the recent increased traffic was tied to oil and gas operations in the Barents. There was also some early seismic work off Northeast Greenland. In addition, the Danish Coast Guard—the Royal Danish Navy—was worried about cruise ships. Carnival Lines had shown up on the Greenland coast in the form of a seven-story cruise liner that carried 4,500 passengers. The company wanted to show their guests the beauties of Scoresby Sound. Greenland's coast was dominated by broken cliffs, calving glaciers, and icebergs the size of small islands. Scoresby Sound was the most complicated bay on the entire southeast coast, and most of it had never even been charted. The largest hospital in Greenland had seventy beds. The Danes were able to field exactly three rescue helicopters along the Greenland coast. And as one Danish cutter commander had put it to Taz, "These idiots have convinced their passengers they're going to see penguins up there."

Still, Taz hadn't yet heard anything truly newsworthy. Until Ingrid mentioned that one of her colleagues had recently had a visit from some consultants working for the Murmansk Shipping Company. The consultants were Finns; they worked for a ship design firm in Helsinki. Her colleague had found the visit odd, and it stuck in her mind.

"Why odd? Don't designers usually consult DNV when they're considering new engineering specs?"

"Sure. But these were Finnish designers working for a Russian company, one that ships almost entirely inside the Russian coastal zone and is required to use Russian service providers. So why were they asking about engine design standards that are going to be applied over the coming decade by the Danish Coast Guard?"

When they finished their coffee, Taz reached over the table to touch Ingrid's hand, gave her a warm thank you. They agreed to talk again as needed.

It took a few calls to track down Bren Stokke. He agreed to join them for a drink at their hotel.

✵✵✵

Taz and Silla arrived at the cantilevered bar early and sat down at a table by the harbor-side window. Taz did his best to greet their server in Norwegian, ordered a martini for Silla and a rye whisky for himself. Watched a sea tug moored on the wharf, lit brightly under its mercury vapor lights.

Bren walked through the low door at six o'clock sharp. He didn't look a day older than the last time they had met over a negotiating table, almost five years before. Tall, gaunt, fit, with a bemused smile. He gave Silla a kiss on both cheeks and held Taz's hand in both of his.

"Taz, my friend. It's been too long."

Their server was occupied at another table full of American tourists. One of them was complaining that the Aquavit he had ordered was undrinkable. He asked for a Cosmopolitan instead. The server, a handsome young woman with her hair in a loose bun, looked Taz's way and rolled her eyes. Silla went to get Bren a scotch at the bar. Taz turned to Stokke.

"Silla says you've been doing very well, that you're now a director at the Foreign Ministry. She also says that you've become the government's senior liaison to StatOil's board. I believe congratulations are in order."

"My colleagues on the board are just waiting for me to stumble. Can you imagine? They think I'm a shill for the foreign minister. I'm treading a bit carefully."

Taz couldn't imagine anyone less likely to shill for politics.

"So, my friend, how've *you* been?" Bren said. His blue eyes were intently focused; he seemed to be trying to read Taz's thoughts. "What's it like to be watching the new bunch from the sidelines?"

"It's a horror show. A slow-motion train wreck."

"You sound almost European. But your life improves, yes?"

"I've had my ups and downs."

"I read about your marriage only a year and a half ago. I was happy for you. I take it the romance didn't translate into something more lasting. I'm sorry."

"I didn't see it coming, that's for sure."

"And so, now?"

Silla came back with Bren's scotch. The conversation turned toward the political situation in Norway. Bren's boss, the foreign minister, was bright, popular, and ambitious. But he would probably never rise to become prime minister, the job he so coveted. The man ahead of him in the polls was just as bright and from a working-class background; Bren's boss had graduated from the Sorbonne and spoke French a bit too well and too often.

Taz asked about the state of play with Russia. He knew about Norway's strategy of seeking Russian partnership in oil development. Also in fishing and other areas. The goal was a more positive relationship that would allow Russia to absorb Norway's technical standards, ultimately leading to better performance and conflict reduction on all fronts. Bren had been a leader in implementing that policy.

"Good news and bad news, as always. We're very close to agreement on the Barents Sea boundary, which would end our forty-year standoff. On the other hand, we had to haul a Russian factory ship into Narvik for illegal fishing. They weren't just over quota, they were fishing illegally in the Svalbard science area and hauling in immense amounts of by-catch. The captain was Russian mafia, but after we arrested him, the Kremlin decided to show their fangs rather than admit they weren't in control of their fishing fleet and face public embarrassment."

"When in doubt, blame the messenger."

"Exactly."

"What do you do now?"

"We'll keep the tub until the fish spoils and then give it back to them. We'll charge the captain and deport him. We'll fine the company, but they'll never pay up. Once the papers move onto other issues, we'll have a serious talk with the right people in Moscow and then forget the whole thing."

"But strategically, what's the next phase? Will StatOil join the consortium to develop Shtokman?"

Shtokman was the largest natural gas reservoir ever discovered on the planet. A single field that could satisfy Europe's natural gas needs for decades. It was also 550 miles from Murmansk on the Barents Sea floor, under 1,000 feet of frigid water where the surface was dominated by million-ton floating ice platforms crunching each other like some geological version of bumper cars.

The fields in the Norwegian Sea were already running dry; the Barents Sea fields would be good for another twenty years at most.

"Then there's Shtokman. But I don't expect very much to happen on it anytime soon. The technology still needs to be developed and the price has to be right. Even then, Gazprom will probably find some way to screw it up."

"So, the future is elsewhere?"

"For joint work with Russia, it has to be."

The rye had been underwhelming, and Taz had switched to scotch, a single malt, but not one of the big smoky ones. It was briny, almost medicinal, with a long technicolor aftertaste. Ardbeg, distilled on Islay.

Bren gave him a sharp look and then smiled. "I can understand why your people would be curious. But I can't do much to satisfy their curiosity. You're my friend, so I'll tell you this. StatOil has a mining subsidiary, a fact I'm sure you're fully aware of. Greenland has more than oil beneath all that ice. And as usual, it's what Russia needs that counts."

Taz took another sip. He looked again at the sea tug. "Bren, when are you next coming to the States? I want to make good on my promise to take you charter fishing out of Chincoteague."

Silla glared at the two of them. "So, this fishing club is men only? I'll have you know I caught a championship ling cod at last year's tournament."

Taz shook his head, soft eyes on Silla. "Some people will do anything for a good fishing charter."

Bren smiled, and Silla gave Taz a gentle punch on the shoulder. The three of them finished their drinks. Silla and Taz saw Bren to his car and watched as he drove off. There was a hint of snow in the air. Silla put her arm through Taz's and snuggled closer for warmth. Two days later Taz flew home. It wasn't until the third hour of the flight, somewhere over the west coast of Ireland, that it sank in that he might not ever see Silla again. She was boarding a train for a new destination. He saw her face in the airplane window, smiling, in a playful scowl. Laughing. He couldn't help smiling himself, though his eyes were moist.

CHAPTER SIX

Ray's Shanty Incident

THE FLIGHT BACK FROM Norway seemed to last an eternity. It didn't help that every mile took Taz farther away from Silla. By the time he arrived at Dulles International Airport, his mood had descended from sorrow to full depression. His horizons had become a sodden gray and he felt the beginnings of a nasty cold. Throat on fire, sinuses plugged, severe ear pain as the Airbus decompressed over the Delmarva Peninsula. He cursed under his breath, damned the plane's canned air and the coughers and sneezers in the rows in front of and behind him.

It was rush hour, and the drive to the island took four hours instead of the usual three. He got home at ten that night and made himself a warm whisky. Stood in the steam of a hot shower, went to bed.

Morning. He didn't want to get up. He stumbled into the bathroom and brushed his teeth, made his way painfully into the kitchen, put on a pot of coffee. This cold was going to be the bad kind.

It was the beginning of October; the air was already hinting at crisp Canadian weather to come. In the Pocomoke forest, a few early trees—maples, poplars, and beeches—were already starting to turn. The marsh grass was donning new colors as well. Ducks flooded in from the north. Taz had always loved the colors of fall.

Now, though, his head ached, his cough racked until his ribs hurt. He climbed back under his bed covers and slept most of the day. Woke in the dimming light of late afternoon. Steeped in the vapors of another shower.

Reentry had always exacted its cost, and he was never very good at it. He felt struck by the absurdity of his existence—sniffling and coughing in his drab little kitchen, on a dark island on the edge of the East Coast of a benighted continent. *So this is what real loneliness is,* he thought. When you realize nobody on Earth gives a flying fuck what happens to you. And why would they?

His mother had died when he was two. All his life, he had sought the company of women. Still, there was no serious woman in his life. He opened a can of crab soup for dinner and turned on the lamp as the last light of the sun darkened in the west. Found his copy of the *Inferno* and reread Dante's opening lines:

> *Nel mezzo del cammin de nostra vita,*
> *Mi retruvai per una selva oscura,*
> *Che la diritta via era smarrita.*
>
> *Midway on our life's journey, I found myself*
> *in dark woods, the right road lost.*

Taz put his dishes in the sink, brushed his teeth, and went back to bed. At first, sleep was hard to come by, and then he had a series of strange, jagged dreams, in which companions left him like leaves blowing away in the wind.

In the morning, he made himself a fresh pot of coffee, sent some emails, cancelled a few scheduled calls, and climbed back into bed. The cottage was cold. He shivered under the covers. Rummaged in the closet to find the old Canadian blanket that his father had bought in the Adirondacks in the 1930s and treasured the rest of his life.

Taz made some strong tea with honey, lemon, and brandy, then wrapped himself in the Canadian blanket and watched Aston Villa fight to a tie with Tottenham Hotspur. Football the English way. Really, the whole world's way. Taz had played midfield in high school and college. But his real education in the sport came later, through a colleague and friend in the British Foreign Ministry, or, as his pal would put it, "a bloke" from Northumberland named Gavin Hart. The year past, Gavin had been posted to Reykjavik.

Tottenham scored first, from a free kick. Villa engineered a great return goal, with a final twenty-yard cross to Agbonlahor, running at top speed, and then firing a driving header into the upper corner.

Taz turned off the television at halftime, ran through his options and, with some trepidation, settled on the garlic cure. He rooted through the freezer until he found his last jar of homemade pesto, full of garlic; his basil crop had come in spectacularly. He thawed the precious green paste, put it in a saucepan above a low flame, added pine nuts and butter. Absorbed as much as he could of the steam from the colander of hot pasta. Crusty garlic bread. Sharp red wine.

He had learned about the cure from Charles McCabe's column in the *San Francisco Chronicle*. McCabe had written about a friend who attacked even the hint of illness by eating whole bulbs of raw garlic for several days running. He didn't bother to separate the cloves, just stripped the outer husk and chewed the greater bulb like an apple. McCabe swore that after three days, he could find his friend in Golden Gate Park just by his odor.

Taz was only starting on the garlic. The next day, he roasted two bulbs in olive oil to have with dinner. On the third day, even his shower smelled of garlic. He pushed it further at lunch by eating four raw cloves with salami, cheese, and half a baguette. Finally, at dinner, he made a Caesar salad from scratch, with homemade croutons fried in olive oil and garlic.

The next morning, he biked to the Dollar Store to pick up some cheap underwear. Found the end of the line behind an old woman he vaguely recognized as a vocal citizen in town meetings.

The girl at the counter looked to be in her early twenties. She sported a shock of purple hair and four or five earrings. A skinny young man with a goatee and three boxes of air fresheners got in line behind Taz. He thought he noticed looks passing among the clerk, the older woman, and the air freshener fan. Just as he was beginning to feel slightly claustrophobic, Dana Bonner appeared from nowhere and joined the end of the line. He stared resolutely out the store window and pretended not to notice. At which point, the old lady turned and asked, loudly, which one of her line mates had just come from "rolling around in a garlic patch." The young Goth at the counter smirked. Taz decided to cop to it; there was nothing else to do.

"I'm afraid it's me, ma'am. Just trying to cure a cold."

She looked him over with a rigorous eye, but not without humor. "Hell, *you* could cure *my* cold." She paid up, thanked the clerk, and left.

Taz put the packet of Hanes on the counter.

The Goth couldn't resist a quip. "At least they're not tidy whiteys."

Taz smiled and paid hurriedly. As he left the counter and headed out the door, he thought he saw Dana rolling her eyes.

Home was the only safe place. Rode back down Pension Street through the rain. Got to the cottage, wiped his bike with a towel and put it in the shed. Once inside, he turned up the heat and picked up the fourth volume of Pocock's *Barbarism and Religion*. Taz had been reminded by more than one of his college professors that he was not a scholar, but he was entirely captivated by Pocock's erudition. The long, well-constructed sentences opened the world of Gibbon and the Enlightenment in a way that few other books had. As the sentences rolled on, Europe's view of Roman antiquity turned out to be an extremely accurate reflection of Europe's own evolving values. Pocock's triumph was that a book said to be about Gibbon and ancient Rome turned out to reveal the subliminal values of the eighteenth-century European literati. It was a strangely insightful anthropological look at the culture that spawned ours. And, given the recent unpleasantness at the Dollar Store, as he would later refer to it, the book had the extra advantage of being extremely long; it could last days, weeks if necessary.

Later that week, Taz showed up at Laney and Richard's house with his tools and a box of shingles. Laney had mentioned that a branch had fallen on the roof in the last big wind. It took four hours to patch the shingled roof, and two more for a game of chess with Richard on the porch. Neither of them was Bobby Fischer, but they knew their openings, and Richard also had some middle-game strategy, which was why he usually won. But this game was still a contest.

"So, I was thinking about this issue of what somebody might know about you."

"Oh, let's talk about me," Taz said, imitating Katharine Hepburn's line in *The Philadelphia Story*.

"Well, do you want to hear it, or not?"

"Yeah, I guess I do."

"Remember Ray's?"

"How could I forget?" A month before, Taz, Ronny, and Tom had headed off-island for the Friday night open mic at Ray's Shanty, a beer, crab, and barbeque place on Route 175 just behind the Wallops Air Station. There were a couple of other acts, not very good, and the crowd was restive. But folks got happier once the threesome started playing. They called themselves the Swamp Possums, and the audience identified with the country style and the old-timey licks.

Everything was going swimmingly until the band hit the Steve Earle tunes. Someone out there made the mistake of actually listening to the lyrics of "City of Immigrants." All hell broke loose. At first, it was a few choice catcalls. Then a half-full Budweiser longneck sailed past Ronny. Tom muttered something about getting out of there, but it was too late. A fat man in the front row got gobsmacked by the second bottle and charged back to find the miscreant. A woman with bleached blonde hair put her face in the way of a flying hamburger. Her boyfriend turned and slugged the unsuspecting innocent at the next table.

Taz and Ronny had already jammed their guitars into their hardshells. Taz was too late with the banjo. An Orpheum 3 from the 1920s. For some reason, his love for it hadn't translated into anything but the old cardboard case it had come in when he bought it twenty years before. Just as he was about to put the banjo away, one of the brawlers stepped backwards to duck a punch and put his foot right through the cardboard. Taz, holding the banjo in his left hand, used his right to give the bonehead a rabbit chop to the back of the neck. The man stumbled over the stage lip and ended up on his face. That's when the police arrived.

No charges were filed. Warnings were given, and restitution was paid. Since the three musicians were more recognizable than the customers—even the regulars—they did most of the paying. Of course it made local headlines.

"You think she got it from the *Beacon*?"

"Or the police blotter."

"But there were no charges."

Richard smiled. "You're the last person I would suspect of naiveté when it comes to the police."

"You have a point."

"Anyway, she said something about not needing another drunk in her life."

"To whom?"

"Laney, of course. They're quite close."

"Holy shit."

"Maybe good for you. Laney thinks you walk on water."

"The last drunk—her husband, the Coast Guard guy?"

"He was famous in town. People suspected he might have been violent with her, or maybe with Moyer."

"Oh." Burning inside.

CHAPTER SEVEN

Tobytown

WHY DID TAZ CARE what she thought of him? Or that she had already decided what kind of man he was? What were the facts the Accomack County authorities might have filed under his name? Taz decided to see for himself.

It was a crisp autumn day. Thursday, October eighteenth, to be exact. He climbed in the truck and headed south on the back roads through the tidy little town of Atlantic. Old Faithful had suffered his driving habits for more than twenty years. She had clocked over 250,000 miles. The first 200,000 on one clutch. He was very proud of that. It wasn't all freeway, either. We're talking two-lane country highways, gravel roads in the Blue Ridge, dirt tracks in the High Plains, and paths ground out of oyster shells in the marshes at the mouth of the Maurice River on the edge of Delaware Bay. The old rust bucket had paid her dues. More than once, she had paid his, too.

He crossed to the bay side of the peninsula and wound his way down to Onancock. Headed to the waterfront, where the old general store had been turned into a decent pub. Had a beer on the porch, read the day's papers, then drove across the peninsula to Accomac.

Accomac, the county seat, omitted the *k*, so as not to be confused with Accomack, the county. The town Accomac didn't have the old town feel of Onancock or Wachapreague. Taz guessed it had always been the domain of the well-off. It didn't feel like a town at all, really, just a loose collection of brick buildings of various ages, all apparently built in the architectural style of the oldest of them, a debtors' prison from the eighteenth century. The buildings were arranged in a loose quadrangle around the axes of Front Street and Courthouse Road. They were surrounded by large, leafy lots and widely separated three-story houses. The whole complex lay about a half mile from the big Virginia Department of Transportation yard on Route 13, only two miles south of one of the biggest chicken slaughterhouses on the peninsula.

He parked on a side street near the courthouse and found the administrative offices. The first two were empty, the desks clean. Behind the third door sat a young woman with tortoiseshell glasses. She was apparently hypnotized by her desktop computer. He coughed to get her attention. She looked up with a tentative smile. Taz introduced himself, pulled out his wallet and let her see his Fish and Wildlife Enforcement badge. It was an honorary badge, but it looked real enough. The Fish and Wildlife Service had given Taz the badge after he persuaded the White House to impose trade sanctions on Taiwan for allowing a flourishing trade in tiger parts. That was when he was playing utility infield for Interior Secretary Talbot.

The local grandees in Taipei and Shanghai had enjoyed garnishing their soup with tiger penises imported from India and Indonesia. Wild tiger populations were in trouble anyway. They didn't really need to have their severed private parts become cult ingredients for rich men's soups in the world's biggest consumer market. No way the White House would let them sanction China, so they decided to send a message through Taiwan.

Turning his attention back to the young woman behind the desk, Taz gave his prepared spiel. "I'm looking for information on a couple of poaching incidents and wanted to see the recent police files."

Her face brightened. "Maybe I can help. I'm bored stiff. " Her scent tasted of rose and citrus.

"Fine. How about if you look at them after I do and make sure I haven't missed anything." She fairly leapt from her desk and through the door behind her, and emerged a few minutes later carrying four large binders with a lot of loose paper tucked into them.

He watched her as she came towards him. She was about five-foot-five, with curly black hair. Early thirties, no ring. Maybe just a little over her target weight, but in a nice way. Dressed conservatively, a gray cardigan over a cream-colored blouse. A cautious smile and a spark behind the glasses.

"Here you are. I'm not sure they're up to date." She gave him an apologetic look. There was honey in her voice.

"You sing?"

"In choir on Sundays." A pause. "Why?"

"You have a nice voice, is all. I didn't catch your name."

"Darly. Darly Exmore." She blushed.

"I'm Taz. Taz Blackwell." He got to work on the binders.

❋❋❋

The first binder had nothing interesting. The usual meth cases, burglaries, stolen cars, domestic incidents. The second one merited more attention. A couple of disputes over leased clam beds in the Chincoteague Channel. Citations issued for hunting over bait in a wildlife management area near Parksley. Notes on a boat stranding on Metompkin, one of the marsh islands bought years ago by The Nature Conservancy. Twenty pounds of heroin in plastic wrap behind the sideboards of a recently purchased twenty-four-foot Velocity 500 speedboat. Nobody found at the scene, no charges, no leads.

He hit the jackpot in the third notebook. There he was, and Tom and Ronny. Officer Rackley reported a fracas at Ray's, got it about right. There were some handwritten notes attached to the formal report. The band hadn't started it, though they had been playing some pretty weird shit. Not clear who threw the first beer, or punch. A couple of hotheads who kept fighting after the police had already told everybody to pipe down got arrested, that was about it. Some broken chairs, but Ray had insurance. So far so good, nothing incriminating.

But the third notebook had something else in it, far more interesting than the story of the Swamp Possums' adventures at Ray's Shanty. The gold medal went to a file on Tobytown, a historically black settlement on the bay south of Onancock. There had been a series of disturbances, the Accomack County police had been called four or five times, enough so that there was a special file folder that had been interleaved into the binder with the title *Tobytown Survey Issues*.

Taz couldn't make out the underlying conflict, but it was clear that the inhabitants of Tobytown weren't all that comfortable with outsiders, and particularly outsiders with theodolites and survey markers. Several survey crews had had trouble—marker stakes pulled, tires slashed, in one case something close to a hit and run, although nothing was hit except survey equipment. In the same folder were some notes of civil disobedience arrests, some in Accomac, one in Annapolis, with residents of Tobytown indicted in both instances. He wrote *Tobytown* on a torn piece of paper.

At first glance, the fourth binder held little of real interest. Several entries tracking wrangles involving farmworkers, and a series of labor disputes at chicken processing plants. Seemed the police were interested in the labor movement in the Delmarva; they were tracking organizers, particularly those who came in from outside. Some of the activists appeared to have been arrested on various charges. Then there was a series of dispatches regarding a two-week dragnet for prostitutes working the Route 13 corridor, and loose pages with other offenses: drunk or disorderly behavior, interference with a police officer, traffic violations. Finally, a page full of real estate property information, including a long litany of violations of building codes, property setbacks, construction permit issues. One thing leapt out at Taz—a surprising number of these last misdemeanors had occurred in or near Tobytown.

He had read too much. He was tired and thirsty. He closed the binder, looked up, and caught Darly watching him.

Thought it best to be polite. "Thank you. I think I've got what I need."

"I bet you came in to see what we had on the fracas at Ray's. You're in that band, aren't you? The one that started the fight." She gave him a quizzical look with a smile tucked right in behind it.

Change the subject. "Do you just sing church music?"

"You're kidding, right? Do I really look so pious?" She took off her glasses and mussed her hair.

"If you're game, there's a bunch that gets together at the bookstore in Chincoteague on Saturday nights. Maybe you should come."

"What sorts of songs do you sing?"

"Folk, Depression-era songs, jug-band tunes, and even an occasional hymn."

"What time do you meet?"

"Usually about seven. With an hour give on either side."

She smiled. "I don't get out to the Island much. Maybe I should."

He couldn't tell whether she meant it or whether she was just being polite. *Don't let the door slam on your way out.*

Taz drove on, heading south and east, angling towards Wachapreague, which was never going to win any tourist awards. There was no beach, just a channel leading to one salt marsh island after another. But Wachapreague's curse was also its salvation. The only outside folks came to catch a fishing charter.

He stopped at the only restaurant on the channel. Took a table on the deck. There were several little groups pulling down beer and cracking crab. Two couples at the farthest table had apparently brought a cabin cruiser up the Intracoastal Waterway from Florida. He looked down at the cruiser, tied up on the floating dock. It was the new style, all aerodynamic sweeps and hardly any actual deck space. There was a Confederate flag rippling from the radar antenna. Still pimping the lost cause, better left in history's refuse pile.

He ordered oysters and a Caesar salad. Caitlyn, his favorite server, brought him a glass of Sauvignon blanc without waiting for him to ask. She was a graduate student at the University of Virginia studying modernism—presumably Ezra Pound and T. S. Eliot.

"Hey, what about Ezra Pound?"

"I don't know, we haven't read his poetry yet."

"I bet the first Cantos will surprise you." She looked perplexed. Taz recited by memory from his old, dog-eared volume from *New Directions*, with the simple burnt orange cover.

> *One year floods rose,*
> *One year they fought in the snows,*
> *One year hail fell, breaking the trees and the walls.*
> *Down here in the marsh they trapped him*
> *In one year,*
> *And he stood in water up to his neck*
> *To keep the hounds off him.*

Caitlyn's eyes were wide. She gave him a quick smile and trotted to the kitchen to pick up an order for another table.

While Taz sat over his wine, a young man with dreadlocks came out of a side door and started to work on the windows. He had a bucket of soapy water and a long applicator with a sponge on one side and a rubber squeegee on the other. He was muttering as if disturbed by something. Taz concentrated on his oysters and looked for Caitlyn to order another glass of wine.

He gave her a desultory wave through the window, but she didn't notice. Finally, he got up to hit the head and get a glass at the bar. Before he had taken his second step, the window washer turned his way.

"Are you okay, sir? Can I do anything for you?"

"Thank you, no. I was just headed to get another glass. Thirstier than your average customer, I guess. Are you from here?"

"Yes sir. Born and raised over in Cashville."

Cashville was only a few miles from Tobytown.

"Family still around these parts?"

"Yes sir, mostly in Cashville, but I still got some cousins in Tobytown, as well."

"What's going on in Tobytown? I've been hearing some things."

"Not much. Never is."

"I don't know. Sounds like folks there are pretty upset about something. What's got them all stirred up?"

"Some big company wants to take a lot of property, that's what I heard."

"For what?"

"Don't know. But there's a big fight over it. They want everybody to sell, but some folks ain't so inclined."

"I can see why."

"Yeah, Tobytown is something special. It's ours, from a long time. Most folks want to keep it that way."

"Good luck to you, then."

✳✳✳

It was close to seven when Taz hit the causeway across the bay and the island came into view. Egrets singly and in groups across the marshes on either side of the Wire Narrows. The last shreds of light on the houses and docks along Main Street. The sunset crowd had already gathered at the outdoor bar at the Chincoteague Inn.

Diane McCloud was presiding over the bar with her usual combination of humor and wit. Or scorn, for the occasional jerk. Taz asked her for a plate of clams casino and a beer, and watched the sun go down. It set in the southwest, the general direction of Tobytown.

CHAPTER EIGHT

Guitar Town

TAZ THOUGHT HE WAS safe on the island, but work crept up on him. The boys at INR wanted a sanitized version of the Norway cable that they could give to the European desk and to his old bureau, Oceans, Environment and Science. It was an assignment that could be done from a remote location, though INR had probably never gotten a briefing from a consultant on a marsh island, the high points of which were ponies and oysters. Taz was finally rid of his bout with influenza, or whatever it was, and could at least sit in front of his laptop for more than half an hour at a time.

Just in time, because a boatload of new work was looming on the horizon. A colleague at the Carnegie Institute was hoping he would agree to speak on a panel as part of a conference on resource use in the Arctic. Soffia Gunnarsdottir, his friend on the Arctic Council Secretariat, called to see if he would help her design a review process to assess progress on the Council's ecosystem management directive, which Taz had negotiated while working at State.

Taz was just starting to scope out the first project when Mother Nature pulled his attention back to the island. There was something besides work looming on the horizon. A tropical depression in the mid-Atlantic had moved west to the Caribbean. The radio jockeys were already frothing with excitement. He called an acquaintance at NOAA, the National Oceanic and Atmospheric Administration.

"Taz, you know as well as I do that these things aren't storms when they come off the African coast. More like waves in the atmosphere—until they cross warmer water." Now the wave had become a loose countercyclical storm headed towards Cuba. They were calling it "Tropical Storm soon-to-be-hurricane Donna" and NOAA showed a storm track coming right up the Atlantic Coast. Which meant taking down his awnings and carting all the furniture off the dock, at the very least. Taz was going to lose a big chunk of his work schedule as well a lot of practice time before the next music night at the bookstore. He biked to the store to pick up a *New Yorker* when Richard flagged him down.

"You know we're playing Saturday night?"

"What time?"

"Seven, as usual. But this time we're going Mexican style." So Taz was going to have to practice a *norteño* or two.

"You need contributions for the tequila?"

"Nah, just bring some limes."

"Good enough."

He almost tripped over Laney on his way out. She grabbed his arm, led him back inside, and gave him a long hug. "And where have you been hiding? I haven't seen you for two weeks. Richard's climbing the walls looking for somebody to talk books with, and he's driving me crazy."

"I had some work, and you know how work makes me sick. Besides, I thought it would be good for my reputation if I kept my head down for a while."

"Oh, that. Maybe I helped you out a little bit."

"What's she like?"

"Dana? She's as brave as they come. A great heart. Maybe she's quick on the draw where her kids are concerned. And maybe she's a little wary on first impression. But burned once, forever careful."

"How bad was the burn?"

"Real bad. So don't go there if you're not serious."

"Right. I've already fucked up twice, by my count. Three strikes and you're out."

Saturday rolled around. Taz spent a couple of hours plunking some songs during the afternoon. He was working on "Poor, Poor Pitiful Me," an offbeat Warren Zevon tune and very witty.

**

Jam nights at Rainy Day were some of his favorite events on the island, right up there with the Saturday morning farmers' market. The back porch was already crowded when he pulled up and turned off his car. He unpacked his guitar next to the romance novels in the back hall and picked his way through the crowd.

A young man he'd never seen before was strumming "500 Miles" on a nylon-string guitar. JoAnne Clayton, a silver-haired Sunday school teacher who never missed a jam, had joined in to offer an upper line. Their voices carried a nice harmony. They got to the end of the song, and there was some polite applause. Tom pulled out his harmonica, looked slyly at Taz, and started in on "Viola Lee Blues." Taz played along, picking the march rhythm on his guitar that Gus Cannon got on his banjo. Ronny strummed the chords in a punchy way that suited the tune.

> *I wrote a letter I mailed in the air,*
> *Mailed it on the air indeed-e,*
> *I wrote a letter, mailed it in the air . . .*
> *You may know by that, I've got a friend somewhere.*

One of the loneliest, proudest lines in the blues.

They played a couple more tunes, and then took a break. There was coffee on a slightly shabby deal table stuck in the corner nearest the back wall of the store. Folks were milling around, catching up on the news in small groups. Taz poured himself a cup and put two bucks in the can. Taz and Tom stood near the back, surveying the scene.

"Hey Mr. Big Spender. The coffee's only a buck."

"I reckon some folks don't pay at all."

"So you're going to make it up? You're probably safe here. Some places I know the deadbeats would bleed you dry and *then* they'd mug you." Tom was nipping on a bottle in a paper bag that he had retrieved from the half-empty bookshelf behind him. Taz didn't make inquiries; everybody knew that Tom favored Jim Beam.

"Thank God we didn't have to do any more folk songs." Tom gave Taz a sideways grin.

"Oh, come on. The kid wasn't too bad a singer, and JoAnne made him sound a lot better."

"Oh, I guess." Another swig.

Just then Taz saw the young folksinger coming his way, waving at him as if he were signaling in semaphore. Right behind him, JoAnne had Dana Bonner by the elbow, talking urgently in her ear. Dana hadn't seen him yet. No matter. His heart was in his throat. He had so wanted to set things right, but how? His mind raced through the options. *Apologize? But for what? Pretend it never happened? Divert to the storm heading our way?*

When the trio was still a few blessed yards away, separated from them by a middle-aged couple who were arguing, pointing fingers at each other and towards the street. JoAnne called out in her best Sunday school voice, "Boys, I've got some people I want you to meet." Tom looked up, saw Dana, nudged Taz with his left elbow. Taz put his coffee down on a shelf. His hand was trembling. The trio arrived.

Dana was wearing a light blue cashmere sweater that clung in all the right places. She was trying to muster a smile. JoAnne introduced the folksinger first.

"Tom, Taz, this is Fred Manchin. Doesn't he have the most wonderful voice? I'm trying to get him to join our choir."

Fred wore his hair early Beatles style. It looked as if it had been cut with the help of a colander. He shook Taz's hand and said, "I love your guitar work. Do you give lessons?" Before Taz could answer, JoAnne said, "And this is Dana Bonner. She's got the best voice in the choir. Have you two met?"

Taz opened his mouth hoping a reply would come of its own accord, but Tom spoke first in a whisper loud enough for anyone nearby to hear.

"Wasn't it a woman named Dana who chewed you out on the beach? You said she was beautiful. Can't be two beautiful Danas on an island this size."

Taz put his hand on Tom's shoulder and tried to muster a semblance of good humor.

Tom scratched his head and continued, with a wicked grin at Taz, to flout pretty much every rule of polite conversation. "She chewed you out before you met? Before you met! Well, I guess it makes it more efficient, don't it. You always end up pissing them off anyway."

Taz gripped his shoulder harder. "And you're not making it any easier."

Taz caught Dana's eye in the moment they both began to search desperately for an escape route. A technicolor blush was rising up to her cheeks. Her lips were slightly parted, as if she were about to say something. At the same time, her nose was crinkling in a way that made him think she was about to laugh. JoAnne, at her side, realized something was up. She turned to Fred and said, "Things are complicated on the island, sometimes."

Just then, Richard extricated himself from the counter and hustled their way. Ignoring all the others, he pointed his finger at Taz. "What you did on our roof, is that going to come through a hurricane?"

"If it doesn't, I'll do it again free. Where's the storm now?"

"Still south of the Carolinas. But they say the core is coming right through the Outer Banks, and the eye will be over us by midday Monday."

"You want to move the books upstairs?"

"Not unless we have to. Don't worry, you'll be the first one I'll call."

"Well I'm not going anywhere. Particularly once they close the causeway."

"Close the causeway?" Fred looked incredulous.

Richard wheeled around and lurched over to his desk, muttering, "All I need. This is all I need."

There were calls from the porch. Taz saw his opening. He looked at Dana, opened his hands, raised his eyebrows, and said with a smile, "I guess now we've met, after all." Then he grabbed Tom by the shoulder, slid between JoAnne and the middle-aged couple, and made his way back into the music.

At nine-thirty, as folks were drifting out, Tom whispered to him over the back of his hand, "Let's go get us a drink before Roxy closes." Taz nodded. *Sounds like a fine idea.*

A half dozen cars and trucks were strewn randomly through the gravel lot at the Pony Pines. The neon fish over the door was casting its unearthly light on the path. Was it a blue? Was it a shad? Maybe a rockfish? There were many drunken discussions on this question. Inside, someone was turning up the jukebox. A boisterous trio of young men were joshing at the table nearest the bar. They were out-of-towners, not even come-heres. They had on starched cowboy shirts, and two of them were wearing brand new Stetsons. Most likely they were working construction on the new bridge. Taz recognized a couple of fishermen at the table by the window, said hello, asked about the catch. Out of the corner of his eye, at a booth in the back corner, he saw Laney and Dana deep in conversation.

Roxy Lopez stood behind the bar, busy totaling some accounts. Taz and Tom sat, careful not to disturb her concentration. She finally looked up. "Haven't seen you two in a while." Taz was grateful for her amnesia. God knows what he might have said when he was drunkenly trying to entice her a few nights before.

Tom ordered a beer, Taz a Maker's on the rocks. The fishermen paid up; the oldest slapped Taz on the back and said he'd better save some money for the next poker game. Taz swallowed half his bourbon, managed a wry smile and coughed out, "What goes around comes around." The fishermen laughed all the way out the door.

Roxy was in her late twenties, skin the color of volcanic sand, and frizzy hair that stood a good two inches off her head in every direction. Taz enjoyed her as much for her take-no-prisoners attitude as for her more obvious qualities. She was wearing a sleeveless T-shirt. No evidence of a bra. Her eyes were bright and direct, and she took no guff from her customers. She lived at Joe's trailer park with her dog, Sasha.

Taz was just starting to chat her up when one of the young rowdies called out, "Hey, brown sugar, why don't you ditch the old man and come and pay a little attention to us?"

She rolled her eyes, picked up her pad, and came around the bar. "What would you like?"

"I'd like it if you'd come sit on my lap." This from the one on the left, who was wearing a blue cowboy shirt with snaps and a pair of Frye boots. They'd clearly had more than one round. Taz turned to look them over. Roxy smiled stiffly at the one who wanted to host her lap dance. "Well, that ain't gonna happen, honey. Not in this life. So what do you want?"

Betty Hunter, the owner, came through the kitchen door and moved to her post at the end of the bar. She'd gotten a drift of what was going on.

John Hiatt was playing on the box. *"Have you ever been sorry, really sorry, for what you done?"* The trio were egging each other on, whispering and laughing.

"How about you come home with us, sweetheart? We'll show you a good time."

Roxy shifted on her feet uneasily.

Tom had enough. "Maybe you should cool it down, boys."

"We don't take marching orders from old hippies." This from the one in the middle, who had his own Frye boots and a suspiciously new-looking ten-gallon hat. He was pudgy.

Taz, loud enough to be heard above the box, said, "How about you set up three beers, Betty?"

Betty nodded, opened three longnecks and put them one by one on the bar. Taz grabbed all three by the necks and turned around to face the rowdies. "Hey gents, these are on me. Let's let Roxy close up, shall we?"

Laney was just approaching the bar to pay her tab. She turned to the three. "Why don't you boys find somewhere else to test your manhood?"

The third one, who looked the youngest, grabbed Roxy's wrist and pulled her towards him. "Stay out of this, bitch. We're just having a little fun."

"Yeah. But maybe your fun's a pain for the rest of us."

"You think I care what a dried-up old whore thinks?" Roxy snatched her arm away, with the young cowpunk struggling out of his chair to grab her again. Taz turned all three bottles upside down at once and poured the cold beer on one rowdy and then the other. They gazed up in astonishment. Then, embarrassed and angry, they all shoved back from the table and came towards him.

The one who had been chasing Roxy rounded on Tom first. Tom head-butted him and knocked him back two full steps. His nose began bleeding profusely. The one in the blue shirt was swinging wildly at Taz. He stepped to the side and rabbit-chopped him in the neck, hard enough to knock him onto the table. The pudgy one had lost his hat. He scurried back around the table, his eyes wide.

Taz picked up the Stetson, threw it on the table. Flattened it the way you kill a roach. "Get your friends and get out of here."

The trio stumbled towards the door. Bloody-nose held a kerchief to his face. The one Taz had punched was trying to stand using Pudgy's shoulder for support. The next thing Taz heard was the sound of tires squealing and throwing gravel.

Taz found he was shaking. Then he felt a slap on the shoulder from Tom, who had a wild look in his eye. "I think that calls for a whisky."

Betty said, "It's on me, boys. Always nice to have a little muscle in the place."

Taz rolled his eyes. "Jesus, Betty, if we're what you call muscle, you're in a heap of trouble."

Laney eyed Taz. "You didn't do so bad."

That brought a laugh from Roxy. She had moved to Taz's side, put her arm around his waist. She looked at Betty apologetically. "It might be a good idea to close up quick so they don't come back with their daddies."

"Don't worry, honey. I'm going to call Jeff and let him know what happened."

Tom grimaced. Jeff was Betty's cousin, one of the town cops. The two already knew each other too well. Betty caught his look. "I won't give them any names. I'll just say a couple of customers helped out. And these two won't say anything either, right, girls?"

Dana was waiting for Laney by the door. She looked his way for a long moment. She seemed stirred up and embarrassed at the same time. Embarrassment won out, and she turned her gaze to the floor. All Taz thought was *strike three.*

CHAPTER NINE

Wild Geese from the West

TAZ FIGURED HE'D BETTER get back home before the police checked in. Back roads only. Drove slowly down the Eastside Road, then on to Ridge and Beebe. Let himself into the cottage through the kitchen door. Found a bottle of rye and a glass; wandered across South Main and down to his dock; sat on the tattered woven plastic chair, watched the base lights at Wallops radar base across the channel.

Slugged down a healthy pour. Another healthy pour. The chagrin on Dana's face was all he could see. She was achingly beautiful. And he had just confirmed every fear she could have about him.

Why do I fuck up everything? Right place, wrong time. *Fucking hot head. Why, oh why, did she have to be here?* Another slug of rye. He savored the aftertaste, realized he was floating. Amber anger management.

Still, Roxy had been thankful for the help. Taz liked Roxy. And Betty, he really liked Betty. And Tom; the boy must have a first-class headache. But not as bad as the other guy. Plastic surgery for him. The bottle had given up its last dose of *woe-be-gone*, a phrase Taz had cadged from Guy

Clark, the Texas songster. Taz managed to assume a vertical position, executed a few dance steps back up the dock, whacked the screen door, grabbed another bottle from the cabinet. A Montecristo for good measure. Came back, sat on the stoop. Struck a safety match, lit up the cigar.

Stars. A crescent moon. The night air cool on his face. Looked for a shooter, but most of what he was seeing was a little blurry. Wispy, high altitude clouds. The sound of geese overhead, talking to each other. Keep in line. Move up. Move back. Passing overhead on their way east to Assateague, leaving shards of sound in the air.

The cigar had a good, relaxing aroma. Not sweet, like a Crooks, or those disgusting cherry smokes they sold in the gas marts. A true tobacco smoke, one leaf, rolled to perfection, with a Connecticut wrapper.

Gradually ceased being mad at himself. What good did it do? The fake cowboys had fucked up, and he had reacted. Nothing more. Hadn't heard from the police yet, so maybe it was okay.

He tried to sort out his feelings. He didn't even know Dana, but she was pulling some kind of a tide in his life; she troubled his mind. They had hardly spoken, except on the beach when she'd told him off. It's not like he was looking for her, he was just trying to talk birds with an eleven-year-old birder. Moyer. But there she was, beautiful, clear-eyed, protective, guarding her nest like an eagle.

Why should I care? She was virtually a stranger, but he could feel his magnetic center being realigned. It didn't make any sense, but wasn't that the definition of love? A tide that carries you even when you can't explain it?

The cigar made sure he wouldn't be going to sleep. At least not anytime soon. He stayed on the front stoop, mulling over his life. A few more flights of Canada geese descended over the Wire Narrows and made their way toward the brackish refuge ponds. He wished he could follow them south.

Blues singer Skip James's high mournful voice echoed in his ears:

> *I laid down last night,*
> *I laid down last night,*
> *I laid down, tried to take my rest.*

My mind got to ramblin',
Like wild geese from the west, from the west.

As he drew down the cigar, Taz recalled that he and Richard had talked about heading down to Cape Charles to see the hawks and flickers gathering to cross the mouth of the Chesapeake Bay. But Richard wouldn't be able leave the store for a few days. It was midnight—perfect timing. If he got to the cape before dawn, he might catch a serious return flight, especially given the good northerly breeze.

Taz got up, made himself strong coffee, tossed his binoculars and some gear into his rucksack, and grabbed a notebook. It was still pitch dark, so he drove straight onto Route 13. Made the left at T's Corner and flipped on the radio. The little Chincoteague independent station was playing some decent jazz. It was close on two when he passed the cut-off for Cape Charles. He decided to head straight to Kiptopeke State Park, almost at the tip of the peninsula. The main park gate was closed, but there was a gravel road at the south boundary that accessed the low forest and dunes just before the beach. He turned in and parked on the flats. Turned off the engine and doused the lights. He was tired. Sleep came easily. His head lolled against the drivers' headrest. When he woke up, he found he'd been drooling.

Just before dawn. Western sky still dark. A mere hint of light blue in the east. He rubbed his eyes and found his plastic water bottle, splashed some water on his face. *Better.* The truck cab smelled funky. He opened the door and stepped out into a cool wet breeze coming off the bay. Last night's northerly had turned. He scrambled up to the top of the dune line. Smelled the salt breeze even more powerfully from higher up. Light gradually increasing, the clouds on the eastern skyline glowing pink. Homer's rosy-fingered dawn. Even before the first shafts of yellow appeared, birds started falling out of the sky. Diving, more accurately, for any bush or tree that offered a perch. They had been flying south at night and found themselves at dawn over the Chesapeake Bay or the Atlantic Ocean. Neither offered great perches or avian rest stops, so the birds dove back to the nearest land. Taz was standing on it. He saw blue jays, flickers, yellow warblers. A black-throated green warbler and two black-throated blues. Goldfinches. Cooper's hawks. Sharpies everywhere, too distracted to hunt. Which was a good thing for the kinglets, sparrows, thrushes, and towhees. It was almost too much, too fast, too many, too quick. The fallout lasted about an hour and a half. When it quieted down, he went off to find breakfast and write down what he had seen.

Nannies in Cape Charles. Scrambled eggs, country ham, biscuits, grits. Smell of grease and coffee. What life had to offer.

The chaos in the Kiptopeke sky was over. A loose line of ibises, flying south over the mouth of the bay. Cormorants, with their crooked necklines and hooked beaks. Ospreys circling, calling. The occasional lucky one carrying a fish fore and aft. Vultures, some the blacks with white-tipped wings and no tail; they looked like B-2 stealth bombers. A few eagles, but no merlins. Geese.

It was quiet and beautiful, and the October breeze was soft and cool. It would have been easy to stay. But he doubted that he would see much beyond what he had already seen. The shorebirds, even the elusive godwits, would be more plentiful back in the salt marshes of the Chincoteague Channel. Taz headed north.

He drove slowly along the country roads on the bay side of Route 13. Farm country where the old men on their front porches waved as you went by. Skirted the Cherrystone Inlet on the way to Eastside. Found the dirt road to the cable ferry across Occohannock Creek at Davis Wharf. The ferryman was sorting some gear by a riverside shed that doubled as the tollhouse. He was glad of the business.

"Not much call for these services anymore," he said. "Route 13 has cut the heart out of life down here. People hurrying from New York to Virginia Beach. What do they care about these little towns, the crabbers and the farmworkers?"

Up through Craddockville and Pungoteague, with their whitewashed houses and carefully tended yards. Worked his way around Pungoteague Creek, then turned left just south of Savageville. Tobytown was a couple of miles downstream, towards the mouth of Pungoteague Creek. Taz loved the east side of the peninsula. Full of bays, inlets, and marshes.

There was a police cruiser at the crossroads. As Taz pulled up to the stop sign, its light began flashing. He waited at the sign and lowered his front windows.

"Everything okay, officer?" he said through the passenger side.

"Aren't you a little out of your way?" Probably looking at his Maryland plates.

"I'm headed into Tobytown."

"What's your business there?"

He had no right to ask, but Taz bit his tongue. "Just going to Ida's for a little late lunch." Ida's was known for its fried chicken and hominy, at least among the locals. "Why's it matter?"

"No tellin.' Just what I'm supposed to ask everybody." Scowling, he added, "You ain't a journalist?"

"Why? Something going on? Either way, I'm not a scribbler. I work on houses."

"Okay. It's just I'm supposed to tell the journalists to get lost."

"Pesky people anyway. Always prying into somebody's business."

"About right. And we don't need any of that just now."

There weren't that many cars at the gravel parking lot at Ida's. Understandable, with a damn police dragnet out on the byways. Taz was getting more curious about Tobytown by the minute. He had never been to Ida's, just heard about the great cooking. A local crowd, mostly black. A couple of Mexicans, maybe farmworkers. That was about it. A lot of eyes turned toward him as he made his way to a seat at the bar. He did his best to smile, unobtrusively.

"What'll it be?" The barman was tall, serious looking.

"Maker's on the rocks, and a glass of water."

The barman seemed to relax. Maybe just a normal customer.

He drank his whisky. Ordered a second. "I wouldn't mind some lunch with that. What are you rolling out today?"

The barman answered with a smile, "Ida's in back. The chicken's good."

"Then I'll have the chicken."

"Good choice. It comes with mashed potatoes or coleslaw."

"I'll take the slaw."

"Good enough."

The next time the barman came by, Taz called him over. "So, I was curious about the police out at the crossroads."

The man's poker face stiffened.

"I mean, it's pretty strange to have some bozo in a cruiser ask you why you want to go someplace. I just want to look around. I live up in Chincoteague. I'm a little new down here."

The barman looked him over carefully. "The cops are in hock to a giant corporation that wants to take our land."

"For what?"

"Not clear. We see the agents and the realtors, that's all. But we started talking to each other about what was going on."

"How long?"

"Been about the last six months."

"So that's why the demonstrations. Salisbury. Annapolis."

"Yep."

A skinny young waitress brought his chicken out from the kitchen. It was crisp and tender, finger-licking good. Just like they said. He lingered over the wings. Got ready to pay up. To the barman he said, "I'd like to help, if I can."

"Got a card?"

"Sure."

He gave him his card. The barman looked at it for a second, then held out his hand. "Glad to meet you, Taz. My name's Rodney."

Out in the parking lot, Taz looked around before getting in his car and heading north. Another police cruiser by the junction at Business Route 13. Passed him without a glance.

CHAPTER TEN

Accomac

THE DRIVE BACK TO the island would take only an hour and half. Taz reckoned he could put the spare time to good use and still get back home by sunset. It was half-past three when he took the turnoff to Accomac. He had decided to stop by the County Lands Office, which was in the same courthouse where he had looked at the police blotter. He entered a rather gloomy office with the shades pulled down and stacks of plat books everywhere in sight. A sallow-faced clerk with thinning hair, in his late thirties, obviously didn't enjoy his job. He was making notes slowly and carefully, apparently too busy to take notice of Taz.

"Excuse me. Where would I find recent real estate transactions around Cashville?" He thought it better not to mention Tobytown.

"The Westside records are all in the volumes on the corner shelf in back." The clerk never raised his gaze.

Taz found a stool near the records and took down a random book the size of a small ping-pong table. Written by hand, it included lists of slaves, of white owners freeing certain slaves, and a few black landowners, some of whom had slaves of their own. There were plats, records of deeds, leases, waivers, quitclaims. Things he didn't fully grasp. Most of the records were from property in Onancock and north. He pulled down another volume. On the fourth try, he found what he was looking for—records from Tobytown and Cashville.

At first, he wasn't sure he was seeing anything significant. The normal sales, liens, assignments. He kept leafing through the book, and eventually came to a section titled "Issues Regarding Mineral Estate." The section had been more recently compiled, and Tobytown showed up prominently. Differing from other places in Virginia, Tobytown's landowners owned the mineral estate of their property. In most Virginia counties, the subsurface had been split off the deeds in colonial times while under British common law. But, according to the equally musty Court Order Books, which Taz had found in a stack on the top shelf behind the plats, Tobytown had been conveyed to a community of free blacks before the Revolution. Most of the transfers were recorded as *"feoffment with livery of seisin,"* which was somehow different from the bargain-and-lease formula that succeeded it. Taz couldn't make it all out. What he could see was that the majority of the Tobytown deeds were for *fee simple* to both land and subsurface. One deed was different. It was a *fee tail* deed for 120 acres. Taz couldn't tell if the difference was significant.

What was clear from the more recent records was that someone had been acquiring a lot of real estate in Tobytown, and some of the mineral estate beneath it as well. The name that kept coming up was *Rinvest*. The Rinvest Company. Rinvest Capital Trust. Rinvest Title Corporation. Rinvest had obviously also been talking to landowners about surface property, seeing who was interested in selling in a down market. They had picked off quite a few takers, but the sales seemed to peter out in September of the year before.

Why? He couldn't tell.

He looked for more, but didn't find much, and shelved the last volume. He thanked the clerk and headed out the door. It occurred to him to see if Darly was in the police administrative office. He took the stairs and found her door. Knocked and peered around the open edge.

Darly was clearly surprised to see him, maybe pleased as well.

"Looking for more records of your escapades?"

"No, I was just in the land office. We missed you at the jam on Saturday."

"How could you miss me? I've never even been there." Very pert. She was wearing a pink blouse with the top button undone.

"We needed your voice. Bunch of scratchy old men. You'd make us sound better."

She smiled. "So when's the next time?"

"Saturday."

"Maybe I'll make it."

"I'll believe it when I see it. But I hope you do."

"Okay, see you. Thanks for stopping by."

He wanted to find out more about Rinvest. But first he wanted to go home and have a whisky out by the dock.

❋

Taz pulled up to the cottage at five-thirty. Sunset was still forty-five minutes away. It had been a warm day, almost Indian summer. Under the circumstances, he decided that a gin and tonic was the better choice. He pulled out a lime, the Bombay and the special tonic from Fever Tree. Dropped in a quick splash of Angostura bitters. He hadn't had the money to build a long dock, so he had started with a thirty-foot deck over the rubble where he could at least dangle his feet in the water. And launch his kayak, at high tide. The marsh grass restoration was proceeding slowly to the right of the deck. Or at least he thought it was. In truth, he couldn't quite tell whether he was gaining ground or losing it. Once the winter storms were over, spring would decide.

Saturday rolled around. Hurricane Doreen had moved off the coast of South Carolina. It was maybe two, three days away. He caught up on a few projects, and then spent some hours clamming off Piney Island. He found some good beds up by the old docks north of Janey's Creek, beyond where the local oystermen had their beds. He dug mostly quahogs—chowder clams. The early Massachusetts settlers adopted the Algonquin name from the Wampanoags, who had first given them the clams. But then the settlers had upset the beds, dug them all out, and a war followed. How could you deliberately destroy your children's harvest?

One way or another, a dozen midsize quahogs, chopped small and lightly sautéed in olive oil, could make a tasty dish of pasta. He was happy with his dinner.

Afterwards, it was time to amble down to Richard's store. He got there late, and the crowd was already pretty thick on the back porch. Darly was there, sitting next to Ronny. He had figured her out fast; they were already busy singing old country hymns. They had just started "In Christ There Is No East or West." Taz stood under the backdoor lintel and listened. Darly had a beautiful voice, and the two of them harmonized well together. Ronny was a natural, and Darly was singing harmonies he hadn't heard in a long time. When the hymn ended, he clapped and said, "Wow."

Darly said, "I thought maybe you were going to stand me up."

"Doesn't look like you were suffering a bit."

She smiled and moved her chair to make room for him to join them.

It was Tom's turn. He had spent the week listening to Paul Butterfield and Charley Musselwhite, and it hadn't done his playing any harm. He started in on "Walking Blues." Taz slotted in the guitar chords and sang back-up. Their voices blended well. It was clear Darly had never heard the song, but by the third time the bridge came by, she was adding an earthy harmony. The night went on like that, Darly surprising them with each song.

Around closing time, Ronny suggested they sing "Amazing Grace." Taz put his guitar down. One of the newer listeners ventured that the song was in G, maybe thinking Taz didn't know the chords.

"No, we're doing this one Acapulco." A few titters of laughter.

Ronny hummed the opening, to get them started.

> *Amazing grace, how sweet the sound,*
> *that saved a wretch like me,*
> *I once was lost, but now am found,*
> *Was blind, but now I see.*

Darly came in on a mournful fourth, like the harmony Roger Sprung sang with Jean Ritchie and Doc Watson so many years ago at Folk City. An unearthly, lonely harmony that set Ronny's voice off perfectly. Taz stopped singing to listen.

The crowd on the porch was silent. The harmonies sailed out through the night. Then Taz joined the singing again, but he was just trying to stay in line. Ronny was leading the tune. Darly had chosen all the boundaries, and she had chosen well.

When they finished, their listeners gasped rather than applauding. Then they cheered. Then they asked for more. It's hard to follow "Amazing Grace." After a spell, Ronny suggested "What Wondrous Love," a shape-note hymn he had started singing at Union Baptist. Taz looked at Darly. She said, "Let's go."

> *What wondrous love is this,*
> *Oh my soul, oh my soul,*
> *What wondrous love is this,*
> *Oh my soul,*
> *What wondrous love is this,*
> *To cause the Lord of Bliss*
> *To set aside his Crown*
> *For my soul, for my soul.*

This time she was singing fifths, gloriously, shiningly. Taz looked out at the crowd on the porch. Laney and Dana were standing at the back, listening intently.

Later, as they packed up guitars and harmonicas, he noticed Darly watching him. He smiled. "Maybe you'd come over for some coffee before you drive?"

"Yes."

She followed him back to the cottage. She leaned softly against him as he fumbled with the keys, and finally let them in.

They didn't need words. The coffee came after they made love. First on the couch, then on the bed, then in the kitchen while the water was boiling.

"You better stay 'til morning." They were sipping coffee side by side, sitting on the floor with their backs to the kitchen counter. Taz had found her some clean boxers and a pink oxford shirt that hung on her all too well. She put her coffee down and reached around his neck. Looked at him softly before they kissed. It was a long kiss.

Only afterwards, did she murmur her answer, but it seemed to be "yes."

***

In the morning he got a call from the barman at Ida's.

"Is this Mr. Blackwell?"

"Yes. Who's this?"

"It's Rodney, from Ida's."

"Oh, hello, how are you?"

"I wanted to let you know there's going to be a demonstration at the courthouse."

"When?"

"Tomorrow at noon."

"Okay, I'll be there."

"You have any friends?"

"Not many on one day's notice."

"Yeah. Okay. See you there."

***

The next day, he got to Accomac at nine thinking it would be good to look around before things got started. Leftover instincts from the resistance in the anti-war days. The district courthouse seemed calm, but there was a police bus behind the Suntrust Bank just across Route 13. Another one to the east of town, behind a gas station on Courthouse Road.

He had alerted Eliza Burkett, his favorite reporter, to the Tobytown story. Now he punched in her number again.

"You coming?"

"If the traffic lights in Pocomoke ever turn green."

About a half-hour away. "Good. Got a photographer?"

"Only our best."

"I should have known. See you soon. Watch out for police north of town. I haven't been up there, but they're everywhere else."

"Thanks for the heads-up."

Eliza Burkett was an up-and-coming reporter at the *Salisbury Daily Times*, the paper of record for Virginia's Eastern Shore. She did double duty as a stringer for the local TV news. Young, lean, and ambitious. They had met at a Shorebirds Minor League game.

Taz parked three blocks from the courthouse and walked over. People were starting to gather. Mostly black, but there was a sprinkling of white farmers as well. Men of both colors in Carhartt overalls and work boots. Women in dresses, some with head scarves. Children in tow. There didn't seem to be a gathering point—they were heading to the courthouse from all sides.

He found himself singing Buffalo Springfield under his breath:

> *There is something happening here,*
> *what it is ain't exactly clear . . .*
> *There's battle lines being drawn . . .*

He noticed another police bus behind the Department of Corrections building off Cross Street.

The crowd gathered slowly, like a cephalopod drawing in its tentacles. Altogether, maybe a couple hundred people. He spotted Rodney on the edge of the crowd, talking into a cell phone. He went over.

"So I did find one friend. She's a reporter for the *Salisbury Daily Times*." He pointed to Eliza and her cameraman, who were now trotting towards the crowd. Rodney smiled.

Nobody had a microphone. One man stood on a bench and addressed the crowd. He was wearing denim overalls over a plaid shirt.

"You know me. I'm Virgil Waite. My family has been on our land since the Articles of Confederation. I grow soybeans and corn. Now they tell me I have to leave, and the police are finding all kinds of problems with my land. First it's my fencing, then it's my shed. They've condemned my barn. *My barn!* How do you condemn a barn? We need it to stop, we need the county to step in. I'm appealing to them."

Murmurs of assent from the crowd.

Virgil had finished his speech. He pointed out the young boy standing beside him.

"My son is here with me. This is Bennett. I want him to have my farm when I'm too old to till. That's not wrong, is it?"

The crowd replied "no," that was not wrong.

Several other citizens got up on the bench to describe the trouble they'd had with the police. Each had appealed to higher authorities.

Taz looked around. He didn't see any higher authorities at the gathering. But he did see the police, and they were moving in. They looked a lot like the tactical squads he remembered from Berkeley in the bad old days. They had truncheons, shields, facemasks and pepper spray. They were approaching in ranks, from the north and east. One, apparently a captain, spoke through a bullhorn.

"This is an illegal gathering. You have no permit. I am ordering you to disperse, now. If you do not disperse, you will be arrested."

A thin man in a black jacket was tugging on his sleeve. There was a quick, intense conversation, during which the thin man pointed towards Virgil and then directly at Taz.

The crowd looked at the Captain balefully. In truth, they had no idea what they were supposed to do. It all happened so fast. The police coming off Courthouse Road charged first. Waded into the crowd, swinging batons. People broke and ran toward Front Street. Taz watched as a special detachment pushed through the crowd toward the speaking bench. The lead cop grabbed Virgil by the arm, the second put him in a headlock with a baton against his Adam's apple. All too familiar.

Screams filled the air as folks ran for the perimeter. The police were beating anyone they could reach. Taz backed up slowly, looking for the exit. Headed south toward Cross Street. Just as he reached the street that paralleled the park, he saw Virgil's son Bennett running in his direction, traumatized and crying. "They're taking my pa! They're taking my pa!"

Taz grabbed the kid by the arm. "Slow down. Everything's going to be all right."

Bennett was shaking, gasping. "What am I going to do?"

"Is your mom here?"

"She's dead."

Taz stopped for a beat. "You have any friends here?"

"I don't know where they are. I'm scared."

"Okay, I understand. Why don't you come with me, and we'll get things sorted out as soon as we can."

Bennett gave him a wary look. "Maybe I better."

"Yeah, I don't think Tobytown is going to be such a great place to stay tonight."

Taz caught sight of the thin man through the stampede. He was about fifty yards to the right, striding towards a small group of police. Taz was pretty sure the man hadn't seen him, and in order to keep it that way, he guided Bennett to a spot in the moving crowd well behind him. That was when Taz noticed what looked like a leather wallet insert half-buried in the mud. He put it in his pocket. They made their way through the police perimeter to Taz's car. Later, he wasn't sure why they hadn't been stopped. Were the cops more intent on cracking skulls than taking names?

✳✳✳

They drove back to Chincoteague in silence. At the marshes, Bennett looked at him with tears in his eyes. "Where are we going?"

"A little town on the water. I live here, and it's a good place. We're going to find somebody to take care of you while I try to figure out what's happened to your father."

"Why do you want to help?" A simple question, but one Taz wasn't sure he could answer.

"I think what your father said at the demonstration was good, and right."

When they got to the cottage, he gave Bennett a glass of orange juice. The child gulped it down.

"You hungry?"

"Yes sir, I am."

"How about some potato salad and a cold drumstick?"

"Okay, thanks."

They sat at the kitchen table. Bennett was hungry and Taz watched him eat. Then he called the bookstore. Laney answered.

"Hi, it's Taz."

"What trouble are you in now?"

"It's not me, it's a ten-year-old kid."

"I'm eleven."

"I mean eleven. His father spoke at the demonstration in Accomac. They got separated. A police attack. I think they arrested his father."

Laney drew a breath. "You brought him back with you?"

"Yes."

"Oh, boy, this is going to be real. I'll call you right back."

"Thanks."

Laney and Richard didn't have kids. And Taz knew he couldn't keep a black eleven-year-old in his house without coming under suspicion for molestation, if not kidnapping. Laney would figure something out.

Meanwhile, he tried to keep young Bennett comfortable.

"The police took my pa, didn't they?"

"I think so."

"What are they going to do with him?"

"They can't do much. He didn't do anything wrong."

Laney called back. "Bring him here. He can stay with Dana. At least he'll have a pal there."

Taz thought Bennett might need a toothbrush and a towel if his father's situation couldn't be sorted out that day. He tossed a few items into a canvas bag and then they drove to the bookstore.

Dana was already there talking to Laney at the desk when they arrived. She turned to look at them. Taz put his hand on Bennett's head, and Bennett looked at him. "Can't I stay with you?"

"This will be better. This nice lady has a son your age."

Dana's eyes were moist, as if she were about to cry. She crouched down to Bennett's height. "I hear your father is very brave."

"Yes, ma'am."

"Well, I think you're brave too, just like your dad. I'd be glad to have you come meet my son Moyer, if you want, and stay with us 'til your dad's back home."

"Yes, ma'am."

They left through the back door.

Taz reached in his pocket for the muddy leather insert. Inside, he found some business cards and a small folded note with his address on it. The cards belonged to Kurt Vogel, senior vice president of Rinvest LLC.

CHAPTER ELEVEN

Calling in Some Chits

TAZ CALLED LANEY FIRST thing in the morning. "I'm going to DC to see if I can find a lawyer."

"Maybe a militia would be better. I watched the local news."

He smiled. "Good thought. But let's start with a lawyer who can get Bennett's dad out of the slammer."

"Cooler heads prevail again. Bummer."

Taz headed out the Chincoteague Road. Officially, Virginia Route 175, but you couldn't find a single local who paid any attention to that. Taz dialed Russ Antrim from a stoplight in Pocomoke. Russ was a product of *L*, the State Department's legal shop.

"Well, well. Long time, no hear," Russ was in a private firm now, raking in the money. Good thing. He had two kids to put through college.

"You doing any *pro bono* work these days?"

"Some. The firm wants more, the bigger backside they have to cover."

"A target-rich environment, I imagine. So I've got something for you."

His next call was to Rick Reed. Rick had been in charge of security for the Secretary of the Interior. Before he transferred to State, Taz had been the secretary's utility infielder. Reed had retired after twenty-five years as the top deputy for law enforcement at the National Park Service. He was built strong, as they say. Had played football at Grambling. Actually, he was a star linebacker, though he'd never say so. Also, the first black man to break into the senior ranks of the National Park Service. But he didn't make a lot of that, either. They had done a fair amount of work together in the old days. "This must be something special. Where you been, brother?"

"Around. Chincoteague, mostly."

"Sweet. What's up?"

"Got a problem with the local constabulary."

"Well that's not new. Didn't you spend some time in the lockup back in the old days?"

"Yeah, but this isn't me. It's a whole neighborhood of black farmers on the Eastern Shore."

"You've got my attention."

"The Accomack County Sheriff's Department is going after a community called Tobytown, down by Cashville and Onancock. I want to know why."

"I'll ask around."

"Rick, I might need some help on this one."

"I figured. Let me ask some questions and get back to you."

The third call he made was to the boys at INR. The assistant secretary was out. Taz ended up talking to his deputy, an ambitious thirty-something who also happened to be very talented. Taz had given him a reference for the job. Later, when he had declined to help INR with a particular errand that wasn't to his taste, they had had some words.

"So, Irvin, I could use some help."

"We like nothing better than to help our alumni. What's the story?"

He told him everything he knew. "Can you check out Rinvest? What the hell do they want with Tobytown?"

"Should be amusing. I'll get back to you when I've cracked the code."

"Thanks."

"Taz, I know we've had our differences before. But we appreciate your taking the Norway trip for us."

"Okay. I'll wait to hear from you."

There was not much else to do until things played out.

CHAPTER TWELVE

Shelter from the Storm

TAZ HAD SET UP what he could. Russ was looking into the charges against Virgil Waite. Rick had assured him he would suss out why the county cops were hassling Tobytown. Irvin had already put a data search in motion for information on Rinvest. Taz just needed to wait to see what turned up. But waiting was the hardest thing. He had done his weeding, and the sea oats he had planted by the dock were flourishing without much help. He refilled the hummingbird feeder. His ruby throated hummingbirds had already left for Venezuela.

As it turned out, he really didn't need to worry about having time on his hands. Mother Nature intervened. Hurricane Doreen, now a Category 3 storm, had passed Charleston seventy miles offshore, topped the approaches to the Oregon Inlet, and carved three new channels through Pea Island in the Outer Banks early in the morning. Chincoteague was a deer in her headlights by four that afternoon. Taz had finished tying up the skiff and blocking the vents in his crawl space. It seemed like a good time to face the storm head-on, the way he'd learned to do in the plains thunderstorms where he grew up. The Fish and Wildlife Service had already closed the auto entrance to Assateague when he bicycled past the barrier and over the causeway bridge. The Forster's terns that normally used the bridge abutments as fishing perches were long gone. The wind howled, the channel frothed. He put his head down and pedaled towards the beach.

He should have known better. It took him half an hour to fight his way past the lighthouse and onto the beach road. By the time he could see the visitors' center, a couple of hundred yards from the normal surf line, the waves from Tom's Cove were overtopping the tarmac and breaking into the brackish ponds just to the north. He actually couldn't get to the beach. The wind drove him back. He could hear the surf pounding, out of any normal rhythm. There was no one in the parking lot, which was good, since it was three feet deep in roiling ocean water.

He pulled the bicycle around and headed back towards the bridge. The spartina marshes off Piney Island were almost unrecognizable. Waves were washing over the flats, and spray off the channel was driving through and flattening the cordgrass. The hurricane hadn't set up the usual steady winds. Instead, it seemed to be spawning micro-bursts and mini tornadoes. In some areas, the treetops were bent over, but chest-level bushes were quiet. In others, the marshes at knee-level couldn't stand the force, but the trees above them seemed tranquil. Meanwhile, low clouds scudded underneath a gray, howling carapace. The whole scene was like something out of Hieronymus Bosch.

He made it back over the causeway, only a hundred yards from the nearest buildings and solid ground. But he couldn't seem to stay on his bicycle. He was blown off in the parking lot of the old oyster museum but kept a hand on the handlebar. He decided it would be better to walk. One of the tall "Welcome" signs at the motel next door was peeling off and looked to be airborne at any moment. He heard howling wind and cracking timber, the sound of shearing metal. He stayed upwind of the peeling sign. Lightning struck just north, followed by a huge and immediate crack of thunder. He was soaked to the skin underneath his windbreaker. His sneakers filled with water. He took his glasses off as he couldn't see through them anyway. Leaves and branches were flying past him as he fought his way behind the museum and the motel, then up Pine where Richard and Laney had their place.

He could just make out the froth on the Assateague Channel behind the houses on his right. A water funnel rose or descended—he couldn't tell which—while he watched. In seconds, it loomed towards him, reversed course, and caromed north. A midsized branch grazed his cheek as it blew by. The jack pines were bent over, throwing their curving tops all in a line. He needed to find shelter somewhere fast. Made it to a shingle house on the water side of Pine that had an open garage. He dragged his bicycle inside. He waited there while the storm gyred and spun, beating itself against the island and anything on it that stood taller than a mailbox.

Finally, the storm changed to a few minutes of merely vertical rain and something like quiet. *Maybe the eye of the storm, passing over.* He took the opportunity to work his way to the house's front door, and holding his breath for courage, knocked twice. Young Moyer opened it and smiled.

Taz had just enough sense to say. "Maybe you should get your mom."

Dana came to the door. She was wearing a man's red plaid flannel shirt and jeans.

Before she could speak, he said, "Sorry. I was trying to get to the beach, but this one beat me back. I took cover in your garage. The door was open."

"You're bleeding. Wait while I find a bandage." Matter of fact. Didn't invite him in. He did his best to shelter under her porch gables.

"You'll have to get out of those clothes. I guess you'd better come in."

They stood by the kitchen table.

"Sorry to intrude like this."

"Forget it."

"It's good to know where Bennett is. I'm grateful to you for taking him in."

"He's upstairs trying to read his way through the storm."

"A better strategy than mine."

A tentative smile. "Wait here. Sit down if you like."

She came back quickly with a kerchief and a small bottle of iodine. "This'll hurt." She dabbed the ragged wound the tree branch had left on his cheek. Taz grimaced as the iodine burned its way into the cut. She gave him a concerned look.

"I'm fine, thanks."

"A stoic, then."

"Not so much. I cry when I stub my toe."

She smirked and found him a shirt and pants that her husband must have left behind. Showed him the bathroom where he could change. Offered hot coffee. Dry again, he sat at the kitchen table, watching as she set the kettle on the gas stove. Her moves were swift and efficient.

There were footfalls on the stairs. Bennett came into the kitchen looking worried. Seeing Taz at the table, he moved quickly to his side. "Mister Taz, where's my pa?"

"He's still with the sheriff. I have some friends working to get him released. He'll be home soon, I promise."

The rain was pelting the windows on the west side of the house. Horizontally. The eye had passed. He got up and wedged his towel into the windowsill. Dana watched from the stove, amused. "Thanks. That one always spits."

"Maybe I should fix it."

"Maybe." She brought Taz his coffee, and then nudged the boy toward the stairs.

He listened as she led Bennett into the upstairs bathroom where Moyer was already brushing his teeth. "You have to get your sleep so you can help your father when he needs you."

When she came back down, slowly, she said to Taz, "There's a cot in the garage." She slipped into the pantry and came back with a pillow and a blanket, stood near him. "You can wash up in the kitchen."

Then she turned to leave, turned back. "What were you doing out there?"

"Trying to ride to the beach."

Her eyes were on him. One eyebrow was raised. "In a hurricane?"

He shrugged, made his way to the garage, sat on the edge of the cot listening to the slackening rain, the occasional burst of wind, the steady thrum of branches turning this way and that. Wondering about Rinvest LLC. The storm was gradually winding down. Dana came in holding an electric heater. "I thought you might be needing this."

His hand touched hers as she passed him the heater. She almost dropped it. He caught the handle before it hit the floor.

He apologized. "I'm sorry. I didn't mean to startle you."

She looked him in the eye. "I've never met anybody like you. You have a shell like a turtle. You risked everything to help young Bennett, but you hide your compassion under that good ol' boy exterior. Laney told me you were a puzzle. She was right."

For one of the few times he could remember, Taz was at a loss for words. Dana patted his hand and turned to leave.

Taz left a little before dawn while the house was still quiet. He had agreed to meet Russ in Accomac. He left a note on the kitchen table with his thanks.

CHAPTER THIRTEEN

Surprise at the Flea Market

TAZ FOUND RUSS AT the Silver Diner on Route 13 a few miles north of Accomac. It was early, and neither of them had eaten breakfast. But for the moment, they only ordered coffee. The waitress bided her time.

"Looks like private practice is treating you well."

"It's not as much fun as negotiating a good treaty. But it pays a lot better."

"A good thing. Who's putting your kids through college?"

"Oh you know, some AID contractors, some international banks, the usual suspects."

"More money than brains. But that's okay, at least they're smart enough to get the right attorney."

"Fuck you."

"No, I mean it."

They always started like this.

"So, what do you think?"

"You mean, can we spring him?"

"You know that's what I mean."

"It'll cost you a pile of pancakes to find out."

He motioned to the waitress and asked for more coffee, eggs and grits, and pancakes for his friend from the city. She looked pleased. At least they weren't just going to take up space.

Russ was in very good shape. He ran marathons. No extra body fat, and no unnecessary muscle either. Great endurance. Handsome and lean. A ready smile, a good sense of humor. Always knew stuff that was still just coming around the corner. It was Russ who had told him, early in the Iraq torture scandal, that there was a lot more to come. The Abu Ghraib mess hit the headlines a month later. Plugged into the State legal office, Justice, and the military's lawyers, he heard things before they were real.

For a few minutes, they ate in silence, hungry. Then, when Russ's last pancake was nearly finished, he said, "Yep, I can spring him. The question is, is he better off out or in?"

Taz hadn't considered that point. *Was Virgil Waite safer in jail?*

"What do you think is going on?"

"I don't have a clue. But the charges are complete bullshit. So that makes me think someone's got an agenda."

"Do you know the judges on this circuit?"

"How would I? I don't usually follow chicken rustling cases. But my guess is that at least one of them is on the take."

"So, assuming he's better off outside, how do we get him out?"

"Easy. We just have to find a judge who still believes in the law."

If anyone could do that, Russ could. Taz paid for breakfast, and dialed Rick on the way to his car.

"Hey bro, how's it goin'?" Rick said.

"'Bout usual, I guess."

"Well, that's not nearly good enough. You should sign up for lessons. What's up?"

"That's what I was calling to ask you."

"Yeah. Well it seems that the Accomack County sheriff is twisted. A lot twisted. The FBI's been listening to him for over six months."

"What's the issue?"

"There were some complaints. Civil rights stuff. Turned out a lot of his boys like to wear sheets on the side."

"And here I thought the KKK was dead."

"Yeah, and pigs are flying in my backyard."

"Anything else?"

"It looks like Sheriff Gaynes is connected. I mean in the corporate direction."

"What did you find?"

"He's got three 401(k)s. The smallest is worth $1.2 million. You don't get that kind of retirement security busting redneck meth labs."

"Rick, how deep does it go? I mean deep in the department."

"Dunno. I'm thinking maybe the recruits get special training."

"Shit."

"S'okay. I've already talked to some friends at DoJ." Before he found his true mission at the Park Service, Rick had spent some time with the Attorney General's security detail.

"Thanks, Rick. Really."

"All in a day's work, my friend, all in a day's work. And I'm not finished yet."

That was Rick. Always the best, with a smile.

Taz's next check-in was with Irvin Friar and INR. But that could wait a day. He'd have to head back into DC. And if they had really come up with something, they'd want something in return.

Taz headed down Route 13 to Temperanceville to get some steaks at a little market that had a butcher you could talk to. He bought a couple of good-looking porterhouse steaks and deposited them in his mobile cooler. On his way back he stopped in at the Latino flea market to pick up some lettuce and jalapeños at the Mexican produce stand. The old building behind the produce stands, full of makeshift stalls, appealed to him and he wandered through the central hall, casting his eye at T-shirt seconds, fake silk scarves, old tools.

The tools always caught him. He was looking at a couple of wood planes and a rip saw when he heard a familiar voice. He turned and saw

Darly bargaining for pillowcases across the corridor. He walked up behind her. "I like the beige ones, myself." She turned, surprised. "Why Taz, what brings you off the island?"

"I was looking for you."

"What a liar you are, Taz. You could have called."

"Didn't have your number."

"But you do remember my name?"

"Not only that. Your voice, which is still ringing in my ears. And your laugh, which I like very much."

She blushed. "You're so full of it. Not that I don't appreciate it."

"When you've figured out your linens, I have something to show you."

She sparked at this and quickly paid for the pillowcases. She moved closer, gave him a peck on the cheek. "Glad to see you."

"Come on. I've got someone I want you to meet." He took her hand and led her down the hall between the stands.

They wound their way through increasingly narrow corridors, off the main hall, where ticky-tacky booths were strung on both sides. He stopped at a booth on the right, with a hand-painted sign that said *Ms. Alice's*. It was surrounded by hanging bedsheets. Taz worked his way through the entrance curtain, drawing Darly behind him.

Alice was a strikingly attractive black woman in her forties who was seated behind a deal table selling burnt CDs. Three black men were poring through cartons of CDs on card tables. Taz figured they were just as likely to be interested in Alice as in the music. But as to music, Alice had an amazing collection. Gospel, R&B, soul. Taz bought two CDs by the Swan Silvertones for five bucks each and introduced Darly. Alice was gracious. In fact, she lavished attention on him, which brought a smile to his face and made Darly giggle in the background.

When they got back outside, Taz said, "You got plans for the day?"

"Not really. You?"

"Well, I know a nice bar in Cape Charles. What do you think?"

"I think a nice bar sounds just fine."

"What about your car?"

"We can leave it here and pick it up on the way back. My place is up in Atlantic."

✳✳✳

They got to Cape Charles a little after two. Found the tavern, a simple but attractive place just off the harbor. They sat at the semi-long wooden saloon bar, with a good view of the sailboats at the marina outside.

"You don't use the phone much, I gather."

"True, but I also had some distractions. Either way, I apologize."

"Distractions?" She was clearly enjoying her position. A very attractive smile was playing across her lips.

"Well, there's been a lot going on. You know. Or maybe the hurricane didn't come your way. There was that demonstration in Accomac. I mean, you couldn't turn around without worrying about something."

Darly was amused.

He was struggling to recover his composure. "White or red?"

"White."

He ordered two glasses of Sauvignon blanc and asked if she was hungry.

"Not really."

"Where did you learn to sing?"

"In church with my parents and then in the choir. It wasn't until I got my own place that I started singing with jazz combos." She put on a wicked little grin. Taz felt her bare toes tickling his shin under the table.

They finished the wine, strolled out to take a look at the harbor. She put her arm in his.

They were standing side by side where they could see Hampton Roads across the mouth of Chesapeake Bay. A great gray Navy ship was moving out in the roads, far enough away that the shape was almost lost in the thermal resonance over the water.

She turned toward him, brushing her breasts against his chest. Her eyes looked into his. "Are you thinking what I'm thinking?"

He couldn't help but smile.

***

He left Darly sleeping in her cottage in Atlantic, headed back to the island. It was almost five, and the sun had just about given up trying to warm a recalcitrant afternoon. Thought of stopping by Captain Fish's for a beer but wanted quiet more. Time to think. Pulled into the oyster shell driveway. The door to the kitchen was open.

Whoever they were, they had done a thorough job. Not a single thing was in its place. Papers, books, spices, pans, clothes were scattered from the kitchen to the bedroom. Chairs were mostly turned over; his old Mission rocking chair was broken. His bed had been torn apart; the stuffing from the mattress was a foot deep on the bedroom floor.

His phone still worked. He called the bookstore and Richard answered.

"Rainy Day. How can I help you?"

"Is anybody using the spare bedroom tonight?"

"Hey, Taz, I don't think so. What gives?"

"Somebody just ransacked my house. I can't deal with it right now."

"Jesus. Well, come on over."

He thought about calling the police, decided that could wait 'til morning. Checked his guitars. The cases were where he had left them. Grabbed a toothbrush, a comb, and his pills. Found his rucksack still hanging on the back of the bedroom door. Waded over to the vicinity of his desk. All the drawers had been emptied on the floor. No laptop. Looked back in the bedroom. Not there either. Well, there wasn't much on it anyway. He had reformatted the hard drive about two weeks back.

Back to the desk. The little black book was opened on the floor. He rifled the pages; about half of them had been ripped out. He laughed mirthlessly at the idea of some corporate Pinkerton trying to read his handwriting.

Laney met him at the back of the store. She looked concerned. "You okay?"

"A little shaky just now."

She wrapped her arms around him and held him for a minute. He took it in.

"Come on in and talk to Richard while I get my stuff."

Richard was cataloguing new arrivals. "You have any idea who did it?"

"Not a clue."

"They take anything?"

"My laptop, I think."

"Your guitars okay?"

"I guess they weren't musically inclined."

"Why don't you and Laney go over to the house. I'm going to close up early."

They were sitting at the kitchen table drinking coffee when Richard came in. Laney made mac and cheese for dinner. Taz offered to get some wine. She said, "You are not going anywhere," and went over to the pantry. Pulled out a bottle of burgundy.

Richard looked at him over his wine glass. "You're getting to be a dangerous person to know."

"I know. I've been thinking about that. I need to make myself scarce for a while."

"You want to stay at our place in Pennsylvania?"

"I think it'll be okay. I suspect I have a trip coming up. I'll be seeing friends at State tomorrow."

"Good timing."

✼✼✼

He drove into DC in the morning. The INR boys were glad to see him. Smiles and handshakes all around. Irvin Friar led them to the SCIF, took their cell phones, gave them to a secretary Taz didn't know.

"She must be new."

"Marjorie? She's been here almost a month."

Once the door was closed, Irvin said, "Gentlemen, we've got two topics today. You're going to hear some information we've been looking into at Envoy Blackwell's request. If it brings anything to mind, feel free to add your two bits. Then we'll turn to the main issue."

Taz noticed the envoy. Said nothing.

Irvin looked at Taz. "This thing you asked us to look into. Tobytown. It's bigger than I hoped."

"I'm getting that impression myself."

"Rinvest is a commercial real estate broker. Big national player. But they're not acting for themselves here. It took us a while to figure out who they're bidding for. It's not the usual mall or estate developer. In fact, they're not interested in the surface at all. Their electronic traffic on all this is going to Australia, to a division of Broken Hill Proprietary."

"BHP Billiton? The mining giant?"

"Exactly."

"What division?"

"Well, it's actually a Canadian company they bought and stripped a year or so ago—Ucor Minerals."

Taz's eyebrows went up.

"That's not the end of the trail. There's a letter agreement between Ucor and Chinalco, the big Chinese mining company."

"And?"

Irvin paused. Jensen, who Taz remembered was with Defense Intelligence, piped up. "It commits that Chinalco will have the option to become a minority partner in any mine that Ucor opens outside of Canada in the next two years."

Taz looked first at Jensen, then at Irvin. "So we're about to evict a bunch of black farmers in Tobytown to pave the way for a Canadian Company and its Chinese partner to open a mine on the Eastern Shore?"

"Not just any mine. They think they're onto a uranium layer in the sediment—the industry gossip is that it's a world-class deposit. Taz, I think you should back off a little here. It's not some little civil rights fight. This is the big money boys, and we've got a lot of complicated relationships at stake."

Taz looked at Irvin carefully. "Okay Irvin, I get it. This one's bigger than all of us."

"That's the way we see it."

Yeah, but I'm not working for the government anymore. "Well, how about this? I'll do my level best just to concentrate on the little pieces."

Irvin decided he had made his point.

"Let's turn to our other matter."

There was a meeting in Reykjavik, a shipping conference. Most of the Arctic players would be there. They had created a consultancy for him with business cards and a rudimentary backstory. Turns out Taz had been doing some political fixing for Bering Shipping, out of Seattle and Unalaska. Mostly a local shipper along the western Alaska coast, they did occasional business across the dateline as well. The spooks gave him some information on the company, a few case histories, some documents confirming his backstory, and a list of names to memorize. His tickets, and a letter from the embassy. He had two days before his plane departed from Dulles.

When he got back to the island, he found that Laney had already put things back into some semblance of their original order. There was a futon where his mattress used to be, and a sign in her inimitable handwriting on the La-Z-Boy she hated, which said, "If you have to break something, try this." When he opened the refrigerator to get a beer, he found himself staring straight at a homemade chicken pot pie.

CHAPTER FOURTEEN

Rotten Shark

REYKJAVIK IN LATE OCTOBER. Clear, crisp winds off the freshly fallen snows up in the Highlands. The city dry and cool, the crowds treasuring the dwindling daylight hours, snaking along the sidewalks of the old town, sunning in the park by the lake, smiling, storing up the last warm shards of fall before the winter storms closed in.

Taz had a day before the conference and only one person to see, and that was for dinner. Most of the shipping company officials weren't coming in until late in the evening. He thought about taking a car up the coast, but hadn't planned anything in advance. By the time he finished breakfast, it was already eight-thirty, too late to start the most interesting trips. He was staying at the Eis-Hotel by the smaller city airport, a little off the city center. The rooms were nice and he had, as was his custom, asked for one overlooking the runways and the ocean beyond.

He put on sneakers, grabbed his binoculars and a light jacket, and started down the bicycle path that skirted the east side of the airport perimeter. He was headed away from town at first, into a kind of warehouse district, but he knew the path would eventually hit the coast and come around to the airport's west side, where he could follow the Suburgata—the main road—up the hill and over into the old port.

He thought it might take an hour—in the end, it took two. But there were oystercatchers, loons, and a couple of jaegers along the coast, and the bracing sea breeze off the North Atlantic.

He had lunch at a little café just above the wharves. Pickled herring, rye bread, beer. Black coffee. The foot traffic here was sparse. Workmen, stevedores, a sailor or two. He had time to consider what he had learned so far: the Russians were clearly up to something. Ingrid's story of the Finnish design team was evidence enough. Bren had made clear it wasn't oil. And he had noticed in passing a few fragments from the Barents Sea news service that raised questions about the glacial research that had gone on over the summer. One article hidden at the end of the feed quoted a senior Danish intelligence official who speculated that the Russian "glaciologists" were actually prospecting for diamonds or rare earth minerals. StatOil's role was less clear—what did they have to gain, and why did Rosneft need them? But the real unknown was: who were they talking to in Nuuk? And, whoever it was, what was in it for them?

He lingered over the coffee. He should've paid more attention in chemistry. Or geochemistry. He didn't know much about rare earth minerals. There were at least fifteen plus, with names like scandium, which makes an alloy for aerospace components, and cerium, a critical catalyst for cracking petroleum in certain refinery operations. Others were essential for lasers, computer memories, nuclear batteries, and God knows what else. They were expensive and scarce, at least in minable concentrations. China controlled ninety-seven percent of the world's production, and also had a bad habit of cutting export quotas for strategic purposes.

The idea of a Chinese monopoly in something so essential to leading-edge technology had become less and less attractive to leaders in the West, to the point where geologists were combing prospective areas in Australia, Brazil, Canada, South Africa, even Montana, in the hope of finding alternative sources of supply. And to that list you could now add Greenland, somewhere on the edge of the Northern Hemisphere's largest ice sheet.

He paid his tab, put on his windbreaker, and ducked out through the low wood atrium. Outside, it was still clear and cool. The wind had died away. Perfect weather for a cigar. Lit a Schimmelpenninck and pulled in a long, slow mouthful of tobacco. Walked up the hill across from the opera house.

If there really were a valuable deposit of rare earth minerals in Greenland, the self-rule government would probably grant the primary concession to a company that was under their control. That's the only way they could be sure of retaining a significant portion of the asset value. A major deposit would build roads, hospitals, and underwrite education and social programs the Greenlanders badly needed. The Inuit leadership, sophisticated as they were, didn't have the technology or the capital to undertake a major mining project. So their company would put it out to bid.

But it wasn't like the Russians to let someone else control the action on a resource that they believed to be strategically essential. So the first thing was to find out which Russian company was bidding. Right after that, he needed to talk to some serious geologists.

His thoughts continued to preoccupy him as he headed semiconsciously back towards the airport and his hotel. He had time—just—for a nap and a shower, before he was to meet Ragnar.

Ragnar Skalldurson had been Iceland's "Senior Arctic Official" when Taz was State's environmental negotiator. To say that Ragnar was unique would be putting it mildly. He had the body of a fencer. He was as tall as Taz but probably thirty pounds lighter, and Taz wasn't anything like fat. Blond hair, a crooked smile, handsome. A linguist, he had been posted to China and spoke perfect Mandarin. As well as Italian, French, and idiomatic English. Or rather American—he had gotten at least some of his schooling at Haverford. It was Ragnar from whom Taz first heard the quip that England and the United States were two cultures divided by a common language.

You would have called him cosmopolitan, but you had to dig to get that far. He was quite content to have you view him as "a minor official in the vast government of Iceland." To that end, he started most conversations with stories of Icelandic culture that only an anthropologist or a confirmed cynic would come up with. The fact that many of the stories were eye-wateringly funny was an added bonus.

Ragnar was to meet Taz by the statue up the hill from Reykjavik's central bus stop. The statue, a bronze, was of a woman and child; it looked like an early work of Botero. But in that case, it was very early—1936. She was wearing a cloak, which she held tightly around the baby. It struck Taz, as he admired the woman's questioning expression in the fiery light of the late afternoon sun, that Icelanders had that Scandinavian instinct for design, but in a peculiarly free way.

"She's hoping you can help her figure out how to get to Paris," was how Ragnar put it, as he came up to Taz's side.

"You think? Just charter the nearest longboat. I hear they went at least that far up the Seine."

"She does look like she just stepped out of *Njál's Saga*, doesn't she?"

"Maybe they took her from Paris before they headed up here, what do you think?"

"I think if they got to Paris, they wouldn't have any obvious reason to sail a thousand miles of the North Atlantic to find an island full of volcanoes."

"Yeah, but your ancestors were berserkers, weren't they? Never saw a voyage they didn't want to try."

"Yes, we learned how to regret it later, after we got here."

Taz smiled. "It's good to see you. Thanks for coming out."

"What, when the great Taz B. comes to Iceland? You think I'd be hiding in a cave on the Vatnajokull?"

"Where are we headed?"

"Well, there's a good French restaurant about two blocks up Tryggvagata, or there's a traditional Icelandic place just behind us."

"Let's try Icelandic."

"You know the most traditional dish in Iceland is rotten shark."

"Even better."

Ragnar led him up the steps off the square to a secondary street, where there was a row of wood-framed buildings with warm lights behind the windows. A sign hanging above the entrance steps said "Laekjarbrekka."

Of course they knew Ragnar. An elegant, fortyish woman came up to them at the entrance and gave Ragnar a kiss on both cheeks, and an endearment in Icelandic.

Ragnar introduced Taz. "Marta, this is my best friend from America. I hope Egil is on his game tonight."

Marta greeted Taz warmly, held both his hands in hers. "Welcome to Iceland." Then she turned to Ragnar with a slight pout, still holding Taz's hands. "Have you ever known Egil to be off his game? But I'll tell him we have a special guest." With a wink in Taz's direction. She led them to a table just to the side of a stone fireplace. The fire was low, but its coals were still glowing, and the occasional ember lit up with flame every so often.

Taz watched Marta sway gracefully back to the foyer, arched an eyebrow at Ragnar.

"She's the daughter of my mentor at the Foreign Ministry. This is her restaurant."

"I would have married her."

"I almost did. But her father sent me to Beijing."

Taz had no response. He put his napkin in his lap and arranged the silverware.

Ragnar was smiling at the irony. "We'd better get a cocktail first. Then I can explain the menu."

Taz ordered a scotch on the rocks, Ragnar a Manhattan.

They sipped in silence for a while. Ragnar looked quizzically at Taz. "It may take more than one, before you're ready."

"Ready for what?" Taz asked.

"Well, for the most Icelandic of appetizers."

"Let's go for the gold."

"But first, the story."

"I was afraid of that. But if you must, I'm all ears."

"Well, we're a seafaring people. Winters were hard. No dirt to grow vegetables. Sea too rough to fish. So we stored what we had already caught, or what ended up dead on the beach."

"Right, dried cod—what do they call it?"

"Well, the Portuguese taught us how to salt it. But that was later. In the beginning, it was just dried without salt—*hardfiskur*. But even that was later, when we learned to go out far enough to find the cod. In the beginning, what we had was shark."

"Not necessarily so bad."

"Right, except the Greenland shark is poisonous. So many toxins in the muscle that it would double you over. So the early Icelanders learned how to ferment it."

"Okay . . ."

"They figured out if you buried it for a year in the volcanic sand, most of the toxins would leach out. But apparently gelatinous, semi-poisonous shark was insufficiently disgusting. Remember, my ancestors had strong stomachs. So they discovered that if you bathe it in its own urine, and bury it in a clay pot, it improves the taste greatly."

Taz was starting to get a little queasy. "A regular Escoffier, whoever thought of that one."

With a widening smile, Ragnar said, "We think of it as *foie gras*, Viking-style. Are you ready for another scotch?"

Well, he was.

"Let's talk about the rest of the menu."

In the end, they ordered Caesar salad, minke whale sushi, and puffin. Just as the waiter was turning towards the kitchen, Taz said, "And the shark appetizer." Ragnar raised an eyebrow, and the waiter looked him over carefully, but at this point Taz's determination was absolute.

"So what brings you out to our fair isle?"

"The shipping conference. I'm hoping to catch up with the state of play."

"Who's your client?"

"A U.S. operation based out of Seattle. They're looking at expanding into the Beaufort."

Ragnar snorted. "There won't be much of that here. They'll all be talking about the Barents cargo routes."

"I know, but I figured some of the technology discussions would be interesting. And maybe some of the regulatory questions. Europe is way ahead of us on this stuff."

"I just did a report for the Parliament about the potential for a transshipment operation in Iceland."

"So I heard. What do you think? And can I cadge a copy? Signed, of course."

"Well, if the Russians open up the Northern Sea Route, they'll have to use shallow draft, ice-hardened ships. They'll need somewhere to transfer their cargoes into Panamax boats that could be unloaded in Rotterdam or Long Beach."

"What about shipments out of Greenland?"

"That's only oil, for the moment. So they don't have a problem."

"I'm hearing that some of the companies are looking at the rules for ore boats, bulk freighters, that kind of thing."

"To carry what—ice?"

"No, rare earth minerals."

Ragnar's crooked smile reappeared. "You've been doing your homework."

The waiter appeared at their table with a small glass jar on a silver tray. The jar was sealed with a gasket and a clamp. Taz noticed that the diners at the tables nearby were looking at him with interest.

Ragnar said, "Our national dish. You asked for it." He looked at the foursome at the next table and shrugged his shoulders, as if to say, "He's American, what can I do?"

The men, very well-dressed, watched Taz warily. The women, even more well-dressed, smiled demurely and carefully eyed their plates.

The waiter put down a glass of transparent liquor. "Brennivin," he said quietly. "It helps if you take some before and after."

Taz lifted the small fork off the tray, opened the jar. A powerful ammoniac smell nearly overpowered him. The thought occurred to him that he might not be able to go through with this.

He belted half the Brennivin, and then picked a cube of translucent shark meat from the jar and put it between his teeth. Chewed, releasing even more of the ammonia taste. And chewed, and chewed. Finally, with vast relief, he swallowed. He belted the rest of the Brennivin. Only two cubes left. When he was finished, the foursome applauded, ever so discreetly.

CHAPTER FIFTEEN

Minding the Minders

ON THE THIRD DAY of the shipping conference, which was about as interesting as such a thing could be, Taz got a call from Richard.

"Hey, buddy boy, how are you?"

"Okay, I think. Missing the quiet life, though."

"Which is not so quiet, lately."

"What now?"

"The Feds have been knocking on doors—a lot of doors. Asking a lot of funny questions about you."

Damn. White had promised no FBI. "Which Feds? What questions?"

"Hey, most of us don't get all feisty once they flash those badges. These guys looked serious. Sunglasses, FBI shoes. Wanted to know how well we knew you. Did we know whether you used drugs. And did we know you'd spent some time in jail."

"Wow. What other tidbits did they drop?"

"Let's see. You were a member of SDS, you don't go to church, and you apparently like gay bars."

"That about covers it, doesn't it. They still in town?"

"No, I think it was a one-day hit, but they've definitely got everybody talking."

"Great. Thanks. Listen, I've got to make a quick call. I'll be home in two days."

"Right. Don't expect a red carpet."

He called John White's direct line. Irvin came on.

"Irvin, I need to speak to John."

"He's at a conference table with half the narco cops in South America."

"He told me, 'no FBI.'"

"So?"

"So why are they all over the island, telling people I was in the SDS?"

"Damned if I know. When did this happen?"

"Two days ago."

"Anybody get a name or a badge ID?"

"No—I've only heard from one friend so far."

"Look, Taz. This isn't us. I don't know what it is, or who it is. I'll see what I can find out."

"Okay. I'm going to be back on Friday, so anything you have by then would be good."

Taz wandered back to the conference rooms, preoccupied. Suddenly the discussions of ice classifications and open sea ballast exchange requirements no longer held his attention. He tried to refocus. The conference was mostly serious professionals—mid-level managers, engineers, and a few executives. Many of them knew each other, but, as in any commercial situation, they were more likely to speak truth to a stranger than to a competitor.

Taz had no trouble starting conversations, and as a negotiator he had an invaluable asset. He knew how to listen attentively and to open a dialogue by leading to his interlocutor's interest. He absorbed himself in his adversary's point of view. It was not just an intellectual exercise, either. He enjoyed learning the other person's perspective, his or her interests, anxieties, boundaries. He had learned early on that the best way to learn what you needed to know was to make the other person feel comfortable, that you admired them, and were on their side in some indefinable way.

In this crowd, that was easy. These were for the most part straightforward people who were good at what they did, and were trying to do more of it and make money into the bargain. Very few complicated motivations.

And a few of them were better than straightforward—they were straightforward, even blunt, intelligent, given to laughter. Like Nils, from Copenship Management, AG. But of course, he'd been all around the industry. Overweight, extroverted, literary. Knew everyone, but more important, everyone knew him. Liked to tell a story or two over scotch. Not afraid of strangers, rather to the contrary. Had been a captain in his time, taken ore boats from Murmansk to Archangelsk. *The cold route*, he called it. Lost two fingers to frostbite one bad February night when the engines went dead and the following seas drove his ore boat perilously close to the shallows on the Kola coast. So when the bankers from Bremen and the professors from Copenhagen expounded on the difficulties of the Northern Sea Route, he just smiled and kept his peace. But later, in the bar, he would tell it like it needed to be told.

The second-to-last night of the conference, Nils found Taz at the back of the meeting room.

"Why don't we get a drink after all the babble is over?"

"Sounds good to me."

"Good. I've got some friends who want to meet you."

Taz thought about that for a moment. He had been keeping a low profile, mostly listening, occasionally saying something anodyne about the situation in the Bering. Nothing to arouse attention.

They met at Finnegan's, a bar in the basement of a mortuary by the same name. The bar had an unusually wide selection of Scotch whiskies. Taz found Nils and crew at a round table in the back. Nils introduced them.

"Taz, this is Erik Nystrom from Agenship, Oleg Krasny from Murmansk, and Irina Tsolkin, who needs no introduction."

The last observation was certainly true. Whoever Irina was, and whatever role she might be playing, introductions could not possibly describe. Erik was tall, grey-blond, glasses, businesslike. Oleg seemed disheveled by comparison, with a low hairline, a heavy beard, and a conspiratorial smile.

Irina was stunning—blonde, blue eyes, a long, graceful neck. An observant, maybe ironic, look, and a mouth that stole the show, even when it was trying hard not to smile.

Nils had made the study of American colloquialisms something of an art form. He brought them all to order.

"First order of business: we attract the bargirl, we order drinks, then we will all learn something from our American friend." *In charge immediately*, thought Taz, who regarded Nils as a kind of Falstaff.

Nils waved somewhat ineffectually at the bar. Taz got up and said hello to the bartender. She smiled and grabbed her order book, followed him to the table. "Good evening to all. What will you have?"

Nils ordered scotch and soda, Erik and Oleg followed suit. Taz asked for an Ardbeg, neat. Irina gave him a considered look. "I'll have the same."

Nils was an amateur anthropologist and liked to start every conversation with a question. "So Taz, what does it mean when the bluesmen say, 'Don't let your deal go down'?"

"Nils, last time I looked, I was white. How do you think I'm going to know the answer to that?"

"I know you better than that, my friend. And I've heard you play guitar. Have you checked your family tree? There's a hint of Africa there somewhere."

"Okay. Most people think the 'deal' refers to a deal in a card game, probably an old game from slave times. If the dealer's card is matched or bettered by the draw, the deal 'goes down'—it goes to the next person."

"But the way some people sing it, it sounds more like it's addressed to a woman." He gave Irina a quick look, smiled.

"And what would it mean, then?"

"Well, it would be an admonition not to sell yourself short, so to speak."

Nils laughed even louder. "That's why I love this man."

The waitress reappeared with the drinks. A toast was raised. Taz sipped the Ardbeg, held it in his mouth, breathed in the incredible flavors, tumbling one over another. When he opened his eyes, he realized Irina was looking at him.

"Breathe over it," he told her.

She took a healthy sip, held it, opened her mouth as if to whistle, breathed in. It took a moment. Then her eyes opened wide in surprise.

The business started. Erik went first. "So, why do you find our Barents Sea so interesting?"

"The challenges are interesting. It's not too long before we will have to deal with the same issues in the Chukchi and the Beaufort."

"Really? I wouldn't have thought so. What's there to transport north of the Straits—a few bulk cargoes for Eskimo villages?"

Irina rolled her eyes. Oleg came back to the point, smiling at Erik. "No, no. They will have some of the same issues, increase in bulk cargoes, search and rescue." He spoke with a thick accent that sounded like a cross between a Scottish burr and some Balkan dialect. Looking at Taz, he added, "But you've solved the big challenges already, haven't you? Because of the Red Dog Mine. So, what can you learn from us?"

Red Dog, near Kotzebue on Alaska's Chukchi coast, sat on top of the world's largest zinc deposit. In the ice-free summer months, the ore was shipped in barges over the shallow shelf near Kotzebue, then loaded onto seagoing ore boats and taken to the smelter complex in Trail, on the British Columbia coast. Taz took a flyer.

"We've never had to ship long distance, like the Greenlanders will. We have a hundred-day shipping season, and we've catered our production to it. The season for an ore operation in southern Greenland might be longer, but it's a lot more sketchy, don't you think?"

"Fish is the only thing the Greenland Inuits are shipping, and that's not the same problem," Erik said.

Oleg interrupted, with a sly look at Erik from under his bushy brows. "But that's not for long, and you know it. They have to figure out an ore route from Kvanefjeld, and where are they going to take it? They're not going to refine it on-site, that's for sure."

That was the first Taz had heard of Kvanefjeld. He made a mental note.

They talked well into the night. Nils demanded that each of them say a few words about the place where they were raised. When Erik quibbled,

Nils said, "For you, a geologic description of the rock that you crawled out from under will do."

Nils went first, with a story of a pie-eating contest in Narvik, on the Norwegian coast. Erik followed with a dry tale of schooldays in Copenhagen. Oleg had grown up in Archangelsk and told of a teenage camping trip to an island full of monasteries that had once also held Stalin's most feared political prisoners.

Irina's story was longer. She had been a tomboy, a word she uttered in a low, serious tone. When she was thirteen, she developed a crush—a devotion she called it—on the star of the school soccer team. He did not notice her, so she decided to make herself more visible. He was also the school's top marksman, and marksmanship was one of the only sports open to girls. Irina surprised her father by declaring that she wanted nothing more than to hunt with him, an activity in which she had shown no interest whatsoever up to that point. He told her she would have to learn to shoot first, and they began by targeting gourds and pumpkins with a vintage carbine from the Second World War. He would set the gourds on fenceposts, and back her away through the wheat and the corn-stubble until she missed. At the end, she was putting holes dead-center at 150 yards.

Then came the day in September when the school held its first shooting competition of the year. Irina, fourteen now, dressed as provocatively as she could manage, to the amusement of both the other competitors and the audience. She won the competition hands down.

"As you can imagine, this was very good for my self-esteem," she said with a grin, "but a terrible failure as tactic for romance." They all laughed. When Taz finally caught his breath, he realized with a start that his turn was up. He brooded openly for a moment, and then decided on the tale of the sand pits.

"I grew up on the Brazos River in Palo Pinto, Texas, not far from Mineral Wells. We used to do strange things for fun. I was about six, and my brother was twelve. He liked to play tricks on me. One summer day, he and his friend Gus took me to the sandpits, an old abandoned sand quarry in the hills south of town. Usually we would go to the flat area at the bottom of the quarry and they'd shoot tin cans while I hunted for lizards. But this time they took me to the very top of the sand cut, where a lip of topsoil held together with roots hung out over a sixty-foot drop. They told me what fun it was to fly, that all you had to do was run at top speed off the lip and wave your arms. I was scared, but they said they'd do it with me. So, we all took a running head start, and of course they stopped dead in their tracks at the edge of the lip. I had already launched myself off the lip—head-first—and was looking down at my certain death. Fortunately, my foot caught the slope's sand so that I rolled, somersaulted down to the pit. Gus and my brother were staring in open-eyed terror at the top of the cut. But I was safe, and we all started to laugh. When I got home, my brother and I both caught hell, and my stepmother hosed me down outside so I wouldn't track sand all over the house."

Irina was giggling, and Oleg guffawed. Nils put his arm over Taz's shoulder, leaned close, and said, "Still diving into the unknown, I see. Keep an eye open!"

Erik, the humorless, was the first to call it quits, as Nils had delved into regaling them with tales of the northern route. Erik left. Oleg was at this point getting deep in his cups, so that Nils finally ceased his storytelling and took him by the arm. "Time for bed, *tovarich*."

The bar had emptied out. Taz gave a long look around that ended on Irina. He patted the seat next to him. She smiled, as if to say, "Why not?" and moved over.

"So how did you like the whisky?"

"It was strange. But spectacular. How could it start with a taste so—briny—and then so many flavors?"

"Exactly. So Nils and Oleg I get. Even Erik. But you I don't get. What brings you here?"

At this, she snorted. Her smile opened even wider. "Well, to watch you, obviously."

"Am I really worth such specialized attention?"

"My friends at the FSB certainly think so."

"Hard to believe."

"Oh, stop. You were State Department. You probably still are State Department. So why is the American government so interested in Greenland?"

Taz didn't see much point in lying. Something about her frankness struck him. Either she knew the truth or she was guessing it, but in any case, denying the obvious wouldn't get him anywhere.

"We'd like to help the Greenlanders go for independence. It's going to happen, with or without us. But we don't want anybody queering the deal."

"So they sent you to find out who's playing in the money game."

"More to help them understand the lay of the land. They're all cooped up in their little cubbyholes, looking at their computer screens."

"Yes. You don't seem to have that problem." She smiled and touched his hair with long, delicate fingers.

"And you? I wouldn't have taken you for a minder."

Her eyes narrowed. "I'm no such thing. I don't even work for them."

"What is it you do, then?"

"I sleep with the ambassador."

Taz looked down the bar. Another technicolor sip of Ardbeg. "So, how did you get here? Where did you start?"

She moved closer, considered her drink, answered softly. "I grew up in Krasnoyarsk. Went to university there. The most beautiful city in all Russia. But hard for a girl alone. After I graduated, a cousin brought me to Moscow. Neither of us had any money. I took a job as a—how would you say—a live mannequin. One of the big department stores. That's where he saw me." She trailed off.

"And now you're in Iceland."

"Yes. From one provincial city to an even more provincial city, connection Moscow." She winked as she said it.

The ambassador had good taste, that was for sure. Taz excused himself, made his way to the bar, paid the tab. Asked for a cold bottle of champagne. Bartender gladly obliged. When he returned to the table, he had a Veuve Clicquot under his arm. Held out his other hand. Irina gave him an inquiring look.

"Are you sure?"

"Never more clear. You?"

She pressed her lips together, nodded and squeezed his hand.

CHAPTER SIXTEEN

All the Things Irina Knew

IRINA WAS NOT JUST good in bed. She was passionate, delicate. Trembled like a leaf the moment before he entered her. Whimpered endearments as they moved together. Tears when she climaxed. Taz raised himself on one elbow, absorbing her beauty.

Later, she smoked languorously. They stood for a while on the balcony, he in his boxers, she in a flimsy nightgown open at the breast. That was when she told him what he had come to learn.

"What you're looking for—I know. Sergei—the ambassador—it's his project. The one that will take him back to Moscow, make his name. He's obsessed with it. What do you call it—'rare earths'?" I don't know what that means. But Russian geologists found it, a big deposit, and his job is to make the commercial arrangements. To get—preferential treatment. Low royalties. The Greenlanders don't know how to bargain. When they try, he threatens. Boundary claims. Fishery wars. I despise him for it."

He slipped behind her, kissed the nape of her neck. She moved against him.

"Does the project have a name?"

"Kvanefjeld. It's close to the southern tip."

"Near Cape Farewell."

"Yes."

"I was there years ago with a group of Inuit seal hunters. It's a beautiful, stark place."

"And we'll ruin it, won't we?" Irina sounded upset.

"Well, I imagine so. At least change it forever."

"The problem is, we're even more capitalist than you, nowadays. What a fucked-up world." And then, imploringly, "I just want to stay here, with you."

She reached back and pulled his arms around her, then reached over her right shoulder to touch his face. He picked her up and carried her back to bed.

In the morning, he got up and showered. When he came back to the bedroom, she was putting on her slip.

"Will they miss you at the embassy?"

"Sergei's in London. I don't report to the staff."

"So much the better. I'm taking a car out to Pingvellir to see the old Viking settlements. Will you join me?"

"I don't know. I already like you too much, and you're just going to disappear, aren't you? I don't know if it would be good for me to go any deeper."

"Look. I don't know where this is going either, but I'd like to find out more about you. We only have this moment. And you only go around once."

She looked quizzical. "Go around what?"

"An American colloquialism. We only live once. No second chances. Your life is your responsibility."

She laughed. "You're an existentialist."

"And you?"

"All Russians are fatalists—you know that."

"Good. Accept fate and get your coat."

✳✳✳

An hour and a half later, they were standing in a brisk wind on the Almannagja escarpment above a 200-foot-deep rift valley, gazing at the Skjaldebreidur Volcano in the distance. The Axe River flowed into the rift below them.

"This is where the first Viking parliament met."

"What a strange place. Powerful. I can feel it. Tell me about the rift. It looks as if it were dug by a giant machine."

"Precise, isn't it? And it goes for miles and miles, right into the interior. We're standing on the very edge of the North American Plate. On the other side, you're in Eurasia."

"But you'd be glad to claim everything up to here, right?" A mischievous gleam.

"As long as you're on this side, yes." She scowled, made as if to punch him, then placed her cheek against his chest.

They made their way back into Reykjavik in the late afternoon. Taz was painfully aware that his plane left in the morning. At the moment, he wished he could just stay. "Would you like to have dinner?"

"I shouldn't. Sergei is coming back in the morning."

"And I fly back then, as well. But we have time."

The slight tip of her head suggested acquiescence.

They ate dinner at a modest fish place near the commercial wharf. Stockfish and potatoes with white wine. Afterward, they made their way to a pub. There was a good crowd, as always in Reykjavik. An Icelandic guitarist was playing a credible version of some Appalachian ballad. Taz ordered a scotch for Irina and a Jim Beam for himself.

The only open table was by the small stage. The Icelandic folksinger had given the guitar to a short, bearded Scot, who declared to no one in particular that he was going to "bring on the blues."

He tried, but it was a long way between a *ceilidh* band and Lightnin' Hopkins. His rhythm was uncertain. He tried to make up for it by pounding the chords. The crowd was growing restive. Finally, he stopped. Looked around. Asked, slurring his English, "Can't anyone here play this thing?"

It was a nice guitar—a Gibson J-50. Taz got halfway up from his chair. "I'll try a tune, if it's okay with the owner."

"Well, I'm the owner. It's okay as long as you sound better than me! I'm Angus."

"I'm Taz."

He held the guitar gently by the neck. It had the sunburst finish, a little nicked up. The action was good, for a Gibson; it must have been worked on. The crowd eyed him warily. Mostly university students and a little anxious about anybody as middle-aged as Taz, particularly in an Oxford shirt.

Taz draped the strap over his neck, made his way to the microphone. "Evening y'all," in his best Texas twang. He strummed an *A* and adjusted a couple of strings.

"This is a song about love." Looking at Irina.

He picked two A chords and started a Bo Diddley beat.

You know love will make fools of men
But you don't care, you're going to try it again.

When you're feelin' sad and blue
You know love's made a fool of you.

Conversation pretty much stopped at that point. Heads turned. A couple of women were already getting up to dance.

Time goes by, it's a-passing fast
You think true love-a has come at last
But by and by you're going to find
Crazy love-a has made you blind.

More people dancing. An appreciative whoop or two. Irina keeping time with the flat of her hand. He was singing Buddy Holly-style, a tenor just below bluegrass.

Love can make you feel so good
When it goes like you think it should,
Or it can make you cry at night,
When your baby don't treat you right.

Jamming the Diddley beat now, thinking about the Grateful Dead hitting the same chords on "Not Fade Away." Cutting them off, like Bob Weir.

When you're feelin' sad and blue,
You know love's made a fool of you,
You know love's made a fool . . . of you.

Shouting from the dance floor. He ripped the chords off the beat, sang a few more choruses. Snapped it to a close. The crowd shouted as one, clapped uproariously. Wanted to touch his shoulder. Wanted more. He just wanted to get back to his room with Irina.

CHAPTER SEVENTEEN

Kvanefjeld

HE WAS ON THE first west-bound plane of the day. Good thing. Meant he had to leave while Irina was still asleep. He crumpled three sheets of paper trying to compose a note. Finally left one that said, *I won't forget you, ever . . . I hope you won't forget me. I know for sure we will see each other again soon.* With his cell number.

With the time change, he got into Dulles by early afternoon. Told the taxi driver to take him to Twenty-first Street and C. Right to State. This time, White was there.

After the preliminaries, Taz said, "Look, I've got to get back home, but I think I've got something for you."

White ushered him into the SCIF. Just then, White's senior counsel, Irvin Friar, came bounding in. Whispered something to White. White nodded, his face betraying some small satisfaction.

"Taz says he's got something." White was discreet, but he couldn't hide a look that said they considered the proposition implausible. They both looked at Taz.

"The deal between Rosneft and StatOil, it's not about oil."

"But oil is their main game."

White waved the back of his hand dismissively. "So what are they moving into?"

"Rare earths."

White put his finger to his lips.

"They've found a world-class deposit, and they're already on the move to tie down the shipping and marketing arrangements."

"Where's the deposit? How did you find this out?"

"The deposit's at Kvanefjeld, on the very southern tip of Greenland—Cape Farewell. There's a whole series of lenses at different depths, embedded in a formation of black *lujavrite* that was uncovered by the glacial retreat. As to how I found it out, let's just say I put it together after a lot of conversations."

Irvin said, "And the Russians have control of this?"

"Not quite. They're bargaining with the Greenland government."

"What do you know about the state of play?"

"The Russians are bargaining hard for the concession, looking for a sweet deal, making threats. Doesn't sound like the Greenlanders are all that happy about the approach. I talked to a friend in the Greenland Parliament. He said the sentiment was to see if there might be a better offer, but they're feeling pressure to close a deal soon."

White looked at Irvin and said, "Let's get them a better deal."

Caught by White's tone, Irvin said a simple, "Yes, sir," turned on his heel and left the room.

White turned to Taz. "Who's leading the Russian effort?"

"Well, at least in negotiating the concession, it's Goncharov, their ambassador to Iceland."

"Makes sense. He's ambitious. This would be a real feather in his cap. He and his mistress would be the toast of Moscow."

Taz bit his lip. So Irina was well-known as Goncharov's mistress.

"Taz, this is good. Better than we hoped for. I have something for you, too."

Taz kept his best poker face.

"But it comes with a note of caution."

"Okay."

"This Eastern Shore thing is complicated. I'm going to tell you what we have, but we may not know everything. One thing we do know is that you're in an exposed position. A very exposed position."

Taz thought about yawning just to throw a wrench into White's carefully planned script. But his more rational mind held him back. Didn't have enough allies to alienate a major one.

"The investigators the other day weren't FBI. They weren't anybody federal."

"Who were they, then?"

"Blackthorn Security contractors, working for Rinvest."

"Can you keep them off me?"

"If you don't keep stirring up trouble, yes."

"John, you've known me for a long time. I'm not going to invite trouble. But maybe you ought to tell whoever you're talking to at Rinvest that their Tobytown project isn't winning them any friends." Taz told White about the thin man.

"You've always been a stubborn son of a bitch."

"Thanks. But I like to think I've matured."

"Yes. Into a crafty, older, stubborn son of a bitch."

He shook the assistant secretary's hand. "Let me know how the Greenland thing goes." Picked up his cell phone and left.

❖❖❖

He got back to the island just before sunset. The marshes were glowing golden across the Wire Narrows. Town lights were just coming on. A big, well-lit ocean tug was powering up the channel.

He parked his car in the gravel lot behind the Chincoteague Inn. A scruffy place, but the open-air deck had the best sunset view in town, and the Clams Casino were tasty. There were a half-dozen locals at the bar—no one he knew. When Diane, the bartender, finally looked his way, he ordered a draft beer and the clams. He was on the last clam but one when

Ben Shefler strode in. Ben was a tugboat captain, former Coast Guard. He took a look at Taz and said, from the other side of the bar, "No way I'm drinking with you, you scofflaw."

Most conversation stopped at that point. But he kept on.

"Bunch of suits combing the whole island like federals. Asking *innocent* questions." He drew out the *innocent*. "Who the hell did you piss off, Buster Brown?" Ben had clearly had a few drinks just to get ready for sunset at the inn.

"Some big mining company. They want all the farmland over in Tobytown."

"Well, do they really? And who the hell are you to say they shouldn't get it?"

"Me? Nobody. Just didn't like the way they were using the law to push folks around."

General murmurs of assent around the bar. A lean-looking fisherman with a worn blue baseball cap said, to no one in particular, "Corporate types is always using the law."

Taz looked around, saw a lot of folks looking his way. "Well, look, I hope I haven't caused anybody a bunch of trouble. Just got a little crosswise with this crew."

The fisherman, still to no one in particular, said, "Don't worry 'bout it. They were assholes."

Diane took the towel off her shoulder, wiped the counter in front of Taz. She was in her late forties and way too elegant to work behind a bar. "They were in here a couple of days ago. Leaving a little message about you. Pissed everybody off." She smiled at him. "Another beer?"

Ben, who had come around to Taz's side of the bar, pushed in next to him. "I'll buy."

CHAPTER EIGHTEEN

Home Again

CRISP FALL WEATHER BEGAN to break sporadically into November's gray dampness. Not every day. Just often enough to remind you that winter approached. The snowy egrets and the night herons had already left for the Carolinas. The terns were wheeling away, too, leaving only the gulls behind. The channel was too rough for fishing, and at forty degrees, Taz wasn't sure he wanted to be out on the water that much anyway. That was one of the things that separated him from some of his local friends. The "Teaguers," as the true old-timers were called, still launched their skiffs to make the regular morning rounds of the crab pots. Men and occasionally women in hip waders raked the oyster beds and shooed the oystercatchers off. The scallop boats moved in and out of the channel past Tom's Cove to the sea.

Taz busied himself insulating his hot water pipes. Stripping, sanding, and treating the windowsills on the front porch, the ones that took the saltwater blast on the days when the wet spray blew in from the west. Paint outside, varnish inside. When he turned on the disc player, it was to listen to Leonard Cohen, the Grateful Dead, or old Appalachian ballads. He knew that he should touch base with Russ and Rick to find out what more they had turned up, but he just didn't have the heart to dive back into the saga of Tobytown.

✻✻✻

Along came a Saturday, finally cloudless and still. The temperature hovered in the high forties. In the late afternoon, he ambled out to the dock, lit up a Flor Dominicana, and sat with his bare feet hanging down, eyeing his spartina. The salt marsh experiment was working, but in its own straggly, unsure way. Still, there were signs of progress. The marsh grass had already grown past the old cinderblock oyster colony and was now starting to extend itself uncertainly towards the first pilings. Little mud crabs were scuttling over the shell beds. That was really all he wanted, that and the smoke from a spicy cigar, and the blue sky and light breeze. Well, sure, if a blue crab or two wanted to make a home there, he'd be even more content. But what it was, was enough. For now.

A good cigar is more than a smoke. It's a vehicle for thought and dreams. Taz sat on the dock as the sun went down and let his mind wander. Just as he started to sink into a deep reverie, an old blue pickup pulled up. Tom stepped out, tipped his cap, and sauntered down the dock.

"Well, ain't you been hard to find. Where you been? Travelin' man?"

"Tom. It's a long story."

"Yeah, I figure. You got people looking for you, and most of 'em ain't your friends. Good time to be gone. But seein' as how you're back, I figure you might want to see somebody who doesn't give a shit about all that stuff."

"Always. How the hell are you?"

"Not so bad. There's a few houses building, and they usually figure out they need finish carpenters, though Lord knows it sometimes takes them a while."

"So I've been doing some business. Glad to be back."

"Where to, you don't mind my askin'." Tom tended to swallow his diphthongs, then his consonants, and occasionally whole words.

"This time Iceland. Big conference on Arctic shipping."

"Iceland—" Stroked the stubble under his chin. "Those boys know how to fish."

"Yeah, they've got that one down cold. You want a beer?"

"Wondered if you was ever gonna ask."

They wandered up the dock toward the cottage. Tom was a true blues man. He lived in an Airstream down in the Bunker Hill Campground. Had a little garden that gave him vegetables, and some chickens that donated eggs on a regular enough basis.

"So what's up in town?"

"Not much. Early birds are closing down for the winter. Jess down at Front Street Supply, he broke his arm fallin' off a ladder."

"Ouch. Didn't he used to play some?"

"Mandolin, on his good days. Not for the next six months, though."

"How're Richard and Laney?"

"You ain't gone by yet? They're going to be righteously pissed, is how they're doing."

"Yeah, I know. This trip took a little getting over."

"There was some thought of playin' tonight, if you was game."

"I'm pretty rusty. You'll all be waiting on me for the changes."

"Well, that's better than noodling around with some damn folk guitarist."

He popped two cans, put one in Tom's waiting hand.

"Okay, what time?"

"Seven. And dress up a little, okay? You look like shit."

"Whatever."

The great thing about Tom—he didn't trim his sails much, if ever. Drank their beers on the dock, spoke little, watched the channel.

After Tom drove off and made the turn at Beebe Road, Taz looked in the mirror. It was hard not to recognize the truth of his friend's fashion commentary. A rumpled sweatshirt with a worn duck stamp on the front, so splattered with paint it looked like the canvasback had been flying through a snowstorm. Hair was sticking out from under his baseball cap, which didn't look any better than the sweatshirt. Taz took off the cap, hung it on the rack on the side of the refrigerator, peeled himself out of the sweatshirt, and turned on the shower.

A half-hour later, he considered himself sufficiently transformed to mingle with other humans. He put on a blue twill shirt and found some khakis that looked more or less pressed. He mustered up a version of dinner—cold cuts, cheese, a little salad—then pulled out his guitar and tentatively fingered some tunes.

Just before seven, he put his guitar in the truck and headed over to the bookstore. A small crowd was gathering as he came through the back door. He saw Terry Carter, his neighbor down Beebe Road who was on the city council. Terry smiled and put his hand on Taz's shoulder. "Glad you're back. Got some late spinach and kale if you come by."

"Kale. I'd definitely go for that. Maybe I'll cook it up with ham, and you and Judy could come over."

"That would be just fine."

CHAPTER NINETEEN

Shape of Time

WHOEVER SAID "TIME DRIVETH onward fast" had it wrong. Time didn't drive on, it didn't pass you like the landscape outside a train, nor did it leave you like the wake behind a trawler. It appeared to Taz more like swimming in a Sierra stream—a cold torrent in one place and just down the creek a deep pool. Rapids where the stream broke up, rivulets running much faster, eddies where a fallen leaf twirled, deep currents where sleek fish worked their way up toward the headwaters. Taz knew he was in an eddy. His thoughts, questions—even the little semi-conscious images and glimmers that disappeared before they were fully formed—were all about the past. But as Faulkner put it, "The past is never dead. It's not even past."

Taz spent as little time as possible guessing what his neighbors thought about him. The ones who knew Taz, at least most of them, had worked out that the badge-men were crooked somehow, so the speculation was, what kind of crooked and why? The rest of the time, he wondered how and what Irina was doing. He kept busy writing up an in-depth report for the boys at INR; everyone he had talked to, the conversations that led to Kvanefjeld. He wasn't surprised that White and Friar had numerous follow-up questions, or even when he found out they were running their own trap lines, asking others to verify even the smallest details of his account. With an opportunity this size, any good analyst would do that. The report took him two days and part of a third, and still there was no word from Irina.

He could have gone back to White, but something in the way the assistant secretary had referred to "Goncharov's mistress" troubled him. The one fact that he had omitted from his report was how he had come to understand that Kvanefjeld was Goncharov's project.

He dialed Marnie Lowenfeld. Marnie was the senior analyst on the Russian desk, probably the smartest one there. Little, wren-like, with sharp features and sharper movements, she followed the traces of the Russian diplomatic service, and their FSB shadows, all over Europe. She was the one to talk to before shipping out to Estonia, or Hungary. She'd give the complete Russian roster with all the pertinent biographical detail—who was worth your time, who to avoid, who to watch. She was a little quirky, and some people avoided her on that account, or because they underestimated her. Taz liked and respected her. During the negotiation of the Stockholm Convention, knowing that Russia would be a critical player, he had sought her out, obtained two hours of her time, brought her flowers and her favorite chocolates, and said, "Please educate me."

Marnie liked the water. She had a place in Lewes, Delaware, not far from the Cape May ferry terminal. It didn't take him long to find her. She was coming out to her place in Lewes for a few days. He told her he was going to Cape May to catch the late hawks on their way south, and asked if he could take her out to dinner. She would be delighted; she had some questions for him as well.

Taz drove up to Lewes on Friday afternoon, caught the last ferry to the New Jersey cape, found a room in one of the old motels by the water tower on the east side of town. In the morning, he got an early coffee at the 7-Eleven and was at Higbee Woods by six-thirty, when the sun was still a glow on the horizon.

It was cold in the predawn hour, with a hint of frost. The jays and the flickers were already on the move, flitting in groups from tree line to tree line. The sparrows and the kinglets scoured the bushes and the old field stands for bugs and seeds.

Once the long beams of the winter sun started to play on the treetops, the young hawks began to appear. Cooper's, sharpies, red-shouldered, all the woodland hawks. A sharpie dived and picked off a dusky-gold finch that had been sheltering on a naked branch only a few yards from Taz's head. He made his way slowly up and down the dirt paths that bordered the old fields, watching the stubble for sparrows and the treeline for warblers.

After about two hours, his feet wet with dew, he began to feel the cold and reluctantly headed back to his truck and drove the back roads down to Cape May Point. He sat with the counters, the pros who could ID a Cooper's hawk when it was still a thousand yards away. They saw the *jizz,* the bird's general shape and impression—and they didn't often miss. He had tried to learn their technique, but he had a long way to go. It didn't help that he always fell asleep during New Jersey Audubon's hawk slideshows.

By midafternoon, he'd been out to the water tower at Sunset Beach to see the peregrines and the merlins, and over to the east side at Wildwood to catch the long lines of scoters bustling over the Atlantic wave break. He even caught some gannets, with their albatross-like wings, diving for menhaden. It was brisk and breezy. He hadn't encountered more than a few other birders, mostly the serious older ones in their Carhartt canvas jackets. Happy, worry-free for the first time in a week, he headed back to the ferry terminal to wait for the next ride south.

✳✳✳

Taz met Marnie at a little Spanish restaurant just a block from the inlet on the north side of town. She was already ensconced by the fire, reading a volume of Akhmatova. "Taz! What trouble are you up to now? I'm glad to see you—it seems like years."

"It *is* years."

"I know, but I don't want to admit it. Life hurries by."

"How are our friends at the Foreign Ministry these days? Any good soap operas?"

"It's all changed, sad to say. Not the professionals we were used to. Businessmen, little oligarchs, mafia types, fast-buck artists. Maybe I should retire."

"When you do, I want to throw the party."

"You've always been the sweet one, my dear. The others just think I'm a file catalog. Consult as needed." She smiled.

They ordered sherry and light tapas. The sherry was bone dry and had a nice mineral finish.

"Marnie, I think I might need some help."

"Yes. Iceland." Her bright gaze met his eyes.

"I should have realized you'd already be on it."

She looked down, took a peck of Spanish rice. "I've been particularly interested in Goncharov, you know, so when John told me what you found, I did some extra digging."

Taz waited.

"He's a dangerous man, Taz. A user. Ambitious. He disposes of people who get in his way, people he doesn't need. He has links to the Russian mafia in Archangelsk and Riga."

"My briefers told me he came up through the fisheries ministry."

"The most corrupt ministry in the government. Yes. You didn't think that meant he had ever cast a line himself, I hope." She looked quickly around the room, then back at Taz.

"Is his role in Kvanefjeld public knowledge?" Taz asked.

"Which role?"

"What do you mean?"

"I mean as the project champion, or as a lead investor?"

"You're sure?"

Marnie snorted. "I had the Agency look into Kvanefjeld's corporate reports right after you gave the lead to INR. Goncharov's got a five percent stake in Kvanefjeld LLC, the holding company. Rosneft has fifty-five percent, StatOil forty. If the project goes to completion, he'll compete with Abramovich to see who can buy the wealthiest Premier League football team."

"And if the project doesn't go through to completion?"

"He'll want to know why not, and if he finds someone responsible, I wouldn't want to be in that person's shoes."

Taz thought over her information uneasily, while she watched him from the side of her eyes. Finally, he met her gaze.

"Marnie, can you help me get Irina out of Iceland?"

"Yes, but we cannot move a finger until INR has put in play its alternative to the Russian concession."

CHAPTER TWENTY

Paying for Your Sins

THE NEXT MORNING, TAZ called Laney.

"Any chance you're free for coffee?"

"I'm never free, honey. But if you're good for it, I could sure use some."

"I'll be right down."

It was only nine-thirty; the bookstore hadn't opened. He went in the back door and looked at Richard. "I'm taking your wife, but I promise I'll bring her back."

"If a hot double espresso comes back with her, all is forgiven."

"This is getting to be an expensive consultation, and it hasn't even started yet."

Laney came out of the back room and pulled her cloak off the hook. She put her arm through his as they walked out the door and across the street.

They sat over their steaming mugs and looked at each other warily. Finally Laney spoke.

"So what happened? It was so promising before you left for Iceland that Richard and I had a shot of tequila to celebrate."

"Maybe you were just a little ahead of yourselves."

"Oh, boy. Tell me."

"I met someone in Iceland."

"Someone really special? Because you're about to blow an opportunity that doesn't ever even happen in most men's lives."

"I know. I didn't know what to do. But the last thing I want to do is to hurt her."

"Credit for that. You want to tell me about Iceland?"

"It's complicated."

"Of course it is, Taz, it's you. You're the most complicated person most of us poor island folk have about ever seen." She had put on a credible Teaguer accent.

"Oh, get off it."

"I wish I was kidding. So are Iceland girls really that awesome?"

"Yes, but this one is Russian. The ambassador's girlfriend."

"You're shitting me, right?"

"Not a bit."

"How?"

"She was sent to spy on me. We hit it off."

"Well I guess."

"She's a woman from Siberia who made it in Moscow by accident. You'd like her."

"I wonder."

"Maybe it doesn't matter. I don't know if I can get her out."

"I thought the old Soviet days were over. Russia's a free country now."

"Not if you're married to the mob. And worse than that, we're about to queer a deal that her boyfriend really wants."

"I guess you don't have a choice then."

"No, I don't think I do."

"You sure about this? Dana won't wait forever."

"I can't do it any other way just now."

"Taz, I love you, but you're really a handful."

"I know. I love you, too."

He picked up Richard's espresso. They made their way back through the drizzle to the warm light of the bookstore.

✤✤✤

When he got back to the cottage, his message machine was blinking. It was Eliza Burkett, the reporter for the Salisbury station who had blown the whistle on the Accomac cops.

"Taz, I've got something I need to run past you. Can we meet?"

They agreed to meet for a drink at the Old Atlantic Hotel in Snow Hill. The hotel was on the Pocomoke River, and had a chef who knew how to cook fish. Taz finished a few notes he was making on the Kvanefjeld deal, threw on an old Filson wool shirt. It was getting dark. Five-thirty. The rain had stopped. The sun was peering bleakly under the clouds on the western horizon.

Headed out across the new bridge. Traffic was light. Got to Snow Hill where Eliza was waiting at the bar. Gave her a kiss on the cheek and sat down on her left.

"I haven't seen you since Accomac. You did a great job on the TV report."

"I owe you a drink or two just for the tip on that one. I've been following it ever since. Virgil Waite has been on at least three times—he's a natural."

"What happened to Sheriff Gaynes?"

"Oh, he's still huffing and puffing, but he's had to pull in his horns. Heard he got some calls from Justice. You wouldn't know anything about that, I guess."

"It's been a long time since I was in government."

"Yeah. And I hear it was a friend of yours who sprang Virgil."

Bartender said they'd better order. Eliza smiled.

"I'm not here digging for a story—not yet anyway."

"What then?"

"Well, I've gotten some information I can't make heads or tails of, and I thought you might be able to help. You used to work at the Interior Department, didn't you?"

"Sure. Six years, before I went to State."

"Did you spend much time with the Geological Survey?

"USGS? Yeah, I worked with them a fair amount. They have all the stream and river science, the geologists, and most of the wildlife biologists. So, when we were trying to deal with the New World Mine, or the push to drill in the Arctic Wildlife Refuge, I always learned from the rock hounds."

"You know much about geology yourself?"

"Only bits and pieces. Salt geology, because we did some work on the search for a high-level waste site. Oil and gas. That kind of thing."

"Is the Eastern Shore a likely place to find radon?"

"Above my pay grade, but I don't think so—not particularly. Most of the East Coast south of Cape Cod on the coast side of the fall line is unconsolidated sediment—sands and loam, residue from the erosion of the Appalachians. Not usually the place you'd go if you wanted to glow, if you know what I mean."

"Then how come the homes in Tobytown have radon counts that are off the charts?"

He looked at the mirror behind the bar, then at her. "Those poor sons of bitches, they just can't catch a break."

"Taz, is this connected in some way with that demonstration?"

"Oh, I think so."

The bartender brought Eliza her Manhattan, came back with a frozen glass and a shaker for him, poured with a flourish.

"How did this come out?"

"It hasn't come out. I got it from a lawyer I know, but I've now confirmed it with a staffer in EPA's regional office." Sip. "In the Indoor Air program. They do a routine monitoring survey, and it's Accomack's turn. They hit zilch until Tobytown, and then the meters were going off the charts." Another sip. "And one more thing—usually this is a problem in tight houses. You know, the tighter the house is in terms of air exchange, the worse the radon problem. But these are old, drafty farmhouses. The staff guy told me Virgil was lucky he didn't grow up in a modern house— or he wouldn't be here now at all."

"Tell me more about this lawyer, the one who gave you the lead."

"I can't. He's a confidential source."

"An ambulance chaser? A personal injury guy?"

"You mean does he have an axe to grind? No. In fact, he does most of his work for big corporations."

She waited while he took a knock from his martini. "So you knew something about this, didn't you?"

"Not about the radon, no. But when I was trying to figure out what was causing all the trouble in Tobytown, I ended up running into a mining company."

"A mining company? The only things we mine out here are sand, gravel, and chicken-shit."

"Yeah I know. But they're interested. That's who's trying to get their hands on the property in Tobytown."

"Thus the cops and the harassment."

"How else are you going to get a bunch of farmers to give up on land they've had since before the Revolution?"

"Can you help me with this, Taz? This is the biggest story I've ever been near." Her lips were glistening. Her eyes were wide with excitement.

"What do you say you buy me dinner?"

She had crab cakes; he had local flounder. He ordered them a bottle of Sancerre, which went down just fine. He found out she had gone to journalism school in Miami at the same time that he was doing work on Everglades restoration for Interior Secretary Talbot.

"Those were crazy times. The state was suing EPA, the Justice Department was suing the sugar industry, and Miccosukee Tribe was suing everybody."

"Aren't they still?"

"Pretty much."

"You're going to laugh. My graduate project was a documentary on the tribal government's response to the restoration plan. You were not their favorite person."

"They didn't even know me."

"They knew you set up the interagency science team, and got the Fish and Wildlife Service to agree with the Park on higher flows out of Okeechobee."

"You were apparently a good student. But most of the credit goes to Buzz Byrd."

Colonel Terrence "Buzz" Byrd, the Florida lead for the Corps of Engineers, was one of the few superstars Taz had met in an eight-year government career. He was the real thing—action-oriented, smart, a natural team leader. Once Taz found him and told the Interior Secretary Talbot that the Corps should lead the science team, logjams broke, seas parted, and a major amount of stuff got done at record speed.

The Secretary wanted to meet him before he made a final decision, since EPA and Fish and the Park Service were also competing for the lead. Taz called Buzz to ask whether he could come to Washington to brief his boss. He still remembered Buzz's response: "Well, now, Taz, does your boss want the standard briefing, or the hot wash and wax?"

"So what about Tobytown? Can you hook me up with your old colleagues at the Survey?"

"I can. But there's something you have to know. This could get dicey. I've been warned off three times—once by friends and twice by thugs working for the company."

"I'm a big girl, Taz." Strictly speaking, not true. She was a bantamweight with the body of a marathon runner.

He smiled. "Eliza, I know you're going to do the story. But you need to keep your eyes open. They broke into my house on the island and sent some fake FBI agents to frighten my neighbors."

"Wow. Okay, I'll talk to my editors. What more can you tell me?"

Over coffee and brandy, he told her what he knew. She took notes in a little spiral-bound book. At the end, she said, "You dug all this out? It's you who should've been a reporter. I'm impressed."

"I've been trying to find a way to impress you ever since that Shorebirds game."

"Really, I don't believe you. But thanks for saying so."

"Just one request. Let me know when you're going to air something, or if you're actually going to interview somebody from Rinvest or BHP, okay?"

"That I can do. Thanks Taz, really. Thanks."

"I'll call GS tomorrow and send you an email about who to talk to."

It was well after dark when they parted company. She was driving a red MG convertible. He waited for her to leave before climbing back into his truck.

CHAPTER TWENTY-ONE

Dinner with Friends

SECOND WEEK OF NOVEMBER. Cold and windy on the clear days, cold and wet on the gray. The island's summer places had gone dark. High-end vacation homes on Piney Island and Oyster Bay stood empty. Main Street deserted. Folks turned inward. If you were here now you knew how to catch supper and cook it, or else you were eating fried chicken from Pantry Pride. Ducks had flown south, and snow geese hadn't yet come in from Hudson's Bay.

Taz picked up Terry's kale. Terry had waited to harvest until the first frost, so the kale had that extra flavor that only comes when you pick it late. Taz hadn't yet hosted a dinner in the cottage, and he figured it was about time. He called Laney and asked her if she'd help put out the word. Laney said she'd bring salad.

He found a salt-cured country ham at a little butcher shop down on Route 13 and soaked it overnight in a pail full of apple cider. Picked up a bag of onions and a dozen white potatoes and started in early on Saturday. Stripped Terry's kale the way his stepmother had taught him, and boiled the leaves for the first hour with the ham and a few of the onions. Used a slotted spoon to take the kale out of the simmering pot, put it in a cast iron skillet with a little sugar, olive oil and bacon fat, cooked it down. Put the ham in a rack to dry, then patted it with brown sugar laced with cognac. At the end, he put the potatoes on to boil. It was four o'clock, and guests would be coming at five. He carved an end off the ham, tasted it, and declared it good. Took a shower, donned a tan flannel shirt, opened a couple of bottles of wine.

Terry and his wife Judy arrived first. Walked down from their house just up Beebe Road, "What have you done to my kale? It smells really nice."

"It's an old German recipe, with a little Kenya thrown in—*sukuma wiki*, the Kenyans call it."

"Taz, are you trying to turn Chincoteague cosmopolitan?"

"I may be crazy, but I'm not stupid. It's just an old family recipe."

"You must have an interesting family. Yes, I'll bet you do."

He got them both apple cider. Neither of them drank alcohol. They sat for a while and talked local politics.

Laney arrived with a giant salad bowl and a plastic bag full of lettuce and peppers.

"Richard's closing up. Where can I do this so I don't get in the way?"

"Don't worry, just use the kitchen table."

Tom came in with a bottle of Stolichnaya. "This go with whatever you're making?"

"Absolutely. Just put it in the freezer, if you can find room."

"Ronny said to make his apologies. He's got to get ready for a big church deal tomorrow."

"We'll save him some ham."

The side door off the kitchen swung open. Ben Shefler, with Diane, the bartender from the Chincoteague Inn. Ben looked around; a little uncertain for such a big man.

"Come on in, Ben. Welcome. And Diane—for once I get to serve you."

Diane grinned. "Sweetheart, why do you think I'm here? And what's that delicious music you're playing?"

"Charlie Byrd."

"I love it." She gave him a kiss on the cheek. He pointed to the wine. The party started to roll. Taz excused himself to deal with the ham.

He moved the drainer to the top of the refrigerator, set up a carving board next to the sink. Laney was shredding lettuce.

"You put together an interesting crowd."

"Oh, there's more. Dana's bringing dessert."

Taz stared at the ham, tried not to smile.

He had just started carving when she came in the front door. She was carrying two homemade pies and a shopping bag. He stuck the fork in the ham, put down his knife, and made space on the counter.

"Those look really good."

"Strawberry-rhubarb."

"My favorite. How did you know?"

"I'm clairvoyant. Also, Laney declared she would kill me if I made anything else."

"Should have known. Can I offer you something?"

"A place to hang my coat?"

Taz pointed to his bed, just off the kitchen, which already sported a mound of miscellaneous coats and scarves. She laughed. "And a white wine spritzer." He turned to get a highball glass.

He filled the glass with ice and got a bottle of Sauvignon blanc out of the refrigerator door. Then the seltzer. When he turned back, Dana was standing by the stove, watching him. She wore a sleeveless black cocktail dress that perfectly accented her figure, which didn't really require any help. A simple silver necklace with a single claw hung in the exact space where the hint of a cleft left a mark on his imagination. The dress ended just above her knees. Her calves showed the sculpted muscles of a cyclist. She had on sandals. Even her feet were beautiful.

"Wow. I mean, you look terrific."

Her eyes twinkled. "Thanks, Taz. Whatever you're cooking smells fantastic."

"It's ham and kale. An old family recipe."

He finished her spritzer with a hint of lemon zest and handed her the glass. They stood together for a moment with their backs to the little pantry table he used for a bar. She surveyed the wood paneling and the framed Aleut bird prints.

"You have a nice place."

"Take a look around. Doesn't take long, and the decorations could use some improvement."

She laughed. "And you think, what? A woman's touch?"

"Something like that."

"Well, maybe I will. I love these old watermen's cottages."

Dana said hello to Judy and Terry, and then slipped up the stairs. Richard had arrived, carrying two bottles of Beaujolais. He was talking to Terry about some local zoning issue. Taz went back to see if he needed to carve more ham.

Like all good parties, little groups were forming, morphing, dissolving. Dana came back down and charmed the living room on her way through to the kitchen. There were at least three separate conversations. Taz carved, turning thin slices onto a warming plate. Diane, Dana, and Laney watched, talking amongst themselves. The gist was that the girls' soccer coach at Chincoteague High was leaving for Richmond, where her boyfriend had landed a big IT job. This was something of a crisis, not least for Suzanne, Dana's daughter, who was a budding midfielder and would need a serious coach for the next couple of years.

Supper went well. Everyone took a plate and ended up anywhere they could find a seat. Diane sat cross-legged on the floor, propping her back on Ben's knees. Taz taught the willing how to chop and mix the kale, potatoes, and ham on their plates German style. Tom looked on.

"I think I'll take mine Irish style."

"How's that?"

"Separately, with a Guinness on the side."

Taz rooted around his refrigerator and came up with a cold bottle of Guinness, "Just like mother's milk."

Judy flinched. Diane fairly snorted. They looked at each other and laughed.

Plates came back to the kitchen for seconds, then back one more time. He started some coffee and looked at Dana.

"I think it's time to drop the sugar bomb." He showed her where the small plates were.

Somehow she had smuggled two pints of vanilla ice cream into the freezer and snuck the pies into the oven, so they had the pie á la mode, with coffee. Terry feigned a heart attack. It was the best dessert any of them had had in months.

People began to drift off. Tom had an early morning date at the boatyard in Wachapreague. Terry and Judy said their goodbyes. Ben gave Diane a warm look. "I've got to take the Georgia-Ann down to Wilmington. Guess we'll cash in our chips early." Diane nibbled his ear. "Probably see you all in a week or so."

Richard and Laney stayed for a nightcap. They had to mind the store in the morning. It had been a better than usual night, they both agreed on that.

Dana smiled at Taz. "Want some help cleaning up?"

Taz looked around the kitchen. "You got a forklift and a flame thrower?"

"It's not that bad. Come on."

When he had dried the last glass and they had put most of the food away, she started wrapping the last of the pie.

"You should take some back for Moyer and Suzanne."

"They're at my sister's house in Baltimore for the weekend. I'll make them one when they come back."

The music had stopped. He switched out the disk for an old album of New Orleans piano tunes.

When he came back to the kitchen, she was looking out the side door. She turned to face him. "Taz, the other night. The coffee we didn't have . . . it made me realize some things. I know I didn't start off very well with you. Can you forgive me for acting like such a bitch?"

"There's nothing to forgive. You were protecting your own. I once saw a black-necked stilt fly off her nest and chase a young red-tailed hawk right into a 320-kilovolt power line. The hawk hit a wing and went up in flames. The stilt had two chicks in her nest, and the hawk just came too close. Mothers sometimes need to be fierce."

"But I chased off the wrong hawk."

"No way for you to know. And you weren't so very wrong. When I first came here, I wasn't exactly in a great place."

"Do you mind talking about it?"

"Do you want some whiskey?"

"I'd take another glass of that Beaujolais, if there's any left."

He poured her the end of the bottle, put a couple of ice cubes into a tumbler, and made himself a rye with some bitters.

They sat on the front porch. Cold air leaked through the walls and windows, but there was a nice view of the water and the lights over on Wallops Island.

"Well. I married someone I was totally smitten by. I thought she loved me too. Except it turned out to be a one-way street. She wanted to go where she thought I could take her, but it was all about my job, her ambition, and a future where we looked like her parents. It wasn't ever about me. Her family hated me because they knew I wasn't one of them. I was oblivious until the storm hit. I ended up losing it all—the marriage, the job, my future. At least it seemed that way."

"It's hard to fail in a marriage. I know."

"It was more that so many things I thought were true, weren't. My life kind of unraveled for a while."

"But your job—you're still doing the same kind of work, yes?"

"Yes and no. I'm still working the same field, but now I'm on my own. Then I had a whole team working with me."

"What were you doing, exactly?"

"Lots of things. At the end, I was negotiating environmental agreements for the State Department."

She raised her eyebrows. "I can't see you as a diplomat at all. You're not stuck up enough, and I can't imagine you in a top hat."

"Yeah, top hats and tails are out these days. But I could be a suit when I needed to be. Mostly that's not what it's all about."

"So what is it all about?"

"Well, for a serious negotiation, it's sort of like managing a baseball team. You have to know what you want, where you need things to come out to make it a good treaty from the US perspective. And you have to build a team that can get you there.

"After that, it's all hit and run. Your objective is to build the coalitions you need in the negotiation to get the outcome you've designed."

"Which is what you're doing on this Tobytown mess, right?"

He hadn't thought of it that way. He really hadn't. She put her hand on his arm. "Laney told me it was a friend of yours who helped Bennett's father. And that you had somebody else back the sheriff down. And that it was you who called the Salisbury television team and got them to the demonstration."

"She's giving me too much credit."

"I know something about power and needing to fight to get justice, Taz. You're doing a good thing."

"Well, it certainly took my mind off my issues, which was probably a good thing for me at least."

"You don't take compliments easily, do you?"

"As a boy, I spent a lot of time avoiding being the object of attention." He stood, walked over to the door, turned. She was looking at him, trying to read him. "Do you want me to go?"

"No . . . no. I like talking to you."

"You know, my ex was always fishing for compliments. It's intriguing to meet someone who shies away from them."

"Tell me a little about your life—before."

She got up to stand beside him. They could see the lights of Ben's tug. The crew were putting on provisions.

She crossed her arms. "I spent my early years in North Carolina, but I really grew up in California, just down from San Francisco. Spent my summers on a ranch in the Sierra foothills. I was good with horses. Came east to go to school. I knew I wanted to work with families, maybe because mine needed some work. My first job was with Rhode Island social services.

That was tough, but it taught me to appreciate what I had. Eventually, I got known a little, and I ran into Norfolk's Director of Social Services at a conference. She invited me down to run her family unit. It was a big break.

"That was where I met Timothy. He was good looking, tall. He kind of swept me off my feet. I think for a California girl it was probably the uniform and the military bearing, as much as anything. Anyway, we started seeing each other, and one thing led to another until I was married with a child on the way. Then the Coast Guard transferred him up here."

"It must have been hard to leave your job in Norfolk."

"Well, I loved my job and I really liked working for Donna, my boss. She's still a friend. But I didn't think I had a choice. That was when we had our first real fight. I found out about a month after we got here that he had requested the transfer."

Taz winced and turned to her, a question on his lips.

She beat him to it. "I think he didn't want me to work outside the house. He never told me that exactly, but when we got settled up here, he kept finding reasons why I should put off looking for work."

"Work is important. It helps you learn. And grow. Sometimes stepping away is the hardest thing. Without it, you're not sure who you are."

"It was that way for me. But by then I had Suzanne. She filled up my time, and my heart. And I made friends. Laney was a big help. We've come to rely on one another.

"I got through, and I got stronger, too, in a funny way. More sure of what I wanted, but that just led to more fighting."

Taz didn't know what to say.

"He was a drinker, but not like you."

Taz cocked an eyebrow.

"Well, don't think I haven't noticed! You get happy and maybe a little silly and loud. But you drink to plus up the fun. Timothy was an angry drunk. I guess he always had it in him, but when he drank, he couldn't hold it back."

Taz put his hand on her shoulder, drew her towards him. She put up a hand and ever so softly held back. "No, it's okay. You should know. The second time it happened, Moyer tried to stop him. He was only five." She was tearing up. He took his kerchief out of his pocket and put it in her hand.

"He hit Moyer. That was the last straw. I left for my sister's that night, and told him I wanted him out by the time I got back."

"Has there been trouble since?"

"No. He went away after the divorce and never came back. I don't even know where he is. He was never a stalker. He just couldn't control himself—his drinking, his anger. It's too bad. It's hard on the kids, not having a dad."

"I know. My mother died when I was little. My dad didn't remarry until I was almost eight." He led the way back into the kitchen, it was warmer there.

"Would you like some coffee?"

"Sure, hot coffee would be good right now." She shivered.

"Decaf or high-test?"

She looked at her watch and gasped. "Better be decaf, or I'll be up 'til dawn."

He busied himself over the stove. The back burner needed a little help getting started. He lit a match.

"So why did you stay on the island?"

"Same reason you will, if our luck holds. It's a great community. People stand up for each other."

He poured the boiled water over the coffee. "I don't know that I'm such an unmixed blessing. My life's a little complicated just now."

"I gather." She caught his eye. "I was hoping we could be friends, at least for now." She surprised him, again and again. "Since that day I pushed you away on the beach, I've had this horrible feeling. It was the way you reacted, I think. You were— Well, I tried to describe it to Laney and she used the word *crestfallen*. But I saw dignity, too."

She stopped to catch her breath. Her eyes were moist.

He pulled her towards him. This time she didn't hold back. He held her close, with his arm around the small of her back and a hand on the nape of her neck. At first, she turned her face past his shoulder, but then she snugged her nose in close to his neck and sniffled. Her hands were between them, palms on his chest. They stood that way for a long time.

They finished their coffee. He put her pie plates in a bag while she put on her coat. Walked her out the door. She was getting in her car, a Volkswagen station wagon. He gave a gentle tug on her sleeve. She turned halfway to him. He touched her lips gently with his fingers. "You're a very special woman. Very beautiful, very strong. Whatever happens, I want you to know how glad I am that I've had the chance to get to know you."

She smiled, rose just far enough to put her lips to his ear, whispered, "Taz, we've hardly touched the surface. Sleep well." Then she slid into the driver's seat, pulled out of the little shell drive, headed north on Main.

CHAPTER TWENTY-TWO

Ton of Bricks

IT WAS EARLY DECEMBER, frosts were hard, snow flurries had made an appearance. Life on the island had slowed to a crawl. The men in their Carolina skiffs still checked their clams, and the clam farmers in Tom's Cove still selected the midday harvest. But Main Street was empty. Even Rainy Day—the bookstore that never closes—had adopted a weekend schedule. Most of the trawlers had moved down to Elizabeth City or points south. The outdoor bar at the Chincoteague Inn was only open on weekends, and then only if the forecast was favorable.

Snow geese had arrived from their breeding grounds, spending days in the corn stubble on the mainland. Evenings they sheltered in the ponds on the refuge. If you were smart enough to walk the refuge loop at dusk, you could watch them fly in at sunset, whistling and gabbling, flight after flight. The sound of the big flights reminded you of the miracle of creation.

Taz spent his days studying. He had taken on the consultancy with the Arctic Council that Soffia had talked to him about. The Council was the forum that the eight Arctic governments had set up to address environmental and development issues in the Circumpolar Arctic region. He was to help the Council secretariat develop a strategy for marine-protected areas. There were a lot of people he needed to talk to, but first he had to master the file—all the past documents from the wildlife working group—to figure out what or who had derailed the original protected-areas effort years before.

The chair of the working group was a longtime friend from Iceland, Magnus Arneson. He gave Taz his personal files, including notes from some of the more delicate meetings, most of which weren't on the public record. Taz was going through them, page by page and hour by hour, trying to understand the arguments of the objectors, first, and then their motivations. Who was pushing them, and why? That was always the question.

Phone started ringing. First call Thursday morning from Marnie. "They're getting close, Taz. They've set up an Australian bid. Who's your friend in the Greenland Parliament?"

Taz thought before he replied. Akannik Olsen had been the one Taz had called to check out the Kvanefjeld story. He was young, smart, and capable. *Good move to bring in the alternate bid, or will it get him in trouble?*

"Tell them to try Akannik. He'll know how to handle it.'"

"Isn't he a little junior for this?"

"Yes, but he's an up and comer. He has good judgment. Besides, he's on the Natural Resource Committee. If someone was going to bring in a new catch, he would be likely anyway."

The next call, Eliza. He picked up the message a little after ten o'clock. He had been over at Nicky's getting some fish when she called.

"Taz, just wanted to let you know, we're going to call Rinvest today for comment on a story about how they're trying to buy up Tobytown. Call me if you want more."

He was just digesting her news when his cell phone lit up. He recognized the Reykjavik exchange. Nils' baritone spoke from the other end, and he appeared to be talking to someone else in the room with him.

"Taz, Taz? Are you there?"

"Hello Nils. How are you?"

"I'm good, but I don't have much time. I'm sorry."

"I'm all ears."

"Taz, I have it on good authority that Irina Tsolkin is flying into Newark tonight."

Taz was still for a moment.

"Taz, are we still connected?"

"Yes. Do you have the flight number?"

"Icelandic Air 270."

"Got it. Anything else I should know?"

"She's hoping you can meet her."

"Of course I will."

"I have to go, Taz."

"Nils. Thanks. You're a true friend."

"When I can be. Keep an open eye, Taz, and don't let your deal go down."

The connection died.

Taz wondered about that last line. What was Nils trying to tell him?

Called Icelandic Air. Flight 270 scheduled to arrive at five-thirty. Didn't have much time. Drove up Highway 13, just in time to catch the Northeast Regional at the Wilmington station. Got settled in the café car and realized he hadn't brought anything to read. Fortunately, his table mate was just finishing the morning *Post*.

"From Washington? How did the Caps do yesterday?"

"Don't know." Not the talkative type.

"Mind if I look at the sports page?"

He shoved the section over to Taz without looking up. Caps beat the Philadelphia Flyers, 5–2. More significantly, Barcelona had routed Chelsea in the first round of the Champions League.

When they reached Philadelphia, Mr. Talkative got off and left the rest of the paper on the table. Taz couldn't concentrate on the news stories. Mind kept drifting back to Irina, to Kvanefjeld, to Nils's puzzling call. Couldn't put it all together. Slept for a spell and woke just as they were braking to make the station at the airport.

Got to the international terminal with half an hour to spare. Paced and looked at the arrival boards. Only one flight from Reykjavik. At last, the board flashed. Plane unloading at Gate 84. Positioned himself just at the exit from the customs area. A trickle of passengers was coming through. Older man confirmed the flight was from Zurich.

Ten minutes passed. A few more passengers came through, then a stream. Taz turned back to make sure he didn't miss her. It was one of the big new airbuses, and Taz guessed it had been full. Scanned the faces.

No Irina.

The stream turned back to a trickle. Finally came the wheelchairs and the crew. He excused himself and asked one of the flight attendants if it was possible to check a passenger manifest.

"I'm afraid we can't give those out, sir, it's a privacy matter."

"Can you confirm whether a particular passenger was on board? "

"I can't, but if you call the airline, they may be able to."

He heard his name over the loudspeaker just as he was dialing his cell. "Mr. Blackwell to the white courtesy phone, please."

Spotted a phone at the end of the empty baggage claim area. Headed over to it but never made it. A serious-looking man in a cheap suit stood in front of him, holding an envelope. "Mr. Blackwell, this is from Miss Tsolkin."

He reached out to take the envelope, sensed someone was behind him, and started to turn. A swift blow to the neck toppled him to his knees. He thought he heard the words, "And this is from the ambassador," before he blacked out.

✳✳✳

When he came to, he was in the back of a limousine. The man who had given him the envelope was driving. Another, larger man was sitting facing him, with a Luger pistol pointed at Taz's stomach.

Suffocating from the heat and the odor of cheap cigarettes and Russian cologne. "Can we open a window?"

"Of course, Mr. Blackwell." Driver pushed a button and both back windows opened a crack. Windows were tinted, but by nicotine. Taz reckoned they were in the Meadowlands.

They turned off the highway onto a two-lane road. Lights went by, then nothing for a while. Taz was thinking furiously.

They turned again, this time onto a dirt road. Finally, they stopped in a gravel parking lot.

"Here." The gunman waited while the driver came back and opened the door. Taz got out, slowly. Looked around. Surrounded by cattail marshes. The dirt road behind them ran over a levee towards some faraway mercury vapor lamps. The gunman put metal in Taz's back and pushed him away from the car. "Walk."

Toward an old warehouse, unlit, large. The two thugs didn't seem to care what he looked at, including their faces, which meant they were going to kill him. Tried to ready himself. The central rolling doors were open; the warehouse empty inside.

The driver stopped. "I forgot the boom box." He walked back to the car.

Just then a violent croaking broke out at the foot of the levee. The gunman, startled, ran over to see what was going on. Taz quickly pulled his cell phone out of his jacket pocket and shoved it down his sock. The herons—there were two—worked their way slowly into the air, croaking at each other and at the gunman.

"Fucking birds."

Taz waited. The gunman waived his pistol towards the cavernous door. The driver came back with the boom box. "We can't have you go out without music, can we, *tovarich*?" he said, slapping Taz's shoulder with his other hand.

Inside—gloomy, damp, cold. Floor littered with bird droppings and old shavings of some kind. Footsteps echoed.

Taz tried to break and run, turning around the driver so that the gunman couldn't reach him. But the big man was fast. He whipped his pistol barrel across the back of Taz's head and he crumpled to his knees in the dirt. Blood oozing on the back of his neck. The gunman pulled him up by the collar and dragged him the few steps back through the open warehouse door.

"It never hurts to try, does it, *tovarich*? Well, maybe a little."

The driver said, "But wait until you hear what I'm going to play for you." He put a tape in the box, leaned to turn it on.

"Wait," said the gunman.

His face came so close Taz could smell the vodka on his breath. "It wasn't just the whore who had a message for you. So does the ambassador—a great man, by the way. The message is this—don't fuck with Sergei Goncharov. Make sure to tell your friends, when you can talk again. Now, put your arms up."

As soon as Taz raised his arms above his head, the ambassador's goon punched his gut. Taz doubled over and fell to the floor, gasping.

The driver knelt near Taz's head. "Somehow, *tovarich*, the ambassador heard that you love music. So I'm to play you something special."

He punched the *play* button. Taz heard the first strains of the overture to "Boris Godunov."

The gunman grabbed him by his collar and yanked him up. Taz stood unsteadily. Then he felt the blow to his kidney and crumpled again. The pain was searing. His legs moved convulsively. Just as the pain subsided to a throb, he imagined Irina's face. He looked at the driver. "*Tovarich*, what will happen to the girl? It's not her fault."

The men laughed. "Touching. She's important, at least for a while. After all, *tovarich*, it's one thing to have a commercial deal stolen by a spy. This everyone understands. But to be betrayed by a department store model? That would be a cause for shame and embarrassment."

Small moment of relief. Then they started in again. The driver would hold him up under the arms, and the gunman would give him a tattoo. At some point, the gunman hit him in the cheek with the butt of the pistol. The *basso profundo* singing Godunov seemed to fill the room. The last thing he saw was a square-toed boot.

CHAPTER TWENTY-THREE

The Light at the End of the Tunnel

FACEDOWN ON BROKEN CEMENT and dirt. Smell of dampness, mold and urine. A gurgling noise. Cold, but he couldn't curl up. Maybe not move at all. Head ached. A deep, throbbing ache that made it hard to think. His left eye closed and swollen. Right hand felt like someone had dug cleats into it. Ribs burned with each breath, no matter how slight.

Gray sunlight filtered in through the dust motes. Tried to close his eyes. Realized he was looking through slits. Pulled his left hand up underneath his shoulder, pressed it into the floor. Ribs screamed, but he managed to sit, somewhat unsteadily, with his right leg curled up underneath him and his left leg outstretched. Reached for his cell phone in his sock, but the fingers on his right hand refused to work. Looked, saw they were swollen to twice the normal size—broken.

Pushed his sock down with his left hand until the phone fell out, and then slowly, slowly dragged his body to a place where he could reach it. Positioned it on his thigh, then used his left hand to tap in Rick Reed's number. Rick answered on the second ring: "Buddy, it's been a while!"

"Rick, I'm in trouble."

"What? I can't hear you."

Taz mumbled. "In trouble." He tried to sound out the syllables.

"Where?"

"Not sure. Warehouse in the Meadowlands."

"What happened?"

"Couple of thugs."

"Somebody rough you up?"

"Oh, yeah."

"All right, just leave your phone on. I'll send somebody with a GPS pinger to get you."

Put the phone down, carefully. Fell over, and his right hand screamed again. Cried in pain and lost track of time.

There was the sound of a siren, at some point. Then it faded.

Finally heard a car pull up, and then footsteps.

"Jesus. They really took you to the cleaners." A woman's voice.

A hand under his head. "God, Rick sent me a picture, but that won't do any good. I guess it must be you."

He mumbled, "Taz."

"Listen, Taz. There's only me, and we have to get you to the car so we can go to the hospital. You're going to have to help me if you can."

Taz squinted up at her. She was wearing an olive green uniform. Park Service.

"Do my best."

"Are your legs hurt?"

"No."

"Back?"

"Kidneys."

"Where else?"

"Ribs. Hand. Head. Face."

"Well, that about covers it, I guess."

Taz tried to smile. "Lips."

She laughed despite herself. Then she put her arms under his shoulders and lifted, slowly.

In the car, Taz slumped against the passenger side door. The woman set his safety belt, put a plastic bottle of water up to his lips. That seemed to help.

On the two-lane road, Taz took another drink. "Name?"

"Deborah Dalton. People call me Dede."

"Dede—where?"

"Have to get you to a hospital. I'm from Long Island. Don't know this area."

"Salisbury."

"In Maryland? That's a long way. You might be bleeding internally."

"Know people there."

She reached over to get the radio phone. "Rick? Got him. Pretty bad. Needs a hospital. He wants to go to Salisbury."

He heard Rick's voice crackling through. Dede said, "I'm no doctor, but I'd say he's going to be in a while. He's pretty broken up."

"Okay, Taz. I'm taking you to Salisbury."

Didn't remember much else about the ride.

❋❋❋

Woke up in a hospital bed, propped up. Sun coming in the window. John White was standing at the foot of his bed.

"You're awake."

Reached for a cup of water that was on a tray table to his left. "What day is it?"

"Monday. You've been out seventy-two hours."

Taz tried to pull himself into a sitting position, but it hurt too much. His right hand was heavily bandaged.

"We had to get you a private room because you were snoring so loud."

"First time that's ever paid off."

"You know, you weren't supposed to go quite so operational on us."

"I didn't plan it, it just happened."

"I know. And you did get what we needed."

Taz looked steadily at him.

"The Greenland government has accepted an Australian bid to operate

Kvanefjeld. Friends of ours. Goncharov has gone back to Moscow to explain what went wrong."

"What about Irina?"

"She's with him. He's putting on a good face. His story is that the Americans got the Kvanefjeld intel by waging cyber war on the Greenland government, and that they sent a senior spy—a Cold War veteran—to discredit him personally."

"I failed, then."

"Not completely. Marnie has uncovered some bodies. When we leak them, he's going to lose a lot—maybe everything."

"Can we protect her?"

"We're working on that. We won't move until we know the situation. And I'll personally let you know."

"Thanks, John."

"No. Thank you. I'll get back on the seventh floor on this one." He smiled, turned on his heel, and closed the door softly as he went out.

Taz felt sleepy. Could be the pain medication. Dozed off and dreamed that Irina was on a boat, floating on the river towards Krasnoyarsk. She seemed happy.

Still light when he woke. He was just going to buzz the nurse for more water when the door opened. Rick Reed.

"Buddy, buddy. What did you get into?"

"More than I bargained for."

"Jeez."

"At least we think we know who was behind it. Embassy go-fers, ex-FSB. Want to see some pictures?"

"Definitely."

Rick showed him four, in sequence.

"First and third."

"You sure?"

Taz nodded.

"Is there anything you need right now?"

"Call the Rainy Day bookstore in Chincoteague and tell Richard or Laney where I am."

"Will do. And I'll see you soon with some scalps."

Taz buzzed the nursing station. In a minute, an older woman, resplendent in starched whites, appeared at his door.

"I see you're feeling better."

"Yes, but a little thirsty."

"Well, this time I'll get it for you," she said, smiling and handing him a paper cup of ice water, "but next time, you're going to get up and get it yourself."

Taz slept well that night, and the next morning he did, indeed, feel able to get out of bed, at least twice. When the doctor came by on his rounds, Taz asked him what they had found. The doctor was a young man, probably from the West Indies, with an easy smile.

"Well, you were pretty mashed up when they brought you in. Broken fingers, broken ribs, some internal bleeding. Looked like you had suffered a concussion from a blow to the back of the head. We put you into a coma and fixed everything we could reach. It took more than thirty stitches, all told."

"How about inside?"

"The internal bleeding usually stops on its own, once the body is stabilized. We wrapped your thorax and restrained you so you couldn't reinjure anything."

"Well, thanks for everything you did."

"You're going to need to stay put for a few more days, until we're sure on the internal side. We'll probably do a scan tomorrow or the next day. But you won't be able to work or seriously exert yourself for at least two weeks."

"Fine."

"Do you mind if I ask what happened?"

"A couple of professionals worked me over to send me a message."

"They knew what they were doing."

"How can you tell?"

"Usually the patients we get have been beaten up around the face and head. Your face was pretty puffed up, but the real damage was to your kidneys and liver. That's why you have to take it easy, even if you feel better."

"Well, if that's all, I guess I can take two weeks."

"And no drinking. Did I say that? No alcohol. Until we do a liver test at the end of the month."

Taz cursed under his breath.

❊❊❊

It was mid-afternoon when Laney arrived.

"Jesus, Taz. What happened?"

"Really? The nurses all say I'm much better looking than I was when they brought me in."

"And when was that?"

"Friday morning."

"You've been here five days? Five days while we've all been going crazy trying to figure out what fool stunt you've pulled this time?" She was beside herself.

"Laney, I was in a coma. I got word to you as soon as I could."

"A coma? Mary, Mother of Jesus. What happened?"

"It's a long story. Goes back to Iceland. The ambassador decided to let me know he didn't appreciate my relationship with Irina."

"Oh, Taz." She had tears in her eyes.

He suddenly remembered the envelope. "Laney, can you fish around in my pockets and see if there's a letter somewhere? It might be in my jacket."

She went to the closet, rummaged for a minute, and returned with it. It was wet and badly crumpled.

"What is it?"

"The goons told me it was from Irina."

"Do you want to be alone?"

"No, stay. Please. I need a friend, I'm grateful you're here."

She had to open the letter. His right hand was useless.

It was written in a shaky longhand. Taz tried to read it, but he couldn't resolve the blur. He asked Laney to read it to him.

Dearest Taz,

I am so, so sorry that I could not fly to meet you. I would . . . The rest
of the line was crossed out. There were water marks on the page.

*Taz, they threatened my family. I have to go with Sergei to
Moscow, to support his story. He wants the minister to believe that
he was targeted, not that he slipped. I must play along.*

*I'm so worried they're going to hurt you. I hope you elude them
somehow. You told me once you could be slippery. Please be slippery.
For me, they can't hurt me—it would damage their story. I will stay
as long as necessary, and then go back home to Krasnoyarsk.*

*The one rule I can't break is—I can't come to you. I can't go to
America. It breaks my heart, Taz. But I'm so glad I met you, really,
so glad in my heart. I will think of you always.*

Your "Rasslablennaya forever."

Taz turned his head to the wall.
"Sorry, Taz, I don't know what to say. I'm sorry, really sorry."
"At least she's safe."
"Yes. At least she's safe."
Pulled himself up, and they sat looking at each other.
"How long do you have to stay here?"
"Probably a couple more days. They have to do an MRI."
"We'll be waiting for you when you come home."
"Thanks, Laney. You're the best. You really are."
After she left, he lay looking out the window for a very long time.

CHAPTER TWENTY-FOUR

Home Is Where the Heart Mends

THE HOSPITAL DISCHARGED HIM two days later. Richard picked him up. Taz moved stiffly and was slow getting into the car.

"At least now when we play the old-timey songs we'll have a real geezer on the guitar."

Taz grimaced. "You're just a fountain of sympathy. Besides, it hurts to laugh."

"Hey, I'm here to get you."

"Yeah."

"You're going to have a hard time playing guitar with that boxing glove on your hand."

"Yeah, they tell me it will be a while."

"How long? People depend on you, dude."

"They said a month. But then I have to do exercises to restore flexibility. If I can. No guarantees."

"Shit. Don't tell me that, bud. You'll just have to pick like Django."

"If I could pick like Django, I'd be living in Paris, not Chincoteague."

Richard laughed.

"Laney and I want to have you over for dinner. You game?"

"I guess. I'm not moving too well. But I don't feel like cooking, either. I wouldn't mind going home first."

"I'll drop you off. Pick you up at seven?"

"Pretty sure I can still drive."

"Whatever you say. Call me when you figure out how much you use your right hand in a manual setup."

It was good to see the cottage again. The door was unlocked. Taz realized he'd left it wide open in his hurry to get to Newark. Everything appeared to be in place, at least as much as usual.

Got out of his clothes with some difficulty. Put a plastic bag over his right hand and took a shower. Shampooing one-handed was a new experience, took longer, but he managed. The hot water ran out just as he was finishing up. Wanted to jump out, but that was out of the question. Sat on the side of the tub, swung his legs over, and then leveraged himself into a standing position.

Struggled into some boxers and put on a flannel shirt. Discovered that he couldn't button his sleeves. Brushing his teeth with his left hand was also an intriguing experience. After a five-minute struggle, he found himself looking longingly at a half-filled whisky bottle.

Eventually got into his jacket, pulled out a bottle of wine, found his keys, and headed over to Richard and Laney's.

Their living room was, well, unique. A low-slung couch on one wall, a sound system worthy of the Grateful Dead on the other. The only other permanent piece of furniture was a giant leather baseball glove that doubled as an armchair. Richard was deeply buried in the baseball glove, listening to Elmore James.

"So you made it here. Good man." He smiled with the banality that only high-grade marijuana can supply.

"You've been getting high without me."

"Me? High? Don't you think I deserve it? You know, worrying about you is stressful."

"Trust me, Richard. Being me is stressful."

Dana came in from the kitchen.

"Hi Taz." Her voice was ultra-delicate, as if she thought a louder sound might break him.

"Dana." He mustered up the best smile he could. Gave her the Burgundy.

"Richard's already stoned. Why don't you come in the kitchen with me?"

Richard gave her a somewhat dazed look. "Whatever."

Taz pointed toward the kitchen, looked at Richard, mouthed the words *must obey.*

Laney was hovering over the stove. "Good to see you, stranger."

Taz tried his best to hug her from behind.

"Now don't think you're going to take advantage just cause Richard's stoned."

"I thought no such thing."

"What are you working on there?"

"*Coq au vin*, Chincoteague-style."

"Even better."

Dana had been leaning quietly against the wall.

"Taz, what are you doing?"

He wasn't sure how to respond. "Just trying to take one day at a time."

"What in the hell does that mean—it's not exactly a life plan, is it?"

"No. I guess I've never held much stock in life plans."

"And so the rest of us are supposed to hang on every accident, and read the obits to see if you're still with us?"

Laney said, "That's not fair, Dana."

"I don't see why not. He can go up north and chase every kind of will-o'-the-wisp and end up half dead in the hospital while we're down here wondering if he's still alive? Is that fair?"

Taz took a step in Dana's direction, reached for her hand. "I'm sorry Dana. I didn't mean to worry everybody, to worry you. Things happened so fast; I didn't have time to tell anyone."

She looked at him. There were tears in her eyes, and anger. But there was also hurt, and something like love. "You know what it's like to watch a shooting star?"

Taz waited.

"Your father teaches you to watch for them. They don't come around all that often. But they're worth waiting for. And so you sit out on the porch night after night and wait. Then, sure enough, there's a shooter. And you put all your hopes on it. You *wish upon a star.* Then the star is gone. Did you dream it? You don't know. All you know is you might not get it back. You know how that feels?"

"I do now. I'm so sorry I've put you through this."

She gave him a gentle push. He had gotten too close. Laney finally came and joined them, put her arms around both, and said, "There, there."

Dana sniffled, worked to compose herself. Laney brought her some tissues.

Dana shook her head. "I'm just so miserable. I'm a wreck."

"I don't know, you look pretty good from here."

"And look at you!" Now she was sniffling and laughing at the same time. "Your eye is black, your cheek is all puffed up, you can't even bend over—" Her voice trailed off.

Laney said, "Yeah, guess we'll have to ditch that Buff Men's Calendar we were going to put out."

All three now, laughing and crying.

They finally settled down. Laney said, "Let's get dinner on. Taz, the silverware is in the drawer behind you. You can do that one-handed."

A few minutes later, they sat. Dana cut Taz's chicken, which he saw was dark and juicy. Richard poured the Burgundy Taz had brought. When he had finished, he looked over at Taz.

"So I think you better tell us all about it."

Laney gave her husband a dirty look. "Couldn't we talk about something else? Sports? Politics? Religion?"

Dana was tentatively picking at her food. Taz looked at her, did his best to smile.

"No, it's all right. You have a right to know. So this goes back to my trip to Iceland. While I was there, I found out about a deal that the Russians were cooking up to get control of a deposit of valuable minerals in Greenland. A world-class deposit. Stuff that everybody wants to get their hands on. The head of the Russian effort was their ambassador to Iceland, a guy with ties to the Russian mob. Corrupt as they come. He was trying to bully the Greenland government to give him a special deal. When I got back, I let the State Department know what I had learned. Then our guys set up an alternative bid, and cut the Russians out. Blew his scheme out of the water."

"Jeez," Richard said. "You're involved in that kinda stuff?"

"Sometimes. Anyhow, the ambassador figured out that I had helped queer his deal. I don't know if he was told, or I was watched, or both. Anyway, on Thursday I got an urgent message to meet the daily flight from Iceland. A key informant was going to be on board. When I got there, I was picked up by two Russian thugs whose idea of anger management therapy was to use me as a punching bag for a few hours. That's about it."

He looked at Laney. Richard and Dana were staring at him, rapt. Richard whistled. "He's a spy! Our over-the-hill guitar picker is a spy! What the hell?"

"No, no. It's nothing like that. You know I do occasional consulting for State. They think it's useful that I know a lot of people in the north, mostly from the Stockholm Convention and the Arctic Council work. So occasionally they send me to a conference, and I keep my ears open. This was a shipping conference."

They took that in.

"And besides, what the hell do you mean, *over-the-hill*? Doc Watson's not over the hill, and he's eighty-two. I'm barely past forty. Okay, okay. Maybe forty-two. You keep talking like that, and I'll swallow your next joint."

This led to a discussion of the prime of life. Richard argued for the twenties. Dana said, "When you're seventeen, and then any time you're in love."

Laney said, "You guys are all wet. The prime of life is when you're forty-eight."

"What year were you born?" Taz asked.

She just gave a Cheshire grin and started clearing plates.

Later, they sat in the living room and drank part of a bottle of Four Roses. Laney and Richard were on the couch. Dana and Taz got the baseball glove. He nestled in the pocket and she sat on the thumb. Richard got up to fiddle with the turntable. He searched a stack and put on an old Mississippi John Hurt LP. Back on the couch, he cocked an eyebrow at Taz.

"So what's it like to get beat up by pros?"

"What do you think? It hurts like hell."

Dana put her hand on his lower back and started rubbing in circles, ever so softly.

"But then it starts to be an almost out-of-body experience. You're watching yourself, listening to your own groans. You think this must be happening to someone else. It gets easier."

"Did you think they were going to kill you?"

"At first. But then I remembered something the gunman said—that the ambassador wanted to send a message, and that I should tell my friends, *when I could talk again.* The message wasn't just for me. So I knew that unless they slipped, I was going be alive in the morning. I tried to think about who I should call."

"Do you think you're still in danger?" Laney asked.

"No, I figure he's made his point. And I have some colleagues who are likely to show up on his radar screen soon. When that happens, he'll have a lot more to deal with than just a busted business deal."

"So, what do you do now?" Dana asked.

"I need to keep a low profile for a while. I've got a few books I want to read for the next couple of weeks, and then I thought, after Christmas, if we get any warm stretches, I might do a little work on my marsh."

"Maybe you'll need some help with that, Mr. Lefty? You can't even put on a pair of rubber boots." Dana said from the thumb.

He looked up at her, saw how beautiful she was. "I thought you were going away."

"For Christmas, to my sister's. But we'll be back the first week of January, and I've got some extra vacation days that I have to use around then. Suzanne and Moyer could help, if it's on a weekend. They love mucking around."

"Well, I like the sound of that."

CHAPTER TWENTY-FIVE

Mucking Around

CHRISTMAS PASSED UNEVENTFULLY. LANEY, whose heritage went back to the English midlands, brought Taz a steak and kidney pie just before she and Richard left for Cancun. It was a better present than Taz had any right to ask for. She made her gravy with Guinness.

Television broadcast the usual slew of soccer matches on Boxing Day and before New Year's. He was reading *The Death of Virgil,* Hermann Broch's sublime novel of the last day in the life of the greatest Roman poet. January showed up almost before he noticed.

He and Dana had decided on a Saturday. She had said that Moyer and Suzanne would simply not hear of such an adventure going ahead without them. He couldn't imagine what she had told them about it.

In the end, Mother Nature was kind. It was only six days into the New Year, but Saturday morning was clear and unseasonably warm. By ten o'clock, it felt like indian summer in October. Taz had picked up a couple of narrow gardening shovels for the kids. He stacked them and his steel rake behind the bulkhead just off the dock.

Low tide. The water had receded thirty feet from the bulkhead. Boat was still floating at the end of the dock, but they'd have to push off before he could put the propeller down. Taz mulled that as Dana pulled up in her van. He walked up the dock as Moyer and Suzanne were spilling out. They looked at him warily. His face had healed well, but he still had a scar under his right eye, and a bandage, though smaller, on his right hand.

"Hi guys. Nice to see you on such a great morning."

Suzanne looked him over carefully. "I haven't met you." She was slight, like Moyer, but a little taller. Bright eyes behind tortoiseshell glasses.

"No, you haven't." He held out his left hand. "My name is Taz. I'm glad to make your acquaintance."

She took his hand. "I know your name. Mama talks about you a lot." Dana was getting gear out of the van. He didn't think she had heard.

"Well, I hope it's not all bad."

"No. She thinks she likes you. She just can't figure you out."

Dana came up with a cooler and a pile of coats. "Suzanne, don't be repeating kitchen talk."

"Well, that's what you say."

Moyer had been standing quietly to the side. Suddenly he walked over and stood closer to Taz. "I saw a merlin yesterday. Flying down the beach."

Taz put his hand on his shoulder. "How did you know it was a merlin?"

"Well, it had that falcon shape. And it was working, not gliding. Moving really fast, practically took my ear off."

"That's a merlin all right. Do you think it was after something?"

"No, I just think they like to fly fast. And when the wind don't help them, they help themselves."

Taz laughed. "Moyer, you're a natural. You know how to look. Do you keep notes?"

"You bet. I have a little notebook in my pack."

"Good. You have a good eye. It gets better when you make yourself remember and write everything down."

Dana had been watching, arms crossed. "Do I get a hello too?"

Taz took a step toward her, gave her a kiss on the cheek. "It's good to see you. You make the morning brighter."

She flushed and mussed her hair. "So, do we have a plan?"

"Well, first we need to go on a little voyage."

That word made Suzanne and Moyer step close. They didn't want to miss anything.

"Voyage?" Dana looked dubious.

"Well, we're going to go up the Wire Narrows to Cockle Creek and get a little special mud, and some more spartina."

"They'll need life vests."

"And I just happen to have some."

"Oh, Mama. It'll be fun!" Squealing.

"Okay, sailors. We need to break open the shed and get some supplies."

They pulled out the life vests and some buckets. Once they got the skiff loaded, Taz got in and lifted them in, one by one. Dana was last. She stepped on the rail; Taz put his left hand out to steady her. She grabbed it and stepped down, a little gingerly.

Moyer and Suzanne sat in back. Dana took a seat up front. Taz used the paddle to push off from the dock. Then he dropped the engine so the propeller could grab water. "Dana, hit that red button, will you?"

The engine started right up. But the boat was turning to the left, headed straight towards Tom Grady's dock. "You have to steer, too."

"Well, you didn't tell me that! I thought you were the captain on this ship."

"I am. So steer out to the channel."

She got behind the wheel and did fine. Before joining her, he checked in with the kids. "Are you guys comfortable?"

"We're fine," Suzanne said.

"This is great!" Moyer agreed.

"Okay. If you want to move around, you can. Just keep your weight low. And tell me if you're going to do anything crazy, like jumping out, okay?"

"Okay."

He moved up to the bow and stood next to Dana. "So we want to head south to get around the marsh. You need to keep us at least fifty yards away from the south end 'cause there's shoals in there. Once we're past that, we head up the Narrows towards the bridge."

"Are you planning to do any work at all, captain?"

"Not if I can help it. Why do you think I drafted such a top-notch crew?"

They rounded the south end of the mudflats and headed north into the Narrows. They were moving well, but still pushing water.

Taz looked at Dana. "Is it okay if I take the wheel for a bit?"

"Well, I was wondering."

He got behind the wheel, pushed the throttle forward. The engine whine picked up a notch, and the boat leapt forward. "Taz, be careful!"

Taz looked back at Moyer and Suzanne who were both all smiles.

"Watch what happens."

"We're gliding."

"Yeah. Hydroplaning. When you get your speed up a little, the boat pulls itself out of the water and glides. There's less friction. Saves gas, too."

Suzanne and Moyer were laughing and yelling in the back.

Taz gunned it under the new bridge and emerged in the channel heading north towards Greenbackville. Eventually, Taz slowed and pulled up to a mudbank with some sad looking spartina scattered around.

Dana looked at him inquiringly.

"The town's been using this as a dump for dredge spoils. The spartina here hasn't got long, anyway. So I figure if we're taking clumps from here, it's more like a rescue."

"Oh, I see."

"You think I shouldn't?"

"No, I just think it's cute that you need a reason."

"I always need a reason. I mean, life would be piracy and anarchy otherwise."

"That's a pretty dark view."

"I think Hobbes knew what he was talking about."

He looked at Suzanne and Moyer. "You got your boots on?"

They nodded.

"Okay. Moyer. Hop out on the flat there. Now grab this anchor. Got it? Drop it in the mud as far away as you can take it."

"How about me?"

"Suzanne, your job is to take this shovel and a bucket and look for some nice plugs of spartina. When you find one, dig deep enough to bring the roots up, okay? We'll be there to help you in a minute."

The kids were gone, each on a mission. He looked at Dana. "Good kids. Really good."

"I know, but thanks for saying it."

He stepped over the gunwale, stood on the flats, held out his hand for her. When she was next to him, he touched her chin with his left hand, gently lifted it up. He kissed her softly on the lips. She put her hands on his jacket and kissed back.

They heard Moyer's voice, "I got it dug in."

"Great, Moyer. Come on back and we'll all do some digging together."

So the morning went. They gathered the spartina and some extra mud. They shared some chocolate that Taz had secreted in the map case. Then they headed back.

When they got to the dock, the tide had risen enough that they could motor in. He cut the engine, glided past the berth towards the shell beach, and put the bow up.

"Dana, if you hop out, we can hand you all the goodies." When that was accomplished, they dug in the spartina. By that time, it was five-thirty and getting cold.

"How about some hot chocolate?" Taz suggested, and the children chorused, "Yes!"

"And pizza."

They shrieked louder.

CHAPTER TWENTY-SIX

Life Gets Complicated

AFTER DANA AND THE children had wolfed down the pizza and headed home, Taz winched the boat onto the floating dock and hosed it down. Then he wrestled the engine onto a wheeled cart and stowed it and most of the gear in the shed. It wasn't likely he'd want to be on the water again until March. When he got back to the house it was almost seven o'clock and his message light was blinking. Irvin's voice.

"Taz, I don't know if you're there, but John would like to have a chat. Can you come in tomorrow?"

Pulled open the refrigerator door, cracked a Modelo, and sat to think. No obvious reason he couldn't go in tomorrow, other than it was a Sunday. Even if it wasn't, he resented having to roust himself at the butt crack of dawn to spend three hours on the road just to get his next assignment.

But John White didn't like talking on the phone, even the encrypted one they used from the SCIF. And he was AS/INR—Assistant Secretary for Intelligence, Narcotics, and Research. He wasn't bad at his job, even if he and Taz hadn't always seen eye to eye.

Taz was still thinking it over when his phone rang. Dana's voice lit up the other end. "Taz, the kids can't stop talking about the adventure you took us on. I wanted to thank you again."

"I'm glad they liked it."

"More than liked. Moyer's busy drawing a map of our route."

Taz smiled. That's what he would have done at that age. He still had some of his old maps showing the bends in the Brazos near his childhood home.

"Taz, I thought maybe tomorrow I could take you out for that coffee we never quite got to?"

Damn, wasn't it always like this? Days of nothing, and then everything layered on top of everything else and the most important things pushed to the back burner.

"I'd love it, but I just got called to the district. One of those meetings—Damn!"

"It's okay, I just thought I'd ask." She said it too lightly. "You're not going to let them send you away again so soon, are you?"

"I don't know what they want."

"Sorry, I don't mean to pry."

"I'll probably stay over and drive back Tuesday. Will you be around then?"

"I have to be at the office."

"Could I come down and take you out to lunch? Would that work?"

She hesitated. "Yes, I'm pretty sure it would. That would be nice."

"Okay, 'til Tuesday, then."

❈❈❈

In the pre-dawn, he could hear the rain before he opened his eyes. Wished he had put new tires on the truck. Current ones weren't far off bald. Imagined various forms of skidding as he stuffed himself in the driver's seat and headed to the 7-Eleven in Atlantic to get coffee.

Got to E Street and Twenty-first around eight fifteen. Called Irvin's number. "Is he ready?"

Irvin came down to meet him at the security desk. Shook hands with Taz. "How are you?"

"Better, thanks. What's up? You don't look so happy."

"There's a glitch. That's what John wants to talk to you about."

They rode up to six in the elevator. Even on a Sunday, there was a skeleton crew on duty. Taz gave his cell phone to a new secretary. This one would definitely be in the SCIF.

Taz left his cell phone on Marjorie's desk. Irvin punched a series of numbers into the keypad, opened the SCIF door, and motioned Taz in. Turner Price and Roland Jensen were there already. White was sitting at one end of the table, Marnie at the other. A young woman Taz didn't recognize occupied the chair across from Marnie.

White stood to shake Taz's hand and motioned him to the chair. "Taz, this is Jessica Lansman." She was about twenty-five, with short blonde hair, and serious. She appraised Taz as she handed him her card that said *NSC*. National Security Council. An assistant to the president. Taz looked at Irvin, who was standing in the corner. White began.

"The Kvanefjeld operation is proceeding as planned. We have set up the alternate bid, which is substantially more favorable to the Greenland government than the Russian offer. Our people in Copenhagen say that it is likely to be accepted."

Taz sat back. *Then what's the glitch?* He already knew the offer had been accepted. He waited.

"Then what's the holdup?" Jessica Lansman said, annoyed.

"These things are complicated."

"Don't patronize me. You said you had assurances from the prime minister." She was referring to Robert Lynge, Greenland's prime minister.

"That's true, but he hasn't signed yet."

"Well, why don't we have Admiral Cray call him?" Robert Cray, the NSC director.

Ms. Lansman looked around the room, moving from face to face.

Finally, Taz piped, "I don't think that's the wisest course of action."

The NSC deputy gave him a fierce look. "And why not?"

"Because Lynge is a proud man. He'll think we're pressuring him, just like the Russians. We have a good deal in front of him, and he knows it.

The question is, what's holding him back?" He thought for a moment. "No. Sorry. *Who's* holding him back."

"Go on."

"He doesn't have that many people he trusts. It's not easy, being the prime minister of an almost country. He's really just a sealing captain. But he's respected by the people. Still, this isn't a role he's used to. He's still trying it on."

"Pop psychology. What does it lead to?"

White interjected. "We need to find out who Lynge is listening to, and why."

"And how do we do that?"

"Taz, how do you feel about a trip to Copenhagen?"

"When?"

"In two weeks."

"I hate Copenhagen. I hate it worse in February."

White agreed. "Don't I know it. Crazy bicyclists, mowing pedestrians down by the dozens. But we need you to go there. And by the time you get there, March will be just around the corner."

Taz looked at him, then at Irvin. "This better be good."

"There's a conference on Greenland's future—The Road to Independence. Lynge will be there. So will Goncharov."

Taz looked down for a moment, considering the job. Jessica Lansman was just about to speak, but before she could get a word out, Taz said, looking at White, "I'll go. That bastard tried to have me killed."

Deputy Lansman looked startled.

White replied, "We're going to work up some intelligence, and we're also going to put some plans in action. As they say, revenge is a dish best served cold."

Deputy Lansman looked at her watch and stood. "I don't have time to sign out. You'll take care of that, Irvin, won't you?"

CHAPTER TWENTY-SEVEN

All Things Come to Those Who Wait

AS TAZ DROVE BACK across the Chesapeake Bay Bridge, his mind swarmed with questions. *Suicide mission?* The last time he got in Goncharov's sights, he had almost died. He was just starting something on the island, something full of promise. *What the hell am I doing?*

His stomach growled. As usual, the bastards hadn't even offered lunch. He decided to stop at Hemingway's and think things over. First bar off the Bay Bridge.

Took the exit to Romancoke and turned immediately back toward the water, down a long lane past some upscale marinas to the bayshore. Hemingway's knew its shellfish. The clams and oysters were top quality, and the bar was a pleasant oasis, next to the large and less-inviting dining room. He sat at the bar. A young and extremely attractive, just-out-of-college bartender smiled. "What'll you have?"

"You know, I'm thirsty. So first of all, a glass of Sauvignon blanc. After that, a dozen oysters, please."

"Rockefeller?"

"No, just the way they came out of the bay, thanks. With some extra horseradish."

"Are you a regular here?"

"No, no. I'm . . . occasional. You know—on the way back and forth."

"I'm Lucy."

"I'm Taz."

"Welcome, Taz. I guess you can tell I'm new here."

"A breath of fresh air."

She smiled and turned to put in his order. She was tall with strong shoulders. He turned his gaze to the television above the bar. The Detroit Lions were ahead of the Los Angeles Rams. No one was watching.

When Lucy came back with his wine, he said, "Do you get NBC Sports?"

"I think so, I don't know."

"Can you change to it? I think Tottenham is playing Newcastle."

She looked nonplussed.

"Soccer."

"Oh, I love soccer. Hold on."

She went back behind the bar for a consultation, then returned, picked up the remote, and found the soccer channel.

The Spurs were driving towards the Newcastle goal. The fans at White Hart Lane were singing, chanting, and generally carrying on. He wished he were there, with all his soul.

Lucy brought out his oysters, plump and sweet to the eye.

"Where're these from?"

"I think we're getting them from down at the mouth of the Rappahannock just now."

"They look good."

He squeezed a lemon wedge over them and added a dash of cocktail sauce to each one, then horseradish. He lifted the shell and swallowed—sweet and tasty. Not at all like the Chincoteague Salts, though the same species. It was all about the water.

"Do you like them?"

"Very much. It's all about where they're from, isn't it? And where are you from?"

"Me? I'm from Missouri."

"How in the world did you get here?"

"I wanted to see the ocean."

"And you're only an hour away."

Newcastle was counterattacking. Tottenham had been banging on their goal, but one of the midfielders had turned over the ball, and the Magpies' new Moroccan striker was racing towards the Spurs' end. His shot just missed the far post.

"You need another glass of wine?"

"Need is not the operative verb, but the answer is yes."

She poured for him, watching him all the while.

"How did you end up being a soccer fan? All the guys I know are fixated on football."

"I played a little, back in the day."

"What position? I played too."

He took another look at her. She had the strong chest and body of a serious athlete. He might have picked her out for a swimmer. It wasn't just the shoulders. When she made her way back to the cash register, it was clear she had the kind of legs that could make a ball curve and sing.

Looking back his way, "What position did you play?"

"I was an attacking midfielder. My idol was Johan Cruyff."

"That's quite a model."

"I fell truly short of the mark. I actually saw him play towards the end of his career, when he and Neeskens were with the Washington Diplomats. It was a lesson on how to play the game. I watched the old films of him at Ajax and on the '74 Dutch World Cup team. How about you?"

"I was a striker. My idol was Mia Hamm."

"I saw her play a few times. She was spectacular. Where did you play?"

"For Washington University, in St. Louis."

"They're serious about their soccer out there."

"You bet they are. It was a wonderful time."

Another customer called her over. She winked at him and left to do her work.

The second half was just beginning. Tottenham had managed a one-goal lead. Newcastle came out swarming. Their young Moroccan was everywhere at once, playing both sides, bewildering the Spurs' defense. Just when things were going seriously south, Newcastle lost the ball in midfield. Gareth Bale picked off the pass and sprinted up the left side. The Newcastle defense had pressed forward, and neither of their center-backs could catch Bale. He danced around the goalie and put the final blow in with his weaker left foot.

"Lucy, you'd better watch this."

She came over to the inside of the bar and turned her eyes on the TV. The announcers were still gasping at Bale's audacity. Then they showed the replay. She put her hands to her cheeks in delight.

"He's like a big, good-looking leprechaun, isn't he? Look at those ears!"

Taz turned to Lucy. "Are you still playing?"

"You know, occasional pick-up games. There's no pro league on our side."

"You must miss it."

"Sure. Don't you?"

"Well, it's been a longer time for me, and my knees are shot anyway."

"Yeah, payback is a bitch."

"Well, we all have to pay for our sins."

"Or our successes." She sounded much older than she looked.

"I'd better take my check."

"It's going to get a lot duller when you leave."

"Well, I've still got a couple of hours ahead of me before I get home."

"Where's home?"

"Chincoteague, down south on the Atlantic side. You should check it out sometime."

Something occurred to him as he was signing the receipt. "You know, you really should check it out. The local high school is looking for a women's soccer coach."

Her eyes widened. "How could you possibly know? That's just the kind of job I've been looking for."

He gave her his card. "Call me in a couple of days. I'll figure out who you should talk to."

CHAPTER TWENTY-EIGHT

Reality Bites

TAZ GOT BACK TO the cottage late, washed up, and fell into bed. In the morning, he called Dana.

"Still game for lunch?"

"Absolutely."

"I'll be at your office about twelve-thirty."

After he had finished showering, he drove one-handed, but carefully, down Route 13 to Accomac. Her building was just down the street from the Accomack County courthouse, and there was little to distinguish it from the other brick buildings, except for a small plaque that said *Child and Family Services*. The lobby was small and unoccupied, without a directory. Taz chose left and headed down the hall. A young woman was sitting behind a desk in the first office.

"Excuse me, but do you know where I could find Dana Bonner?"

"Two doors down." She looked at him with curiosity.

Dana's door was open, but he knocked anyway. Her desk was facing the only window, and she turned around to see who it was. She smiled. "Taz."

"Do you have enough time to go down to Onancock?"

"I think so."

She put on a nice-looking blue wool coat and cinched the belt as they walked to his truck. He drove them to the old wharf-side supply store in Onancock, which had been turned into a pub-style restaurant. They sat inside by the fire. Dana ordered crab cakes, Taz a fried oyster po' boy.

"Wine?"

"I shouldn't—have to work. Just one?"

"I promise."

"You're a bad influence, you know."

"But I like to occasionally find ways to redeem myself."

"And?"

"I just found your new girls' soccer coach."

Astonishment filled her face. "Where, who? How did you know?"

"My agents are everywhere. Her name is Lucy. She's working as a bartender at Hemingway's."

Dana looked doubtful.

"She was an All American striker for Washington University in St. Louis. If there was a women's pro league, she'd be a poster on Suzanne's wall right now."

Dana sat back. "You're a recruiter. That's what you do."

"Sometimes."

"No, all the time. Am I a recruit too? And if so, for what?"

"Not at all."

Taz hadn't expected to encounter heavy weather so close to shore. He gazed outside, where a few boats were rocking at anchor. There was a fishing skiff and a modest-sized keelboat, which looked like it would be fun to sail. He looked back at her.

"You are one of the most attractive women I've ever met. But you're a challenge. I wonder if I could live up to you. I don't even know what that means, but I wonder. You trouble me. No woman has ever done that before."

She put down her napkin, put her chin on her hands, looked at him.

"Oh, Taz. You make it so complicated."

"I'm sorry, I really am."

The waitress came over. They ordered coffee.

"So, where do they want you to go now?"

"Copenhagen."

"I've always wanted to see Copenhagen."

"It's not bad. But I prefer Oslo."

"Go ahead, dash my dreams."

"What dream did you have that involved Copenhagen?"

"The Little Mermaid, of course. I was the Little Mermaid."

"Because you like the water?"

"No, because I would sacrifice everything for love."

Taz couldn't reply. He sipped his coffee, considered what he was up against. She sat across from him. She held her head high, her eyes on him, and when he returned her gaze, he was astonished at their intensity. He reached across the table and touched her cheek.

✻✻✻

Taz got in his truck and headed north towards home. His cell phone jangled in his pocket.

"Hello?"

"Is this Taz Blackwell?"

"Last I heard."

"My name is Brian Radford. I'm an attorney."

"Good for you."

"I'm doing some work for Broken Hill Proprietary, LLC."

Taz pulled over in front of the Coast Guard station. "So, Brian. What would cause you to call me?"

"I'd like to talk to you, that's all."

"Shouldn't you be talking to Virgil Waite and the folks in Tobytown?"

"Well, that isn't going so well."

"No, I guess not."

"It was mishandled. I've been brought in to see if we can put it back on track."

"And what makes you think I would be helpful?"

"Well, my people tell me you have the best interests of the folks in Tobytown at heart. And we think there's actually something to talk about."

"You realize I can't represent anybody there. They may have their own lawyer. And for what it's worth, I'm not a lawyer."

"We know all that. They don't have a lawyer. Still, they seem to have some trust in you. And you're a negotiator."

"Not on this kind of stuff."

"Taz, come on. You negotiated two treaties in two years at State. You reached the government's goals both times, and at least one of them came out spectacularly, with a win for all parties, which you designed. We've done our homework."

"It's so nice to be appreciated. I guess I should be willing to at least hear the pitch."

"Good. Can you meet me for breakfast next Thursday at the diner at Tom's Corner?"

"Sure, what time?"

"At seven, if that's not too early."

"No, that's fine."

He pulled out onto Main and headed south, wondering. Decided he'd better go see Virgil Waite.

❈❈❈

He got to Tobytown just after one o'clock in the afternoon. Good time to stop at Ida's. Rodney was behind the bar. Taz sat on the stool nearest the door.

Rodney came over, shook his hand. "Good to see you, Taz."

"Good to see you too, Rodney. How are things going?"

"Smoother, since you stepped in."

"I noticed the police cruisers are gone."

"Yeah, they pretty much disappeared. We heard somebody put the arm on the sheriff."

"Well, I wouldn't know about that."

"Of course not. What brings you to town?"

"Well, I wanted to talk to Virgil. But maybe you should join us."

Rodney gave him a look. "I don't know why you would want me there."

"Well, because you're the organizer. And when the talk gets serious, you want to talk to the organizer."

"I'll be there if you think it will help."

Taz reached for a menu.

Rodney stopped him. "Don't bother. Just have the chicken. Ida's in back."

"Sounds good. With a ginger ale and coleslaw, okay?"

By two-thirty, the crowd had cleared. Rodney took off his apron. "Virgil's probably down in his shed. He was going to work on his tractor today."

They went to Virgil's place. When they walked up to the shed, young Bennett came running out.

"Pa, Mr. Taz is here!" He hugged Taz's knee. Taz rubbed his head, said "Hi, Bennett. You've grown since I saw you last."

"Taz, I didn't know you were coming. We would have put on lunch."

"I know, Virgil, it was kind of a surprise to me, too. I would have warned you otherwise. I stopped off at Ida's, and Rodney was kind enough to help me find you."

"Well, you know Rodney, he keeps track of everybody."

"So, could we talk a bit?"

"Sure Taz, come on in the kitchen."

Virgil's kitchen was small, but well-appointed. There was an oak table just big enough for four.

"You want some coffee?"

"That would be great. Thanks."

Virgil busied himself at the stove. When the coffee was ready, he sat down.

Taz looked at Virgil, then at Rodney. "So, I got a call out of the blue. From a lawyer for the mining company. I think they want to make some kind of offer."

Virgil leaned back in his chair. "Why wouldn't they just come here and spell it out?"

"I'm not sure. I think they know things between you and them are at a pretty bad pass. They've brought in someone new to find a way to smooth things out. Whoever it is, they want to open up a line of communication."

Rodney interjected. "How do you know it's someone new?"

"The attorney who called me wasn't part of the company, he'd been brought in just for this. He said the new team pulled him in to 'see if he could get things back on track.'"

"Well, so what? I still don't see what there is to talk about," Virgil replied.

"Well, my experience is, it's never bad to have that opening conversation. Not to commit to anything, but just to check out what they want to put on the table."

"Rodney?"

"Well, like he says. Let's see what they want to put on the table. I sure don't see it right now."

"Okay, Taz, if you say so," Virgil conceded.

"So I'm going to have this first conversation. That's all. I will let you know everything they say. I'll make it clear that I'm only there to listen and report back. I won't commit to anything—not even to a direct meeting, which is probably what they want—until we've talked. Is that okay?"

Virgil looked at Rodney. Rodney nodded.

CHAPTER TWENTY-NINE

Too Good to Refuse

TAZ ARRIVED AT THE diner and waited to see if Radford came in a limousine, or if not, what he was driving. Whether he showed up alone or with a squad of suits. He sat at a booth by the window, facing the entrance.

While he sipped contentedly on his second cup of coffee, a dark blue sports car squealed to a stop in the gravel parking lot. Very sleek, with an open grille that made it look like a four-wheeled jet engine. At first Taz couldn't place it. Then the driver revved the engine once or twice. The whine immediately brought back the afternoon in Monte Carlo when Taz had watched his only live Grand Prix. Looked more closely—*a Maserati.* Had to have cost at least two hundred thousand.

The man stepping out was of average height, in his forties, good looking, wearing a dark green poplin jacket. Taz would have pegged him for a Beamer jockey, but his ride spoke to a greater need for speed, and an even deeper wallet.

He came through the door, coolly scanned the room, turned and walked deliberately over to Taz's table. "Mr. Blackwell?"

"Call me Taz. Are you Brian?"

"Indeed."

He was wearing blue jeans with creases. His Bass Weejun loafers were properly scuffed. But the shirt was the telltale sign. Cowboy style, with snaps and a starched collar. Taz recognized the pattern from Brooks Brothers.

"Have a seat. Gina'll be over in a second to get your coffee."

"I'm afraid I don't drink—" Gina was already standing there, looking him over with a somewhat jaundiced early morning gaze.

"Do you have tea? I'd like some Earl Grey."

"Twinings do?"

"That'll be fine, thanks."

Gina looked at Taz. "You finally eating?"

"We both will, I expect."

She returned with a couple of menus and then went behind the counter to get the hot water.

"So, Brian, how did BHP rope you into this one?"

"Oh, I do this kind of thing for them on occasion."

"Where else?"

"The last one was in Malaysia. A gold mine in Sarawak."

"How did that go?"

Brian gestured to the Maserati. "Well enough. The biggest problem was the workforce. A remote area. The villagers wanted employment, but nobody had the skills. If we had brought in the whole workforce, it would have tripled the size of the village and destroyed the culture. We ended up putting the workers on a hospital ship offshore and paying the villagers to stay away from the mine."

"The price of progress."

"Oh, it was worth it. The mine is netting three hundred and fifty million a year, and the villagers have almost forgotten it's there."

"A win-win, then."

"I understand your cynicism, but I'll argue those villagers have medical care now, and indoor plumbing."

"Tobytown already has indoor plumbing."

"And medical care. But they're still dying a decade early compared to the rest of the Eastern Shore."

"News to me."

"I can show you the EPA field report, if you'd like."

"That's okay. I'll take your word for it. It's just that I've spent quite a bit of time down there, and nobody's ever mentioned radon, cancer clusters, anything like that."

Gina reappeared, notepad in hand.

Taz ordered. "I'll have the corned beef hash with two eggs over medium."

She looked at Brian. "The seasonal berries and yogurt, please." Gina turned to Taz and rolled her eyes.

Taz waited.

"Look, Taz. Suppose I was to tell you that we could take all the uranium out, in twenty years, using a one hundred and twenty-acre platform? And that when we were finished, Tobytown's radon problem would be history?"

"Sounds like an engineer's fantasy."

"It's real. I can prove it to you."

"Let's say you can. What about the folks who are there now?"

"We'll seal their floors and walls and vent their houses. All of them. No cost to them. We'll reduce the indoor radiation by ninety percent."

"How about their farms?"

"They can keep planting and harvesting to their heart's content."

"Except?"

Brian looked at him steadily. "Except for the one hundred and twenty acres. We need exclusive access there."

"How are you going to get the ore out?"

"By barge, to the Port of Baltimore."

"So you need access to the bayshore. Virgil's place. I don't think he's going to sell."

Gina reappeared, a plate in one hand and a bowl in the other. Before he could even ask, she whipped a bottle of Tabasco out of her pocket.

"This is what you're looking for, I expect."

"You know me too well."

"Or not well enough." She sighed and turned on her heels.

"Seems you know your way around," Brian remarked.

"Oh, I've been coming here for a long time. It's just a game we play."

"We'll make Virgil a good offer. A really good offer."

"I don't think money is what motivates him."

"What then?"

"He wants to know that Tobytown will endure, that it will be better for his people, and that he can help it thrive."

"Thank you, Taz. That insight might really help."

"What exactly is it that you want me to help you with?"

"Just tell them what we're prepared to do. They've got a leukemia cluster there. We can make sure it doesn't continue. I'd like to meet with them to explain it in person."

"How do I check out whether your engineering solution is real?"

"Talk with EPA, or even with your friends at USGS. They'll tell you."

Brian pulled a case out of his inside jacket pocket and offered Taz two cards—his, and an EPA business card with the name of someone in the Air division.

Taz busied himself buttering toast and administering salt, pepper, and Tabasco. Radford picked at his yogurt. He gave Taz an appraising look.

"So, what leads a successful diplomat—a star, they tell me—to give it all up and move to Podunk-by-the-sea?"

Taz wasn't sure he liked the question. "I got tired of negotiating good deals that the Senate was too stupid to ratify."

Radford looked sympathetic. "Anyone would get tired of that, I imagine. But wasn't there something about a divorce, too? I'm sure I read something about it."

He's not really prying, Taz decided. He wanted Taz to know that he'd taken time to ferret out his weaknesses.

"I felt that if I was going to change my life, I might as well be thorough."

"You like taking risks, don't you?"

"I guess. Probably the way you like making money."

Radford froze his smile. "What I really like is winning. Making money is just an incidental benefit."

Sure, Taz thought.

"So, Taz, tell me about the Eastern Shore. It's not a place where I've spent much time."

"Where do you spend your time?"

"In the States, I work out of Miami. When I'm in Asia, I have a place in Singapore."

"Well, that explains why you don't spend much time on the Eastern Shore."

"But now it looks like I might be here for a while, off and on. You know your way around. Where should I go?"

"Well, that would depend on what kind of experience you're looking for."

"Wine, women, and song, of course." A quick pause. "Just kidding. No, I'd like to see the places that make the Eastern Shore such a legend to my friends in Washington."

Taz doubted seriously that Brian Radford ever kidded. He withheld his response to the second part of the question.

"The DC set likes Easton, Oxford, and most of all St. Michaels, on the bay side. Lets them one-up the old money in Annapolis."

"But there's a beach scene on the ocean side as well, isn't there? With nightlife?"

"The nightlife is a little spotty unless you go to Ocean City, and then it's just sleazy. The smart set goes to Bethany and Rehoboth."

"And in-between?"

"Farm country. Canola, corn. Chickens. White towns and black villages."

"Oh, well. But you chose Chincoteague. I don't guess it was for the nightlife."

"Or I could say with Bogart that I was just misinformed."

Taz agreed to see about putting together a meeting to see if the folks at Tobytown were willing to reopen the discussion.

Radford insisted on taking the check. As he roared off in his lavish toy, it occurred to Taz that the breakfast was probably the only free thing he'd ever get from BHP.

CHAPTER THIRTY

Guidance from the Elders

TAZ TURNED THE CONVERSATION over in his mind as he drove back towards the causeway. Wasn't sure what to make of Radford. Slick, for sure. The aura of self-confidence that comes with a long winning streak. But Taz sensed insecurity behind the arrogance. How else to explain the show of force, dropping the tidbits about Taz's divorce, the "wine, women, and song" nonsense.

Still, he decided it would be better to talk to Rodney and Virgil before he left for Europe. There was a chance that Radford was holding a real offer. And he wanted to find out more about the health issues Radford had mentioned. He hadn't heard of a leukemia problem in Tobytown, but he hadn't been looking for health issues, either.

He called Rodney to see about a time. After a few seconds and a side conversation with someone at the bar, Rodney asked if he could come down in two days. Something about a village meeting that had already been planned. Taz said yes. The two days would give him time to check out BHP's miracle technology and to look into the Sarawak mine.

His next call was to Kirby Johnson. Kirby was a geologist who had spent twenty years researching bedrock structures for the Geological Survey, USGS. There wasn't much about minerals he didn't know.

"Kirby, if someone told me they could extract all the economically valuable uranium in a lens of some kind under the Eastern Shore of Virginia from a hundred-acre platform, what would you say?"

"Well, technology has gotten better. But this is a geological question. How deep is the deposit?"

"Shit, Kirby, I don't know."

"Well, that's important. Most uranium deposits are close enough to the surface that you get them by surface mining. In that case, the mine plan has to cover the extent of the deposit."

"So, just for argument's sake, let's say the deposit is deep enough that it would require an underground approach. Is that possible?"

"Well it's possible, but it's not real likely." He waited a second, then realized that he needed to talk down to his audience. "I mean, you might find deep uranium in a geology with some rock in it, like those old volcanic necks that they found in northern Canada. But the Eastern Shore is basically a pile of debris from the Appalachians. I don't see how there would be a deep deposit in that geology. I suppose it's possible that an archaic Appalachian river might have drained a uranium-rich headwaters area. But then the uranium would be at the mouth of the ancient river, and close to the surface."

"Thanks, Kirby. It's always an education to . . . "

"Wait . . . wait. There is one other possibility."

"Oh?"

"It's a long shot—it has to do with a meteor."

"A meteor?"

"Don't feel bad if it doesn't ring a bell. It was a little before your time. Thirty-four million years before your time, to be exact."

"I'm on the edge of my seat."

"Whether you know it or not, you're sitting on top of the Chesapeake Impact Crater—one of the largest meteor-impact craters on the continent. It's fifty miles in diameter and three-quarters of a mile deep."

"Must have made quite a bang."

He could hear Kirby chuckling. "The loudest since the Big Bang, I'm sure. My marine geologist friends say the tsunami reached Europe and Africa."

"So . . . what does one of these meteors do to the rock where the meteor hits?"

"Explodes everything—the sediment, the bedrock, and itself. A lot vaporizes. What's left under you is a two-mile-thick layer of what we call *breccia*."

"Breccia. I've heard the word but honestly that's about it. I'm guessing there might be uranium in the mix?"

"Yup, but not a lot—I mean not in commercial quantities. Your breccia is a mix of fragments composed of everything that was there before the collision, including the meteorite itself, all melded into a conglomerate rock. The Aguas Zarcas meteor left several pieces of carbonaceous chondrite as big as cinderblocks. Unfortunately, most of them were scooped up by local villagers before my colleagues could test them."

"I get the breccia part. But the rest—the carbonaceous stuff—that's above my pay grade."

"The 'carbonaceous stuff' contains the succession of molecular codes that enabled the emergence of life."

Taz grabbed an old grocery receipt and a well-chewed pencil and began taking notes. "Kirby, are you pulling my leg? Are we really talking about rocks that hold the spark that . . . Jesus."

"Bingo. It could be that some of the most valuable chunks of rock on the planet are mixed in there along with everything else."

"Okay . . . so this whole business may not be about uranium at all." More a muse than a declaration. "Thanks, Kirby."

"You're not so bad at this, really. Maybe you should have been a geologist."

"I couldn't. You're the only geologist I know with a funnybone. And that's the most comic thing you've ever said."

Taz refilled his coffee. Took a moment to digest what Kirby had told him. Then he looked up the area code for Kitty Hawk, North Carolina.

Bob Pelham had retired down there, after spending thirty years as a senior scientist in EPA's Air office in Research Triangle Park. Bob had been one of Taz's senior advisors in negotiating the Stockholm Convention to eliminate persistent organic pollutants. His wit was legendary. He kept a land-line, mostly to amuse his friends. A Gilbert and Sullivan fanatic.

"Robert, how's tricks?"

"The Outer Banks have been berry, berry good to me. You should'a been here."

"I bet. I have enough trouble with the inner banks. How'd you fare in the storm?"

"Well, it cut up Pea Island pretty bad—I guess you heard. But for some reason it didn't do Nags Head much damage. The sand washed away under about a dozen houses at the south end, but that's about it."

"Glad to hear it. Up here, it was just a deluge. I'm told we took seven inches. The drains are still flooded."

"Yeah, same where I used to live, in Carroll County. They got hammered."

"So I heard."

"So, what's up, chief?"

"Well, I could use a little advice. Have you ever heard of radon being a problem on the Delmarva?"

"I don't think so."

"The regional office apparently found a lot of radon in houses in the Tobytown area, just south of Onancock. It was in the press up here about a month ago."

"Okay."

"But something about it feels a little hinky."

"And you're involved how?"

"A big mining company has been trying to buy up the mineral estate in the same area. I've been looking into it."

"Can you get me the press notice?"

"I think so."

"Great. I'll see what I can find out."

❊❊❊

Taz spent the rest of the two days rigging his kayak, sanding his windowsills, then treating them with old-fashioned varnish. Taz wasn't a big fan of varathane. All gloss and no depth.

About four o'clock on Friday, he put his truck in gear and was in Tobytown by five. The staff at Ida's was getting ready for dinner. He sat at the bar. There was a new bartender studiously ignoring Taz, polishing glasses and chatting with a young woman whose role was unclear. Taz decided not to press the point; he pulled out his cell phone and scrolled through his email. Just then Rodney came out from the kitchen. He gave a quick look around, ducked behind the bar, picked a highball glass off the shelf, half-filled it with ice and Maker's Mark, and slid it down to Taz. The young bartender, looking on, realized maybe he had missed something.

"Taz, good to see you."

"You too, Rodney. How's tricks?"

"Still quiet, mostly."

"I guess that's good."

"Yeah. We had enough excitement last fall. But something tells me it's not over. What do you think?"

"It's not over. They want to try a new approach, though. It's up to you whether what they're offering makes sense."

"What's the new line?"

"The new line is that they think they can extract the ore without taking as much land as they thought. They say they only need Virgil's place for the mining and barge loading. They can get it all out in twenty years. Meanwhile, they'll deal with the radon problem and put a lot of money into the community. That's the gist."

"The radon problem?"

"Apparently Tobytown—a lot of the houses, anyway—has high levels of indoor radiation. Which would explain the leukemia rates."

"Taz, this community hasn't had a leukemia case in my lifetime. What are you talking about?"

"It was in the press a month ago. You didn't see it?"

"We saw it, and we were scratching our heads. I don't know what community they were talking about, but it couldn't have been this one."

Now Taz was scratching his head. *If there's no radon problem, why's EPA saying there is? If there's no leukemia cluster either, somebody's really put one over on Eliza.*

"Okay, Taz. Finish that, and then let's go meet the elders. By the way, the drink is on the house, which means on Elvin." Pointing his thumb towards the younger bartender.

The elders. It occurred to Taz that he could have studied more about his clients' leadership framework.

He finished his drink, thinking hard about what he wanted to say. Rodney motioned, and they climbed into the cab of his pickup. They pulled out through the gravel of Ida's back parking lot and onto a road to the Bay. Just before they would have rounded the slight curve to Virgil's place, Rodney turned left on a dirt road. It went up the shoulder of a small hill. Rodney stopped short of the high point. "We'll walk from here."

They got out and walked up a dirt path through some scrubby pin oaks. Taz found himself in a rough clearing marked by low, uneven stone walls. Some older black women with headscarves were preparing a fire. Rodney motioned him towards a fallen log. "Wait here."

Taz looked around. Where there was grass, it had been tamped down by regular use. The rest was bare, and the clay looked as polished as an old dance floor. The fire women gave him no notice. They worked steadily, bringing wood and stacking it in separate piles by size—a high stack of kindling, and a pile of branches. Just behind the branches, two women were bringing larger limbs and adding them to a tangle of driftwood and logs. Soon, they busied themselves building the fire. They built it log cabin style. A younger woman brought kindling and duff to put in the center. Taz watched, fascinated.

Taz sensed that they weren't alone. Other women started to arrive, from all sides. Some carried wood, others half-gallon jugs that they set down near where the fire-makers were working. Then they moved to the side, and sat on rocks or on their heels, eyes cast down.

Taz waited. After a few minutes, men arrived and entered the fire circle. He saw a few faces he remembered from the demonstration. Rodney and Virgil showed up with young Bennett alongside. Bennett saw him and ran over.

"Mr. Taz, Mr. Taz!" A big smile as he held out his hand. Taz shook his hand—he already had some callouses but the palm still had that tenderness that children are blessed with.

"Bennett, how are you?"

"My dad and I have been working together." He was bouncing on his feet. Virgil had come over to shake Taz's hand. "Taz. Good to see you. Welcome to our little gathering."

One by one, the men came over to say hello. "Taz. I'm Charley Wilson. Good to meet you." He met Boo Blackwell, Hubert Shadwell . . . seven all counted. Then they all sat on rocks, stumps, or on the ground. There was some desultory conversation, and hand-rolled cigarettes. The fire crackled; Taz noticed that three good-size clean-cut stumps close to the flames remained unoccupied.

Rodney reached for one of the bottles of clear liquid, pulled out the cork with his teeth, and took a swig. Passed it to Hubert, who took a pull and passed it. Taz put it to his lips, heard a gravel voice say, "Watch this," and took a mouthful of some of the fiercest firewater that had ever passed his lips. He wiped his mouth with the back of his hand and smiled at Hubert. Mouthed the word *thanks,* but no sound was forthcoming. He passed the bottle to Charley, who clapped him on the back. "Good man."

Taz looked at the ground to hide the fact that his mouth was on fire. Heard a twig snap and looked up to see three figures approaching the circle. First, an old man with dark pants and suspenders and a starched white shirt, leaning on a cane. Behind him, two even older women, who could have been sisters. They both had long calico skirts, yellow blouses, and bright woven caftans. One had a feathered hat that wouldn't have been out of place at an Easter parade. The other, who was smoking a long-stemmed corncob pipe, wore a traditional indigo headdress. Taz could hear murmurs. The man was apparently called *Uncle.* He motioned for all to sit. The women were Auntie Em and Auntie Kate. There was silence as they settled on their stumps.

Auntie Em spoke first. Her eyes were rheumy, and her voice quavered. "Children, ain't it a beautiful evening." A murmur of assent. "And I understand we're welcoming a friend to our midst." She turned her face in Taz's general direction. "Welcome."

"Thank you, ma'am."

Auntie Kate broke in. She gave Taz a piercing look. "What did Rodney say your name was?"

"Taz Blackwell, ma'am."

"Do you smoke tobacco, Mr. Blackwell?"

"On occasion."

"Good. She produced a handmade cheroot from somewhere in her caftan and handed it to Hubert, who handed it on to Taz.

The cheroot smelled good, the way dry-cured whole leaf tobacco does. Taz bit off the end and fished in his pocket for a match. Unsuccessfully.

Auntie Kate took a long draw from her corn cob pipe. Hubert produced a twig and dipped the thin end into the fire. After a few seconds, he pulled it out and blew on it, and it burst into flame. He turned towards Taz and held the flame to the end of the cheroot.

Taz drew his breath and pulled in the first smoke. It was slightly spicy. He savored it for a few seconds, then let it escape into the dimming air. Smiled. "Much appreciated, ma'am."

"We are glad you could join us, Mr. Blackwell. We are told you are a friend."

"I'm honored to be here."

"But what was it that caused you to want to help us, Mr. Blackwell?"

"I don't like to see political power misused."

"Weren't you in politics yourself?"

"Yes, I was."

"Seems that people with power find it hard not to misuse it occasionally."

"Some find it harder than others, I guess."

"Yes, perhaps you're right. Those who can refrain are the wise ones, don't you think?"

"Well, wise—I don't know. Maybe just well-grounded."

"Ah, Mr. Blackwell. You are indeed, as Rodney said, different than most of those we encounter."

Taz had sense enough to keep quiet.

There was a long silence. Taz smoked his cheroot and marveled at the scene around him. The fire was going strong now, and it was fully dark. Faces were lit up by sparks or flames or not at all. The three elders sat upright, absorbed in their thoughts. Rodney and Virgil, sitting off to the right side, whispered together.

Finally, Auntie Kate spoke again. "Mr. Blackwell, you have spoken to the men of the mining company, am I correct?"

"I've spoken to someone who represents himself as an agent for the mining company."

"You parse things very carefully, I see."

"I find that in certain situations, it's best to be precise."

"How right you are, Mr. Blackwell. How right you are."

"Rodney." Auntie Kate's piercing glare turned to him. "I believe that you have found our true friend."

She turned back to Taz. "Mr. Blackwell. Our friend. We are going to tell you something that we have shared with no one outside our circle. Will you promise us to hold it as if it were your own?"

"Yes, ma'am. I promise."

"There is a particular reason that your mining company is so interested in Virgil's property, Mr. Blackwell. Oh, I know they say they need access to the water, but they could get that access in Cashville or Crisfield. What they really want is Virgil's deed."

"I'm sorry, but I don't understand."

"Mr. Blackwell, Virgil is the heir to a colonial deed—the first grant ever given to the land around Tobytown. It was done by livery of seisin, and signed by Lord Baltimore himself. And confirmed by the son of Kiptopeke, the grandson of Debedeavon, the Paramount Chief of the Accomacs."

"But how—"

"We were free before the war, Mr. Blackwell. Before Lincoln's Emancipation. In truth, before the Revolution. Our freedom is guaranteed by a patent signed by King George—and not in his senility."

Taz absorbed this.

"Our deed—Virgil's deed, by direct inheritance—is in *fee tail*. As long as his line prospers, that deed is ours. And that deed controls all things beneath the ground throughout the Bay side of Accomack County."

"As long as Virgil and young Bennett are alive, you mean? My God." Taz couldn't hide his astonishment.

"Yes, Mr. Blackwell. That's what the Chinese are after."

Taz was reeling. This ninety-five-year-old woman in an eighteenth-century headdress had just given him the complete analysis of the play that Radford and BHP were making. They wanted an unfettered chance to sample the breccia underneath the Eastern Shore. If they found carbonaceous chondrites, they'd be millionaires. If they then sold the drilling rights, billions of dollars were at stake. He was truly humbled.

"Thank you, Auntie Kate, for clarifying my understanding of the situation."

"We look to you, Mr. Blackwell, as to how we should address this challenge."

"To me?"

"Yes, Mr. Blackwell. Are you afraid?"

"Auntie Kate, it is a large responsibility."

"I'm aware of that, Mr. Blackwell. Do you feel unequal?"

"No, Auntie Kate. I can do this."

"Yes, I thought you would say so. Nevertheless, we would hope that by tomorrow midday you would be able to present a plan of action."

"Yes, ma'am. I will do my best."

"See that you do, Mr. Blackwell. And thank you very much."

CHAPTER THIRTY-ONE

Push Comes to Shove

TAZ WAS WIDE AWAKE by five in the morning. Spent most of the night mulling the whole thing over. By six, he had composed a brief memo to Rodney outlining his thoughts. Not that complicated, really. Brian and his employer wanted a deed that they thought was in Virgil's possession. They were happy to negotiate a deal in which Virgil transferred the deed voluntarily—less messy that way. But they wanted that deed, one way or the other. All the talks were a sideshow.

The deed was worth enough that they would kill to get it. Of that, Taz was sure. Game plan: keep the possibility of a negotiation on the table until he and Rodney could drop a bomb big enough to chase BHP and Chinalco out of the county.

And what bomb would that be, exactly? Taz did not have an answer to that, but he was determined to find one.

***

At six-thirty Irvin called to give him the logistical details for Iceland. By seven, Taz had showered and shaved, a zen process that allowed him to calm and center.

He packed, preoccupied. Needs: a suit and three or four shirts and ties. Waxed canvas overcoat.

After he had gone through his trip list for the nth time, he called Rodney. Gave him the outline of his plan. Rodney thought it just might work.

It's a long way from Chincoteague to a diplomatic conference in Copenhagen. Space like that is measured in ambience—not miles. In one place, khakis and a collared shirt were dress clothes. In the other, you couldn't appear at breakfast without a suit. On the island, merit was measured by what you could catch, what you could play, how well you could sing, whether you could make your friends laugh, and for how long. In the other world, merit synced with power and seniority. Wit and logic might help. But in the end, influence at the argument table told the tale.

Taz booked a room at a waterfront hotel in the old brick customs house off Nyhavn, an old fishing inlet that extended four blocks off the harbor towards Konigstrasse. Pronounced *Nee-hahven.* Surrounded by waterfront restaurants, some catering to the tourist trade, some quite good. The best was Den Raven. They served fresh Baltic fish and venison with wild mushrooms.

Taz had stayed at the hotel before. Comfortable, and a good breakfast spread. And he would need all the comfort and security he could get, this time around. Irvin had told him that the embassy had been instructed to be helpful. He'd see.

Threw his bags in the back of the truck. No need to water, rain was in the forecast and anyway, the garden plants were mostly dormant. Looked around the cottage, straightened a picture or two. Gathered old papers for recycling at the dump. Put the recycling box in the back of the truck, threw his briefcase onto the passenger seat.

On the front stoop, just about to lock up, when Dana's van turned the corner. She opened the door and ran to him. Reached for his hands, then freed her right hand to push the hair out of her eyes. A north wind gusted. Put her hand back in his. He looked at her, searching. She was tearing up.

"You come back here in one piece, Taz Blackwell. I don't want to have to nurse you back to health again, please."

He smiled. "I'll do my best."

"And I don't want to be reading about you, either."

She wore an old flannel shirt. The top two buttons undone, and the curve of her breasts apparent with each breath. She put her knuckles to her lips and looked quickly out at the water. A sea tug was moving up the channel to an anchorage near the new bridge. He touched her cheek with his hand, turned her head gently back towards him.

He kissed her, lightly. "Dana, I'm coming back."

"Are you sure?"

"Yes, I'm sure. I like you—very much—and I'd like to get to know you better. I know I've done some crazy things in my life, but I'm not stupid. I'll come back."

She nuzzled her cheek against his chest, put her arms around his waist, and just held on for a while. Then she pulled up, smiled, turned and got in her van.

Checked the cottage one last time, got in his truck and headed for the bridge. At least a four-hour drive to Dulles.

❄❄❄

Parked in the daily lot. State could afford it, and he hated waiting for the buses from the long-term lots. When he got to the ticketing desk, he called the number that Irvin had given him. Minutes later, a young man in a suit approached.

"Mr. Blackwell?"

"Yes."

"I'm Cedric. This is from Irvin Friar." Cedric handed him a large manila envelope.

"Thank you, Cedric."

"Good luck, sir."

White had gotten him a diplomatic passport. Went through the crew line at security. Passed by the Starbucks without stopping, determined to get a decent few hours of sleep on the plane. They were just starting to board business class when he got to the gate.

He went through the rest of the envelope before the stewards came out with dinner.

His first stop was to be at the Embassy, where he would receive a briefing about security arrangements. The logistics after that were pretty straightforward. Hotel, the conference center, alternate routes back and forth. Metro and bus information. An envelope with a thousand euros.

A separate large envelope, light blue, with a *Confidential* stamp. The first thing he pulled out was a photograph, on glossy paper, of a reasonably good-looking man, about his age, with a solid jaw and a dark stubble. His hair was cropped short, and his cheeks had the florid look of someone who had enjoyed more than his share of vodka. His eyes seemed to look through the photographer, with a dark and somewhat dissipated gaze. Goncharov.

Various bits and pieces followed. A concise biography, probably written by Marnie. Not exactly a self-made man—his father had been in the Brezhnev Politburo. A list of his past positions. A diagram of his reporting chain, which surprised Taz. He was a full two levels down from Nilitin, the Deputy Foreign Minister.

Then some material about the conference itself, which hardly merited a "confidential" label. The agenda was pretty standard stuff, with ministers and ambassadors giving opening remarks, Lynge giving a keynote, and then a series of expert panels in plenary. Attached to the agenda was an interim list of participants. He flipped to the national delegations. The US del was being led by Stewart Robson, a senior lawyer from the European desk. He noticed with pleasure that Gavin Hart was listed as a counselor to the British delegation. Then he turned to Russia. The seventh and final name on the Russian list—Irina Tsolkin. He leaned back in his seat and rubbed his eyes. Called the steward, asked for a double scotch. Sleep plans up in smoke.

CHAPTER THIRTY-TWO

Reinforcements

TAZ DOZED OFF FOR an hour or so. The plane landed in the gray Copenhagen dawn. By the time he gathered his papers into his briefcase, the Danish passengers already had their coats on. His diplomatic passport ensured a quick turn through passport control. There was no bag search at customs. He took the first cab to the US Embassy. It was a long, low, not very architecturally interesting structure just west of the Kastellet on the Dag Hammarskjold Allee, an address that Taz found somewhat ironic.

He went through security and ended up in the lobby, speaking to a severe-looking woman with a tight hair bun and horn rim glasses. Explained that he was scheduled to meet with the ambassador.

"Unfortunately, Mr. Tanner is on leave." She was a Danish national.

"On leave? But I was specifically told to look him up."

"As I say, he's on leave."

"In that case, I'd like to speak to the DCM." The Deputy Chief of Mission was second in command, and usually the operational director of the embassy.

"That won't be possible."

"Why isn't that possible?" Taz was tired, irritated.

Several embassy employees had gathered on the other side of the lobby. They were looking uncertainly in Taz's direction.

"It's just not possible. I'm sure you understand." Uttered with extreme condescension.

Taz decided to make a point.

"No, I don't understand. Who the hell are you to tell me what's possible?" He slammed his palm down on the counter for emphasis.

Startled, she reached towards the left side of the desk.

Under his breath he said, "Before you hit that buzzer, let me tell you that I'm here on the direct request of John White at INR. If you screw this up, you'll be back milking cows in Arnhagen by the end of the week. Now get me in to see the DCM." Her eyes widened, then squinted at him.

One of the employees, a slight man of about forty, detached himself from the group and came towards them. "Can I help you?"

"Yes, you can tell the DCM. I want to see him. Directly."

"And you are?"

"Taz Blackwell. "

The slight man brightened. "Weren't you the deputy assistant secretary for Environment under Secretary Albright?"

"I was, yes. Sorry for being irritable, but I've been flying all night."

"No problem, Mr. Blackwell. We'll find the DCM."

The berated clerk busied herself straightening magazines for the occasional guest. Neither looked at the other while Taz waited. The group at the other side of the lobby talked among themselves. Finally, the elevator door opened, and out stepped a sallow-looking figure in a three-piece suit.

"Mr. Blackwell, I'm Ferdinand Triguet. I'm the DCM. Would you care to accompany me to my office?"

Taz stepped into the elevator. Triguet waited, then pressed the button for the third floor. His office was on the corner opposite the ambassador's suite. The ambassador looked out on to the Kastellet and the harbor, Triguet looked northwest towards Norrebro and the lake.

Taz decided to go first. "I knew Samelson. Where is he now?" Samelson was the former DCM.

"He's in Helmand Province by now, I expect. Got sucked into the whirlwind."

"Good for you, then."

"Yes. I was the science officer in Brussels. Not a bad job, but this is more . . . interesting."

Taz couldn't imagine what he meant. The science officer in Brussels had the responsibility to keep track of all the EU's regulatory moves, and to help the US government figure out how to respond to them. It was a great job, if you liked to work.

"I suppose."

"After all, Copenhagen is a much more interesting city."

Taz figured it was time to get down to business.

"John White told me the Embassy would help with security while I'm here in your interesting city."

Triguet sniffed. "We generally defer to the Copenhagen police for those kinds of things."

He evidently hadn't a clue what Taz was talking about. "So you haven't had any communication from INR?"

"None that I'm aware of."

Taz didn't see much point in going on. "Thank you for your time."

"My pleasure, Mr. Blackwell. Do call us if you need further assistance."

Taz bit his lip. He allowed Triguet to accompany him to the elevator.

***

On the way to his hotel, Taz dialed Gavin Hart's cell number. He felt positively grateful when he heard Hart's gravelly voice on the other end of the line. "It's Hart."

"It's Taz, Gavin."

"Well, I'll be damned. I saw your name on the list, but I didn't really think you'd be fool enough to show up here."

"What? You thought I'd be in hiding?"

"I should have known, shouldn't I."

"Yeah. Where are you?"

"At the Sheraton. Our people have no imagination."

"You up for dinner?"

"Where."

"Den Raven."

"I'll be there at seven."

Cold, dark, and wet. The cobblestones were slick. There were a few barges moored in the Nyhavn Canal that looked like they had been there a long time, and were probably going to end there. In one of them, a light was on. Taz realized it was being used as a houseboat.

Taz waited just off the stone steps to the half-basement where Den Raven's owner, Denis Derkamp, had established his restaurant. There was a light-boat out in the harbor, moving slowly towards the Kattegat. Wondered where it moored. Just then, he felt a hand on his shoulder. He hadn't heard a thing. He turned—Gavin.

"You know, if it's dark enough, you don't look so bad."

"Gavin, glad to see you."

"Let's get out of this shite, shall we?" He pronounced it to rhyme with *light*.

Taz went down the wet stone steps and opened the door. Inside, the warm room was lit entirely by candles. They hung their coats and found their way to a table in the corner. There were only two other parties in the room, a couple who seemed very intensely dug into their own world, and a quartet who were working on dessert.

When the waiter inquired, Gavin ordered a single malt scotch, neat. Taz followed suit.

"So, Taz, how did you let yourself get out on the flank with no center back support?"

"Sheer stupidity. They dangled the bait, and I bit."

"And the bait was herself, I suppose?"

"Of course. Why I didn't see it coming, I don't know."

Gavin sipped his scotch. "You're a gallant, that's all. They read you like a book."

"I didn't think I was so obvious."

"Bollocks. You were the talk of the Reykie diplo cocktail circuit for at least a month."

Taz must have shown a hint of surprise.

"So, you thought it was all undercover? Taz, lad. You have a lot to learn."

The waiter returned. Gavin ordered venison, Taz the cod.

"Well, what are we going to do for wine? Not some *foocking* split-the-difference rosé, I hope."

"How about a Beaujolais. Last year was spectacular, and they must have some bottles left. It's that time of year."

"You're smarter than you look. Of course, with that scar under your eye, it's not a high bar. Watch out, people might think you were a pugilist."

"Right. But my last fight didn't go so well."

"I got a full report. I understand the boys who did it ran into some local justice."

"For sure." With some satisfaction. "They were picked up by the NYPD, and somehow their diplomatic ID's got lost. They spent ten days on Riker's Island before their ambassador could get them out and back on a plane to the motherland."

"I always had a warm place in my heart for New York's finest. Now I know why."

"They put them in with a gang of Crips from the South Bronx."

"I'm sure you enjoyed hearing that."

"Well, I did. Not that I'm proud of it. But they did a real thorough job on me, so the thought of the Crips giving them some extra tattoos wasn't actually that displeasing."

"That all would have been reported back. And if I saw your name on the list, so did he."

"Why do you think I'm buying you dinner?"

Gavin grinned, dug into his venison.

While they were waiting for dessert, they caught up on the Premier League and ordered coffee. The Blues at Manchester City were making a run, and across town, Alec Ferguson was having conniptions. This was all very pleasing to Gavin.

After dessert, Gavin gave Taz a card with a private cell number. "I've made it clear to my head of delegation that I may have some extracurricular duties. I have an open schedule. You need anything, just ring me up."

They shook hands outside in the cold. Gavin gave Taz an appraising glance, all the while holding his hand.

"You know, you're tougher than you look. That's a good quality for a midfielder. Frankie Lampard, for instance, he's like that. Looks like a choirboy and kicks like a mule."

CHAPTER THIRTY-THREE

A Dish Best Served Cold

THE CONFERENCE STARTED IN the morning. The opening plenary was led off by the Danish prime minister, who made it sound like a glorious future was indeed in store for his unruly home rule province, though he couldn't quite articulate what that future would look like or when it might occur.

One thing was clear, though. Mineral development was a big part of the picture. To support Greenland in the future, and to help pay for Danish generosity in the transition. He didn't actually say the last part, but Taz understood the subtext.

The PM was followed by Robert Lynge who welcomed the assembled dignitaries, and particularly the "leaders of the private sector, who are here to help us build Greenland's future." Taz noticed a trio of empty seats behind the Russian flag. The Russian ambassador to Denmark was apparently occupied elsewhere.

There followed some high-level panels discussing Greenland's new mining and oil and gas policies, followed by a panel on human development efforts, education, and health issues. Taz wandered out to the lobby. A few delegates were getting coffee. From the back, he saw Akkanik. Taz filled two cups and headed over to the table where Akkanik was talking on a cell phone.

Taz gave him the cup. Akkanik wound up his call and took an appreciative sip.

"Taz, my friend."

"Aki." They shook, and then clasped forearms for good measure.

"I'd rather have a beer."

"Well, let's go then."

They retrieved their coats, stepped down the courtyard to the little pub at the end of the quay. Aki looked at Taz seriously as they sat. "This one's on me, friend."

Taz ordered a Tuborg on draft. They clinked glasses.

"Taz, I don't know what you did. But it gave Lynge a second chance."

"Is he going to take it?"

"Yes, but there are complications. The Danes are leaning on him. They're very unhappy that he's crossed the Russians."

"How unhappy?"

"Lavrov was here last week." Lavrov, the Foreign Minister. Taz whistled under his breath.

"Who's doing the talking for the Danes?"

"Nykvist, the PM's chief of staff."

Taz took a long pull on his Tuborg. "I think I'll need more than one."

"Me, too, friend. Me, too."

"So what happens next?"

"I don't know. I don't think Lynge can go back on the deal with BHP. It's too good, and the Parliamentary leaders are all for it."

They had a second round. Taz turned the conversation to other things. The Council, and the EU's sealing policy, which never could quite take the Greenlanders into account.

Eventually, Aki said, "I have to get back. Lynge will think I've abandoned him."

The program was to end at five o'clock. Dinner on your own. Tomorrow was the big day, with a final plenary led by the Danish foreign minister and Lynge, and featuring the chairman of Royal Dutch Shell. That was to be followed by a reception and an intimate dinner for ambassadors and heads of delegations at the Danish Foreign Ministry.

Taz paid the tab and started back to his hotel. There were taxis ranked outside on the cobblestone courtyard near the quay. He stepped past them and walked over the first bridge. It was still blustery, but the rain had stopped, and he needed to think. Wound his way through the streets behind the old opera house, until he reached Nyhavn. There, a traditional Danish restaurant on the east side that he remembered had a good fish soup.

Whatever else the Russians were up to, they weren't hiding their displeasure at the loss of the Kvanefjeld concession. Maybe they were trying to make a point to the Danes. *Trying to undercut Lynge?* He wouldn't take that lightly. Even though he hadn't signed the contract yet, he wasn't going to reverse course on Kvanefjeld. *What other irons do they have in the fire?*

Excellent fish soup. A dark bisque with good size morsels of lobster and a dollop of strong garlic aioli. Homemade croutons to give it some texture. Taz asked for a glass of Meursault.

When he got back to his room, he called White. Irvin's voice came on the line.

"Irvin, can you encrypt this?"

"Where are you?"

"In my hotel room."

"Can you go to the embassy? They have a SCIF."

"No way. They're a hinky bunch, Irvin. Didn't seem very glad to see me."

"Triguet. Slimy little bastard."

"You got it."

"Our technician is out sick."

"Okay, fine, don't worry about it. But let me tell you a baseball story."

"I don't even like baseball."

"Don't I know it. But you'll like this story."

"Okay." Hesitantly. Irvin really didn't like baseball.

"So, I'm down in Arizona at spring training. Royals against the Giants."

A sigh. "You're going to give me this in technicolor, aren't you?"

"Just for you, Irvin. But I can't tell a good baseball story any other way. So the Giants have a great infield defense, and a good pitcher on the mound. But he's given up a walk, and the Royals have a man on base. They're down a run, so getting him in scoring position is a high priority. They put on a hit and run."

"What's a hit and run?"

"Well, in this case, it's almost a run and hit. You start the runner from first when the pitcher comes to the plate, in the hope that your man can beat out a ground ball."

"Well, that's clear as mud."

"Okay, but the Giant's manager has stolen their sign, so he's on to them. They pitch out and the catcher nails the runner at second."

"And?" Another sigh.

"Well that's it. The Giants fans are gleeful, and the Royals fans are suffering. But two innings later, the Royals get on base again. Except this time, they put two men on. The Giants' pitcher is tired. He walks the lead-off man. Hits the number two batter. So it's two men on base, no outs."

"How long do these games go on?"

"Long, Irvin. Long. The key thing is that the Royals have two on, and a good hitter at the plate. The Giants need a double play. You know what that is, I hope?"

"Even I know what that is."

"Irvin, someday I'm going to get to actually like you. I'll take you to a game."

"I can't wait."

"The Royals put on a double steal. The catcher is quick, but he has to choose which runner to peg. He should go to third to get the lead runner. But the batter is a righty, and the pitcher throws a fastball low and outside. The catcher has to go to second. They get the trailing runner, but the lead runner is in scoring position."

"Okay."

"So the question is, how did we miss their lead runner? Because they're definitely playing for a run here."

"You mean?"

"You know exactly what I mean. Can you get me something to work with tonight?"

"I'll do my best, Taz. I'll do my best."

CHAPTER THIRTY-FOUR

Nailing the Lead Runner

TAZ WOKE UP AT five-thirty. Still dark. The garbage trucks and the all-night lorries rattled through the streets. He splashed cold water on his face, switched on his laptop. Took a minute to open various programs.

A new email from Irvin. *Call me when you wake up. I don't care what time it is.* The message was followed by a cell phone number. Taz did a quick calculation. Half-past midnight in Washington.

Irvin's voice came through on the other end. "Taz, there's a car coming to pick you up at seven. You'll be taken to the SCIF at the embassy. I'll brief you then."

"Okay, I better hop in the shower."

"Talk to you in half an hour."

Irvin pulled an all-nighter on this one. It must be pretty good.

When he got to the embassy, he was ushered immediately to an elevator at the back of the lobby. The staffer who was taking care of him was notably deferential. They got out on the fourth floor, the staffer led the way down a long hall to a suite of offices. No one in any of them, except for a lone secretary in the anteroom to the SCIF. He handed her his cell phone and went in.

He expected a phone hookup and was surprised when, instead, the large flat screen flickered and showed a conference room. Irvin soon appeared and sat. His lips moved, but there was no sound. Taz cupped his ear with his hand and gave Irvin a questioning look, assuming the folks at State could see him. Irvin uttered a few more silent sentences, then looked in the direction of the screen. Taz kept his hand up to his ear. Irvin turned and spoke sharply to someone. The screen flickered.

"Can you hear me now?"

"Yes, I can hear you fine."

"And I can finally hear you. Let's get started. Taz, your theory about two runners was correct."

"So tell me about the lead runner."

"The Russians are working on an exclusive commodity transport contract for Murmansk Shipping Company."

"Meaning?"

"Murmansk will have the right to ship every boatload of mineral ore that leaves Greenland for the next thirty years, or Greenland will pay a penalty equivalent to twenty percent of the value of the ore."

"A thirty-year lock-in? No one in Greenland would do that."

"They don't have to. Prime Minister Paulsen will do it for them under the Kingdom's plenary authority over foreign policy."

"So that's where Nykvist comes in."

"Yes, and that's not all. All hell is about to break loose, at least for your friend Goncharov."

"What? Why?"

"He's the one who's been paying off Nykvist. We have proof. As of tomorrow morning, so will the *Dagbladet Politiken* and the *Jyllands-Posten*." Denmark's most influential newspapers.

"So that was the body White was telling me about?"

"One of them, yes. This guy's got a closetful. And we're going to out them all before we're done."

Taz savored the news for a second. "How did you find all this, Irvin?"

"We had some help from some unlikely friends. The FSB. Russia's internal security service. The closest thing they have to the FBI."

"Okay, now I'm really lost."

"Well, all I can tell you is that someone decided he wasn't just in it for Mother Russia. And that someone slipped us his financial codes and passwords. Turns out Goncharov has been taking a little too much off the top of too many deals. These kinds of things don't go down with Putin. We need to call him out in public. Can you do it?"

"Can you get me some concrete evidence I can wave around? I may have a golden opportunity at lunch today."

When Taz left the SCIF, he was more than usually anxious to get to the conference. He found a taxi and paid the exorbitant tab without a second thought.

Nykvist had arranged an intimate lunch to be hosted by Prime Minister Paulsen for one p.m. Foreign Minister Lavrov would be there, as would Goncharov and the ambassadors of all the Arctic Council states. Except for the US. Its ambassador to Denmark was in the Canary Islands, enjoying a well-deserved vacation. Deputy Chief of Mission Triguet looked forward to taking his place.

Taz suggested to Irvin that Assistant Secretary White might call the embassy and make clear the building's view that the US Arctic envoy should attend the lunch, rather than the DCM. He later learned that Triguet felt profoundly humiliated by what he regarded as an unforgivable slight; he actually put those words in a cable directed to the assistant secretary for Europe. Months later, over a martini, the AS/EU told Taz that he regarded Triguet as "an insufferable hemorrhoid at his best." At the time, the AS/EU merely declined to intervene.

Hated dressing like a penguin. Still, he dutifully pulled his suit from the armoire, found a suitable tie for a gray suit—scarlet, with a Haida fish design. A little like what you might see on a modern totem pole.

The Danes had arranged a special room in Noma, widely considered the most creative of the New Wave restaurants sweeping Europe. Taz didn't remember much about the meal itself, except that there was dish that consisted entirely of seafoam, somehow transformed through contact with liquid nitrogen. There was also a seaweed salad that tasted like it might have come from the Baltic. That one chilled Taz's spine.

After the lunch plates were taken away, Foreign Minister Lavrov proposed a toast to the "gratifying progress in the Danish-Russian partnership." He congratulated Prime Minister Paulsen on his "far-sighted leadership," and did not forget to mention the "excellent staff work, for which we all must thank the Prime Minister's Executive Secretary Emil Nykvist."

Prime Minister Paulsen, who was apparently somewhat deep in his cups, gave a florid reply. He praised the Russian "spirit of innovation," and expressed his devout wish that relations between the two nations would continue to prosper, and would, in fact, only grow over the coming years, and become an example for others to follow.

Paulsen was followed by fulsome words from the Canadian ambassador, who was also at pains to celebrate the "new spirit of collaboration" between Russia and the West.

Finally, Taz stood. Eyes turned skeptically in his direction—he was not known to the Copenhagen diplo circuit. But he was speaking from behind the small US flag that marked his position at the table, and so they all tried to look attentive.

Taz started by recognizing the importance of the occasion, with nods to Foreign Minister Lavrov and Prime Minister Paulsen. The United States, too, wished to recognize the new relationship between Denmark and Russia, and not only because it had inspired the wonderful lunch that they had all just shared. The new arrangement would confer extraordinary benefits on both Denmark and Russia. Secretary General Nykvist was to be congratulated for his role in crafting the agreement.

Just as the collected ambassadors were starting to nod off, having consumed a wonderful dessert torte after a filling lunch, Taz dropped the bomb. But not all at once.

"Of course, there is one ambassador missing from the table today— the ambassador from Greenland. You might ask why. Well, I have talked to him, and I am authorized to say that in our conversation, he expressed the concern of the Greenland government that the deal that Secretary Nykvist had constructed, while it is beneficial to Denmark and Russia, does not confer similar benefits on Greenland."

All eyes shifted to Taz. Lavrov whispered to an aide. Prime Minister Paulsen looked distinctly uncomfortable. He motioned for one of the retinue of foreign ministry officials who had accompanied him.

"Still, echoing my colleagues, I must congratulate Secretary Nykvist on the cleverness of the new arrangement. It may appear extraordinary that a partnership designed and pursued with such perseverance by a Danish civil servant would confer such benefits on Russia, at the expense of Greenland. Which is, after all, still under the care of Denmark."

"And yet, there are reasons for Mr. Nykvist's very creative efforts. I am holding one of them in my hand."

At this point, Prime Minister Paulsen found that he had to leave the lunch for an emergency. Foreign Minister Lavrov also departed, without explanation. He did, however, glare in Taz's direction on his way out. Goncharov scurried after him.

Eyes again turned to Taz, who continued hold the paper above his head, in his right hand.

"This a bank daft from Rosbank, which, as you're undoubtedly aware, has close ties to the Kremlin."

Nykvist jumped out of his chair, "Stop this right now! I've heard enough! He has no proof of anything. This is all lies! It's a CIA plot to discredit the Danish government and undermine the deal."

Nykvist began bundling up his papers. Taz waited a suitable amount of time. He smiled at the remaining diners. He now had their rapt attention.

"The document I'm holding in my hand is the record of a twenty-million euro transfer, dated April ten, to a bank account in the Cayman Islands. The bank account belongs to Executive Secretary Nykvist."

Nykvist was trying to shout, but what came out was in a strangled voice, "All a terrible misunderstanding! There is an explanation. You are all making a big mistake."

All eyes turned in his direction. More quietly, "This farcical charade must be stopped." To which, the ambassador from Iceland said, "No, no. I find this quite fascinating. I would hope that our colleague from the US might continue until we have heard the full story." He then quite deliberately looked around the room. One by one, the other six ambassadors nodded. Nykvist finished bundling his papers and scurried out of the room.

Taz, in a level, emotionless tone said, "The account number that is designated in the transfer belongs to Mr. Nykvist. I also have proof, should any of my esteemed colleagues would care to inquire further."

Murmuring and whispered conversations as the ambassadors left the room. With the exception of the ambassador from Iceland, Thorgild Magnusson. He introduced himself to Taz. Then said, "Nykvist needed to be scotched. You did it. Thank you."

Taz put the paper back in his file envelope. Only one more to go.

CHAPTER THIRTY-FIVE

Float Like a Butterfly

THERE WAS NOT MUCH point in staying for hallway talk. Taz got his coat and walked out onto the cobblestone quay, facing back across the canal towards town. The sky had begun to clear. A cold wind bore shreds of clouds away to the east. A Danish Coast Guard cutter motored past the opera house and out to sea. Looked around for a taxi but saw only a black Mercedes Benz idling by the conference entrance. He turned and walked towards the Torvegade Bridge. Hundreds of cyclists were heading towards him. They wore suits and overcoats. Woolen scarves everywhere. Friday afternoon—time to forget work and start the weekend.

There was a good bistro off the second canal. He could get some soup there, and a glass of wine. He walked briskly, the cold made sure of that. He knew he should feel vindicated by what had happened, and he did in fact feel a modest sense of victory. Nykvist's exposure put Goncharov in an extremely vulnerable position. He had gone from hunter to hunted.

If Nykvist has been bribed, who had done the bribing? Taz appreciated the irony. Goncharov was a bully who confused money with power.

Whereas money is really a quite separate form of power, with different rules entirely. One has to know which universe one is in. But the victory was incomplete. Goncharov was by no means dead and buried. *Much more to be done. But what exactly?*

As he approached the canal, he took no notice of the Mercedes following him a half block behind.

Taz poked his head into the café to make sure they were still serving, closed the door behind him. It was almost two-thirty. He hung his coat on the wooden coat tree and found a small table in the corner. The room was warm, and the smell of pastries and garlic and coffee swirled slowly in the air.

The waitress stood at his table and smiled. He smiled back and turned to the menu. A familiar voice said, "He'll have a bowl of seafood soup, a crust of bread, and a bottle of Sauvignon blanc. And would you mind setting an extra place? I'll have the same."

Irina looked deeply at Taz.

"I thought I had missed you."

"I didn't even dare to hope you would come."

He stood to hold her hands. "I'm so glad you're still here."

"Taz, Taz. What was I going to do? I had to stay."

"How much time do we have?"

"There is a lunch tomorrow at the Embassy, and then I must act the part of his consort at the ministerial dinner tomorrow night. So we have tonight and tomorrow morning."

"And Sergei?"

"He was required to accompany Lavrov to Berlin. I expect he will be trying to explain the embarrassment of what's now known as the *Nykvist Affair.* Your toast left quite an impression! In fact, my friends tell me it's still echoing in Moscow." With a smile. "In any case, we must leave in the early morning Tuesday." She looked away.

"Are you okay?"

"Am I okay? Am I okay?" Her voice was almost shrill. "I was told what they did to you. That was when I decided he had to be stopped." She reached across and, with her forefinger, gently caressed the scar under his eye.

"You decided?"

"Taz, who do you think gave the Americans his financial codes?"

Momentarily stunned, as it hadn't occurred to him. "I'm such a fool. I had things exactly backwards."

"Oh, Taz. You're such a man. Of course you didn't guess it. Anyway, I don't wish to talk about him. He created a mess for Russia to clean up. It's only getting worse here in Copenhagen. Once we get back to Moscow, he'll have a different kind of trouble. It should keep him quite busy."

"Will he try to get back at you?"

"He is a vengeful man, Taz. And he still has some allies, including some dark ones. Still, if my friends and I are successful, he will be gone, and I expect he will stay gone."

Taz wasn't sure he liked the uncertainty of all this.

"And you?"

"Some friends have arranged a position at the University in Krasnoyarsk. I will be a counselor for the women students and perhaps even teach a course."

"You're looking forward to going back."

Irina smiled. "Yes, it's ironic. But my father is quite old. I want to be near him. And Krasnoyarsk is—"

"The most beautiful city in all Russia." Taz smiled. Irina glared, and then laughed.

"Irina, there's something you should know."

Squinting just a little. "Yes?"

"Murmansk Shipping can still bid for a Greenland contract."

"But they would laugh at us now, spit in our faces."

"Maybe some, but Akkavik won't, and he'll be influential."

"Why would he ignore what's happened?"

"He won't. It won't be an exclusive contract. But he'll have an open mind. He's aware of the design work that Murmansk commissioned from the Finns."

"How?"

"I told him."

Her eyes widened. "Now it's I who should have known."

"It occurred to me that people appreciate messengers who come home with good news."

"I do love you, Taz. I do."

"Perhaps, this evening—"

"Yes. I will show you."

The waitress brought the fish soup and the wine. After they toasted and Taz broke the bread and gave Irina half, they tucked in and ate in silence for a few minutes.

Irina dabbed her mouth with her napkin. "Taz, do you know this man at the embassy, Triguet?"

"Yes, I know him."

"I just want to say, that in my country, he would be shot."

"Yes. In my country, he will be promoted."

"How can you run a Foreign Service like this?"

"Well, that's the question, isn't it. How did you encounter him?"

"He was supposed to convey information to you which he did not do. Instead, he passed it to the Danes."

"What information?"

"Now it's not important. Just that he is playing his own game."

"I will let people know, but I think they already do. We would have to be able to prove something."

"Maybe it doesn't matter."

"Irina, what matters is that you're here. And I thought I knew who you were, but now I'm not so sure."

"No. No. That's what doesn't matter. You found my heart. You know my heart. That's what matters."

Taz absorbed that. The waitress came over to clear their soup bowls. "Coffee?"

Irina ordered a latte. Taz had a double espresso, cut short. They sat across from each other, content for the moment in each other's company. The coffee came. They sipped in silence. Around them, the last of the lunch crowd headed reluctantly back to work.

"Irina, are you sure I can't convince you to come with me to the States?"

"Taz, don't."

He was struck again by her beauty, by the vulnerability of it, the fierce gaze when she was angry.

"I must go, Taz. I must. Because we have something special, but if we try to hold it, to pin it down, it won't last. We're in different worlds, Taz. I thought about leaving for you, I really did. But I can't leave Russia, at least not forever. The thought of living again in Krasnoyarsk makes my heart thrill. I think of all the places, the friends who play music there, the conversation at parties, the constant arguments over ideas and books. Things I can't get anywhere else."

Taz's thoughts wandered to other scenes. Meeting her at the bar in Tromsoe. Standing on the edge of the rift valley in the wind. Her eyes when she tasted Ardbeg for the first time. Dana's smile on the sand bar when Suzanne brought back the first clump of spartina. Dana caught halfway between embarrassment and laughter the night that Tom blurted out his version of their very first encounter, on the beach. Dana looking on in horror as Taz and Tom rocked out on a ragged version of "High-heeled Sneakers" at the end of a long whisky-fueled jam.

Taz couldn't help himself—he started laughing. A laugh that turned into a giggle, then into a snort, until, finally, he ended up with a most beatific smile, as Irina described it to him later that night, with her head on his chest. He knew how they were going to do it.

Put on your red dress, baby
Lord, we goin' out tonight
Put on your red dress baby
Lord, we goin' out tonight
And-a bring some boxin' gloves
In case some fool might wanna fight

Put on your high-heel sneakers
Wear your wig hat on your head

Put on your high-heel sneakers
Wear your wig hat on your head
I'm pretty sure now baby
Don't you know, you know, you gonna knock 'em dead

❊ ❊ ❊

They woke together. Taz rolled, Irina sighed and moved against him. He draped his arm over her breasts. Afterwards, Taz thought in silence for a little. Started hesitantly, "Irina—I think I know how we can do it." She put her finger on his lips and shushed him. She was watching a young mother cradling a baby just outside the window.

"Do what?"

"Put the hex on Goncharov so he's never in a position to hurt either of us again."

A penetrating gaze. "*Hex*? What is a hex? Oh, what does it matter? How is it that you say it? I'm all ears."

They started at a high-end shop in Magasin du Nord, the grand old department store just off the Kongens Nytorv, one of the city's most glamorous squares. From there, they went to Storm, Noa Noa, and, of course, Cos.

In each, Irina would survey the racks, pick a few possibilities, and retire to the dressing room, emerging a few minutes later flashing and twirling for Taz's viewing pleasure. He would smile, laugh, hide his eyes, or give her a thumbs-up.

They finally arrived at Holly Golightly, the most exclusive boutique in Copenhagen. Famous for new designer collections. Edgy, hip beyond imagination. No racks at all. Rather, a supremely elegant young woman who introduced herself, suggested a place to sit, offered them coffee, Chablis, or cognac. She was dressed to the nines, a pleasure to watch. Spoke nine languages, four of them fluently. Taz winked at Irina to show her he had no intention of becoming distracted. At least not right then.

After they had gotten to know one another, the young woman named Kirsten excused herself and disappeared behind a silk curtain towards the back of the room. She reappeared a few minutes later with three dresses draped over her arm. Folded them carefully over the back of a Bauhaus chair, selected one at a time, each time with a sidelong look at Irina, then displayed them, holding them by the shoulders in front of her so they could imagine how good they would look if she were wearing them.

The first was a dark blue caftan that looked like it might have been made for a Moroccan princess. Irina nodded appreciatively. Taz gazed, dreaming. The second was by Maison Baylé—a terrific black-on-white print on silk, but cut like an asymmetric frock worn by a nineteenth-century schoolmarm. Irina giggled, Taz smiled. The young woman tossed it over the back of a nearby love seat.

Now she was holding a handmade poppy dress from Vita Kin. It was made from terracotta-orange linen, with beautiful blue and brown embroidery. The young woman explained that the pattern was based on traditional *vyshyvanka* embroidery from the Ukraine. Round neckline, with a center-front V-slit held by blue and brown tassel fastening. Long sleeves and a loose, flowing silhouette.

Taz put two fingers to his lips, looked at Irina. She had a look of pure desire that would have made him blush if only it had been aimed in his direction. The young woman took Irina by the hand. This time they both disappeared.

Irina came out alone. She was resplendent. A goddess that only appears once in a blue moon. Taz was open-mouthed, astonished. The young woman appeared silently behind Irina, took one look at Taz, put her hand to her mouth and laughed, ever so delicately.

They watched as she put the dress in a gift box. Said their goodbyes and headed out the front door, laughing with pleasure.

It was a brisk day, cool, blue, and beautiful. The sun warmed their backs as they walked down the esplanade, stopped into a high-end men's shop. Taz picked out a tuxedo that, with a quick adjustment to the sleeves by the house tailor, fit him almost perfectly.

Outside, they gave each other a look, laughed, and headed to the wine bar next to the Angleterre. It was only two blocks away.

CHAPTER THIRTY-SIX

Sting Like a Bee

THE RECEPTION WAS SCHEDULED for seven p.m. at the new Opera House on the harbor. Although the stage would be dark, the building and its surrounding plaza were already lit and humming.

Taz dropped Irina at her hotel at four-thirty. They had gone over their plan at the wine bar while working their way through a delightful bottle of Pol Roger. It seemed only appropriate to launch their little escapade with Winston Churchill's favorite champagne. Just like Churchill's ventures, the possible results ranged from glorious success to ignominious failure. By the time the bottle reached the dregs, they were giggling at some of the more absurd scenarios. Irina laughed so hard her eyes watered.

Still feeling the last electric clutch of her hand, Taz began his way back to the opera over the Norrebro Bridge. Attempted a more serious review of the possible scenarios for the evening. Which would have been helpful, but his mind kept wandering to other scenes, with Irina in Iceland, with Dana on Chincoteague, with Jaclyn at the Inaugural Ball. All the while, his attention was training itself on the traffic on the bridge, the strange perspective of the opera building, the boats in the channel moving out towards the sea.

The Prime Minister and Foreign Minister Lavrov were to co-chair the formal dinner. All the Arctic ministers would attend. The Danes had put on extra security measures. There were rope lines leading to five screening machines. The security folks were reviewing the procedures for patting down anyone whose belt buckle tripped the alarm. In the event, the screening was conducted politely, without the kind of barely subliminal paranoia Taz had grown used to in American airports. Taz's embassy ID badge exempted him from any pat-down.

He made his way to the ballroom. A dozen plainclothes types were scattered strategically around the lobby and the hallways. Taz wandered wherever he wanted. The stage and podium where the formal addresses would be given were on one side of the room. There were exits on either side. He tried checking to see where they led, but they were locked.

The bar was set up on the opposite wall. Again, exits on either side. About a hundred and twenty feet between bar and podium. No obvious sign of any control board, or any control switches for the two microphones that were placed on the podium. One was apparently meant to attach to a stand, one to float free.

No sign of Russian goons, which he reported with some relief to Gavin when they met at six forty-five, just outside the freight ramp. "I scouted the place. Nothing unusual, as far as I could see."

"Sure, and did you notice the white van just off the rear entrance? The one with all the listening equipment? And, in your 'scouting tour,' did you happen to see that one of the stage-side exits—the one on the left—led directly to the Russian Embassy's hospitality suite?"

"The exit door was locked."

"Of course it was, my dear." Gavin grinned. "And so is the Russkies' suite. Don't worry, it's empty. They're all in a last-minute meeting with Lavrov himself at the embassy. But by the time this fiasco starts, they will have at least three goons in there with the dignitaries." The last word was spit out with an unfamiliar venom.

"It's all right, amigo. Just think of me as a kind of sweeper, like the eighties used in the World Cup. Franco Baresi. Brazil would have aced them without him. Once you go up, we'll put up the wall. Catenaccio. All tied up. Clean sheet. The end." For Gavin, there was a football metaphor for every occasion. Crazy, but it worked, at least for Taz. But Taz had to go up, to score first.

Other people began drifting in—caterers, opera staff, perhaps some dignitaries' personal assistants. Checking out the venue. Taz and Gavin slipped out one of the stage-side entrances.

They found themselves in an antiseptic white-sided hall that zig-zagged towards the back of the building. As they passed the second of several crossing corridors, Taz caught movement out of the corner of his eye. Halfway down the hall, two heavyset men in ill-fitting suits were sharing cigarettes and what looked like a pint of vodka. When he looked again, Taz recognized one as the driver who had taken him to the abandoned warehouse in the Meadowlands. *Goncharov's man.* He had a lot to answer for.

The heavies turned towards them slowly, as if waking from a dream. Taz smelled pot. Stoned or not, as they moved to either side of the corridor where Taz and Gavin were standing, the goons looked plenty menacing. The one on Gavin's left took the first swing. Gavin ducked and devastated its author with a right hook that made a sickening sound that might mean a broken cheekbone. The second came after Taz. He fended him off, blocking what might have been a lethal left with his forearm, which hurt for a week. While the heavy was gathering his wits for a second effort, Gavin stepped in and touched his Adam's apple ever so lightly with a knuckle or maybe two. The goon crumpled, clutching his throat, gagging and coughing.

At that point, both of Goncharov's men were hugging linoleum, one barely conscious and the other whimpering in pain. Gavin stepped over to check for pistols. It was a good thing. They both had full shoulder holsters. Those two babies would be at the bottom of the canal in a few minutes. Meanwhile, Goncharov was nowhere in sight. Still, Taz reckoned he'd soon get the message.

They left through the emergency exit a floor down. Wound up on a fire escape two stories off the street. Laughed and dropped the ladder. No security at all. Walked a hundred yards to the bulkheads by the harbor, watching the water. A sea-tug was making its way past them, no doubt to the Kattegat.

"Nice forearm block." As close as Gavin got to a compliment.

Taz ditched the pistols, dangling each one first before sending it to its watery grave. "What next?"

"Well, Goncharov will know we're onto him. He'll either bring reinforcements, or change course. I'm betting on reinforcements."

"Good enough. I haven't had a really proper fight since the last time my boys played Stoke City."

They strolled around the south side of the opera towards the main entrance, off the plaza. They were facing Nyhaven across the Kobenhavn canal. Gavin lit a cigarette. Taz gave him an inquiring look.

"What the . . . Socrates smoked four packs a day, didn't he. The greatest midfielder since Cruyff." Having made his point, he offered Taz a Gauloise. No filter, just pure nicotine and the powerful aromatics of Latakia and Virginia tobacco. Taz took pleasure, puff after puff.

It was time. Gavin headed directly to the opera's stage entrance. Taz made his way to his car, retrieved his tuxedo, and followed. He changed in an empty dressing room.

The ballroom was already humming when he slipped in. Early arrivals, more or less, and those who hadn't been invited to the VIP cocktail hour were finding their tables, standing in small groups, holding wine glasses or champagne flutes, looking discreetly to see when the important people would make their entrance. Not wanting to scoop his own surprise, Taz milled around the ballroom as well. He stood near the entrance farthest from the bandstand. He was focused on the semi-circular head table, empty on its low platform, where Lavrov and the Prime Minister would soon be seated. Wondered how he would feel when Irina was sitting there too, as Goncharov's consort. Reminded himself that this was all part of the plan.

He was startled from his reverie by a soft touch on his elbow. Looked to his left to see a young woman—black hair cut to fall just below her ears, long neck, aquiline nose, sparkling blue eyes, deep set. Regarding him intently, but with a slow smile gradually lighting up as her amusement gathered.

"Lost in thought? I didn't think you Yanks were set up to be introspective." The smile broadened.

Taz smiled back. "Well, lost—yes. But thought? I wouldn't call it that. More a train of images than a train of thoughts—like a waking dream."

"Oh! I do that too. I've just never known what to call it. I'm Maeve, by the way." With the merest hint of a curtsy. "And you?"

"Taz. Taz Blackwell. I'm—"

"Oh, no need! You're famous. Or notorious, depending on one's point of view."

"And your point of view?

"Agnostic for now. I'm with the British Embassy." *Yes, of course.*

"Ahh, that's why you have such a low opinion of Yanks. Can we just take a moment and remember who it was that surrendered at Yorktown?"

"Not to worry! Just here as an observer. The ambassador will be along shortly, and if there is anything to be said on our side, he will say it."

"But let me guess. You will write it. On a napkin, if necessary."

"You've seen through me already." She looked downcast. "I must be an open book." Gazing into his eyes. Smiling again, more softly.

"Just putting two and two together."

"You're pretty good at that, so I hear." Gavin. No other explanation. "I'm told there may be some dancing after dinner." An arched eyebrow and a slightly crooked smile said she wouldn't turn down an offer.

"I'd be honored if you would consent to share the first dance."

"How wonderfully retro of you. All my friends would sputter or say, 'Wow. Really? Totally cool.'"

"I'm sure they're eloquent in their own way."

"Oh, for sure. After they bonk you, they light up a cigarette and say thanks."

Taz considered that for a second, looked her over once again. "I wonder if you would consider one other possible dance partner. Perhaps for the second dance?"

"And who would that be?" Amusement and surprise, at once.

"Ambassador Goncharov. He'll be coming in soon. It wouldn't be at all difficult for you to catch his eye."

"Is that a compliment? Or merely a very awkward proposition? I think you're a bad man. A very bad man." A half-turn away, eyes looking beguilingly over her shoulder. "Anyway, what's in it for me?"

"It'll be like acting in a play. If you pull it off, legions of fans will adore you."

"And you?"

"Yes. In fact, I will be your most ardent fan of all."

"Ardent. Hmm. I like that word." Maeve slipped out the nearest exit. Taz moved through the swelling crowd, trying to get a feel for the room, the way a jazz player scouts a club. Hip crowd, a dancing crowd? Or a collection of lonely civil servants whose response would prove all-too-predictably slack? Would they play in when the time came? Or stand aside?

The crowd noise began to swell with sheer human density, stifling one-to-one communication. Some guests resorted to shouting to make themselves heard. Others innovated various forms of sign language. And then, just for a few moments, the room went silent as Prime Minister Paulsen and Foreign Minister Lavrov entered. They were talking easily, seemingly taking no notice of the crowd that parted like the Red Sea to allow them unobstructed passage. They reached the head table, sat in the two center seats, to applause.

The leading lights were followed by other dignitaries. The foreign minister of Norway and his wife. Their Swedish counterparts. The head table was arranged as a flattened semicircle, so the VIPs could see each other as well as the audience. Each stood or sat behind their flag placard. Arctic Council state members were represented by their ambassadors. One or two by environment ministers.

Finally, Goncharov. And, on his arm, Irina, looking way beyond dazzling. Taz took a deep breath. Waited until they were all standing behind their seats to walk up and take his seat at the opposite extreme of the head table, behind the small American flag.

After a suitable amount of small talk while the first of the wine was poured, the prime minister stood to give an opening toast. Gracious and urbane as he welcomed all to his wonderful city. He particularly celebrated the presence of the Russian foreign minister, a "true friend" of Denmark. He looked forward to a splendid evening, and to the opportunity to dance with at least a few of the very beautiful women in attendance. Glancing here and there about the room and finally gazing fondly at Irina. Sergei flushed. Put his hands on the table as if to rise from his seat. Irina clutched his arm, poured him another vodka.

Foreign Minister Lavrov rose and clinked his glass once. With a sweep of his arm, he noted the growing economic ties between Denmark and Russia, and the fellowship that Russia felt for the people of Greenland in particular. To his disappointment, the Russian government's most recent effort to assist Greenland's economic development had not yet been able to move from dream to reality. However, when more such opportunities arose in coming years, he felt sure that future Danish governments would look favorably on them.

Taz looked around the room to see if anyone had caught the reference to "future Danish governments," but saw only a few seasoned diplomats whispering to each other behind their hands.

Prime Minister Paulsen rose once more, motioned to a dozen seated musicians on the bandstand, and called on all to enjoy "a little music and dancing before dinner."

At which point he strode to the left extreme of the head table and offered Irina his hand. Taz couldn't suppress a smile. It was working out even better than they had planned. The prime minister of Denmark had taken his place as Irina's first partner. Goncharov's discomfort was rising, along with his vodka levels.

Just as Prime Minister Paulsen and the Russian ambassador's consort were showing signs of enjoying their waltz, Maeve appeared by the side of the table to Goncharov's left. She was wearing a dark blue cocktail dress trimmed in gold, cut low, and a diamond brooch that accented the lovely curve of her breasts. She smiled invitingly. Goncharov stepped on the draped tablecloth, spilling two water glasses in his haste to leave his seat and insinuate his thick hand around her waist. Other couples were now joining the dance.

Just as Goncharov was stepping unsteadily off the platform, Taz swooped in and slipped his hand between Maeve's arm and her ribs, whispered in her ear. They ran onto the dance floor together. Taz looked back as they took their first turn. Goncharov was glaring daggers.

Irina was still twirling with the PM. As they passed Goncharov still standing alone, she said something in Russian. He jumped at her, thought better of it, stepped back, looking over his shoulder. Two Danish security types were talking into their lapel mics as they moved to stand on either side of him.

The waltz ended with a flourish. Irina disengaged from the PM, who thanked her in flowery terms. Maeve gave Taz a soft peck on the check, brushed his ear with her nose, whispered, "I enjoyed that." Then she slipped off through the crowd.

Irina wended her way to Taz's side. "So. Who was your extra? You would have to pick a professional dancer."

"Doesn't matter. Everyone's eyes were on you. Including mine. What did you say to Goncharov that set him off so badly?"

"I told him that even in your hospital bed, you were twice the man he was."

Most of the dancers remained standing and talking on the dance floor. Taz looked over at Goncharov. He was talking into a cell phone and gesticulating wildly. Gavin Hart stood about a yard behind him. As Taz turned back to gaze at Irina, he saw several young women placing pamphlets on the empty chairs around the dinner tables. They were working quickly and efficiently. Waiters were circulating through the dance crowd with trays of champagne. Taz picked one for Irina, then one for himself. They toasted, smiling.

After a few minutes more, the call came to take seats for dinner.

Waiters began serving appetizers and pouring white wine. As the guests bent to take their seats, they discovered an advance copy of the next morning's *Jyllands-Posten*. Next to a prominent picture of Ambassador Goncharov on the front page was the lead headline: "Source of Nykvist Bribe Uncovered—Russia's Ambassador."

As the head table reassembled, all eyes turned towards Russian Ambassador Goncharov, who was still on his cell phone, yelling in Russian, facing the now almost empty dance floor.

Goncharov must have felt the collective stare burning through the back of his suit. He flipped his phone closed and stepped onto the platform. As he did, the hissing started. It came from all over, from every table except the head table, and it grew in volume. It was only then that Goncharov saw the newspaper. He stared at it, bug-eyed with anger, reached down, held it up for all to see, and tore it in half. At which point the hisses turned to boos and yells. Prime Minister Paulsen made a motion to his aides. Lavrov's seat was empty. Two of the prime minister's aides hurried quickly over to Goncharov and showed him to the exit.

CHAPTER THIRTY-SEVEN

Da Svedanya

THE DEAL HAD BEEN played. Goncharov had lost—big time. The rest would just be explanations and mopping up. Taz looked at Irina, "Shall we?"

Irina was caught halfway between smiling and crying. She hid her face behind the back of her hand. Taz found her coat on the rack, then his. She reached for his hand and led him out the door.

They walked across the bridge to her hotel, on the water across from the opera house. Taz's attention was on her in the glow of Copenhagen lights reflecting from the water. His mind was flitting between thoughts, never settling on one or the other. The night's excitement. The expression on Goncharov's face when he realized that he was the butt of the joke. But he wasn't the only one who had misread the situation.

Taz's head was still spinning from his lunch with Irina the day before. How had he misunderstood so much? The Irina he knew was a wildflower in a thunderstorm. Now she was the lightning. It occurred to him that when he bought the champagne in Tromsoe, just when he was most confident of being in charge, he was actually walking straight into her script.

They wound up at the entrance to an old hotel, with the kind of ornate lobby that only occurs in Agatha Christie's Poirot stories. The rooms still had high ceilings and sash windows that opened to the evening winds. He looked around while she moved some things.

"I have something for you." His face indicated his surprise, because she laughed, that lovely tingling laugh that reminded him that she was still a girl from Krasnoyarsk.

She opened a cabinet door to reveal a well-hidden refrigerator. Reached in and handed Taz a bottle of Veuve Clicquot. "One good turn deserves another." She put two champagne flutes on the table, and looked meaningfully at him. He stripped the foil, twisted the cork, and held it down as it worked its way out of the neck. After a few long seconds there was a quick, soft release.

"Just like a woman's sigh." She said it with a smile as she poured.

"Taz, I don't want you to think this was all planned. It wasn't. I told you I was sent to watch you, and that was true. But then I fell for you, and that was true, too." She pursed her lips.

"It's just . . . it's just that I—"

She paused.

"You thought I was a little girl, and I wasn't. I told you I wasn't a minder, and I wasn't. But I knew Sergei was corrupt, and at some point I said so to my cousin, who is FSB. After that, a man in the embassy asked only that I let him know if the ambassador was courting trouble. So I began . . . keeping tabs. The FSB wanted to protect the integrity of the embassy. Corruption in an ambassador is embarrassing to the Kremlin. And Sergei—well, once he acquired me, he became a different, less pleasing person. Demanding, dictatorial. I didn't like that. So I was glad to tell the FSB about his little schemes."

Taz held up his glass. Irina touched hers to his. *"Zha lyubov!"* He gave a questioning look.

"To love!"

"To you, in Krasnoyarsk."

"And how about you, Taz? How about you?"

"I've met someone on the island. I think it might be serious."

Irina didn't flinch, at least at first. But then she stood and looked toward the window. "What makes you think so? Tell me about her."

"Well, she's the only woman I've ever met who is as beautiful as you."

"Good start. Go on."

"She's a single mom with two kids."

"Not advantageous, my mother would say."

"No. Not only that. We haven't even slept together."

"Good. I'd like to think there's hope that I might see you in Krasnoyarsk one day."

She turned, with a hand on hip. "Do you still think I'm attractive?"

"Irina, no woman has ever attracted me so completely."

"Well, what are you going to do about it?"

He stood up and went over to her. She had a questioning look in her eyes. All attitude, all desire. He touched her cheek, her shoulder, her hip. She tapped her foot, put her forefinger to her lips, said, "Here."

Later, he couldn't remember the exact sequence. It was a slow, sensual blur of touching, caressing, feeling. He was determined to make her lose control first. He remembered unbuttoning her blouse, kissing her nipples. He remembered her scent of citrus and arousal, and the strange, vulnerable sensation when she unbuckled his belt. He picked her up, carried her to the bed. Took off her panties with his teeth. Kissed his way back up her thighs, until he was in deep enjoyment, and she was moaning and lifting her hips off the mattress.

Making love on the bed, at first slowly, then with growing intensity. His hands sliding up and down her ribcage, moving to cup her breasts. Her nails digging into his back, his buttocks. Holding her hair from behind, and her hips. Until she begged, that was in his mind. And she did, but with music in her voice. Finally tumbling onto the floor, catching their breath and, as time slowed down, laughing. Until they collapsed together, exhausted, deep into the night. They fell asleep on the floor, spooning, with him nuzzling the nape of her neck and with his ankle between hers.

In the morning, even before coffee, they made love again, slowly. In the shower, as he was soaping her back, he said, "I'll never forget you."

"Don't say that, it sounds so final. Just say, 'farewell for now.'"

He dried her, and she him, taking extra care on his chest and ribs with the soft towel. He made coffee while they dressed.

"How are you getting out to Keflavik?"

"The embassy driver will pick me up." She turned his wrist towards her, to look at his watch. "In twenty minutes."

He pulled her up, opened the doors to the balcony, and led her out. It was cold, but there was a good view of the city and the harbor. She embraced him from behind as they shivered in the cold wind.

"I've never met anyone like you, Irina."

"Or I you."

"I think I would burn inside if I thought you were unhappy. Will you be happy?"

"Yes. Yes, I think I will." Her nose was pressed between his shoulder blades.

Finally, she pulled away to look at his watch again. "I have to go."

"Farewell for now, my beautiful Irina."

"*Da Svedanya*, Taz. Fare well."

✻✻✻

Later, Taz searched for the right words to encapsulate Irina's indelible impact on his life. Found some lines of Anna Akhmatova, the great Russian lyric poet. Willing sufferer, open-hearted victim:

> *As if on the rim of a cloud,*
> *I remember your words,*
>
> *And because of my words to you,*
> *Night became brighter than day.*
>
> *Thus, torn from the earth,*
> *We rose up, like stars.*

There was neither despair nor shame,
Not now, not afterward, not at the time.

But in real life, right now,
You hear how I am calling you.

And that door that you half opened,
I don't have the strength to slam.

CHAPTER THIRTY-EIGHT

One for the Road

THE LIMOUSINE HAD COME and gone. Irina was on a plane to Moscow. Copenhagen was back to its cold, gray, wet self. Taz was utterly lonely. It seemed very cold on the bridge. He stood with his hands on the iron rail and looked over the canal.

He had always hated absences. His mother died when he was two. Taz carried her absence in his heart like a secret abscess. Needing and treasuring the company of women, he'd learned to charm, and listen. And yet they left, time and again. The canal water gurgled and swept out with the waning tide.

Taz walked down to the wharf, found a little fish place whose kitchen advertised a breakfast menu. Asked for coffee and a couple of eggs over easy. They were served with fried ham and sautéed tomatoes. A Tuborg to wash them down. Pulled the *International Herald Tribune* off the rack. Asked for a coffee refill. Called Gavin, left a message saying thanks for everything and see you next time. He didn't see much point in going back to his room. Instead, he walked up the slight incline towards Kongens Nytorv—the King's Square. Stopped at a little wine bar with a black signboard advertising an attractive menu. Distractedly ordered a bottle of burgundy and a fish pie. A chapter had closed, and he had no idea what came next. His heart had left on Irina's plane. He felt a grim pleasure at Goncharov's fall, but there was no pride in it. He had made a lot of mistakes, and had finally done what was necessary, that was all.

Then there was Dana, whose portrait appeared first in sepia and then in technicolor, at the occasional times when he felt her heart opening to him. Right behind her in his floating mental collage, Tobytown. He had left both threads untied, and God knows what had transpired while he was shadow boxing in Copenhagen. He guessed he could reconnect with a phone call, but he wouldn't know what to say. Even to Laney.

As the golden winter light turned toward dusk, he continued to amble the streets north of the square. Taz found himself on the steps of the Hotel Angleterre, the old doyenne of the King's Square. There was a young blonde behind the bar. She had a smart smile and a gentle demeanor. He registered her surprise when he asked for the bottle of Ballantine's, but after a moment she set it in front of him, with a two-ounce whisky glass.

Irina was right. They were from two different worlds. Irina from Krasnoyarsk was a city girl. She lived for culture, conversation, the wit of cities. He had once been that way too. But the longer he absorbed the flavors and friendships of the Island, the less romance he had found in the life of the nation's capital. Chincoteague was his home now. He loved it. But it wasn't for everyone.

All fine, except that he was losing the one woman who could thrill him with a single touch, or one whisper in his ear. She was laughter, drama, mystery. The sight of her gave him chills. Now she was heading for the exit. Soon she would be a memory.

He poured a second double shot. It was always this way. The ones you loved the most disappeared. And then where were you, really? You reach out to the world, but it's like sand running through your fingers.

Sometimes you win some. A quip brings a laugh, a compliment begets a smile. That's what you should hope for, aim for. Moments of pleasure unappreciated even when they wash over us. God knows, it should be enough. The glance received, appreciated. The appraising look. The harmony that appears from nowhere.

"By the rivers of Babylon, where we sat down, and there we wept, when we remembered Zion."

He finished his shot and poured another. The barmaid wiped the bar just to his left, looked at him with a question in her eyes. He smiled at her.

"Are you all right?"

"Never better. Well, maybe a few days. Those have been better, for sure."

"Not to worry. Things will turn around. Don't they always?"

When you're young they do. The last time he had seen Laney, she'd said something about him being a drifter. Drifting in and out of their lives. Was that how he came across? To his closest friends on the island?

I am a poor wayfaring stranger
I'm only here to see my mother
She said she'd meet me when I come
I'm only going over Jordan
I'm only going over home.

He wondered about Dana. In her deepest heart, Irina had a touch of fire. Her heart was his for the asking. The contrast was stark. There was no free love at Dana's door. To reach her heart would require a test of some kind, a long trek through a dark forest or a climb up a risky cliff. And when he got there, Dana's love would be guarded by beasts, spells, and incantations, a ruby inside a golden statue. Indiana Jones, here we come.

He heard the creak of the door from the lobby. The barmaid looked up, surprised to see a new customer so late in the evening. Taz kept his eye on the Ballantine's. He was enjoying his isolation, not wanting it to end. Not wanting to talk to some businessman who'd had a bad day.

Then he felt a familiar touch on his shoulder. Maeve, watching him warily. Her left elbow was on the bar, she was leaning her cheek against her left hand. Her right hand was on his shoulder, working a small circle towards his collarbone.

"That bad, is it? I'm so sorry."

"Just trying to put two worlds together. It's not working. No harm though. It never does."

She was wearing a dark blue button-down shirt, silk, open at the top. It hung very nicely. "Do you want to talk about it? About the two worlds?"

He asked the young barmaid for a second glass, poured Maeve a double. "Okay. Imagine an island, a small town. Real people who've brought you in out of the cold. Someone there you could love, someone wonderful. But your timing is always wrong. You fuck up. Leave her wondering if you're really worth it. You don't think you are. Then, out of the blue and half a world away, you find your soulmate. You fall head over heels. But it's impossible. She's from another planet, that's how far the distance is. You don't know what to do, you just don't know."

Maeve covered his hand with hers, looked in his eyes. "Maybe you keep that door open. Maybe it's not as hopeless as you think. Or, maybe you let chance be your guide. Or fate, if that's what you call it. Your river has channels. Which channel are you in?"

"I wish I could tell you. I will, when I know."

More a question than an answer.

CHAPTER THIRTY-NINE

Odysseus Returns to Ithaca

THE NEXT MORNING WAS gray, damp, and cold. Maeve was still deep asleep, smiling and murmuring. Taz kissed her on the cheek and left as quietly as he could. Walked back towards Nyhavn. Gathered his things and found a taxi. Made the gate with a few minutes to spare.

He was asleep before they lifted off. Didn't wake up until they were off the southern tip of Greenland. The clouds had broken up west of Iceland and he could make out the coast near Cape Farewell. There was a fair amount of ice in the water offshore, everything from bergie bits to sheared-off plates of shorefast ice. He wondered how a bulk loader would maneuver in those waters.

Went back to sleep over the waters of the Davis Strait. When he next woke, they were somewhere over Labrador. It was clear. He could make out the marks the glaciers left on the Canadian Shield as they retreated north. They had left elongated valleys running south to north, many with lakes in them. A barren, stony land, and yet beautiful. Most of the lakes were still frozen, but a few were glistening in the afternoon sun. Warmer than usual for early March.

They landed at Dulles in the late afternoon. Taz found his car and thought briefly about the four-hour drive to Chincoteague. Decided it would be better to stay in town. It was eleven at night Copenhagen time, and he was feeling the effect. White would want to debrief him in the morning, provided he wasn't out on some junket of his own.

He found a room on N Street, not far from the Tabard Inn, a Washington institution. He could eat there and sleep down the block for half the price.

As soon as he got settled, he called Irvin. White would be happy to see him first thing in the morning. He took a long shower to wash away the stickiness of the airplane. While he was drying off, he called Laney.

"Hey there, just wanted to let you know I'm back on our side of the Atlantic."

"About time. Did everything go okay?"

"About as well as it could, I guess. Goncharov pretty much set himself on fire."

"So are you happy?"

"I should have enjoyed it more, since he did it in front of his own foreign minister and half the Danish upper crust, but it's still tough to watch an *auto-da-fé*. Even if it's your worst enemy."

"What about Irina?"

"She's going back to Krasnoyarsk."

"And I was so looking forward to meeting her."

"Don't be sarcastic, it doesn't become you."

"It was only half in sarcasm, to be honest. I really was curious about her."

"How are things on the island?"

"How long have you been gone—ten days? A lot happens in ten days."

"On the sleepiest of all islands? Like what?"

"Well, Richard's scheme to reopen the movie theater as an arts center got a clean *yes* vote in the Council."

"Laney, that's great."

"I wish that was all."

"Laney, stop playing with me. What's up?"

"Dana has a suitor—a serious one."

"Jesus. How does a suitor get serious in ten days?"

"It's been too long since your last bout with Homer, I can tell. I'll save a copy for you at the counter."

"Laney, I don't think I'm ready for this."

"Well, Taz, what can I say? I guess sometimes things that are meant to be just don't show up, after all."

He didn't know what to say either, so he said nothing.

"When are you coming out? Richard is pining for you."

"It'll be a couple of days. I've got to brief the folks at State."

"Well, don't be too long. Check in when you get here."

"I will. Thanks, Laney."

He hung up and sat for a while on the bed. He should have seen it coming. She was a beautiful, spirited woman. Only a fool would think a treasure like Dana would stay unnoticed. *How long did you actually think you'd have her for yourself? You pulled the 'oblivious Taz' act, and now you're going to pay for it. Great.*

He kicked the chair in front of him so hard his toe bled. Cursed a blue streak. Cleaned it with iodine. Stung like a bee. Pressed a tissue to it until the bleeding slowed. Then he put on his socks and dressed for dinner.

He walked the few yards to the Tabard and sat at the bar. They had a good menu, including Blue Point oysters on the half shell. He started with a dozen, and a salad.

"What'll you have to drink with that?" The barman was young, serious looking.

"How are you at making a Sazerac?"

"I've been practicing. You be the judge."

"Okay. Give me one of those, not too much Pernod."

"I use Herbsaint."

Taz smiled. The young man was clearly serious about his work. "Even better. Not too much Herbsaint, then. And when the oysters come, I'll have a Sauvignon blanc."

The barman went to work. He filled a highball glass with ice and water. Next he dropped a sugar cube in a mixing glass, added ice, rye, and bitters. Muddled the sugar, stirred, and eyed his concoction. Then he tossed the ice, swirled the Herbsaint in the frozen glass, tossed that, poured in the rye mix, and cut an orange peel for the garnish.

When he presented it, Taz said, "The last time I had one made that way was in New Orleans."

"Hope you like it."

Taz sipped it appreciatively. It took his mind off the fact that his life was turning to ashes.

CHAPTER FORTY

Debriefing INR

THE DEBRIEF WITH INR was exceptional only because it was to be attended by Jessica Lansman, the whippet from the White House.

Irvin met Taz at the Twenty-first Street entrance at eight, as usual. By the time they got to the INR offices, White and the spooks were already in the SCIF. He handed over his cell phone and went in, said his hellos. They seemed to regard him as an old friend. Some chitchat. Finally Taz ventured, "I suppose you'd like to hear a few things about Copenhagen."

White motioned him to desist. "Let's wait for Jessica." Price, the CIA case officer, rolled his eyes.

Taz was not fond of waiting in silence. As the last one to the party, he would've felt awkward saying nothing at all. "So Irvin, are you going down for spring training?"

"Down where? What's spring training?" Price and Jensen snickered. Irvin flushed. "Taz. Give me a break."

To the others Taz said, "It's okay. He's just learning the game. Right, Irvin?"

"I guess. But we did get the lead runner."

"Yes, we did. Because of good work on your part."

White smiled at Taz. "Yes, I understand you two developed your own private code."

"Any port in a storm."

"Taz, you'd be good at this, if you wanted to take it on full-time."

Roland Jensen looked first at Irvin, then at Taz. "Our boys think this was a bang-up job. My director asked me to convey his congratulations." His director was the deputy director for operations, so that meant something.

White clapped Irvin on the back. Irvin smiled. He had been brought into the boys' club.

Just then Jessica entered. She sat at the other end of the table from White and looked at him expectantly. "Well?"

"The prime minister has signed the contract for Kvanefjeld. The Danish police have arrested Nykvist on bribery charges. Goncharov has been recalled and is presumably on his way to a desk job in Novosibirsk. We're tying this one up."

"So far, so good."

All eyes turned to her. *Just what she wanted,* Taz thought.

"So, if this is all tied up, why are the Greenlanders still talking to Murmansk Shipping about the bulk transport contract?"

Nobody spoke. Ms. Lansman looked at White, then at Irvin, then at Taz.

"Well, Mr. Blackwell?"

"My guess is that one's being decided on the merits."

"I don't see how the merits have anything to do with it. We're not in the business of setting up lucrative deals for Russian shipping companies, are we?"

Taz didn't like the tone. He took a deep breath.

She looked at White, and then again at Taz. "I thought the NSC guidance was pretty clear. The White House promised Senator Glanville that his people would have a shot." Glanville was from Mississippi.

Taz cut her off. "Ms. Lansman, this is on me, not on any of my colleagues here. If there was something about shipping in the guidance that I missed, I apologize. I don't believe I was ever informed of any deal involving Senator Glanville. I did give a friend from the Greenland Parliament my assessment of the shipping options that they had identified, only because he specifically asked me to do so. I felt that assisting in that way was well within the scope of the guidance, given its essential goal of assisting Greenland in its effort to establish an autonomous government with real decision-making authority."

Ms. Lansman raised her voice. "Don't presume to lecture me on NSC policy." Riffled her papers. To regain her composure? "I'm not sure you have our interests entirely at heart, Mr. Blackwell."

White was rising from his seat, hands out, palms down, trying to pour oil on the water. "I don't think the shipping issue was part of Mr. Blackwell's brief. Don't you think you're being a little harsh?"

"I think Mr. Blackwell does what he wants to do, for reasons that are more personal than policy oriented."

Despite himself, Taz was impressed. She was sharp. She was exceedingly well-informed, and she had an agenda. Did his best to keep his temper and to continue in a civil tone.

"Look, Ms. Lansman. *Jessica.* Some things can't be torqued to fit policy made in log-rolling deals with Capitol Hill. There are only two or three shipping companies in the world that can do what the Greenlanders will need. Kvanefjeld is designed to be a three-hundred-and-sixty-five-day-a-year, twenty-four-hour-a-day operation, with ore boats lining up to take on loads in the March darkness just as much as the August sun. The Swedes, and Wallenius Logistics, know how to operate in ice, but their ice boats are all built for the Gulf of Bothnia. The Finns design the boats for all the big Arctic shippers, but they don't do the shipping. The Norwegians would be able to do it, but all their boats are tied up servicing their oil fields in the Barents Sea. That leaves Murmansk Shipping. They've been working on ice-hardened bulk-loading designs for the Greenland trade for three years. The Finns are already building their first three boats. They'll be ready next summer. If BHP wants to start shipping anytime in the next decade, they don't have much choice. And at this point, the Murmansk directors are panicking. They have a half-billion dollar investment that's about to go up in smoke. They will accept a non-exclusive contract, and they'll do it at a competitive price. So, for once, the Greenland government has the upper hand. I didn't tell them what to do. I just laid out the situation for them."

He took a breath, surveyed the room. "They need a shipper that knows how to navigate in the Arctic, has boats of the proper design. Do you really think some shipbuilder in Biloxi is going to know what it takes to carry ore through the ice in winter, from Greenland? Have you ever even seen what it looks like up there? Have you? I flew over Kvanefjeld yesterday, and the Greenland Sea was full of icebergs and floating sea ice the size of small islands. So you have to decide. Which is more important? Establishing friendly relations with a pro-western Greenland, which the last I heard was your responsibility as part of your NSC portfolio, or selling the Greenlanders out in the hope of squeezing a few ungettable votes out of a failing shipyard in the most conservative district of a conservative state?"

Ms. Lansman seemed momentarily lost for words. She was scribbling in a note pad. When she looked up, it was at Taz.

"I appreciate your explanation, Mr. Blackwell. Thank you." She was struggling with her composure. "Overall, the effort went very well." She looked around the table. "The NSC director will receive a full report. Thank you for your time, gentlemen." She gathered up her notebook and purse. Irvin opened the SCIF door to let her out.

Turner Price smiled at Taz. "Thank you. I think you may have saved our little project. She'll probably never speak to you again, but now she'll be scurrying off to the NSC director to tell him how her Greenland initiative almost went belly up doing the legislative shop's bidding. What a joy, to have the freedom of an alum."

✳✳✳

Taz decided he could wait for lunch until he crossed the Bay Bridge. He loaded his gear into the truck, headed east on New York Avenue. As he passed Sixth Street, he looked mournfully at the vacant building that used to be the home of A.V. Ristorante, a truly quirky but great Italian restaurant that had finally sold out to a developer after a forty-year run.

He had a vision of the dark, long dining room, with its giant fireplace and five-foot dragon andirons. Cheap Chianti and good clams. Old 78s of Maria Callas. It had been too long.

Washington wasn't what it had been. When Taz first encountered the nation's capital, the chairman of the House Science Committee would hold court in the spring on the Capitol steps, smoking a barrel-sized cigar. All were welcome. Interns or colleagues, it didn't matter. If you wanted to sit and talk, he would listen and talk back. Members from both parties argued and then met at the Monocle to drink and talk family and compare notes. The town was not so upscale, but it was friendly.

The House Interior and Natural Resources Committee was Taz's first real home in Washington. Its chairman was Mo Udall, from Arizona, one of the wisest and wittiest men ever to grace the Capitol's halls. He and his sidekick, John Seiberling, from the Cuyahoga Valley of Ohio, had done their level best to save Alaska's wilderness lands.

Taz continued out past Bladensburg Road and the beautiful green expanse of the Arboretum. Over the Anacostia, the benighted second river of Washington. Before long he was on Route 50, passing the Beltway, heading towards Annapolis deep in thought.

He had burnt some bridges that probably couldn't be rebuilt. You don't dress down a White House staffer without consequence. He doubted seriously if he would be getting assignments from INR, at least not in the foreseeable future. But maybe that was a good thing. His fees for the Kvanefjeld work would cover expenses for at least six months. He could figure out something after that.

And he could stop being a drifter. But what good would that do, if he was too late? If Dana was really headed towards someone else?

He crossed the Severn River. There was the usual slowdown, but before long he was out the other side, headed towards Sandy Point State Park and the bridge. It was late enough that the usual lunch crowd would have already left Hemingway's. He decided that might be a good place to stop.

There was a cold, stiff bay breeze blowing as he got out of the truck and walked across the parking lot. The boats in the marina were rocking against their moorings. The ones that hadn't been tied down properly were bumping the dock. Some so-called yachtsmen had more money than skill.

He climbed the steps a little stiffly and let himself in. There were a few people at tables, but only one couple at the bar. He sat down. Lucy came in from the dining room, took one look, slipped around the bar to give him a hug.

"Taz, I'm so glad to see you."

"Lucy. I didn't know if you'd be here."

"It's my last day!"

"Well, I hope they're throwing you a party."

"Oh, we'll have some fun. But Taz, I got the job!"

His mind was elsewhere. It must have shown.

"Taz, the coaching job you told me about. I got it!"

She was so happy she could hardly contain herself.

"Lucy, that's great."

"I talked to Dana Bonner. And she introduced me to everyone. She's wonderful. She put me up in her home while I interviewed. I've found a house to rent and everything."

"When do you start?"

"I don't really start until September, but the principal agreed I should get to know everybody this spring. So I'll start training with the team in April. We'll work together through the end of the school year, and then I'll go see my family and come back in August."

"I'm really glad it worked out."

"It was because of you. My God, I forgot what I'm doing here. What can I get you?"

He laughed. "The usual, I guess. A dozen oysters and a glass of wine."

"Sauvignon blanc."

"The very one."

She brought back a very full glass, wiped off the base with her towel. She hovered while he tasted it.

"This will do fine."

"Taz, I have a question."

"Sure."

"Would you be willing to show me the island? I mean, take me around? Introduce me to people?"

"Of course, but I figure Dana and the school moms will want to do that."

"Sure, they've been great. But I want to see your side of the island, too."

"My side of the island?"

"Taz, you're kind of, you know, well-known on the island."

"As a troublemaker, mainly."

"I was poking around, and it's like there's all these little groups on the island. The school families, the folks who hang out at the bookstore, the upscale tourists on Piney Island, the fishermen, the ex-hippies down at the trailer park at the south end. Somehow a lot of them know you, and, believe it or not, they like you. I dropped your name in more than a few places, and it worked every time."

"Must have been your effervescent personality." He took a long sip of wine.

Lucy smiled and flushed. "*Effervescent?* That's a nice thing to say."

"Well, I'd be happy to show you around, in any case."

"I'll be getting your oysters now." She ran off.

The oysters were good, and the wine tasted clean and sharp. Another waitress came up and whispered in Lucy's ear.

"Taz, I have to go. See you in Chincoteague?" He said yes, and she was gone, most likely to her party. He left a fat tip and walked out, smiling to himself.

On the way east on Route 404, he found himself humming the old reggae song by the great Jimmy Cliff:

> *You can get it if you really want,*
> *you can get it if you really want,*
> *you can get it if you really want,*
> *but you must try, try, and try,*

try and try,
you'll succeed at last.

He drove out Route 50 over the Kent Island Narrows. Traffic was light, but he decided to take the Route 404 cut-off anyway. Slowed through Denton and Bridgeville, finally turning south onto Route 113 near Berlin, where you could almost smell the sea breeze. When he got to Snow Hill, he made a left on Route 12, took the country road down through Stockton and Girdletree towards Atlantic. Then turned out to the island, past the Wallops Island airfield. When he rounded the last curve to cross the marshes, he opened the windows to breathe it all in. The cold hit him first, then the salty, slightly sulfurous smell of the marsh. It was good to be home.

By the time he hit Main Street it was ten. Too late to call Laney or Dana. He put his gear in the porch, found his way through the modest living room in the dark, and turned on the heat. The great thing about his small house—it heated up fast.

He looked around. It had been a long time since he'd been home, but everything appeared to be in its place. His message machine was blinking. He'd check it in the morning. He slipped off his shoes and poured himself a double shot of scotch. Got his wool Filson shirt out of the closet. Better than a pea coat. Found a cigar and matches in the cabinet. Opened the side door and stepped out into the cold night air. Barefoot through the cold grass, then the sidewalk, cheap aggregate concrete, over the asphalt of South Main, then the cold sand and sea oats he'd planted, finally the wood planks of the dock. Wood never feels cold, even when it is. Out to the T at the end of the dock. He sat on a cinderblock and looked out over the channel. The night was on the cool side, but the cigar tasted good, and the breeze was clean and fresh.

Night sky full of stars. Bright and plentiful. Big Dipper halfway up from the horizon. He could trace the handle's arc to Arcturus. His birth star was up there in the diamond of Libra. *Zuban ubi.* No clue what that meant in Arabic. The language of the best astronomers after the classical Greeks. One of the fifty-seven navigational stars. That much he knew. Long ago, he had decided that the correct translation was, *Lucky, sometimes.*

The channel was quiet, except for the occasional squawk of a heron in the marshes across the way. There were a few lights up towards town. He was tired, a tired man. He was conscious of a strange river of half-formed questions coursing through his mind. He felt at a crossroads. Where was his life supposed to play out? He had left DC for the island, and sheltered there through the fall. He loved being there. The simple things about it. The marshes. Sipping beer on the porch with friends. Bicycling to the beach, or the Church Street produce stand. But if the island is enough, why did he keep leaving?

If you're going to end up alone, where would you rather be? A dock in Chincoteague, or a café in Oslo? Does it really matter? Places aren't what matters. What matters most is who you share them with. One man alone might as well be on a strange dock, in a foreign café, or on a down escalator to Hell. He took a gulp of scotch.

He recalled the ironic story of the last two Jews in Kabul. As jihad and its attendant destruction came to Afghanistan, most of Kabul's Jews fled to countries nearby where they could at least cling to life and community. Two old men were left behind, the last members of what had once been a thriving religious community. They hated each other, and refused to speak. Like the Grateful Dead said:

I may be going to Hell in a bucket, Babe,
but at least I'm enjoying the ride,
At least I'm enjoying the ride.

Yeah. And he was going to keep enjoying it. Life is full of opportunities for experience. How do you stand on the bank of a river like that, and not dive in? How is that living? But somehow that wasn't the point, was it? Maybe timing was the point. There's a time to swim, and a time to get hold of a tree root and cling. But his timing was all askew. The women in his life came along on their own timelines, not his. Like Darly. She came along on her time. Whereas if he had a sign out front, it would read *always open*. Then he met the woman who captured his focus at first sight, and he wasn't ready. Timing's everything.

Her beauty was a match for Irina's. Just more tentative and less dangerous.

He smoked on. The stars moved in their slow rotation. He watched the lights of a tug that was holding a dredge barge in place down the channel. The band Nazareth had it right:

> *Love hurts, love scars*
> *Love wounds, and mars*
> *any heart, not tough*
> *or strong enough,*
> *to take a lot of pain,*
> *take a lot of pain.*
>
> *Some fools rave of happiness,*
> *blissfulness, togetherness*
> *some fools fool themselves I guess,*
> *but they're not fooling me.*

It was high tide. He took off his jacket, then his shirt and pants. Dove off the dock towards the channel. Hit the water and came up like a jumping mullet, gasping at the cold. But the flash of cold felt good. He took a few strokes, realized the outgoing tide was taking him south. His legs were already feeling numb. Dug in and kicked to get back to the dock. It was what he needed. He climbed up the ladder and shivered. Gathered his clothes, and wandered slowly back towards the warm cottage.

CHAPTER FORTY-ONE

Stepping Twice into the Same River

HERACLITUS SAID IT ALL those thousands of years ago: you can't step into the same river twice. The island was a river, in its own way. Constantly flowing, defined by the interactions of its own population and its visitors as they touched each other, circled, eddied, or collided. Summer was high water, winter generally still, slow, and cold. By March, the winter was occasionally giving way to signs of spring. On an Arctic river, you would call it break up, and bet on what day the ice dams would give way.

Taz woke early, made coffee, walked barefoot out to the dock. It was foggy, and he could just make out the lights of the tug that had been so prominent a few hours earlier. The dim gray ambient light, the mist, and the tug's rumble combined to suppress the early morning. Things seemed slower, dimmer, warmer. A new weather system had come in overnight, he guessed from the Gulf. He absorbed it for a while. The water lapping at the pilings, the cries of gulls and the sharp whistles of the oystercatchers. He couldn't see any of them.

He made his way back to the cottage. His little salt-marsh experiment was doing well. In the dim morning light, he could just make out some small crabs scuttling on the mud just underneath the dock. He let the screen door bang on his way in. Unpacked his suitcase and started a load of laundry. He would have to spend at least some of the day drafting a report for INR. He realized he was deliberately avoiding the moment when he would sit down and start on it.

Later in the morning, he would bike into town and check in on Richard and Laney. But he was avoiding that, too. Not sure he wanted to hear any more about Dana's new love interest, if that's what it was. Didn't want to run into her by accident.

Made a second pot of coffee, realized there was nothing in the refrigerator that even resembled breakfast makings: he'd finished the eggs and tossed the milk before he left. Reckoned it had been almost two weeks. Made the bed and straightened a few things. The quiet was almost supernatural. Dawned on him that it was Sunday. No parade of pickups on the way to work. Mid-March, so the campgrounds at the south end of the island were empty. He liked it this way.

His stomach didn't like it so much. It had been grumbling for some time, and now it was getting louder. He figured he'd go out and see Gina at the diner.

Almost eight when he got there. Gina was behind the counter. Sat in his usual booth, put the Sunday *Times* on the table. After a decent interval, she sauntered over with a pot of coffee. Put a hand on her hip and looked him over.

"It's been awhile, stranger. Something I said?"

"Gina, you know you'd have to use buckshot to keep me from coming back."

"Hadn't thought of that."

"No, I was just traveling."

"Where to this time?"

"Copenhagen."

"You do pick the strangest places. Now me, in March, I'd be looking at Miami Beach."

"Yeah, they'd be looking at you, too." Gina was 'of a certain age,' but she had held her shape very well.

"You're sweet. What'll you have?"

"Just some eggs over easy and home fries, I think."

"Okay, sweetheart. I'll be right back."

She returned with a glass of grapefruit juice. "Your snappy friend with the Maserati has been by a few times."

"Really?"

"Asking a lot of questions too. Kind of a nosy sort."

"Yeah, he's not really a friend. More like a business associate."

Gina sat down across from him. She spoke in a low voice. "I guessed as much. He was asking about you, sometimes."

"And what else?"

"Oh, the island. How it works."

"And what did you tell him?"

"I fed him a bunch of bullshit. Made it up as I went along. It was kind of fun." Wicked smile.

Taz laughed "Gina, what am I going to do with you?"

"I can think of a few things, darlin'. You just tell me when you're ready."

He reached across the table, caressed her cheek with the back of his hand. "You deserve better than me, you know that."

"Well, and when it comes walking in, I'll be walking out. Until then, you're the best I've got."

She smiled and got up to pour coffee for an old man who had just seated himself at the counter. "Henry, you old goat. How are you?"

The eggs were good and the home fries were, as ever, terrific. The place gradually filled up. Early church must have just let out. Folks weren't dressed fancy, but they weren't in work clothes, either. Pressed shirts, the occasional tie. The women in dresses. Taz left a ten on the table, paid his check at the counter, waved at Gina on the way out. She blew him a kiss.

❊❊❊

On the way back out over the marshes, he dialed Russ from his cell.

"Taz, to what do I owe the honor?"

"I need to get the skinny on one of your legal colleagues."

"Well, I figured you weren't inviting me to a golf tournament."

"No, but I am inviting you and your lovely wife to join me for a weekend out here when it starts to get nice, which is not too long now."

"Is fishing involved?"

"For you, Russ, no fishing. Just fresh local seafood cooked to perfection."

"Delightful. You know how I feel about fish guts and slime."

"Not to worry. All the dirty work will be done out of sight."

"Then we're on. Just let us know what weekend. We're not going anywhere in April."

"Okay. In the meantime, what can you find out about Brian Radford?"

"Isn't he kind of a freelance fixer for the corporate big boys? Works out of Latham and Watkins?"

"Yeah, he's been brought in by BHP to restart discussions with Tobytown."

"Ummm. Well, I don't know much, except that he's a hot shot. I'll see what I can find out."

"Thanks, bud."

His next call was to Irvin Friar. He got a machine. "Irvin, it's me, Taz. Need to talk. Give me a call Monday, okay?"

By then he was pulling up in front of his cottage. There was a girl's bicycle leaning on the front stoop. He went around the side, and found Suzanne sitting on the steps.

"Suzanne, hey. How long have you been here?"

"Hi Taz. Just a few minutes."

He gave her a hug, said, "Come on in." Unlocked the door.

"You want some juice or something?"

She looked around the kitchen. "It's kind of cold." She was a perfect thirteen-year-old.

"How about some hot chocolate, then?"

She brightened up. "That would be fabulous."

He had bought some basic supplies at the Shore Market on the way back. He pulled the milk out of its bag. "How are you at opening these?"

While she was trying to get the cardboard spout to open, he pulled the cocoa from the top of the spice cabinet. Then he poured milk into the pot and turned on the flame, low. Suzanne was fidgeting at the kitchen table.

"So, what brings you down to my side of the island?"

"Umm, you know, just biking around."

"Yeah. Does your mom know you're here?"

"I told her I was headed to the playground to meet some friends."

He let that one sit. The milk was hot. He spooned out two big helpings of cocoa and poured the hot milk. Put a spoon in each. Gave Suzanne hers, and sat opposite.

"Taz, Mom's got a new boyfriend."

"So I hear."

"Well, at least someone who wants to be her boyfriend."

"That's kind of a different thing."

"But Moyer and I—" she hesitated.

Taz looked at her, said, "Don't worry Suzanne, I won't tell anybody."

"We like you," she blurted.

He considered her for a while. *So brave.* Would he have ever intervened in the world of his father like this? Not on your life.

"Say something, Taz."

"Suzanne, you're the bravest girl I've ever met, other than maybe your mom. I like you too. Very much."

Suzanne sipped her cocoa. Her eyes were alternately on Taz, and downcast towards the table.

"But your mom has her own life, and she has to do what she believes is best for herself and her future, as well as for the two of you."

"But don't you love her, Taz? Laney said you do."

"Your mom is a wonderful woman. But we're still just getting to know one another. With some people that happens fast. With others, it can take a long time."

Suzanne had tears in her eyes.

"Don't take too long, Taz, please?"

He walked behind her and put a hand on her shoulder. "Whatever happens, Suzanne, you and Moyer and I will always be friends."

Suzanne pushed her chair back, put on her jacket. "I've got to go find my friends."

Taz walked her out the front door. When she got on her bike, he put a finger gently under her chin, lifted it to look in her eyes. "Thanks for coming by, Suzanne. It means a lot. And don't worry, it's all between us."

She smiled and wheeled out on to the sidewalk.

"Give Moyer a hug for me, okay? Tell him I saw a black-bellied plover out on the salt flats."

"I will Taz. Thanks for the hot chocolate."

And she was gone.

CHAPTER FORTY-TWO

Kayak Trouble

TAZ WENT BACK INTO the cottage, found himself in the kitchen doing dishes. Suzanne's cup, the little aluminum pot he had used to boil the milk. Wiped the counters, which didn't really need it. Straightened here and there. Couldn't stop moving, even if it was to no purpose. He was as agitated as a songbird without a perch.

He would have to present himself at the bookstore at some point. He was supposed to bring his guitar to a kids' poetry reading—Dana was involved. He had promised to play a few tunes around the edges. He realized with a start that the reading was tonight. Supposed to show up at six. Dreaded the face-to-face with Laney almost as much as he wanted to avoid running into Dana.

The island suddenly appeared to be a place where there was really no space to hide. Particularly when you had managed to make a complete hash out of your life.

He had a list of all the little jobs that needed doing around the cottage. Couldn't find it. Would have tacked it up next to the refrigerator; it wasn't there. Cursed, first under his breath, then out loud. What did it matter? There was no one to hear him. He was turning circles in frustration.

Caught himself, started to laugh. He wasn't this frantic even when his Russian friends were setting up to beat him to death. Now here he was, shaking at the thought of the slightest contact with a woman who he wasn't even sure he wanted to be with. He needed to go someplace, do something that would let his head and heart sort things out.

He went out to the shed, got his kayak paddle and a small dry bag. Put binoculars and a full water bottle in the bag, rolled up the mouth and tightened the side strapping so it was waterproof. Grabbed an old Pea Island baseball cap, muscled his kayak into the back of the truck, and took off for Piney Island.

There was a public landing off Pine Drive. He turned down the dirt road through the loblolly pines and parked on the needle duff in a little swale off to the side. Slid the kayak down the old decayed cement ramp, centered himself and the pack and pushed off into the water.

Paddled into a little channel facing a small marsh island festooned with 'No Trespassing' signs. Somebody's crab sanctuary. He had forgotten his knee braces. Blake had taught him how to rig bungee cords for extra leverage, but he figured he'd be okay without them.

Maneuvered up the side channel and came out into the main tide across from the south end of Janey's Creek Marsh. Could feel the tide trying to turn his bow up-channel. An uneven breeze blew from the north. Decided to cross there and go up the opposite side, in the lee of the Assateague shore. There were a few great egrets and even bigger blue herons; their smaller cousins hadn't come up from the Carolinas yet. Made it across and then turned north. Past the Janey's Creek Marsh and about a half-mile of open water to the south side of the next marsh island, whose name he didn't know. Then angled east towards the Assateague shoreline, opening from forest to a kind of sandy meadow area. Further north, there was a pronounced bay with old fishing weirs still in place, and a barbed wire enclosure, probably for ponies. On the other side of the channel some old duck hunting houses and a rudimentary wooden dock. He beached his kayak above the weirs and waded through a wet meadow to get to shore. He had forgotten his water shoes as well, but his Tevas managed to hang on through the sucking mud.

Dragged the kayak into some bayberry bushes where it was partly hidden, slid the paddle in next to it. Headed across the levee and the dirt road that the fish and wildlife rangers used to patrol the wilderness sections of the barrier island. A mown field immediately on the other side, and then some hedgerows leading to a series of bayberry copses.

Taz followed the winding paths in between the bayberry islands, and finally reached the dune line. Found a place to cross that looked like it had been used before. Ended up on a broad section of beach, not another soul in sight. There was a mixed group of sanderlings and willets feeding on the surf line about fifty yards to the south. The tide was low, and the waves were breaking on the sand bar offshore. The inshore re-break was nothing to get excited about. A little breezy, but otherwise, a pleasant day.

Taz dropped his rucksack and sat on the sand berm. The sun felt warm on his skin. Took off his shirt and let the warmth sink in. In half an hour, he was finally warm enough. Stripped, rolled his clothes into a ball, put his sunglasses in his baseball cap, walked down to the surf line. The water was deliciously cold on his feet.

He'd have to move fast. Once his feet started to ache, it would be too late. He let one wavelet crash just in front of him and then charged in. Dove into the foam of the next wave and came up gasping for air. One more dive, a few quick strokes, and he had to come out. Enough. Enough to give that clean feeling, the one where all the tangles have been washed out of your mind. He loved the ocean.

Climbed up the loose sand, over the sea wrack on the berm, and lay down on his shirt. Sun warmed his skin. Noticed high clouds in the sky, and some darker clouds forming in the south. Then fell asleep.

Rain woke him. More precisely, a single, large, hail-like drop that hit him dead in the forehead. By then the beach was showing the telltale pockmarks of a building storm. The sky was dark, a gusty wind had picked up out of the south. Taz sat up, shivered, and realized he was in big trouble. He glanced at his watch. Four-thirty. He would have to hug the shoreline, going back. He probably wouldn't even get to the ramp until six. He was definitely going to be late for the poetry party.

Struggled into his pants and flicked his shirt in the wind to loosen the sand. Put it on as he made his way to the dune line. When he got to the top, he had a better look at the sky. It was not a pretty sight. Dark to the south, the strange greenish hue that occasionally accompanies lightning storms. The lower cloud layer right above him held a lighter tinge, but the rain was already getting thicker. A storm curtain on the bay beyond the marsh and the duck blinds. Moving towards him. Dragged the kayak and paddle out of the bayberry and hauled them across the muck into the wind. Maybe he could make it across to the hunting shack before the worst of the rain.

Aimed the bow out into the water and pushed off. The wind turned him upstream and he found himself struggling to right his course. Finally realized if he paddled entirely on the right side he could work his way crabwise across the current. He grounded the kayak about a hundred feet above the disused dock. Dragged the kayak down under the dock and pulled some rope from his dry bag to tie it to a piling. Then scrambled up the slick mud embankment and crawled across the deck to shelter under the shack's broken roof.

Not much of a shelter. Only one corner of the floor that was still dry, and it was full of chewed newspaper and woodrat droppings. Rain came straight through the open roof at the peak of the shack, and dripping steadily through cracks elsewhere. Wind had a free time with the open windows and the place where the door used to be. Still, it was better shelter than a bayberry bush.

Lightning lit up the sky. Most of it was still south, beyond the rain curtain, now less than a couple hundred yards away. The storm opened quickly toward him, and gushers of rain came through the window and the roof openings. The shack trembled, and gave every sign of lifting off the marsh, but then settled down again. A board that had been nailed across one of the windows flew off and grazed his cheek and shoulder on the way by. He could hear the kayak banging against the pilings. More cracks of lightning, this time to the east. The bayberries at his landing were repeatedly lit up by the unearthly blue light.

Most of the lightning was now east, over the ocean. The storm took an hour to pass. Rummaged in his dry bag and found a half-full flask of rye whiskey. Tasted good against the wet and the salt wind.

The rain died away slowly until Taz felt able to walk the few steps to the dock. The kayak was still there. By the looks of it and the twists on the tie line, it had turned over a few times. He went back to the shack and stuffed his gear into the dry bag, slid down the embankment and untied the kayak. The sky was opening up overhead, and there was still a glow of sunset to the west. A few stars were emerging through ragged clouds overhead. It was after eight.

He paddled south along the shore, looking for signs of damage. Lots of limbs down, but not too many trees, at least that he could see in the murky evening light. There was still some chop in the channel, but he had to cross at some point, so he maneuvered above the mudbank at the north end of Janey's Creek. No boats out. Paddled over to the Piney Island shore just above the most northerly house. He could see what looked like a fire on a dock a few hundred yards down the shore, and he made his way in that general direction.

As he got closer, he picked up the sound of women's voices across the smoother water on the lee shore. One of the voices was surely Laney's. "Can't believe it. I really can't." She wasn't saying it rhetorically, but with finality. "Be careful. Maybe he has a reason to tell you these things."

Taz was only four docks up the channel, about forty yards away. He touched against the pilings on his starboard side, laid his paddle across his lap. The brackish water lapped gently, and the smell of pine tar permeated the air next to the piling. He knew he shouldn't listen, but he couldn't stop himself. The second voice was lower, more tentative. Dana.

"I know, I know. But why would Brian say these things if they weren't true? There's a lot Taz doesn't tell us. What about all that trouble he got in? Do you still believe that a Russian ambassador would do that because he lost a business deal?"

"Dana, I love you like a sister. But why would you trust someone you've only known for a week instead of following your heart? You have feelings for Taz, you said so yourself."

"My heart led me astray once before. That's enough. And Brian's not mercurial, like Taz. He has a good job, and he shows up when he says he will. He solves problems, he doesn't create them. He feels safe, and that's something, isn't it?"

"Baby, you're too young and too alive to settle for safe. I know it must be scary sometimes, but—"

"But Taz couldn't even show up for the kids tonight! He told you he would come, didn't he? Where was he?"

Stuck. He didn't dare move for fear they would hear him and realize he had been listening. He didn't want to hear more, but there was not a lot he could do about it. He tried to concentrate on the guttural noises of the herons on Janey's marsh. Thought about what he had heard. *So Brian Radford's the suitor.* Didn't strike Taz as the marrying kind. More of a player. On the other hand, Dana could definitely turn a head, maybe even change a player's mind. It's not just that she was great looking, but she exuded a kind of emotional vulnerability and quiet sexuality that had powerful effects on men. So maybe Brian was just an accidental bystander, after all.

Maybe, but that didn't explain how he got to the island. The only other connection between here and Tobytown was sitting wet and uncomfortable on a kayak waiting for the magical moment when he could slip back to the ramp and get home to some dry clothes. Brian was more suited to the player's Eastern Shore—Easton, Bethany Beach. So why had he shown up in Chincoteague?

CHAPTER FORTY-THREE

No Coincidence

TAZ WAS FINALLY RELEASED from limbo when Dana and Laney ran out of wine. There was some desultory conversation about getting a refill, then the sounds of Adirondack chairs scraping the woodwork and bare feet padding down the dock towards the house. Taz pushed away from the piling, and carefully paddled out into the current. In what seemed like a rather long time, he glided past Dana's dock and was on his way back to the muddy ramp where he could take out his kayak and head for home.

It was after eleven by the time he got back to the east side of the island. He left the kayak in the back of the truck and fell into bed.

Strange hyperkinetic dreams dominated his sleep. Cities were burning, he was fleeing, but the pathways were complicated, maybe impossible. He chose one that led into the forest behind his childhood home. He had outrun the crowds, but something was still missing. He awoke not knowing what it was.

He couldn't shake the sense that there were noises in the kitchen. Pots gently kissing, touching burners. Tableware being laid. Coffee perking.

The coffee smell finally opened his eyes. His bedroom formed around him; it took some time. At some point, he was ready to sit up and feel the floor under his feet. He entertained the crazy thought that Dana was making him breakfast.

Struggled into some cotton shorts and pushed his door open. Laney was standing over the stove; she hardly gave him a look.

"Well, if it isn't sleepyhead."

"Guilty as charged. What time is it?"

"Time for you to get up and take control of your life, that's what time it is."

"I'm going back to bed."

"Like hell you are. Come get your coffee."

He did as he was told. Sat at his kitchen table, watching Laney move around his kitchen as if she owned it. Sipped the coffee. It was strong and sweet.

"If I was Richard, I'd be jealous."

"If you were Richard, you'd be in San Francisco."

"What's he doing out there?"

"Looking for music."

"How long?"

"Not clear. At least the week."

"Cool. You can move in."

"Don't flatter yourself. I'm just here to drop a reality bomb."

"Can it wait until after breakfast?"

"Just that long, my friend, just that long."

She made fried eggs and scrapple for two, with English muffins. They ate in silence, punctuated by an occasional hum of satisfaction from Taz.

Scraped the last of the yolk off his plate with his final edge of English muffin.

"I'm wondering why the service isn't like this all the time. Or maybe I should ask: to what do I owe the honor?"

'What happened to you last night?"

"I miscalculated the weather."

"Oh, fine. Tell that to Dana."

"I know. Sorry. But that's really what happened." She was looking at him as if he was some kind of specimen.

"And what the hell happened to your cheek?" He felt his left cheek, instinctively. There was a rough, uneven line of crusted blood that didn't seem to belong there.

"I was in the duck house up at the gap when the storm hit. A board kissed me on the way by."

She wet a paper towel and started dabbing at the cut. "Jesus, Taz. What were you doing up there?"

"I kayaked up there to sort things out. Fell asleep on the beach. Woke up to dark blue clouds and lightning bolts. The most hellish storm I've seen in a while. Didn't get back here 'til after ten."

"Dana and I were on her dock. You should have stopped by."

He lied. "I came back on the other side of Janey's Marsh. Anyway, I'm sorry. I'll apologize to Dana."

"She's supposed to come by the store after lunch, if that helps."

"I'm thinking maybe I should go over to her place."

"Good idea. But you better call first."

"Is the mystery man there that often?"

"You are so oblivious."

"True, I guess."

"Look, Taz. You've been dilly-dallying long enough. It's time to fish or cut bait. Shit or get off the pot. Either—"

"God, please, no more clichés."

"Okay, so maybe I'm not Ms. Eloquence. I don't care. I do care about you, and you're throwing away your life. Your whole fucking life. Do you get what I'm saying?"

Taz was indeed wide awake at this point.

"I understand you got burned once. But this is different. Dana's real. She would like nothing better than to be in love with someone who loves her. And you do. But you won't admit it. So of course she's going to be interested when some hotshot lawyer tells her how beautiful she is."

"Does she know who he works for?"

"What do you mean?"

"I mean, does she know who Brian Radford works for."

"How do you know his name? Never mind. Who does he work for?"

"BHP. Or rather, BHP's Chinese affiliate. The ones who want to dig a uranium mine at Tobytown."

Laney stood stock still. "Oh, no."

"Oh, yes."

"You know him."

"I've met him—once."

"So this whole thing—not an accident."

"I don't know, but I don't think so."

"Jesus. Poor Dana."

CHAPTER FORTY-FOUR

Truth Ain't an Easy Road

"TAZ, YOU HAVE TO tell her."

"No way on God's Green Earth am I going to be the one."

Looked over his shoulder at her to make the point while doing the dishes.

"But I can't, for God's sake. I got it from you, and she'd think I'd been talking behind her back. She'd never trust me again. Taz, she needs someone she can trust."

"Then she's going to have to learn it the hard way."

"But can't you see where that's going to put her? How can we let her be used like this?"

She was sitting at the table, searching him for an answer.

"Laney, she has a choice to make for herself. I can't weight the scale."

"But it's not. It's not a real choice. You're acting like some Good Time Charley who thinks honesty will win out, and meanwhile this guy is a shark with a strategy. How do you expect her to make the right choice?"

"But what's the right choice for Dana? Do you know? I know what I hope for, sure. But I can't see things from her side. Maybe she's looking at the difference between being with a very successful, rich lawyer who can put her kids in the international school in Singapore, or living her life with a beach bum who can barely get his head on straight on a good morning."

"Oh, Taz."

"Look at it this way. When she figures out what the game is, she'll be standing on her own two feet. Then she can choose."

"Taz, was there some kind of scandal that led to you leaving government?"

He turned back from the dishes again.

"I wasn't going to say anything. But Brian told Dana that he had heard of you, or maybe read about you in the papers."

"And?"

"Well, Dana was telling him about the people on the island. When he heard your name, he said he had heard of you. That there was some misuse of money and they forced you out."

Taz whistled. He really hadn't thought that one would follow him. Brian wasn't kidding about having done his homework. He must have had a small research team on the case.

"Wow. I left government because of a scandal, all right. It was a five-to-four decision in a case called *Bush v. Gore*. I was political, and once the Supremes took things into their own hands, it was only a matter of time, so I resigned. But yes, there was a money fracas. I suppose you want the details. Have you got some time?"

"You know I do."

"So, in November, while the election was still being argued in the Florida courts, we larcenous bureaucrats were trying to make sure we had fully spent all the money we had been appropriated for the fiscal year. My budget guy told me we had about a hundred and thirty-five thousand unspent in various accounts. We were trying to figure out how to use it to pay advance expenses for a spring workshop we and the South Africans had agreed to put together on non-chemical malaria control. Malaria kills a million people a year, including a lot of babies. When we heard that the Supreme Court had decided for Bush, we realized there would probably never be a South African workshop.

"We were ready to throw the money back. But then I got a call from a pal at Interior who was working with SEMARNAP, the Mexican conservation agency. SEMARNAP had a plan to protect the last reserve for an endangered parrot species in Tamaulipas, the province right across the Rio Grande from Texas. A Mexican NGO actually came up with the idea. There was a development proposal for an agricultural valley that the parrots used for foraging. Up in the mountains above Saltillo. The NGO was prepared to buy the land and put it in a conservancy, and the owner was willing to sell it to them for less than market price—in fact, for a quarter million. But nobody had any money. Interior was tapped out, and anyway, we couldn't use US government money to buy land in Mexico. Bad politics on both sides of the border." Taz paused.

"But?"

"Yes. It turned out that the San Diego Zoo had a grant fund for conservation in Mexico. They were willing to use a hundred and twenty-five grand they had in the fund if they could get a match. And they had a contract relationship with Interior for wildlife conservation efforts. So we transferred the funds to Interior, they funneled it to the Zoo, the Zoo put together a grant with the Mexican NGO, and the NGO bought the land."

"Very creative."

"I thought so. I went down with my top staff person, Tanya Churchill—the woman who had put together all the nuts and bolts. Of course she had perfect Spanish, the best deputy I've ever worked with. Those mountains are beautiful. I mean, if I wasn't holed up here on our lovely sinking marsh island, I'd really think hard about it. It's like you're in Switzerland.

"Ernesto Yglesias, the head of the NGO, took us up. A beautiful valley with scattered orchards, nestled against an escarpment. The parrots nested in the highest part of the cliffs. About four hundred of them. Very pretty. They loved the apples in the orchards. So there's a picture of me and Ernesto, and Tanya, in front of a cactus full of maroon-fronted parrots, and it gets in the Interior Department's newsletter. And to put a cap on it, Ernesto is now the Director General of the Mexican Park Service. Nice conservation victory." He paused again.

"Except?"

"Except the Bush transition team was already on the warpath against last-minute deals by our side. We were the outgoing team, and we were apparently supposed to sit at our desks twiddling our thumbs and gnashing our teeth until they were ready to take over. So some bloodhound reads the Department newsletter, puts two and two together, and gets five. There were some charges of improper use of funds, but we had run it all through the State legal shop, so that was all covered. Still, they did their best to make it look bad. They even had the chairman of the House Resources Committee threaten to pull me up under oath."

"So that was what Brian was referring to?"

"Had to be. There was nothing else. And his minions would have found it in a ten-minute Google search."

Laney looked at her coffee, then out the window. In an official sounding voice, she said, "Sure glad we cleared that one up."

"Me, too. Keeping this dark secret has been giving me nightmares for years." They laughed together. A good sound.

Laney looked at him. "Taz, what are you going to do now?"

"I don't know. He's going to trip. Soon. Maybe he already has. And then we'll see."

CHAPTER FORTY-FIVE

Cold, Cold Heart

TAZ HAD ALMOST EVERYTHING he needed to close the trap on Brian Radford. Once he had the documentation from Russ, it would be time. Meanwhile, he needed to make an apology.

It was April, wildflowers were blooming all over the island. Pedaling down Pine Drive, he was struck again by the beauty of it all. When he got to Dana's house, he was relieved that there was no Maserati outside. She was on her knees in the garden, pulling some weeds with a gardening fork.

He wheeled up and dismounted. She didn't turn to him at first.

"Dana, I came over to apologize."

Very slowly, she straightened up and looked in his direction. She pulled her hair out of her eyes.

"Oh, Taz. The kids were so disappointed."

"I imagine. I'm really sorry."

"But you're being sorry doesn't help, Taz. You're just—just not really reliable."

He absorbed that for a few seconds. She was kneeling in the dirt, holding her fork. Her shirt was open at the top. Her eyes were wet, her disappointment complete.

"I could try to make it up—to the kids I mean."

Her look said it all. She didn't believe him. She shook her head.

"Dana—"

"You know I've been seeing someone."

"Yes, I heard."

"Well, maybe we—you and I—we should try just being friends."

"Friends."

"You're too dangerous for me, Taz. I never know where I am with you." She moved her hair out of her eyes. "I can't . . . I don't want to live that way."

"But I—"

"No *buts,* Taz. They don't change who you are. You can't change who I am. I think it's the best thing, really."

Taz looked at the ground, gave a little futile kick in the mud. She was still watching him.

Finally, he picked up his bike.

"Goodbye, Dana."

"Goodbye, Taz." He put his left foot on the pedal, pushed off with his right until he was in the saddle. Then he turned and pedaled towards town. He didn't look back.

✳✳✳

It was about three and half miles to the bookstore. Seemed like it took forever.

Leant his bike across the recess in the front window.

Laney knew right away that something was wrong. "Taz. What's going on?"

All he could think of to say was, "Strike three."

"Let's get coffee." He nodded.

"Richard, can you mind the register? It's coffee time."

Richard came out from the office. Looked at Taz. "What happened?" Taz rolled his eyes.

They walked the three blocks to the coffee shop in silence. When they got there, Laney ordered their usual: two double espressos. Taz said "Let's sit outside."

Laney brought the espressos. Taz had taken a seat at a brushed aluminum table on the front deck, which faced the bridge and a little knick-knack shop they both loved.

Laney put down the cups, sat, and looked at him.

"What happened?"

"I went over to apologize. She was in the garden. I said how sorry I was, and she blew me off."

"Oh Taz, I'm so sorry."

"There's more. She told me she was seeing somebody."

"But Taz, why didn't you—"

"That's the one thing I can't do. You know that."

"Yes, I know."

"I'm unreliable."

"Jesus. But did you tell her about the storm?"

"She never asked why I didn't make it. And I felt . . . well I just didn't feel there was any point in telling her. It wasn't going to change her mind."

"Taz, Dana feels so strongly for you—"

"No. She told me we should just be friends. She said I was too dangerous. It's over, Laney."

"And how does that feel to you? Are you okay with that?"

"Okay with that? No, not likely. I'm devastated, if I have to find a word. I don't know what to do."

"So what are you going to do?"

"Radford has been lying to everybody. I'm going to burn him like he's never been burned before."

"But what about Dana?"

"She's made her decision, Laney. I just have to accept it."

"Taz—"

"No, Laney. I can't. This happened to me once before. Right now I just need to do what I have to do. If I wallow around, I'm just going to get lost again. Last time it took me more than a year to get back on my feet. I don't want to go back to sleeping on the docks."

She looked at him across the table. "Taz, I love you. Richard does, too. We just want what's best, for you to be on the island with us. Whatever I can do to make that happen, I want to do it."

"Thanks, Laney. Really."

✽✽✽

Saturday came around, as Saturdays do. Ronny dropped by in the early morning to remind him that the jam was on. Later, Taz sat on his stoop, practicing some licks, trying to get a Mike Bloomfield blues riff down once and for all. A few people went by with appreciative smiles.

A van with four Amish women smiling out the windows slowed to a stop by the next house down, then backed up until they were just opposite. He thought they might be asking for directions.

"Can I help you, ladies?" Noticed that the girl in the passenger seat had buried her head in embarrassment. The driver, a clear-eyed young woman with a beautiful smile, replied, "No, just keep playing. We wanted to hear more." Taz complied. Smiled to himself. Considered what it would be like to love an Amish girl.

Most of the day he worked on putting in his new floating dock. His existing dock, known to his amused neighbors as "Shorty," extended across the rip-rap but not a whole lot farther. Its lower deck and ladder were still twenty yards short of the channel. He needed a way to put in his kayak and canoe. He had asked Bill Burton, the local who had built Shorty, to put the floater in. Bill and his crew were too busy on other projects for the moment. Taz decided he could do it himself. He was busy trying to anchor the rubber for the harnesses.

When Cliff found him, he was chest-deep, down towards the end of his dock, bolting harnesses and measuring lift. Cliff was a third-generation Teaguer. He had been everywhere with the Air Force. He was more cosmopolitan than some of the top officials at State. Also a first-class storyteller. He could smell a storm before it even showed up on the horizon.

"Looks like a fool's errand to me. There's a storm headed this way tomorrow."

"Shit. I've got to get this thing hooked up and anchored before then, I guess."

"You got the hawsers and brackets?"

"In my truck."

"Well, let's get started."

Cliff had been working with his clam sets and was already in his hip boots. He climbed in next to Taz. They bolted the U-shaped brackets to the floating dock and then looped the hawsers around the posts and tied them to the cleats on the floater. They had a reasonably stable result within an hour and a half.

"I owe you, amigo," Taz told Cliff.

"Not between friends. But the next round's on you, and that could be a big round."

Cliff had a lot of friends, most of whom showed up when he arrived weekly at AJ's Restaurant.

Taz nodded. As Cliff climbed back up the ladder of his own dock, Taz headed out for a swim. The water was clear and calm. Porpoises disported across the channel, diving for croaker. Cliff had told him the porpoises surround the croaker first, and then send in a second group to dive on them. He figured out that was pretty much what he was trying to do, except his prey wouldn't be nearly as tasty.

He came out of the water at five, showered. Put on one of his more presentable shirts, and some Bay Rum from Dominica. Grabbed a piece of scrap paper and started a playlist. Rustled some potato salad and a little leftover skirt steak for dinner. Washed it all down with a decent red blend that he found cheap at the Sysco Cash and Carry up in Pocomoke.

He parked in back of the bookstore, by the little town park on the channel. There were four or five other cars there before him. He heard Tom's harmonica wailing as he came in. Put his guitar case down and poked his head around the door frame to the back porch. Ronny was playing guitar—a spiritual. A local he had run into back in the fall was unpacking a banjo.

A couple who looked like they might be in for the decoy festival were listening with tentative expressions. Taz went back to the hall and unpacked his guitar. He had brought Big Mama, his apple-backed twelve-string. A Guild F-512, built back in the seventies when there was still good Brazilian rosewood available to specialty importers in New Orleans and New York. He had re-strung her over the weekend; she was sounding bright and sure.

He sat down in a straight-backed wooden chair with his back against the wall. The chair had no arms, which made it easier to handle Big Mama, with the added advantage that he had a good view of the dirt parking lot and the dark channel beyond.

Tom finished his song and looked over at him. "Howdy, stranger. I see you brought the heavy artillery. Good stuff."

"Long as I don't have to re-tune."

"Where's your A?"

Taz plucked his doubled A string.

"A perfect G. You're in."

Like Blind Willie McTell and a lot of other twelve-string players before him, Taz tuned his guitar a whole note down so as to reduce the tremendous pressure the strings exert on the neck. "I'll follow you."

"Let's make it easy on you and do some things in G."

They started in on "Sweet Sunny South," the way Taz learned it from the Ramblers. You play a minor scale against major chords, which makes for a strange, haunting kind of melody. Tom was there ahead of him. People were trickling in from the store.

Ronny followed with a tune of his own that sounded like a Piedmont blues. It was about the days before the great 1962 storm, when everybody on the island kept chickens. It had a great chorus for people to sing along with, and quite a few joined in.

The musicians were chatting among themselves, after. Taz was in mid-sentence; looked up to see Laney at the back of the crowd give him a meaningful look, followed by an exaggerated shoulder shrug. Right behind Dana, with his hand on Dana's hip, Brian Radford. Dana looked radiant in a blue version of the black cocktail dress she had worn at his dinner party in November. She had put her hair up. Radford was wearing a plaid golfing sweater.

Ronny caught his attention. "Taz, where you wandering off to? It's your turn."

Turned to refocus. "Sorry, Ronny. I'm back."

They started in on "Cold, Cold Heart:"

Another love before my time made your heart sad and blue
And so my heart is paying now for things I didn't do
In anger, unkind words are said that make the teardrops start,
Why can't you free your doubtful mind, and melt your cold, cold heart?

Ronny came in with a perfect harmony. Just as they were finishing, Taz saw headlights through the windows as another car pulled up outside. Darly Exmore stepped out and came in the back door. There were about twenty people on the porch, so she had to snake her way in. He saw Radford give her an appraising look as she passed him. He avoided catching Dana's eye.

Darly smiled warmly at Taz. She was wearing dark pants and a beige cashmere top that accented her figure. He gave up half his chair so she'd have a place to sit. Tom and Ronny doffed their caps to her, then went to talking back and forth, obviously cooking up something. At that point Ronny played the slow opening cadence of "I Still Miss Someone."

At my door, the leaves are falling,
A cold, wild wind has come,
Sweethearts walk by together,
But I still miss someone.

Darly's harmony was perfect and piercing. She reminded Taz of the great hillbilly singer Iris Dement. For Taz, *hillbilly* was a compliment, as opposed to *country*. Hillbilly meant plain and pure, no vibrato in the fiddle or the voice. No false moves, just the notes, and the timing, and the melody. Darly had it down.

Taz watched as Brian turned and slid back into the bookstore. Dana was still there, standing next to Laney, looking alternately defiant and stricken. Tom fished through his harmonica bag and pulled out a D harp. Looked at Taz, said, "Why don't you do something in A and I'll play cross harp."

Taz said, "Let's do 'Love's Made a Fool of You.'"

He capoed at the second fret and then hit the Bo Diddley beat in A.

They banged the chords together. Ronny was picking out a top solo. Tom was wailing the beat onto a pail with both hands. Some folks in the crowd were clapping along. Whooping and applause at the end.

Ronny said, "Let's do two more and take a break."

"How about a couple of jug tunes?"

Some of the regulars started chanting, "Washboard, washboard."

Ronny looked around, grumbled, said, "I knowed I shouldn't've brought that thing. Now I'm going to have find my thimbles, too." Rummaged through his pockets, secretly pleased. Tom dropped his harmonica back in the case and picked up the jug, which had been behind his chair. Cheers from the regulars. They looked at Taz.

"Let's start with "Keep Your Hands Off Her."

Tom blew into the jug a few times to get the cobwebs out. Taz started in G. They played it through once, then started singing:

> *I got a woman got great big legs*
> *I got a woman got great big legs*
> *Got a woman got great big legs*
> *Like rolling on soft boiled eggs.*

By the time he hit the refrain, most of the crowd joined in.

> *I got a woman, she's so tall*
> *Got a woman, she's so tall*
> *She sleeps in the bed*
> *With her feet in the hall.*

Keep your hands off her,
Keep your hands off her,
Keep your hands off her,
She sure don't belong to you.

Taz stopped playing so Ronny and Tom could do a percussion cadenza. They sang the chorus one more time, and then banged it a close, to wild applause and cheering. Except from Dana.

They looked at Taz again. He said, "How about 'Stealin'?"

Put your arms around me like a circle 'round the sun
Darlin' will you rock me like my easy rider done
You don't believe I love you, look at the fool I've been
You don't believe I love you, look at the shape I'm in.

Stealin', stealin',
Pretty mama don't you tell on me
'Cause I'm stealin' back
To my same old used-to-be.

Taz picked a little on this one, with Ronny and Tom providing a raucous underpinning. They sang one more chorus, this time with virtually everybody joining in. Then they put their instruments down, laughing, and Ronny called out, "We'll be back in twenty. There's coffee and tea in the store for a dollar a cup."

People moved towards the main part of the store. Taz stowed his guitar on a chair. A young woman he hadn't met touched his shoulder, "That was wonderful."

Darly moved to stand next to him, "You're sure in a broken heart mood tonight."

"A little, yes." He recovered, partly. "Old memories."

"I brought some whiskey. Would that help?"

He put his arm around her shoulder. "You know, I think it would."

They went out the back. She drove a Morris Minor. Opened the door, reached into the back, pulled out a fifth of Jim Beam Black. Taz said his Hail Mary's and took a swig. Waited for the inevitable impact, worked his elbows and quacked twice, and took a second. Darly was laughing.

"My uncle does that. The quacking." She looked puzzled.

"You have to acknowledge the hit—it just feels right."

"Okay . . ."

Richard came out, worried that the local constabulary would bust somebody for drinking in his parking lot. They each took one more pull. Darly reluctantly put the bottle away. Taz just bided his time until she was ready to go back in.

A few people were still sitting on the porch, as if they were tied down. The rest of the crowd was mingling in the main part of the bookstore, browsing, talking, and laughing. Darly went off towards the fiction section, where Ronny was holding court. Taz started towards the small magazine stand. Tom was entertaining a young tourist.

He was intercepted by Laney. She looked at him meaningfully, and said, somewhat loudly, "Taz, I have someone I'd like you to meet." She turned and gestured in an almost theatrical way towards Brian Radford, who was standing next to the checkout desk with his hand on Dana Bonner's ass.

Radford held out his hand. "Taz Blackwell, very nice to meet you." Why he thought Taz would cooperate in his charade only he knew.

Taz looked him in the eye. Radford was about two inches the shorter. He was still holding out his hand. Taz put his own hand back in his pocket.

"Brian. This is the second time we've met. Or maybe you forgot? Anyway, I've consulted with the Tobytown elders about the question you put to me last Thursday. They're willing to talk, but only to the top executives—the CEO of BHP and the Chair of the Chinalco Board."

Radford forgot his stage show for the moment. "You and I both know that's ridiculous. Do you really think that the CEO of a multinational mining firm is going to come to Salisbury to sit down with a bunch of smalltime farmers who are blocking a major mine that's on the company's priority list? We've got a thousand other ways to take care of that problem."

Taz cut him off in midstream. "I'm sure you do."

To the small group that had assembled to catch the scent of conflict. "Brian's been trying to get me to help him put a land purchase proposal in front of the Tobytown community. They don't want to sell, but he thinks he can convince them that a sale would be in their *best interest*. Does that about cover it, Brian?"

The room grew silent. Darly and the others watched.

"You haven't forgotten that first conversation, have you, Brian? You were driving a blue Maserati that you were very proud of. Bought with the proceeds of your last mining deal, as I recall, the one in Malaysia."

Dana was looking questioningly at Radford, and her eyes were just starting to tear up. The seconds seemed to last, as if time's envelope had suddenly been stretched out of all recognition. Then she turned and looked towards Taz. He met her eyes for a moment. He shook his head. He wasn't interested in hiding his disappointment. He was sad to the depths of his soul.

Taz looked away and turned to start his journey back towards the porch. He heard Brian say, tersely, "Let's go."

Then Laney's voice, "Jesus, Dana, call me."

And Dana, "What is this about, Brian?" He turned to hear Radford's answer but he couldn't make it out. Radford had his hand on the small of Dana's back, pushing her ahead of him towards the front door.

Richard said to no one in particular, "Now, that's entertainment."

A few people left, but most stayed, and gradually resumed talking, until Ronny called them back to the porch. He led the musicians through a few more tunes. Mostly mournful ballads; he sensed the mood. Finally, he looked at Taz, and said, "Do you still play 'Omie Wise'?"

"Omie Wise" was a great, dark Appalachian ballad that Taz had learned off Doc Watson. In A minor. He started up, Darly came in on a perfect fourth. A hollow harmony that fits ballads well. When they were finished, there was no whooping at all.

They were packing up the instruments. Darly was sitting cross-legged on the floor beside Taz's guitar case. He didn't know what to say. He was exhausted.

She looked at him, "I don't want to feel like a consolation."

He came out of his misery long enough to touch her cheek. "You're much more than that."

She gave a wan smile. "Thanks, Taz. I'll catch you next time."

"Okay, I understand. Drive safe, Darly."

While she was still making her way to the door, Tom slid by her, tipped his cap in her direction, and said to Taz, "Looks like you could use a whisky."

"Or three," Taz replied

Tom, normally taciturn, brightened considerably. "Back to the scene of the crime."

Richard came by with a stack of books. "To the scene of the crime! I close in fifteen minutes."

Tom said, "We'll be on number three by then, I expect."

"Fuck you."

"Don't delay. Time and whisky are passing things."

"Why, Tom, that's poetry."

"Thanks, professor."

✻✻✻

They drove to the Pony Pines in Tom's VW Beatle, circa 1969. There was a lot of baling wire involved. A few other cars and two pickups in the lot. They crowded in through the wooden screen door, let it rebound against the sill. A little too hard. Said their hellos and sat at the round table by the bar that the bridge engineers had used the night of the brawl.

Roxy came over, pulled a pencil from behind her ear, all seriousness. "What'll it be, gents? First one's free." Now with a mischievous smile.

Tom said to Taz, "Told you we might get lucky." To Roxy, "I'll take a rye. Please."

Taz echoed, "The same, beautiful. Thanks."

She came back with the drinks, and some bar nuts. Looked at Taz, said, "Who died? I mean, you look like you just lost your best friend."

Tom replied, "Somebody just as important, but not necessarily a friend, if you know what I mean."

Looking at Taz, "Sorry, babe. You know I'm here for you."

"Sweetheart, if that were only as true as I want it to be."

They turned to talking. Richard arrived, earlier than expected. "I got Laney to close. Didn't want to have to catch up to three."

"More agile than I was giving you credit for," Tom said.

Roxy looked up from polishing glasses, saw Richard. "Bookman! What can I do for you?"

Taz could think of any number of possible replies to this question. Richard said, "I'd love a scotch on the rocks."

"Dewar's? Cutty Sark? Johnnie Walker?"

Taz called out, "Test him. Give him a Famous Grouse or Teachers."

"Really."

"No kidding."

"We have Famous Grouse. Nobody ever orders it."

Richard laughed. "Typical Taz recommendation. I'll try the thing nobody ever orders." Emphasizing the last three words, and looking at Taz.

Taz shrugged. "The price of freedom is unpopularity."

"Oh. Yeah, freedom." They pretty much all chanted this at once.

"I thought this was supposed to be a feel-good drink," Richard said.

Everyone looked at him in utter astonishment, as if to say, "What the fuck?"

"Oh, I get it."

Roxy brought the whiskies. They touched rim to rim, threw down their drinks. Taz was first. He placed his glass upside down with great delicacy, looked at Roxy, and said, "Good appetizer. How about you just bring over the bottle. You can put it on my tab."

Roxy rolled her eyes. Got the bottle, worked it over with the bar towel, walked to their table with her hips rolling in an extremely provocative way, said, "Here it is." Then, looking, directly at Taz, "But if you think I'm taking you home after this, you better think twice."

"Darlin' Roxy, keep hope alive!"

"Taz, when was the last time you read *Macbeth*?"

"Terrible bloody play. Haven't read it in years."

She put her hands on her hips, looked at the ceiling for a second, then back at him, scowling:

". . . much drink
may be said to be an equivocator with lechery:
it makes him, and it mars him; it sets
him on, and it takes him off; it persuades him,
and disheartens him; makes him stand to, and
not stand to; in conclusion, equivocates him
in a sleep, and, giving him the lie, leaves him."

She wagged her finger at him, deepened her scowl, threw her head back, turned, and resumed her place behind the bar, polishing glasses, no longer deigning to notice them at all.

Richard glanced at Taz, and then back at Roxy. "Was it something you said? Or have you two actually tested this theory?"

Taz grabbed the bottle, filled their glasses, said, "Shut it, Richard."

Tom finally unveiled the elephant. "So, this time she really shut you down for sure."

"Worse. She took up with my existential adversary."

"With who?"

"With *whom.* With a complete con artist who's trying to fuck up pretty much everything I care about."

"That sounds bad. If I knew what it meant."

"The guy she came in with is a corporate lawyer who's trying to steal all the land in Tobytown so his Chinese overlords can put in a fucking mine."

"You mean the city slicker who had his hand on her ass?"

"I couldn't have put it better myself."

Richard tried to get in, "Taz, Laney—"

Tom just kept rolling along, "Buddy, I'm really, truly sorry. I thought you two were made for each other. 'Course, I get this kind of shit wrong all the time. But I really did. And you, well, you seemed more directional around her, if you know what I mean."

Taz looked at Tom for a long time, then smiled. "This is why you are my buddy. And you haven't got this shit wrong at all."

Richard sighed, "Oh, boy. This is going to be a long night."

CHAPTER FORTY-SIX

No Defense Like a Good Offense

SIX IN THE MORNING. Taz woke up on his dock with a banging hangover. Shivering in the cold April dawn. Looked blearily around, developed a rudimentary concept of where he was, and rolled off the dock into four feet of cold, salty water. The result was extremely edifying. He felt like a new man, except that his head was still ringing like a gong. Climbed somewhat uncertainly up his ladder, made his wet way into the cottage and took two Advil and a shower. Threw his wet clothes into the washing machine and turned it on. It occurred to him later that he had forgotten the detergent.

Morning turned from its marginally hopeful start to the kind of gray day that couldn't decide whether it was winter or summer. It certainly wasn't spring. Spattering rain from the north. Hardly enough to get you wet. Taz sat on his stoop, smoking a cigar, pretending to think. His cell cawed; he almost jumped off the dock. Russ's number. "Taz here."

"Hey, chief. You don't sound so hot."

"Well, if you don't count the fact that the most beautiful woman I ever met is heading to a nunnery in Krasnoyarsk, and the potential love of my life has taken up with my existential adversary, everything is okay. Really okay."

"That good, huh?"

"Never better. And how about yourself?"

"Self, good. Family, better. You should try it someday."

"I did. You saw what happened."

"That was then, this is now."

"Yeah, well, now, the guy I asked you to look into is hitting on the only woman I could imagine spending a life with. Have you got anything for me?"

"You're sooo impatient. Think I called without something to report?"

"Sorry. I'm just a little strung out on this one."

"Well, that's understandable. Both ends of your life are collapsing towards the middle."

"Meanwhile, I've been trying to find the solution to this one and I honestly don't have a clue."

"That's why you have a team, my man. That's why you have a team. So I think you're going to be in a better mood after you hear what I found. Radford is a hotshot lawyer, but you won't find him in court in Maryland or Virginia, or anywhere in the country, for that matter."

"Oh?"

"He was disbarred eight years ago."

"What for?"

"Election law violations. He was a Republican operative in New Jersey. I didn't get all the gory details, but I will after my intern gets finished combing the Newark *Star-Ledger* archives. It must have been pretty bad, though. They don't disbar you for penny-ante stuff."

"You're right. I am getting in a better mood."

"Oh, that's not all. Not by a long shot. He was expelled from Malaysia. Deported and told never to come back."

"Really. What's the rap on that one?"

"The BHP mine deal he negotiated with the village elders on Borneo? Three years after the mine went into operation, the dam on the tailings pond failed and a toxic mudslide killed sixty villagers. He had told them that the dam was guaranteed to be safe by the US government. No such guarantee had ever been made."

"Jesus, let's hope not."

"Right. So when he asked the US Embassy to protest his deportation, they shut the door in his face."

"If I were the ambassador, he would have been taken out and shot."

"Watch it. You're talking to an officer of the court. If he turns up dead tomorrow, I'll have to turn you in."

"I'd be a prime suspect anyway. Yeah, okay, so I'm now in a much better mood. You've made my day, in fact. Can you get me any documentary evidence on either incident?"

"How about both?"

"You're too good. Really."

"Well, the ambassador's cable about the Malaysian mine disaster was in the Wikileaks dump, and Brandi will be back from Newark today, so we'll see what she's got."

"Your intern's name is really Brandi? But Russ, truly. I can't thank you enough."

"Once a delegation lawyer, always a delegation lawyer. It's generally a good idea to answer when the Head of Del calls."

✷✷✷

Taz spent the next day sorting materials that Russ and his team had sent his way, gathering documentation for Eliza and putzing around the house. Sanded a few windowsills. Scrubbed his old oak table with Murphy's oil soap. About four, he headed out to the dock with a Macanudo to think. He was sure of his course of action. He also knew the repercussions were going to be power-packed and hard to predict.

Walked back into his cottage. Put on Tom Waits' version of Screamin' Jay Hawkins' "Heart Attack and Vine."

Liar, liar with your drawers on fire
White spades hangin' on the telephone wire

Gamblers reevaluate along the dotted line
You'll never recognize yourself on Heart Attack and Vine.

Taz considered the relative merits of the two versions. For the first time, he understood the line about there being no devil, just God when he's drunk. It was clear to him that God was drunk at least as often as he was, and with much more powerful results.

He gathered his file of clippings together, straightened his shirt, grabbed a windbreaker and a baseball cap, got in the truck. Turned the key and listened to the cough and rumble. Backed on to Main Street. His cell phone cawed. Again. He finally picked it up.

It was Laney. "Taz, Dana just called me to take her to the health clinic. When I asked what happened, all she would say was that she was giving Brian holy hell for lying to her, and he hit her. I'm worried she's in danger."

"Where are the urchins?"

"Thank heaven they're at their grandmother's."

"It's going to be okay. Take her to the clinic. Stay with her, then take her back home with you. He's going to be too busy to come after her again. And by two days from now, he's not going to be in a position to hurt anybody."

Taz headed north to the bridge. He was late, and Eliza was edgy. "I thought you were going to stand me up."

"Not likely." He was sitting across from her at a small table. There was a candle. The waitress had already brought water. She asked for a Cosmopolitan. He ordered a double Jim Beam on the rocks.

"Taz, what's going on? You're so grim it's scary."

"Sorry, Eliza. I really am. A lot is going on. And I have to tell you some hard things."

"Hard things? Are you breaking up with me?" Trying to inject some levity.

"Eliza, the radon story."

"What about the radon story?" Suddenly she had a rabbit in the headlights look.

"The whole Tobytown radon story was a put-up job."

"No way in hell. I had three sources."

"Who was your primary source? The one who put you on the story?"

"I can't tell you, you know that."

The waitress brought their drinks. Taz took a good sip. Eliza gulped half of hers in one take.

"You told me it was an attorney."

"Right."

"Tell me it wasn't Brian Radford."

Eliza went pale. She looked at Taz with eyes that seemed on the verge of being hollow.

"And your source in the EPA regional office. Radford paid him off." He had never seen Eliza speechless. "Did Brian tell you that his biggest account for the last decade has been Broken Hill Proprietary, out of Australia? Or that he's currently on contract to Chinalco, the state-owned Chinese mining company?"

"Oh, Jesus, Taz. Why the hell would he do it?"

"To get your help in persuading the folks in Tobytown to get lost. Voluntarily."

"Taz, I am so fucked. This is my career. That was my breakthrough story. Oh my good Christ."

Taz waited. He took another drink while the reality set in.

She was close to tears, but she straightened up and held them back. "How did you find this out?"

"He asked me to help him sucker Virgil Waite into a deal. And that's not all. To make sure I was sufficiently distracted, he moved in on the woman I was dating. Well, hoping to date, I guess is more the truth."

"So you want me to get back at him."

"No. I'm just being honest with you, which is more than he did. I'm hoping you will help me set things right for Tobytown. And if you're willing, I think you can get back some of the truth he stole from you."

"And how am I supposed to set things right for Tobytown? I'm just a reporter, you know. And apparently not a very good one."

"On the contrary. You're a terrific reporter. And he used that to suck you in."

She smiled ruefully.

He slid the manila folder he had brought across to her. "What's in there is enough to reset the balance. I don't think you'll have any trouble figuring out how to use it."

"Taz, you know I'll do anything I can to make this right."

"Yes, Eliza, I know. If you have any questions, call me."

❊❊❊

When he got back home, Taz called Rick.

"So the shit's going to start flying on Saturday at six."

"Are you talking six hundred, or eighteen?"

"Eighteen hundred sharp, commander."

"Got to get you coached up into military mode, brother. This is now a military operation."

"Gotcha."

"You mean 'Roger.'"

"Roger."

"So we'll be there by noon. You can give us the layout over lunch."

"Roger and out."

"Bingo."

Taz felt strangely reassured. Rick had been an Army Ranger before he decided the security business paid better and was a whole lot less risky.

His next call was to Ida's. He didn't even know if Virgil had a telephone.

A strange male voice picked up. A little gruff. It was Elvin, the young bartender.

"Elvin. This is Taz Blackwell."

"Hello, Mr. Blackwell. What can I do for you?"

"Call me Taz. That'll be a start. And get me Rodney, if he's there."

"Sorry, Taz. Rodney's down in Norfolk on business."

"Shit. Listen Elvin, do you know if Virgil Waite is home?"

"Pretty sure. He don't normally go anywhere."

"Does he have a telephone number that you can give me?"

"No, Virgil, he don't believe in all the modern equipment, as he calls it."

Taz thought for a second. Could he trust him? He didn't have much choice.

"Elvin, I know we didn't get off to a great start. But are you willing to do a big favor for me?"

"I'm really sorry, Taz. I didn't know who you were, what you done, nothing like that."

"It's all okay. But right now Virgil needs help, and he doesn't know it yet. Can you give him a message from me?"

"Sure can."

"Okay. Just tell him that the shitstorm we talked about is going to break tomorrow afternoon at six. I'm going to bring some friends down to make sure he and Bennett are safe."

"I'll tell him, Taz. I'll sure tell him as soon as we close."

"Thank you, Elvin. If this all works out, I'll be the one buying you a drink."

Elvin laughed, "Well, that would be something."

CHAPTER FORTY-SEVEN

Calm Before the Storm

TAZ WOKE AT FOUR-THIRTY in the morning, his mind already pacing. Brushed his teeth, thinking about the potential pathways the action could take. Not much he could do, really. At least not if he had designed the sequence of events properly. The whole thing should unroll like the German mobilization in 1914.

Got his bicycle out of the shed and headed up Beebe to Ridge. Turned right on the Eastside Road, sensing the beginning of pink in the sky above Assateague. North on Chicken City to Maddox, right turn, out past the ticky-tacky miniature golf world, around the circle, then on the beach road. Low tide. Stopped before the bridge to see if he could make out any rails in the murk. He could hear them, but that was all.

Once he was over the arch of the Assateague causeway, he sped up. Ratcheted the gears gradually, until he was in the second highest ratio the bike could handle. Pedaling with all his might. Had no idea how fast he was going, but it was a lot better than his normal twelve to fifteen miles per hour.

A cold wind pushed back as he pedaled toward the beach. There were a few shorebirds in the brackish lagoon north of the road. He'd look them over on the way back.

The sun was still a thought below the horizon as he parked his bike at the beach parking lot. Put his Tevas under the front wheel and walked out over the soft, cool sand. Nobody in sight. Not even the early morning shell hunters.

By the sound, he guessed the waves were pretty good-sized. It had reached mid-tide, which normally made for a good ride in this section of the beach. He put his glasses and his watch in his pants pocket, stripped, and made his way out through the foam to the first surf line.

The waves were breaking smoothly, though some sounded powerful. Those would require serious attention. As he waded and swam out to the bar in the half dark, he realized there were some big boys coming in sets, at irregular intervals. He had to dive several for cosmetic purposes, one to stay alive.

He could just make out the horizon. Reading the waves was difficult. Tried looking at the cresting pattern over the bar. Finally read one right, caught it just as it was curling to a roll, slid down the surface, felt the crash on his feet, and the powerful push towards shore as it enveloped him and drove him foaming downwards towards the sand. He held his body rigid like a surfboard. Threw his right arm out front, tried to steer with his left. The force of the wave turned him sideways, and finally, flipped him. He landed on his shoulder in the sand at the beach edge. A great ride.

He took wave after wave, as the sun rose above the ocean horizon and lit up Assateague's loblolly pines. Royal terns flew low above him, chanting to each other about where to find the first catch of the day. Hundreds of willets on the beach to the north, working the deeper part of the wave wash while the ever-present sanderlings worked the surf line. Perfectly dull gray shorebirds—until they lift off in flight. Then their wings flashed a black and white pattern worthy of a Burchell's zebra. Two ruddy turnstones in full color. Lines of pelicans following the wave line from the north. April, so mostly adults. You could tell them by their white foreheads. By early June their chicks would be perched on pilings, begging to feed by probing Mom's bill pouch.

After about ninety minutes, well and truly exhausted, he struggled out of the surf, and sat on his pants on the soft sand above the tide line, thinking. Mostly about Dana. So beautiful, with her slim waist, red-brunette hair slightly curling just to her shoulders, flashing eyes, tentative smile. So courageous. A single mom, fierce and proud. Such loyalty as a friend, and moral clarity. And yet, and yet. She didn't trust her own heart. He didn't—*couldn't*—understand.

He lay on his back in the cool sand and watched whatever crossed above him. Over a half an hour he saw three herring gulls, two royal terns, three common terns, innumerable laughing gulls, a lone osprey carrying its fish fore and aft, and a monarch butterfly, which one might argue should have been suffering from Seasonal Affective Disorder.

Put on his pants and walked north on the beach. Ocean City was a mere thirty-five miles away as the crow flies. The sanderlings gave him no notice. The willets, on the other hand, took flight at the first sign of trouble. Walked past the bicycle beach at the north end of the refuge, kept walking. More willets now. Thought he saw a red knot, but that would be early. They usually waited to come through 'til the first full moon of May, when the horseshoe crabs laid their eggs on the beaches of Delaware Bay. But there were always outliers.

Kept walking up the beach. Eventually, he found himself in unfamiliar territory. Higher dunes, stranger surf line. Then he saw her. A mother turtle, a big leatherback, digging in her eggs. He stayed back so as not to disturb her. *Must weigh four hundred pounds.* She was throwing sand with her hind flippers, covering up the gift she had just given to the earth. Her carapace was the size of a VW bug's roof. *Old, very old.* But her eye was young, as she looked him over and pushed her painful way back to the surf line. When she worked her way far enough out to float, she dived, and transformed into an elegant sea creature.

Taz thrilled, thunderstruck. Followed her trail to the surf line, his bare feet in the short foam, reveled in astonishment. Then he turned and walked back towards his bike.

Pedaled back to the cottage at mid-morning. He had work to do before he met Rick and his crew.

✴✴✴

Taz had worked up a good sweat. He put his bike in back. Opened the side door and pulled a towel off the hook. Headed to the dock. The tide was getting along towards full. He dove towards the channel and swam a ways out and back. Climbed back on the ladder on the north side, sat for a while as the water ran off his body. Went back to the cottage, showered and brushed his teeth. Put on Buddy Guy's "Mary Had a Little Lamb." The great bluesman's reading of the fairy tale was far from politically correct, but highly entertaining nonetheless.

He dressed carefully. Pressed khakis, blue oxford shirt. His wallet, cell phone, best French folding knife. Brushed his hair. Looked in the mirror. Saw a somewhat grizzled man. A combat veteran from a different kind of war. A little silver around the edges, a little grim. But maybe that was all right.

Parked at the diner at a little before noon. Sidled in through the front door as a heavyset couple was leaving. Sat at his usual window. After a suitable interval, Gina came over.

"A little late for breakfast, aren't we?"

"I guess. I've got some friends coming to share lunch. But I'll have the same thing as always, if Ramon will make it."

"Darlin', Ramon would make you corned beef hash at midnight."

"That's why I love you guys, Gina. But not the only reason."

She came back with two glasses of water, sat down in the booth opposite him.

"Are you okay, Taz? You're looking a little on the grim side."

"It's a grim day. But it will all be over soon."

"This has to do with that pumped-up jackass, doesn't it?"

"How is it possible that the co-owner of my favorite diner knows more about my life than I do?"

"You know, Taz, what I do is collect stories. The usual stories, and the weird ones. And sometimes the stories weave into each other. In bizarre ways."

"Gina, how long have you had this place?"

"It's been ten years since Ramon and I bought it."

"But you were working here before."

"Yeah, for me, it's seventeen years altogether. Crazy, right?"

With Gina, age was not an issue. Somehow she had kept the attitude that is the deep ground of all attraction. It was in her eyes, her walk, her stance, her speech.

"Not so crazy, I think. It's a good living in a good place."

"You're sweet, you know? That's why I'd run away with you in a second."

"I've got my not-so-sweet side, too."

"Which is today. I understand."

"I'm afraid so."

"Well, you come back when your troubles are done. Give me a full report. I'll show you a good time."

Her smile made Taz ache.

It was about then that two black Chevy Suburbans pulled up. The doors opened and Rick and two large teammates got out. Rick was in the door first, came over to the table.

"Taz, buddy." Looking at Gina, "Well, yes! Good morning, indeed."

Taz stood. "Rick, meet Gina. She owns this place."

"Wow. You do know where to dine."

Gina. Charmed, despite herself, "Pleased to meet you, Mr.—"

"Reed. Rick Reed."

"Coffee?"

"For three, thank you."

Rick's teammates were just then coming in through the doorway. No swagger about them, just a certain kind of confidence and a watchful look. They were black and white, but otherwise you could have substituted one for the other. Obviously pushed weights. Both very trim. No extra pounds. If they had been playing soccer, it would have been at midfield. The guys who can run both ways all day, tackle hard, and still get off a good thirty-yard shot. Alert. Rick introduced them.

"Taz, this is Bruce Tarrant, and this is Ken Berner. Boys, this is the famous Taz Blackwell."

Lots of "Pleased to meet ya's."

Gina brought three coffees and got out her pad.

Taz said, "This one's on me, friends. You might need a dose of protein."

Rick and the boys had steak and home fries. Taz had eggs and corned beef hash, as usual. When Gina came back with the food, Taz ordered a round of beer to go with. The boys brightened up considerably. They ate in silence, appreciatively. As you should. Only then picked up the beers.

Rick spoke first. "Suppose you give Bruce and Ken the basic layout. I've given them the picture from our phone conversation, but I think it might be good for them to hear some more detail."

Taz took a sip of coffee, pushed his plate away.

"Okay. Tobytown is a little black village that's been on the Eastern Shore almost forever. Not a slave place. It was founded by free blacks before the Revolution. It's south of Onancock, and has some purchase on the Bay through one piece of property that's owned by Virgil Waite, a farmer. Well, they're all farmers, pretty much. About two years back, they started getting pressure to sell, but they didn't know from where. There were offers to buy almost every property, and survey teams coming in uninvited. They got together and had a kind of village meeting to sort things out, run by the three oldest people I've ever seen in my life." Bruce and Ken laughed.

"Well, the oldest is Auntie Kate, and let me just tell you, she's as sharp as a tack and can see for miles and miles and miles." Just when they had decided he was certifiably delusional, Taz smiled at them. "You boys are just too young. It's a song by The Who." They appreciated the reference.

"So they decided not to sell, to hang in. Then they started getting pressure from the local cops. Accomack County sheriffs. Citations for all kinds of crap—not painting your fence, driving a '37 pickup with no taillights, you name it. So they started resisting. Survey stakes got pulled. Real estate agents looking to buy got doors shoved in their faces. Folks started getting arrested for all kinds of little shit that wouldn't matter to anybody. Believe me, I looked at the police blotter."

Rick added, "Turns out the sheriff's crew were all hooked up with the Klan." Bruce and Ken gave each other looks that meant business.

"Yeah, and with a big mining company out of Australia. They think they've found a world-class deposit under Tobytown. And they want it bad. But that's not all. They have a deal with Chinalco, the state-owned Chinese mining company. That's who would get the ore."

"Jesus Christ Almighty," Bruce said.

"Right. But even with the government pressure, the folks at Tobytown refused to fold up and sell. So the company sent in a high-priced fixer to persuade them to sell. He's been talking to me, because he knows I've been trying to help them. He created this whole fantasy about a radon problem in their houses, and that all they need to do is give him Virgil Waite's property, because the company has a new technology that will allow them to recover all the ore from even that small a platform."

"Well, mining technology has improved," Ken said.

"For sure. But that's not what this is about. What they really want is Virgil Waite's land deed. It's a special deed, used in Colonial times, that controls all the subsurface on the west side of Accomack County. If they had that, they could drill and blast anywhere they wanted to, and no landowner could stand in their way. They've been trying to get Virgil to sell, 'for the good of the community,' so to speak."

Ken, again, "So when they find out he isn't going to sell—"

"Exactly. Especially since the deed is in a particular form that only lasts as long as he and the *direct heirs of his body* are alive."

Rick put everything together. "So we're here to protect Virgil and his eleven-year-old son when the shit hits the fan. Which is tonight."

"Guess we better have a look around Tobytown," Bruce said.

"That's where we're going next. But before you do, let me show you a picture," Taz said. He pulled out a picture of Brian Radford.

"This is the Philadelphia lawyer who's been trying to put this deal down. He's clever, and he doesn't mind telling lies to get where he wants to go. He's also capable of violence. It's possible that the company would send in professionals to do what has to be done. But it's occurred to me that this asshole may have skin of his own in the game. If he does, it's possible he would try something himself."

Rick looked at his men. "Boys?"

"Got it." In unison. Then Bruce added, "Let's go take a look."

CHAPTER FORTY-EIGHT

All Hell Breaks Loose

AS THEY WERE HEADING out to the cars, Rick caught Taz's elbow. "Let's leave your car here and ride down there together."

"Okay." Not having a clue why this was a good idea. But his car would be fine with Gina.

Rick turned to Bruce, who was driving the second Suburban, "We'll regroup at the Onancock Wharf."

"Roger."

Taz slid into the passenger side of the Suburban. Rick was already revving the engine.

They pulled out of the parking lot in silence. Finally, Rick said, "Who is that woman?"

"Like I said, she's the co-owner. We're kind of sweet on each other."

Rick was disappointed. "Well, if you're in first—"

"Rick, I'm just tweaking you. I saw your tip."

"And I thought I was so smooth."

"Like a baby's bottom."

"Yeah. So is she seeing anyone?"

"There is Ramon, her longtime business partner. Maybe there was something there long ago, but she seems interested in making new acquaintances these days."

"And you and her?"

"Oh, we joke about it all the time. But that's about it. She's a great gal, though, Rick. So don't do it if it's just recreation, okay?"

"Hey bro, it's already more than that. She has magnetism, you know what I mean?"

"I believe I do."

A little more silence as they cruised down Route 13 towards the Onancock Road. Finally, Rick said, "I really hope they're not pros."

"What's got you worried?"

"Well, we don't know the place. For all we know, they might already be there. We're trying to defend against gunners we won't recognize, in terrain we don't know, and if they're smart, they'll come at night. You got any bright ideas?"

"Figured that's why I brought you."

"No, no, Taz. I'm a gunner. My boys are gunners. We're very good. You're the bright idea man. Give it some thought."

Which Taz did, as they continued to cruise past Accomac.

It took about ten minutes. As they turned off to the northern road to Onancock, Taz said, "I've been to Virgil's—only once or twice, but still. Maybe I do have an idea."

"Now we're cooking. I can see your wheels turning."

"There's a little hill to the side of the village. It's where they have their town meetings. Bald crown on top, surrounded by beech woods. What if we took Virgil and Bennett up there to do a little camping? Off to the side, of course. Or, two of us could do the hill and two could watch Virgil's house."

"You know, you actually have some potential." A wicked smile. "With about four years of basic and advanced training."

"Thanks, bud. I appreciate the thought. But basic and marijuana don't work that well together."

"You're such a hippie. Other than that, I could probably get to like you."

"What are we going to do with the dirigibles?"

"What?"

"Well, been a long time since two armored Suburbans pulled into Tobytown."

"Oh, that. We've got a friend with a garage just south of Onancock. We're going to stow them there."

They did just that. Stopped at Rick's friend's garage, which was just off the Bobtown Road down by Whealton's wharf, climbed into an old Dodge pickup for the last leg. Taz watched as Rick and the boys loaded their hardware into the toolbox in back. They had clearly done this more than once. Routine. Quiet and efficient, with deadly certainty. Within a few minutes, they were on the way to Tobytown. They approached Ida's from the south, slipping unnoticed inside the perimeter monitored by the county police.

They parked in the bare dirt lot behind Ida's. From there, Ida's looked more like a crab-picker's ramble than a successful restaurant. While the boys unloaded their gear, Taz and Rick went in to pay their respects to Rodney. Then all three walked the few hundred yards to Virgil's place.

Taz introduced his friend to Virgil and Rodney. "This is Rick Reed. He and his team are going to help you and Bennett stay safe while things play out."

Virgil turned to Bennett, who was standing behind him with a worried expression on his face. "Bennett, the side garden needs weeding. You take care of that, hear?"

"Yessir." Bennett pulled a weeding fork from a fruit basket full of tools by the door and headed out.

Virgil turned to Taz. "Do you really think there's danger?"

"I think we have to assume that Radford has done his research on you, just like he did on me. Deeds are public documents. If he knows about the *fee tail*, or if the company's landmen do, then the danger is between the time that he figures out we're not dealing and when we kick him out of the state for good. "

"Okay, Taz. What do we do?"

"I've got some friends on top of Council Hill. They're good—former Army Rangers. I'm going to go up there with you and Bennett, and then Rick and I are going to watch your house."

Virgil got up slowly and walked to the door, feeling the gravity of the situation. Taz got up to stand by him. "It's going to come out fine, Virgil. This is the last chapter."

Rick came over, looked them both in the eye. "My colleagues and I, we don't make a practice of losing clients." A slight smile and glint in his eye.

Virgil laughed to himself. Opened the door, called out to Bennett. "Son, you've done enough for now. We're going to go camping. Get your sleeping bag and a couple of water bottles, okay?"

It seemed that this sudden turn of events did not displease the young Mr. Waite.

After Taz had deposited Virgil and Bennett with Bruce and Ken, he jogged back down to the house. Rick was walking around looking the scene over, standing by one window or another, peering out at the road.

"I don't like the sight lines. The thing is clapboard, so there's no protection, once they have a sense of where we are. They'll just fire bursts. I feel like the first little piggy."

Taz surveyed the scene, trying to see it through Rick's eyes. Their shadows were getting long. The house was an old gray clapboard structure, one story, resting uncertainly on brick pillars, which raised it about three feet off the ground—a good idea in an area so close to the marsh. Most of the house was surrounded by azaleas and rhododendrons. There was a large metal propane tank out back. Probably for the stove and the hot water heater. Having been under his own house a lot recently, Taz knelt to look between two rhododendrons. The ground under the house was uneven but dry. There were no ducts, since Virgil didn't believe in air conditioning. In one corner, there were some rolls of metal screen.

He looked at Rick. "How about if we wait underneath?"

Rick took a quick look. "Right. Let's get the gear."

They went back to the truck and pulled two more duffels from the tool can. Taz was surprised by their weight.

By the time he had lugged his duffel back to the house, Rick was already underneath, rearranging things. He arranged a firing position underneath the front porch, and put two rolls of wire in front of it in an L-shape. Did the same under the right rear corner. They would be about twenty feet apart, but it would be easy to cover each other.

Next, he went to the opposite side from Taz's position, marked his way ten feet from the house, and put a clay stake ankle deep in the dirt. Another ten feet off the left rear corner, another off the center of the back wall, and another off Taz's corner. He strung trigger wire between the stakes, and attached what looked like percussion grenades every dozen feet or so, except for Taz's corner. Covered the grenades with leaves and dry grass.

"Don't want to deafen you—at least not permanently."

"Yeah, that wouldn't be good for my career as a rock guitarist."

"Aren't you rock and roll boys all deaf anyway?"

"Our strategy is to die before we go deaf."

"Better get some water. It could be a long night."

They got some plastic water bottles out of the truck. Pulled on sweatshirts—it was cooling off. Headed back to the house. Rick reached into the duffel Taz had lugged onto the front porch and handed him a very compact assault rifle.

"You ever use one of these?"

"No." Taz looked it over. He'd never seen anything like it. It was short, but the barrel length was still substantial. The manufacturer had apparently figured out how to mount the bolt carrier behind the pistol grip. It looked for all the world like an advanced industrial stapler. With a barrel full of hollow-point 5.56 millimeter bullets.

"It's a Heckler & Koch 9mm submachine gun. So, what have you shot?"

"A twenty-two."

"Jesus save us."

"With my dad. I was twelve. In the side yard. Aiming at paper targets."

"And that was when? In nineteen seventy-five? Lord, at least tell me you hit them."

"I hit them."

After Rick showed him the basic operation of the firearm, as he called it, they discussed what he called the rules of engagement. The idea was to wait, at least until there was a breaking and entering, or a shot fired, before they unloaded. Aim for the legs first. If he brought pals along, make sure to take them down before going after Radford.

⚹⚹⚹

They took their positions and chatted back and forth for a while, mostly to quiet Taz's nerves. But the distance was enough that the talk eventually died away, and Taz was left to his own thoughts. It was dusk.

Taz sipped some water. Rick had put flashlights in their duffels, but they weren't to use them except in an emergency. About ten, the moon rose, and Taz could see a little better, though his own position was still black as coal.

Night sounds. The moon had brought out the chorus frogs down the marsh. The occasional bark of a leopard frog. Toads trilling from somewhere near the creek. Crickets pretty much all around. A croak from a great blue heron, then the sound of those huge wings flapping and lifting off. Two raccoons crept silently across the lane towards the water line.

He was brought fully alert by the sound of cars rolling to a stop in dirt and loose gravel. He rubbed his eyes and saw Radford's Maserati, followed by a BMW sedan. He snapped a twig. Rick snapped back. Two men got out of the BMW. After a suitable interval, the Maserati's door opened and Radford emerged.

The moon was high and the three of them were clearly delineated in the silver light. Radford was carrying a pistol. The other two had what looked like AK-47s. Radford motioned one of them around towards the back of the house. He moved to his right, in the direction of Taz's corner. The other one positioned himself behind and to the left of Radford as he approached the door.

Taz, who had been watching over his shoulder, now turned to face the gunman behind the house. He had positioned himself to cover anyone who might try to prevent Virgil from getting away through the back door or window.

He heard Radford knocking, then pounding the front door. "Virgil Waite? It's Brian Radford. I need to talk to you."

Silence. Frogs. A screech owl's quaver.

Then the sound of a boot kicking in Virgil Waite's door.

A sharp series of cracks as Rick took out the front gunman.

The gunman opposite Taz yelled something in Chinese, fired a random burst towards the house, and then started moving quickly around towards the front. Taz opened up on his legs, just as one of the pressure grenades went off with a deafening boom. The gunman fell like a stone, twitching and screaming.

Taz's head was spinning and he had a high-pitched buzzing in his ears. He crawled out from the crawl space, looked through the rear screen door, and saw Radford cross the back bedroom. Now he was moving quickly from room to room, checking any drawer, any shelf. He was tossing books, looking under mattresses, cursing a blue streak. He finally exited the room, heading back towards the front door. Then a muffled but still startling crack, and a loud "Fuck!"

Rick called, "Taz—over here!"

Taz straightened from his crouch. Walked a little unsteadily around the corner to the front door. Brian Radford was sitting splay-legged on the dirt with a look of astonishment on his face. His knee appeared to have been shattered. Rick was standing with his Tavor pointed at Radford's head.

Rick looked at Taz. "I had to drag his sorry ass out here before he bled all over the floor. Time to call the police?"

"Not just yet."

He bent down to look his nemesis in the eye.

"Which hand did you use?"

Brian seemed to be trying to come to.

"Use?"

"When you hit her."

"Does it matter?"

Taz produced a piece of paper and a pen.

"Write your confession."

Brian looked at him blankly.

"Look. I'm going to let you bleed to death right here unless you put down what you came here to do."

He started writing, with his right hand.

Taz let him finish. Rick was now looking at both of them.

Radford finished, dropped the pen.

Taz grabbed him by the collar and pulled him up. He screamed in pain.

Taz turned to Rick. "One more thing. Can you help me get him into the kitchen?"

They dragged Radford down the hall and into the kitchen. Taz jammed a chair close to the stove, pushed him into the chair. Turned on the front burner. The son-of-a-bitch had just enough time to squeal, "Don't!"

Taz grabbed his wrist with both hands. "Rick—hold him." He pulled the hand to the burner. Radford screamed and twisted. Taz slammed his hand palm down on the iron grill. Rick held him fast by the shoulders. Taz pressed his all-time least favorite lawyer's right hand on the grill until it smoked and he could smell burnt flesh.

When the police got there, about half an hour later, Radford was whimpering in the corner. The two Chinese toughs were tied up outside, bleeding. Taz suddenly felt very tired.

CHAPTER FORTY-NINE

The Rubble is Still Smoking

IT WAS ALMOST DAWN by the time they had finished answering the local cops' questions and given their statements to the FBI agent whom Rick had called in. The ambulances had come and gone, with Radford and the gunmen bandaged, in manacles. When one of the paramedics objected to the cuffs, Rick said, "They're only leg-shot, you know. They deserved worse."

Bruce and Ken had come down from the hill with Virgil and Bennett in tow. Virgil made a pot of coffee and invited them all in to sit before they went their separate ways.

When he had finished filling their cups, Virgil said grace.

"Oh God, how precious is this life you have given us. Thank you for sending these capable men to protect us in our time of need. Bless them, Lord. And thank you for helping us to find Taz, our friend. Please look after him with special care. Amen."

To which Rick said, "Amen, indeed." Looked at Taz. "And he could sure use it."

They laughed. There was some discussion recounting the events. Virgil and Bennett had camped in the beech woods, just off the Council circle. Bennett had a good sleep. Virgil couldn't sleep, sat up with Bruce and Ken, who had established covering positions. When they heard the shooting, Virgil wanted to come down to help but Bruce made clear that they should wait until they got the okay call from Rick.

Rick talked a little about how it went down at the house. Taz could see the sky lightening in the east, figured it was time to go. Rick was already rising from his chair. Virgil grabbed his hand. "Go well, Rick."

Rick turned to Taz, gave him a bear hug. "You were steady out there, buddy, steady. There's no better word."

It took Taz a few seconds to refill his lungs. "You've been steady for me for years. I owed you fifteen minutes, at least."

Smiles all around. Rick and the boys threw their gear into the truck and clambered in after the duffels. Bennett had gone off to get a little extra shuteye. Virgil looked at Taz.

"You got a few minutes more?"

"Sure."

"You've done so much, Taz, I don't like to ask more. But what happens now?"

"Well, if everything has gone the way we planned, last night's Salisbury TV news had the whole story on Mr. Radford. What he was doing, who he was working for, and why. In addition, the report would have had the fact that he's lawyering illegally, since he was disbarred years ago. Also that he was kicked out of Malaysia for similar shenanigans five years back, and because his mine there killed more than sixty local villagers."

Virgil's eyes widened perceptibly. "How?"

"The dam on the tailings pond failed. The village was downstream. He had promised the village head man that they would be safe."

"My God. That boy is going to have a hard time with Saint Peter. "

"Yes, he is. And in between now and then, he's going to spend a lot of time in jail."

"But the county D.A. is in their pocket, right?"

"Maybe. But the charges will be brought by the US Attorney for Northern Virginia."

Virgil looked at Taz. "I'm a good farmer. I know what it is to plan, plant, care, and harvest. What I see is that you're a good farmer, too. I'm not sure how you did this, but I . . . we all of us owe you a debt of gratitude."

Taz fought back tears. "Coming from you, Virgil, that means a lot. You're one of the bravest men I've ever met."

CHAPTER FIFTY

Finding His Way Back Home

RICK WAS PROBABLY HALFWAY back to DC when Taz hitched a ride with Hubert Shadwell to Salisbury later in the morning. Wandered around the center of town for a half hour or so, found a bus to Temperanceville. That still left him about seven miles from home. He started walking on the country road towards Atlantic. Thought about hitching, but there weren't many cars on the road, and anyway people were too scared to pick each other up anymore.

It wasn't an unpleasant day—a little overcast, but that cooled it off, too. He had walked about two miles when an antique farm truck passed, barely doing twenty. It was followed closely by a retinue of irritated drivers. The last car pulled over just twenty yards beyond Taz, and started backing up towards him. His adrenalin spiked until he realized it was Laney.

She looked through the open passenger window. "Goin' my way, handsome?"

"Believe I am."

"Well, you know where the handle is."

He got in. She pulled out. The radio was on, playing a Charlie Pride song that he hadn't heard in ages. He said, "Thanks," and just listened for a while.

Laney looked his way when the song finished. "Dana came back from the hospital last night. She's not doing so good."

"Did he hurt her that bad?"

"No, it's not that. She said he only punched her three times, and she's a fast healer, physically. It's the spiritual side. She's broken up seven ways from Sunday."

Taz looked out the window and thought that one over.

"It's not your fault, you know. Really not. Sometimes things that ought to work out just don't. But she's lost everything emotional she thought she had. Except her kids. She doesn't trust herself anymore."

They were passing the road to the lobster lady's shed in Atlantic. East on the same road led to a nice marsh landing that the state, for some reason, didn't maintain, or tell anybody about, either.

"And she's afraid, too. Nobody knows where Brian is."

"Well, you can tell her that one's taken care of."

"What do you mean?"

"I mean he's taken care of. He's in the county lockup over at Exmore. In about two days, he'll be transferred to a federal maximum-security prison in Delaware."

"Taz, what are you talking about?"

"He did his best to kill Virgil and Bennett Waite last night. Some friends and I stopped him. He's got a shattered knee and a badly burnt hand that will take a long time to heal," Taz said evenly.

Laney pulled over. "Why would he want to kill Virgil and Bennett? I know he and his Chinese company were dragged over the coals on TV last night, but that wouldn't have been Virgil's doing. But how did you . . . I mean, what the hell have you been up to?"

"It's a long story. I suspected he might try something desperate to get the deed they want in Tobytown. So I called some friends, and we were ready when he and his Chinese pals showed up."

"Chinese pals? I thought it was an Australian company."

"BHP might not have even known much about it. I think he had an independent relationship with Chinalco, the Chinese company that really wanted this mine to go forward."

She gave him a look. "How did his hand get burned, Taz?"

"Well, after my friend Rick shot his knee through, I dragged his sorry ass into the house and put his hand on the stove with an open burner. I made sure it was the one he hit Dana with."

"My God, Taz."

She was silent for a long while. Tears rolled down her cheeks. She pulled back onto the road, turned right on Route 175, passed the airstrip and radar complex at the Wallops airfield. The road turned east towards the end of the runway. They were facing Chincoteague across the bay. The marshes opened on either side of the causeway. The little blue herons had still not come in, but there were plenty of egrets—snowies and greats.

She dropped him off in front of his house. As he was opening the door she reached over and put her hand on his shoulder.

"You know, Taz, I was feeling sorry for Dana. But now I'm feeling sorry for you, too."

"Thanks for the ride, Laney."

✻✻✻

That evening he put on a sweatshirt and popped the top on a can of Modelo. Went out to the dock. There were still some ragged clouds in the sky, the stars were a little random. Still worth watching. He looked up and wondered whether the early warblers were already flying. Warblers generally migrate at night, high in the sky. Some of them come from as far away as Venezuela and the Guianas. Nobody knows exactly how they do it. Some think they navigate by starlight, and others say they're reading the earth's magnetic field. What he did know was how much he loved seeing them return from the south, these little penny-weight beings, full of beautiful spring color, inexplicable descendants of the dinosaurs. He made a mental note to clean the lenses on his binoculars.

He finished the beer and went inside. Almost immediately fell into bed and a very, very deep sleep.

CHAPTER FIFTY-ONE

Ashes of Love

THE LOCAL PAPERS HAD most of the story, if you put two or three articles together. The headlines told it: *Feds Throw Book at Disbarred Attorney; BHP Lawyer Accused in Attempted Murder for Hire; Australian Mining Giant Disclaims Interest in Delmarva.*

The *Shore Daily News* reported that Radford had been working on commission for Chinalco. It also noted that he had been badly injured "in the course of being brought to justice." *The Daily Times,* out of Salisbury, spent more time on the Tobytown side of the story, recounting the radon fraud and Chinalco's stake in the uranium play. He figured Eliza had probably helped them put the story together. There was a pullout interview with Virgil, who thanked God for intervening on their behalf in what had been a difficult time. Said the folks of Tobytown appreciated the help they had gotten from "a number of friends from outside." He finished by expressing the hope that the community could soon "put all this excitement behind us," and get back to farming and the quiet life by the bay.

The last paragraph of the story credited "a number of good samaritans," who had tried to help the residents of Tobytown, including "Russ Antrim, a senior partner at Watkins-Cole, who, working *pro bono*, brought a number of legal actions on behalf of the community," "Richard Reed, recently retired from the US Park Police," and "Taz Blackwell, a former State Department official now resident on Chincoteague."

So, Eliza had continued digging. He hoped to hell she wasn't writing a book.

He bought the papers, and an energy drink. Only fair, since he had already read the juicy parts, standing just inside the entrance to the Church Street station. Just before seven. A blustery April morning. Bundled the papers in a roll behind the seat of his bicycle and headed east on Church Street. Past Fillmore, the little lane by the gut that was always filled with flowers. On to Eastside Drive, turning south at the Assateague marshes. Down past the giant oyster piles, where he crossed through Memorial Park and then cut his way down through the trailer park to the marshes of the Black Drain. Should have been taking a victory lap, like Bale and the Spurs after a soccer derby victory against Arsenal. But didn't feel like that at all.

The marsh complex extended south all the way to the very tip of the island. It was a great place to see rails at the right tide. Usually Virginia rails, or the occasional *sora* or king. On one memorable morning in the late summer he had seen black rail chicks there. They looked for all the world like little black cotton swabs on sticks. Of course, no camera.

He rode, feeling careless. Found the secret entrance to Bunker Hill and the dirt road that paralleled the marshes to the marina. The sun was just above the horizon, but its light was already warming everything it touched. He gloried in it. And why would you not? He was determined to put the dark spot behind him, but on this road, there was no dark spot to worry about. The early morning light was finding silver reflections in the marshes. Red-winged blackbirds were hoarsely calling out their territory. Saw an early palm warbler hunting for grubs in the bushes just off the marsh. Called it out by the maroon splash on its forehead. One of the first birds up from South America.

Throughout his life, Taz had harbored the hope that he would find love. He had smelled the scent of love, tasted the true flavor, finally found his other true being in Dana. In all the ways he had ever imagined his life, he never imagined that he would lose the trail. But he had.

How did you let her slip through your fingers? He considered all the moments. The ones where he could have declared himself, if he had been ready. But he wasn't ready. And then, all of a sudden, she had moved on. What the hell, honestly. What the hell.

So now, here he was, in the place he loved most, an island not four miles across or seven long, so never more than three miles away from her. And there was a gulf between them as wide as the blue Atlantic. He would just have to get used to it. Breathing and biking and with every breath, knowing she was less than three miles away, living on a different constellation. He told himself not to think about her. It's like not thinking about a tiger. You say no, you ban the tiger from consciousness, you think about anything else. Meanwhile, the tiger is there, lurking in the forests of the mind. And of course it's an Amur tiger, the most beautiful and striking of all.

The following morning Taz woke to bright sun. It was well after his normal hour. In his final dream, the one that edges closer and closer to wakefulness, a big ugly man with a heavy sledgehammer was trying to knock down his house. When he had risen far enough from the depths, he realized someone was indeed knocking on his door. Called, as loudly as his froggy voice could muster, "Be right there." He pulled on a pair of baggy gym shorts and a T-shirt, opened the door, rubbing his eyes to ward off the sun's dazzle. Dana was sitting on his stoop, watching a scallop trawler chugging out with the tide. He blinked at her, and again at the morning sun.

"What time is it?"

"Half past nine."

"Sorry. I don't usually sleep so late."

"I know. People on the island call you the six a.m. bicycler."

"No idea . . . honest?" He felt vaguely uncomfortable.

"It was Juliet at Church Street Produce who coined it. She sees you coming off the Eastside Road every morning when she's out rinsing her pots."

He thought about it, scratched the back of his neck. "I like bicycler instead of bicyclist." He looked out at the dock. Wanted desperately to dive in.

She fidgeted.

"Can I come in?"

"Is that what you want?"

"You could offer to make some coffee, you know."

He stood aside so she could enter. "I don't think I've ever made you coffee before. How do you like yours?"

"With a little cream."

"Milk do? I'm a black coffee guy."

"Sure."

He pointed to a seat at the kitchen table. Busied himself with the coffee. Trying to sort out his feelings. She was wearing an old blue T-shirt and jean shorts. She looked great at both levels. He noticed a small pink scar under her left eye, and the little tinge of yellow on her cheek. The sign that remains after the more vivid bruise begins to fade. He hair fell just a little to the side of her left eye. With a flip of her fingers, she could bring it over to hide the bruise.

He excused himself to freshen up. Splashed his face with cold water, brushed his hair, swiped at his teeth with last night's toothbrush. Back in the kitchen, he pulled two Arctic Club cups from the shelf and poured. Handed her one and the quart of milk.

"I'd just get it wrong." Sat down opposite.

"What's the Arctic Club?" She was looking at her cup. It was ceramic, cream-colored, and unusually thick. It had a drawing of a walrus, in brown, with the words *The Arctic Club* underneath, and a nicely curved lip.

"A hotel in Seattle. Also, the extended family of people who work around the Arctic Council. Including me."

She ran her forefinger around the lip of her cup, thinking. Looked out the window at his crepe myrtle, and then the old fig tree, and the juniper next to it. Moved her hair out of her eyes.

"Taz, Laney told me what you did."

He waited. No idea where this conversation was headed.

"I don't know what to say. I came here to thank you, but I feel like such a miserable idiot." She breathed deep. Looked down at her cup. Touched the little pink scar under her eye, unconsciously, tearing up.

"Anybody can make a mistake," he said flatly.

"Not at this level. This is major league. Truly epic. That night in the bookstore, I just wanted to crawl in a hole and die."

"Me, too, for what it's worth."

A tentative smile. She took a sip of coffee.

Then a piercing look. "Taz, why didn't you tell me?"

"Would you have believed me if I had? Anyway, I didn't know who it was until way past the burn date. By that time, I was in Denmark, and you were doing your best to show Brian that you really loved him."

"Oh, Taz."

"I'm curious. When did you first sleep with him?"

"On our second date." Taz flinched and turned his face away. "Please don't do this to me." She said it quietly. "That night in the crowd at Rainy Day, I finally realized that I was not the person he was interested in. Not at all."

Taz reached over the table to stroke her cheek. "Right. When he pushed you out the door, I worried about you."

"You know what? The humiliation was much more painful than the beating." A lone tear rolled down her cheek.

"Do you know what I did to him for hitting you? Did Laney tell you that?"

She looked at the window as if for an escape route. Yet when she turned to him, she still had the courage to meet his eyes. "No, she didn't. What do you mean?"

"Well, you do understand that he was going to kill Virgil Waite, right? And young Bennett?" This last with extra emphasis. "That he brought two freaking Chinese gunmen with AK-47s to kill them in the middle of the night?" He wanted to shake her.

"I . . . I didn't know."

"So he could get the deed that controls the mineral estate around Tobytown?"

"He didn't tell me anything, Taz."

"No, I expect not. So, after he kicked in Virgil's door at three in the morning, with a pistol in his hand, my friend Rick shattered his kneecap with a hollow point bullet. I dragged him whimpering into Virgil's kitchen."

"I jammed his open palm down on the burner, and I held it there. He screamed bloody murder then. I didn't care. I wanted to smell his flesh burn. I wanted to know for damn sure that he will never, never in life, use that hand again. Never write another letter, never hit another woman."

He felt his eyes moistening, pushed his chair back and went to the window. She was working desperately to hold her own tears back.

"Taz, why are you telling me this?"

"I don't know—maybe because you tossed me off. For a cold-blooded confidence man. I guess I took out my anger on him so I wouldn't blame you." An extraordinarily bright goldfinch caught his eye. He turned to her, looked at his hands. Turned back towards the window. "I did what I did. I have to live with it. And I sure as hell want you to live with it, too."

"Do you hate me so much, Taz?" Her voice trembled.

He turned back towards her. "I don't hate you at all. No. I loved you too much. I had sworn that I wouldn't ever do that—go head over heels ever again. I have absolutely no right to be angry with you for sleeping with him. That's not it at all. But I put my hope in you. It's that you turned your back on whatever we were starting—for him. I didn't understand why then . . . and I still don't. I want to, but I can't. I realize now that you can't trust your own heart, and you sure can't bring yourself to trust me. That's my fault. But how can you love someone you can't trust?"

"Taz, it's just that you have such an impact, and I never know which way you're headed. I just can't deal with that kind of uncertainty."

"So you decided to play it safe. How did that work out?"

"You see how it's worked out, Taz."

"Laney says I'm too much of a risk taker. The irony is that there are some risks I just can't take anymore. I just can't stand up to it. I can't risk giving my heart only to have it kicked to the curb. I did that once, and it took me years to recover."

She pushed her chair back and stood up. Her eyes rested for a moment on his, she reached to touch him, perhaps to say goodbye. He was just far enough away that she couldn't. She turned and left, without another word.

After Taz heard her car cough and hum, he found an old disc of Cecilia Bartoli's. He turned up the volume on his little CD player and listened to *bel canto* arias as he sat in his gym shorts at the kitchen table, sipping his coffee.

Once again, Bob Dylan put it best, in "One of Us Must Know:"

I didn't mean to treat you SO bad,
You shouldn't take it so personal.
I didn't mean to make you SO sad,
You just happened to be there, that's all . . .

Sooner or later, one of us must know,
That you just did what you were supposed to do,
Sooner or later, one of us must know
That I really did try to get close to you.

I couldn't see what you could SHOW me,
Your scarf had kept your mouth well hid,
I couldn't see how you could KNOW me,
But you said you knew and I believed you did . . .

CHAPTER FIFTY-TWO

Love Hurts

MORNING. TAZ NURSED HIS second beer, brooded. His thoughts weren't getting any clearer. He'd been awake since six. Took his first swim at six-thirty. Maybe if he biked down to the bookstore, played a little chess.

He opened the shed, tossed the beer bottle in the bin, pulled his bicycle out of the shadows. An old Gitane he'd had since college. Rust spots here and there, but in good shape, after all the years. He checked the tires, found the pump, loosened the fasteners on the Schrader valves. When he was finished, both tires were hard and clean. He wheeled the bike out through the yard to the street, and mounted on a hop, as he had done since he was six.

A girlfriend once told him nobody did it that way. You sat on your bike and tugged yourself into motion. Not Taz. He stood to the side, took a couple of strides, put his left foot on the pedal, swung over, found the right pedal and cruised. The way you would mount a pony. Maybe it was just the way a West Texas boy does it when he's riding the five miles to Ladentown to see his best friend. And to eat his friend's mother's chocolate chip cookies.

Aunt Betty. From Butte, Montana. A straight shooter with a good sense of humor and complete disdain for pretension. The way they made them in the West, in the old days. A long way to go, no time to waste.

Cruised past the carnival grounds and the Coast Guard Station, the Chincoteague Inn and the firehouse. Pulled up behind the bookstore in the dirt lot by the City Park. In through the back. Richard looked up from the laptop on his desk.

"You want to try that Queen's Knight opening one more time?"

"Jesus, have you been reading Nimzovich again? Do you ever sleep?"

"Not so much, honestly. Revenge is a dish best served after a night of whisky and chess online. Offhand, it might be argued that you had forgotten that precept."

There were a couple of casual customers to attend to. Taz looked around at the familiar shelves, saw Laney come in the back. She ducked quickly into the office. To compose herself, he supposed. Storm coming his way.

He waited. When she reappeared, he walked her way. "Laney. You okay?"

"Aside from the fact that my fondest hopes have been dashed, I'll soldier on. More importantly, how are you? I talked to Dana this morning."

Taz considered his options. All things considered, he decided it was best to take his punishment like a man, standing up.

"Tell me."

Laney searched his eyes. "You don't think you were a little hard on her?"

"Look, Laney, if you want to call me a hypocrite, go ahead. I won't say you're wrong. But at the point where the two of us . . . when it seemed like we might really have something . . . I was ready to drop it all to see where we could go."

"So she missed the takeoff point?"

"Or she felt it and it scared her."

"You know I love her like a sister."

"I do."

"I know she wounded you. I don't think she meant to. She was just trying to protect herself."

"I wish it wasn't this way."

"I know you do. I hate to see you both so hurt."

She looked to the side. Came back to him, her head in a quizzical tilt. "What are you going to do now?"

"I don't know, Laney. I guess, really, I'm totally fucked. She's just on the other side of the island, but we might as well be separated by the Gulf Stream. I'm going to run into her at the market, at Church Street Supply, at Steve's, here, everywhere. And it's going to kill me, time after time. So what are my options, honestly? Get on Captain Charlie's fishing charter and dive off at the top of the Baltimore Canyon?"

"Well, at least you still have a flair for the dramatic."

"Oh, thanks."

"Maybe it's not so hopeless, if you think long-term."

"Long-term, I'll be dead." She cocked her head and continued to probe his eyes. "Laney, I didn't mean to make it all so complicated."

"Sometimes life just does that on its own. "

"Still friends?"

She blanched. "You thought that—?" She gasped, clapped her hand to her open mouth. Stared at him in horror. Then, with the same hand, reached and touched his cheek. "Never more."

"Thanks, Laney."

"Yeah. You owe me an espresso. Maybe two."

The words "maybe two" echoed in his mind as he made his way back out to the desk, where Richard had the chess board set up.

He played his Queen's Knight opening. Richard responded with a straight up the middle attack, as Nimzovich says you should.

CHAPTER FIFTY-THREE

Mr. Tambourine Man

MID-MORNING IN LATE APRIL. Taz on his stoop, looking out at the dock. He had finally acquired the sign he intended to raise by the dock—the one that would, without saying so, warn strangers that maybe they shouldn't assume this was a public ramp. The sign was really quite beautiful. Three feet long, only about nine inches wide, in license plate metal, enameled in scarlet and black. The words, *Fear the Turtle.* A slogan of the Terrapins of the University of Maryland, otherwise known as the Terps, but uniquely suited to be erected here with a different meaning entirely.

He had figured his strategy for putting the sign up the day before. He wanted to get the job done today. Naturally, that required at least three trips to Church Street Supply, the first for the right size lag screws, the second for shorter mounting bolts, the third for an extended quarter-inch drill bit to bite through the four-by-four post into the pressure-treated wood of the bulkhead.

He had assembled the sign in the work shed in his backyard. A ten-foot four-by-four would serve as the stanchion. The placard was a two-by-six cut to the exact length of the sign. The two-by-six bolted onto the stanchion, and the sign bolted on to the two-by-six. All with stainless steel to hold off the salt, rust, and general corruption of metal on the coast. The phrase "my cross to bear" kept echoing in his mind.

Low tide. The water had receded almost forty feet from the bulkhead. He stood in the sea lettuce, mud, and detritus and looked the situation over. He decided to tie the stanchion to the bulkhead, but also to the first post. That way it wouldn't peel off, even in a hurricane. Got two of the longest extension cords he had and strung them together, out his front porch and across Main Street. Coiled the strand once around a cinderblock and then plugged in the drill. Put it on the bulkhead. Clambered back down into the muck, grabbed an old cinderblock to use as a footing. Still not high enough, so he topped it with a brick. About right. Lifted the foot of the stanchion and positioned it on the brick, so it was hugging the bulkhead on one side, and the first post on the other. The drilling was the easy part. Then the lag screws, four into the bulkhead and two into the post. Ratchet them down until they were biting wood. By the time he was finished, the dock would come apart before the sign came down.

It was eleven, and the tide had turned. Climbed up onto the bulkhead and gathered his tools. Put everything in its place in the shed, locked it behind him. Pulled a longneck out of the refrigerator and sat on the front stoop, admiring his handiwork.

Pretty much at the point where he was getting just slightly jaded contemplating his street art, two bicycles came tearing around the corner of Beebe and Main. They screeched to a stop just short of his perch on the front stoop. Suzanne was in the lead coming off Beebe; Moyer had done his best to catch up by hopping the curb and riding across the grass of the house next door. If the lawn had been recently cut, his gamble might have worked.

"Hi Taz." Suzanne was smiling.

"Hey, buttercup, how are you?"

"I'm okay, but I could be better." Intense seriousness over her horn rims. "You taught me that."

"I don't see how you could be any better." The ritual formulation.

"But let's concede the point for the sake of argument. In that case, what would make you better?"

The point of the game here was honesty.

"If you and Mom got together again."

Moyer was waiting, semi-patiently.

"Buttercup, you know how to aim for the heart. If that option wasn't so easy, for the moment, is there something else that would help?"

"If Moyer and I got to hang out with you more."

Moyer popped in. "Taz, we had three palm warblers in our yard yesterday. In our yard!"

"Well I guess you better put them down on your backyard bird list, right?"

"Right-o." Another ritual formulation.

To Suzanne, gently, "So where does your mom think you are just now?"

"Riding around."

"Well, that's certainly true." He thought for a while. "I was going to play some guitar. Do you two want hot chocolate?"

Big smile from Moyer. Raised fist pump from Suzanne.

Fortunately he had milk that hadn't turned. They made the hot chocolate, returned to the stoop. He opened Little Sister's case and brought her out to the porch. Strummed a few chords to get the feel back.

"Do the fox song?" Moyer. "Please?"

He first heard Burl Ives sing it when he was Moyer's age, or even younger. That reedy voice with the burr in it.

> *Well, the fox went out on a moonlit night,*
> *prayed for the moon to give him light,*
> *He had many a mile to go that night,*
> *before he reached the town-o, town-o, town-o,*
> *Many a mile to go that night,*
> *before he reached the town-o.*

The song had a zillion verses. He remembered most of them, and Moyer supplied the others.

> *. . . ran right up to the great big pen,*
> *the geese and the ducks were kept therein,*
> *A couple of you are going to slick my chin,*
> *before I leave this town-o.*

That fox was a genuine bad boy.
> *Grabbed the grey goose by the neck,*
> *slung a little duck over his back,*
> *He didn't mind the quack-quack-quack,*
> *Or the legs all dangling down-o.*

They sang on together. Suzanne ventured a harmony line at various places.

> *He ran back home to his cozy den.*
> *There were his little ones, eight, nine, ten.*
> *They cried Daddy, better go back again,*
> *'cause it must be a mighty fine town-o.*
> *They never had such a dinner in their life,*
> *And the little ones chewed on the bones-o.*

When he had pinged the last note, he suggested to Moyer that he check the crab pots at the end of the dock.

Turned to Suzanne. "Buttercup. You know you're family here. Anytime you want to be. You and Moyer mean the world to me."

"Oh, Taz." She looked older and wiser than her fourteen years.

"But I think we have to be straight up with your mom."

"I guess so." Reluctantly.

"So here's what I suggest. Tell your mom that you swung by here. Tell her we had hot chocolate and did some singing. She knows you're safe here. Say I offered to pay you both a little if you wanted to work on the marsh grass restoration or a few other projects. But only as long as it's all right with her. See what she says."

"Okay, Taz. You're the best." She gave him a hug.

Moyer was running back down the dock with a jimmy in each hand. "You got two!"

Taz had him hold up the first one, then the second, measuring the carapaces with his thumb and pinkie. "Well, technically, they're legal, but they're pretty small, don't you think?"

"I guess so, Taz."

"So what does a good conservationist do in this situation?"

"Throw 'em back."

"And?"

"And, throw a couple of chicken necks in behind them so they grow up faster."

"You da' man, Moyer."

Suzanne put her arm around Moyer's shoulder. "We better go, brother. I need to have a talk with Mom." With a smile for Taz. Then they were on their bikes, zipping up Main.

CHAPTER FIFTY-FOUR

Capital of Pain

EVENING. LEAFING THROUGH A few of his favorite poets. Neruda and Vallejo were too full of color. Wanted something bleaker, something to match his mood. The future he had nurtured in his heart had slipped away. He had been twirling a beautiful long-stemmed rose. Now he was holding a handful of dust.

Finally, he came across a lyric from Eluard:

> *She is standing on my eyelids,*
> *And her hair is in mine,*
> *She has the shape of my hands,*
> *She has the color of my eyes,*
> *In my shadow she is engulfed*
> *Like a stone on the sky.*
>
> *She always has open eyes*
> *And does not let me sleep.*

Her dreams in broad daylight
Make suns evaporate,
Make me laugh, cry and laugh,
Speak having nothing to say.

Taz poured himself a hit of Brennivin, Iceland's "Black Death." Found his tattered pink copy of Attila Jozsef, turned to page thirty-five:

Heavy peasants are straggling home
from the fields without a word.
The river and I are lying side by side.
Fresh grasses sleep under my heart.
A deep calm is rolling in the river.
My heavy cares are now as light as dew.
The man lying here is ageless, without
enemies or brothers—just a tired man.

Evening ladles out the quiet.
I am a warm slice from its loaf of bread.
The sky is resting, the stars come out
to sit on the river and shine on my head.

ACKNOWLEDGMENTS

THE TOWN OF CHINCOTEAGUE, on Virginia's Eastern shore, is situated on the island of the same name. The island has no beaches of its own, protected as it is by the barrier island of Assateague, whose sandy southern reaches curl past Tom's Cove and appear to be moving steadily to cut off the Chincoteague Channel. Chincoteague is a mix of marsh and loblolly pine forest. The island has been inhabited for thousands of years, first by oyster-gathering Indians and then by white and black settlers who made their living from the sea or by raising chickens and small gardens. Today, the island is still changing. The fishermen, oystermen and clammers still work the waters, but now summer tourists and retirees form a significant part of the economy and the social scene.

My wife Cindy and I started coming to Chincoteague over thirty-five years ago. In some sense, we raised my daughters here. Hannah and Liesel are now pursuing their own careers and adult lives, but each of them would tell you, if asked, that Chincoteague formed an important part of their upbringing. Together, the four of us rented so many different houses on the island that we've lived in almost every neighborhood, from Down the Marsh to Piney Island. So perhaps it's not surprising that in October of 2011, Cindy and I bought a little hundred-year old waterman's cottage on the south side of Main Street, down by Beebe Road.

The surprise of it all was the welcome we received once it became known that we were moving in for real. Our neighbors were anxious to introduce themselves, and happy to talk about their island with us. Terry Howard, the dean of our neighborhood, deserves special mention. He arrived at our doorstep one October morning with a bushel of vegetables from his garden. At first, he was reluctant to accept my invitation to come in and sit. But once he did, he regaled me with stories and anecdotes that gradually helped me understand Chincoteague's true heart. Terry is a leader and a city councilman, also a sage. People stop by his house on Beebe Road daily during the spring and summer to buy heritage tomatoes and other produce from his garden, but also to trade stories with Terry and his lovely wife Judy. Terry's tomatoes are legendary among his neighbors, and I can testify that his eggplant is also second to none.

Setting a novel in a place like Chincoteague should give any author at least a little trepidation. It's a place where, when all is said and done, everybody does know everybody else. The situation makes it doubly important to clarify that, with the exception of Terry and Judy, who have cameo roles, no character in this story is based on any living person in Chincoteague. In some cases, for instance with regard to the proprietors of the town bookstore, actual people have provided the starting point for characters in the novel. But none of the characters are, as they say, "drawn from life." Rather, they are entirely imaginary creations, and their foibles and occasional moments of valor or wisdom are entirely the product of the author's somewhat fevered imagination.

With that said, welcome to Chincoteague. I can only hope I have captured some small bit of the charm and mystery of the island, and of Virginia's Eastern Shore.

This is the appropriate place to thank my wonderful editor Diane MacEachern, an accomplished writer in her own right who, out of the goodness of her heart, volunteered to edit my novel when it was still in its infancy. There are not enough superlatives to describe her efforts, her good judgment, or her "bedside manner" as she conveyed the hardest news for any author to hear—yes, radical surgery was required—more than once. Let's just say that her excisions were just as important as her many adjustments, revisions, or additions. Without her help, this book would not exist in the form it now has.

I want to thank my beautiful wife Cindy for her vast patience and her encouragement of this project and for her indefatigable effort to ready it for publication. And, most importantly, the wisdom of her comments as she read what I was writing. A favorite phrase in our house is, "You put up with a lot, but I'm a lot to put up with." Cindy's love has been, and is now, the mainstay of my life.

Brooks B. Yeager
September 2020